PENGUIN BOOKS

THE SPARKLE PAGES

Meg Bignell grew up in a sprawling garden on the banks of the Derwent River in Tasmania's Derwent Valley. She now lives with her husband and three children on a dairy farm at Bream Creek on the east coast of Tasmania. She is the author of *Welcome to Nowhere River* and *The Angry Women's Choir*.

www.megbignell.com.au

Praise for Meg Bignell

'If you have forgotten why you're angry, if you've forgotten that you *are* angry, this laugh-out-loud, sob-out-loud, sing-out-loud book will remind you.'
MINNIE DARKE

'Entertaining, emotional, full of lunatic charm and startlingly honest, *The Sparkle Pages* takes you on an unforgettable journey deep into the heart of a woman, her marriage and her family.'
BETTER READING

'*The Angry Women's Choir* is an uplifting story about female friendship, bubbling rage, and finally taking a stand.'
MAMAMIA

'A boisterous tale of music, friendship and women's rights.'
BOOKS + PUBLISHING

'A small town in Tasmania given the warm spotlight it deserves. Funny, sad, relatable, full of people who continue to breathe well after the last page. A beautifully nuanced read from start to finish.'
MARTA DUSSELDORP

'*The Sparkle Pages* is witty, light, dark and insightfully addictive all at once.'
SAMANTHA BOND

'An unputdownable celebration of all women.'
BRISBANISTA

'This book was witty, charming, at times hysterically funny and heartbreakingly sad. A call to arms for women around the world and a testament to the power we can harness when we band together and hold each other up.'
CLAUDINE TINELLIS

'*Welcome to Nowhere River* is a captivating and tender-hearted story of a country town and its rhythms.'
BETTER READING

THE
SPARKLE
PAGES

MEG BIGNELL

PENGUIN BOOKS

PENGUIN BOOKS

UK | USA | Canada | Ireland | Australia
India | New Zealand | South Africa | China

Penguin Books is part of the Penguin Random House group of companies
whose addresses can be found at global.penguinrandomhouse.com.

First published by Michael Joseph, 2019
This edition published by Penguin Books, 2023

Cover design by Christabella Designs © Penguin Random House Australia Pty Ltd
Cover photographs by Shutterstock
Text design by Louisa Maggio © Penguin Random House Australia Pty Ltd
Typeset in Sabon by Midland Typesetters, Australia

Printed and bound in Australia by Griffin Press, an accredited
ISO AS/NZS 14001 Environmental Management Systems printer

A catalogue record for this
book is available from the
National Library of Australia

ISBN 978 1 76134 403 9

penguin.com.au

For Mum, who has the most sparkle of anyone I know.
For Dad, who taught me the importance of silliness.

For Em and for Dickie.

With thanks to Maggie.

This journal belongs to: Susannah Parks
Address: 14 Mathwin Avenue,
West Hobart, Tasmania 7004

Reward for return: $100. Thank you.
$150 if you don't read it. I will know.

P.S. If I'm incapacitated, vanished or dead,
please send directly to Ria Mirrin,
35 Great Windmill Street,
Soho, London, UK. Thank you.

Prelude

☆

♡ ♪♪

SATURDAY 31st DECEMBER

I have been hiding in the wardrobe for eleven and a half minutes. I've done ten and a half minutes of deep breathing and a bit of meditation and still I don't trust myself to come out. I am sitting on Hugh's shoes, amid his hanging trousers. It might appear a bit childish, this hiding in the wardrobe, but actually I'm very sensibly not losing my temper. Trying at least; I can still feel some shouts threatening to burst out and screech all over the house. I must clutch on to them and stay here a bit longer. If I lose my temper, I might not find it in time for the New Year's Eve guest arrivals . . .

Right, those deep breaths made me quite dizzy and my mind's not made for meditation, so I've decided instead to turn my potential maelstrom into quietly written words that mar only this paper and not the impressionable, developing brains of my four darling children. Oh, I could say some things. Things that would end this year on a very bad note.

Here's what the ~~little knobheads~~ dear little blossoms have done today:

- Offered to make New Year's Eve cupcakes but instead decorated the kitchen with icing sugar, egg, milk and sprinkles.

- Let the (morbidly obese) dog clean up the sprinkles.
- Eaten most of the icing and all the tiny silver balls and lied about it (Jimmy, I suspect).
- Spilt purple food colouring on the couch and lied about it (Mary-Lou – she has purple tones in her hair, which is not ideal for long dark ringlets. She looks like a modern-day witch's familiar).
- Burnt the cupcakes (Rafferty).
- Licked all the windows in the front hall (Jimmy and Mary-Lou).
- Turned the spare bed into a lifeboat and filled it with every pillow, cushion, dolly and stuffed animal in the house (all of them).
- Ignored me altogether (Eloise).
- Brought home a baby possum (Jimmy).
- Owned up to nothing, told lies, blamed one another and said bugger. Twice (all of them).

The possum was The Last Straw (I shouted, before shutting the rest of the shouts in the wardrobe). It is a ringtail possum so we have to save it, apparently. Jimmy was firm about this. 'He's fallen out of his nest, Mum.'

'They don't have nests, darling,' I said. 'It's a possum, not a bird. Put it back. Its mother will be looking for it.'

'They do have nests,' he said, all outraged. 'We did it in science. It's a common ringtail. They build nests and have a declining population. He's cold. He'll die from the cold and his mother's asleep. They're mocturnal.'

I peered at the possum in his hands. It looked like a tiny alien foetus, all hairless and curled up, with very long fingers. Somehow quite sweet, especially in the hands of Jimmy, who is tough and sporty but goes all tender and soggy around animals. 'Why are they called "common" if they're in decline?'

'That's their name. Like you're called Mum.'

'Well, really I'm called Susannah.'

'And he's called Peter.'

Honestly. I long for the days of the schoolroom and mother-knows-best. A possum rescue is the last thing I need when the children are in a sugar frenzy and we're hosting a dinner party.

Calm, calm, Susannah. Calm calm calm . . . Funny word, calm.

I wasn't going to start writing in this diary until the actual new year. But we're very nearly there, aren't we, and the diary happened to be here, waiting in the wardrobe when I dived in for refuge. Its pages are so clean and inviting, like washed sheets. Already I feel better for sinking into them. (Must remember to redo the spare bed before tonight.)

Just to be clear, this is a large walk-in wardrobe, not the closed-up cupboardy sort, so there's really no reason why I should be crouched in the trousers, just that it's more muffled and hidey. (Although the cupboard kind of wardrobe might open up to a whole new Narnia world into which I could run and vanish for a decently extended time without possums to keep alive or beds to make.) There's even a chair in here; the grey velvet rocking chair that Mum gave me years ago for breastfeeding. It's quite nice, that chair, even though it makes me feel sad about not having babies any more (and a bit tingly in the nipples). Perhaps I could do an upholstery course and re-cover it with something a bit less dull. Donkey-grey is probably the colour of disappointment. Floral? Yellow? Apricot? I've always liked apricot; reminds me of Mum. She has a velvet apricot dressing-gown.

The first dinner I ever cooked after Hugh and I were married was quite grey-looking. Beef stroganoff. Deeply disappointing. Hugh might have done well to treat it as a warning sign.

My viola is in the wardrobe too. Sometimes I come in here and look at it, give it a little 'hello, how are you?' No need for anything more than that; no need for any actual music playing. That really would end the year on very bad notes. All notes made by me from now on are the notes I make on these pages. So there we are . . .

And, anyway, viola playing would certainly wake the baby possum. It's here with me, staying warm inside my shirt (and away from Barky, who wouldn't eat it, I don't think, but might possibly bark it to death). Jimmy's sick of it already and has left me to deal with it. I've phoned the animal rescue people. Even they sounded possum-weary, despite me telling them it's a precious ringtail.

'Yes, they're everywhere in West Hobart,' they said. 'Eating everyone's lettuce seedlings. We can't take it for three or four days, if it survives. Just feed it with a dropper.'

Hugh's going to sigh and roll his eyeballs at me when he gets home. Oh, and:

While I'm sitting on his shoes trying to avert disastrous parenting fallout, Hugh has gone diving somewhere down the Tasman Peninsula. He claims to be hunting and gathering for tonight, but I know better. What a hardship, being in the peaceful underwater, filling your catch bag and listening to your own breaths in the static of the kelp forests. A bit like being among hanging trousers and hyperventilating with a hairless possum down your front. For goodness sake.

I'm in the rocking chair now. Rocking the possum. Or am I rocking myself, like a mad person? It's quite soothing actually, and much more comfortable. My limbs were getting numb. I'm too tall to scrunch myself up into a hidey hole. I should reupholster this chair in apricot velvet and come here whenever I need a dose of dressing-gown comfort . . . and some diary writing.

I must not enter the new year in this present state. I will not be the one rocking in the wardrobe with a bald possum in my shirt. I will not be resentful of abalone, nor impatient with children being ~~arseholes~~ children. I will emerge from this wardrobe all pulled together and entertain our friends and family with utmost ease, good humour and very good hair. I will face the sugary, messy music in the kitchen, laugh with my spirited children, whip up some bruschetta and clean the windows. We will start the year on Very Good Notes.

And perhaps Hugh will fall properly back in love with me.

That's my New Year's Resolution, to help my husband love me again. That's why I bought this diary, to record all my resolution notes – thoughts, plans, progress, research, etc. Perhaps I should write some sort of contract with myself, make it official right here at the start. Yes.

I, Susannah Parks, have lost the passion in my marriage, somewhere in the slippery, rushing, last-straw hours, and I need to find it. I *will* find it.

S. Parks

Sparks. Passion and sparks. And when there are no sparks, at least just a little sparkle.

So there we are, a contract. This is not one of my whims. I have also discussed it fully with Ria (my best friend, confidante and very wise person) and she has endorsed my proactivity. She would absolutely tell me if she thought I was being ridiculous. Actually, she did tell me I was being ridiculous, but that was before Christmas when I made noises about wanting to sell our chaotic house and move to the upper Derwent Valley, where Hugh and I can recalibrate, team-parent our free-range children, grow mangel-wurzels and milk a house cow. She reined me in, which – along with piano, flute and cello – she is very practised at.

'Susannah,' she said (I know to listen when she calls me Susannah), 'you don't need a house cow, you idiot. You need some passion.'

'What? But I'm very passionate.'

'About hiding vegetables in lasagne.'

'That's not fair, Ria. And shut up if you're about to tell me to pick up the viola.'

'Pick up the viola.'

I stayed silent.

'Well, pick up your husband, then. Have you noticed him lately? He's lovely.'

'I notice him more than he notices me,' I said. The words came out like those of a petulant teen, reminding me of Eloise when I ask her if she has any washing.

'Have you also noticed that when you talk to him, it's in that weird flat marriage monotone?'

'What?'

'There's no light in your voice. Put some fucking light in your voice.'

'Right.' Something in her words was starting to ring true.

'Look, we both know I'm no relationship expert but it seems to me there are two things you need to do when things are getting a bit stale: one, be interested, and two, be interesting.'

'I am interested.'

'Be really interested. In the world, in other people, and mostly in Hugh.'

'I *am* interested in Hugh.'

'How often do you have sex?'

'A lot.'

'Is that a lie?'

'Yes.'

'How often?'

'Well, you know, we have busy lives. It's easy to just sail past one another in the hallway for a week before we actually spend time together.'

'You'd go a whole week without sex?' She sounded incredulous. (Ah, bless these idealistic single people.)

'Sometimes,' I said (also a lie – I don't actually like to think too hard about how long it's been since Hugh and I last made love).

'Jesus, that *is* stale. You wouldn't leave bread for a week without making a sandwich.'

'Am I not interesting?' I asked, trying to steer things away from sex.

'Well, I think you're endlessly fascinating, you know that. But we're talking about Hugh. When was the last time you felt compelled to tell him all about something you've done, with light in your voice? When did you last try something new?'

I tried to think but could only come up with learning to make a pumpkin costume for Mary-Lou's school play. I knew better than to volunteer that.

Ria put a knowing 'hmm' into the silence.

'Well, I think interesting things, don't I?'

'You think weird things.'

'Like what?'

'Like making kale into chips. And buying a fucking farmlet in Ouse.'

'I really like Ouse.'

'See, weird.'

I had to be silent again. There's no arguing with Ria, especially when she's a little bit right. She was virtually raised by three older brothers and had to compensate for a lack of brawn with a very good brain. Its dispute centre is well exercised and in robust, rude health. It has to be said that, beyond the children, there's ~~hardly any~~ no interest in my life. Incoming or outgoing.

'Look,' she said, just as the last of my reinvention zeal dissolved into dismay, 'this isn't that hard. You two are the best couple I know, honestly you are. Just resolve to work at it.'

'You mean a resolution?' I said. 'I do love a New Year's resolution.'

'If you like,' she said, then added, 'but, for fuck's sake, don't run a mile with the idea. Take it quietly. Simple things. No enrolling in sexology degrees or getting your labia reduced.'

'There are sexology degrees?' I asked, with mock excitement.

'No.'

'Joking.'

But later I looked up 'sexology'. And did a small assessment of my labia.

So, anyway, I should come out of the wardrobe. I'm not feeling so angry now. In fact, I'm feeling quite sad, remembering how not interesting I am. Even in this rocking chair I can feel the rising beat of my scaredy-cat heart. It's disturbing the possum. There's a lump the size of a plum pip forming in the back of my throat. *Not now, not now.* I have a New Year's Eve party to throw. I'll get to New Year's resolutions tomorrow; I can be brave then. A brave new year. I don't, at least, feel as though I'm going to shout. Sadness is easier to hide than fury. Also sparkly windows are easier to achieve than sparkly hearts, so I'll get on with those.

I hope we have Windex.

SUNDAY 1st JANUARY

It's one o'clock in the morning. Our guests have departed – most of them before midnight, actually. My family are all asleep. I am not drunk, but I've had enough to keep me wide awake. And I'm sitting in the wardrobe again.

There's a small glass of sparkling wine with me, with which I can have a private little toast to the sparkly New Year. A year that's so brand new it hasn't even opened its eyes yet – much like Peter the Possum (still here, in a pillow case around my neck). Furled, innocent, waiting. I have so many plans for this year. I hope it doesn't grow up to growl at the windows, wee on the fence and eat all the roses.

Not being drunk is a slight disappointment; if I'd had more champagne, I might have handled things differently. Or been tucked up in bed already.

Things got a bit out of hand.

To begin with, the dynamic was all wrong. I was more concerned with paying off all our accumulated dinner debts in one shebang than thinking about compatibility and diplomacy. I invited:

- Hugh's parents (Laurence barely counts due to the fact that he doesn't speak, although Alison makes up for that).
- Josh and Isobel Hadley and their two children, from three doors up. Our children have virtually lived in their pool since they moved in last September so I had to have them.
- Dear Henry, who told me weeks ago that he's left the orchestra to open a bookshop and still hasn't given me full details.

- Mum and Dad.
- Valda from next door, who would complain about the noise and blast us with *La Traviata* for a week if we didn't ask her.

Alison arrived first, with prickly remarks about the year's disappointments and how people (me) can improve. 'We don't usually bother with New Year's Eve,' she said, 'but we thought it would be nice to see the children in their natural habitat before they get a postgraduate degree, marry a foreigner and send a telegram to my funeral.'

Why do they blame me for not visiting them more often? Isn't that Hugh's job? I don't remember him ever dropping in on my parents without me.

Then came the general deflatery that arrives with Josh and Isobel. Perfection surrounds them like a Vaseline vignette, blurring all else in the vicinity, no matter how much time you've spent ~~plucking your chin hairs~~ shining your shoes or coaxing some volume and grace into your stupid feathery hair.

For a start, Josh is so incredibly good-looking up close! (I realised I've only ever waved to him from his driveway or from across the park.) He's very nice, in an ever so slightly slimy kind of way. His conversation is dotted with innuendo and he tends to loom on the edges of your personal space. This is not unpleasant. It's unfair what beautiful people can get away with. His wife, Isobel, is tiny and so perfectly made that she can wear a kimono and goddess plaits without looking even faintly ridiculous.

And to add insult to injury, they are quite scarily intelligent. She's a scientist at the Menzies Research Centre – something world-changey, probably. He's a fertility specialist. I'm pleased to report that I didn't carry on about my surprisingly fertile gonads. (There are advantages to remaining sober.)

Josh and Isobel have a lot of money. Their children, Thomas and Ava, have perfect manners and say things like 'No, thank you. I don't like fizzy drinks.' Ava plays footy in the state under-twelves and Thomas is in his school's gifted program. I'm hoping some of their focus will rub off on Raffy, whose favourite pastime is being upside down on the couch. I'm also hoping the smiles I gave them didn't look as sucked-lemon as they felt.

Even perpetually grumpy Valda seemed quite taken with the Hadleys. She was irritated with Eloise for being late to fetch her over but, when she spotted our glamorous guests, she gave them a beauteous smile, a pot of her homemade marmalade and the words, 'I want to thank you for what you've done with your landscaping. It's raised the neighbourhood's garden bar back to where it belongs.' This was followed by a pointed look at me. I suppressed a twitch in my middle finger as our unpruned apple tree waved at me through the window. (It's worth noting that Valda didn't show the slightest interest when Princess Mary was residing a street away for the holidays and frequented the chemist on the corner, so the Hadley spellbind must be potent.)

Thank goodness for Henry, who never notices glamour (or a lack thereof) and who hasn't changed a bit since I met him in my orchestra days. He arrived late, greeted everyone with equal warmth and a handshake, then went and played sardines with the children. He's a joy, is Henry, in his expensive shoes, his well-made jumpers with leather patches on the elbows and a hankie in the sleeve. He is seven years younger than me, but twenty years more grown-up. I was proud to introduce him to the Hadleys. (He is very handsome but blushes if you tell him so. Ria had a fleeting crush on him until we noticed that his hankie was white linen with a lace corner and he called it a 'handkersniff'.)

It turns out that Henry hasn't left the orchestra for his bookshop after all. Not completely. He is still on as a casual cellist. Of course he is; they would be mad to let him go completely, and he could never give up his music. I had a vague fantasy that he might declare himself 'spent!' and join me in a tiny exclusive club of professional musicians who have downed their instruments for good. We could have little support meetings once a month in his shop. But of course he must never stop. That divine sound, he carries it in his face; I can hear it when I look at him.

His shop opens in a few weeks! It's in Battery Point, it's called Lettercello and I just know he'll make a success of it. People are drawn to Henry in the same way they are to leather-bound books.

Mum was very drawn to Josh Hadley, though. She had a lovely time with him, God help us. Thankfully he appears to have a sense of humour. She put her hand over his at the table, leaned in and said, 'I read a very interesting article about how baboons' bottoms inflate and turn bright red when they're ovulating.' She glanced at Alison and raised her voice a touch. 'And the male baboons have lilac scrotums – imagine that! Sort of like mating beacons.'

At that point there was a sudden wail from Mary-Lou and a shout from Jimmy. The usual bickering. Dad glanced from them to Hugh and said, 'Shame Susannah didn't have an inflatable bottom. A warning beacon might have saved you some trouble.' Alison looked cross (she's over Mum and Dad's attempts to shock) and Laurence turned redder than a baboon's bottom.

Luckily the subject was changed by Hugh bringing in his seafood platter. Yes, Hugh, our hunting and gathering hero, had of course brought home the bacon in the form of two crayfish and a pile of abalone. I should be grateful for his efforts but no one ever makes a fuss about women who do the groceries with four unwieldy offspring and a wobbly trolley. ('Oh, Hugh, you've out-done yourself,' etc.)

Then it was time to turn our attentions to the children, because Jimmy decided to stage a talent show. This sounds like a lovely, wholesome way to bring children together, but 'Jimmy's show-offs' (as Raffy calls them) are produced as a means to display his latest feat of coordination. He is supremely, infuriatingly nimble. Trampoline acrobatics, magic shows, miming, juggling, balancing, he can do it all, with style. His New Year's Eve performance featured a mashup of undeniably cool dance moves he's picked up from some hideous computer game. With his dark curls bouncing and his smile giving away his dimples (my dimples too, but they look perfect on him – mine just look goofy), he was quite a fetching spectacle. Aside from Eloise (who could teach the *Mona Lisa* a thing or two about indifference), everyone was impressed. The other children instantly wanted to try the moves themselves and soon it was as though they'd all submitted to some terrible spasmodic limb contagion. It was funny to watch, but Mary-Lou, who dreams fiercely of being as smooth as Jimmy, didn't take the hilarity well. She sent out one of her best wails, along with some very fat tears.

'Oh, Mary-Lou,' said Mum, 'we're laughing with joy because you did it so well. Shall we see how Granny Frannie goes? I can throw some awesome shapes, you know.'

'Frannie, remember your knees,' Dad warned. But Mum was already centre-stage with her best groovy expression and possibly the most startling array of manoeuvres ever attempted by a 68-year-old woman. Mary-Lou had to laugh. Goodness, even grinchy old Alison laughed. Hearing Alison laugh is a bit like seeing a cat swim. Rare and unsettling.

Henry and I joined Mum on the stage, where Jimmy's flawless rhythm sped up amid the indignity of the mature-age people and their shapes. Even Valda threw a feeble arm or two in the air, as if adding her pump to the Mary-Lou tyres. It was brilliant.

Later the show was ~~ruined~~ nudged back on the talent track by Thomas, who can solve a Rubik's cube in under a minute, and by Ava, who sang 'Listen' by Beyoncé and took everyone's breath away. Valda had that taken face on again and said, 'Pitch wasn't perfect but very good technique. *Very* good. And that's what matters.' I felt a nasty sneer of jealousy in the back of my throat. It shamed me into overzealous applause.

'Mum, how about you play your viola?' asked Jimmy, whose competitive spirit knows no bounds.

'No, darling, it's time for sparklers,' I said.

'Come on, Zannah,' said Hugh. 'While we're talking talent.'

I sent him a daggery stare and said, 'No.'

'Can I play it, then?' Raffy asked with a strange sort of beseeching expression on his face that looked a bit like enthusiasm (more cats swimming).

I responded with, 'I'll show you talent,' and took to the stage to belt out my best, but the world's worst, rendition of 'Hit Me with Your Best Shot', which didn't go for long because I couldn't remember the words of the second verse. Dad came to the rescue by shouting, 'Talent shmalent,' turning off all the lights, putting pen torches up his nostrils and switching them on. His nose is substantial. In full glowing glory it stole the show. Dear Dad, he knows when I'm flailing.

To finish things off, Mum rewarded every performer with a kiss and a hedgehog sticker.

Now that I'm sitting in the wardrobe alone with my champagne flute (empty), I realise that Hugh spent most of the evening chatting with Josh and Isobel, or his parents. Everyone else (the people with the hedgehogs, as it turns out) sort of larked about. Hugh was clearly much more at home with the normal people. And at the end of the night, once we'd finished the washing-up (who washes up on New Year's Eve?) he said, 'That was a pretty brave performance, Susannah. Next time you might be brave enough for the viola?'

'Heck no,' I said. 'Talent shows are so last year.' We laughed, and he kissed me briefly but I didn't notice any sparkles, just the sensation that a vaguely distant threat was actually much closer and much more terrible than I thought . . . What's the opposite of sparkle? Darkle?

That wasn't actual bravery I showed, it was bravado. I've always been full of it when there's a stage. Real-world courage eludes me. Much like the admiring eyes of my husband, which were there once, weren't they?

Valda and Henry got along well, which is something. 'What a delight to meet Valda,' Henry said in his best Classic FM voice. 'She has an uncommon knowledge of the Baroque operas.'

I must ask her about that.

No, but I won't. I will focus. It's resolution time. *Resolve, resolve.*

I've removed my hedgehog sticker. And perhaps tomorrow I'll start this diary again, in a better temper, with a brand-new happy new year to wield against negative attitudes. And a quiver of ideas to throw at the Hugh problem. All my best shots.

Goodness, it's after two. Must sleep.

TOMORROW I WILL MAP OUT MY RESOLUTION AND RESCUE MY MARRIAGE.

♫

Coloratura

TUESDAY 3rd JANUARY

The Sparkle Project. That's what I've named this resolution. And this diary is the Sparkle Pages. There *will* be sparkles. I am determined. And I'm back in the wardrobe with my next update.

We've had a nice family day at the beach. Well, mostly nice. Mary-Lou had a tantrum about ice cream, Raffy lost his towel and Hugh did quite a lot of looking at a beautiful woman in a microscopic bikini.

He had the grace to look sheepish when I caught him. He said, 'Ahem, isn't she on the telly or something?' And then, 'She's nothing on you,' but in a half-hearted way that made me aware of my thighs. She's not a celebrity. We don't have those in Tasmania. They all leave. Unless you count newsreaders, pollies and that nice bloke from *Play School*.

Then we had to take Peter Possum to his wildlife carer and she looked just like Helena Christensen. *Oh, come on, Hobart*, I thought. *Now is not the time to be wheeling out your beautiful people.* She was wearing a gypsy dress and bare feet and had the sort of wafty presence that excuses itself from the hubbub of the mainstream.

'Hello, hello,' she said in a soothing voice, smiling at the children. 'Well done, rescuers. Ringtails are delicate little souls.'

Hugh was looking at her as though he'd like to stop in and have his delicate little soul rescued too. Can't blame him, really. I'd only just finished huffing about the lost towel. (How does anyone lose a towel, for goodness sake? Perhaps I should be feeding Rafferty more oily fish. He's so infuriatingly vague. Kind, though, which is more important.)

We all said goodbye to Peter. It was quite sad. As his primary carer I felt so essential. Perhaps I should sign up for wildlife rescue. Wait, no, that would be asking for trouble, and Barky has been very put out with Peter around. But I will miss that little warm weight next to my heart.

Anyway, it was a good day. Hugh's going to try to stay on holidays until Monday. I am sceptical but hopeful. It's nice to have him around. And good for him to see how annoying all the children can be even when we don't have to do spelling tests and rush to sports games. He can experience just how much time it takes to cut up watermelons and apply everyone's sunscreen.

Having Hugh home also highlights a few of our weak spots. For instance, this morning I couldn't help but get prickly about him NEVER putting things in the dishwasher. If he can put his cup on top of the dishwasher, then surely he can put it in. And he got unreasonably irritated when I suggested he check his pockets before putting his trousers in the wash pile. (An important business card went through the wash.) Small things, but they can build up until there's very little light in our voices, or any light at all . . . Here comes the throat lump again . . .

I shouldn't get prickly. I forgot to clean my toenail clippings from the bath so we're probably even.

So, weak spots. We have them. Clearly I need to stop delaying and dive into this resolution before Hugh gets swallowed up into another work matter.

I realise I should probably begin from the beginning . . . Hello! I'm Susannah – wife, mother, cleaner of surfaces, runner of household.

My husband, Hugh, and I have four children: Eloise, who is thirteen; Raffy, who is nine; Jimmy, eight; and Mary-Lou, six.

We didn't quite set out to have so many children, but certain things happened and before long it seemed as though motherhood was the only thing I could manage. Only I wasn't very good at it. Did I keep having babies to try to get it right? The way people keep trying to bake sponge cakes? Anyway, four it is, and of course now the thought of not having them all gives me a horrible pain.

We live in a medium-sized, creaky but good-natured blue house on a hill in West Hobart with a tangly garden, a lovely view of Hobart and an overweight dog called Barky. My best friend, Ria, who is mostly in London being a very famous pianist and composer, says that our house has a really contented look on its Federation face, and that she sleeps much better here than she does anywhere else. I know very well what she means. At least, I used to. Lately there are times when I look at our house and it seems to look back at me with a weary expression. Only last week I was doing one of my regular nude runs to the laundry in search of underwear and Eloise said, 'God, Mum, even the house is embarrassed.' Perhaps she's right. Not that long ago Eloise was laughing at my jokes and charging around the house in the nude as well. Soon she'll be giving me mortgage advice.

By the way, I got a text from Ria last night. It said:

On a scale of 1 to 10, my New Year's hangover
is a solid 9. Hoping yours is nothing less than a 7
and that your night was super. Happy New Year.
Let's kick this one in the balls. Love always, R xx
PS Hope NY resolution is off to a sizzling start.

PPS You know you could always pick up a certain stringed instrument; I hear a good serenade is quite the thing.

But I digress . . .

Hugh is a forensic structural engineer, which means he is called on to investigate structural failures that lead to litigation. For instance, someone might lose money, limbs, life or other vital things because something went structurally wrong. He has worked very hard to build up his business and career. Very, very hard. Study and more study and seminars, etc. And now he employs three other engineers with various specialties and his consultancy is called upon to investigate all kinds of things. Sometimes I hear him on the radio talking about buckled iron or something. He is an expert, we are very proud of him and I don't know why these words are sounding insincere and uncomfortable.

I do not resent my husband's success. I am grateful for all his hard work. I just wish he could be more present (perhaps with more presents, which sounds materialistic but I haven't had a birthday gift in five years. He writes a good card, though, so . . .). It's just that we have four children and years and years of ~~drudgery~~ challenging parenting ahead and no amount of Hugh saying he will take on less work in the future leaves me believing this will happen. He is ~~mental~~ passionate about his work; he adores it. It saves lives, etc. He needs me to support that, and I'm happy to be the reinforced girders. I just wish he found me at least half as interesting as his work. Or a quarter, let's not be greedy.

This interest factor seems to be a recurring resolution theme . . . I mean, he *adores* his work and I don't necessarily have time for that level of extreme adoration. Just something a bit sparklier than simple fondness would be perfect. I suppose that something would be love, wouldn't it? Does he properly love me?

Once he went to Antarctica for five months. He left his comfortable home, three and a half children and loving wife to go and sleep in cramped quarters and work as a labourer on a continent made of ice. And he *really, properly* loved it. He still gazes at the photos, watches the videos.

There's a video of him and his fellow expeditioners daring one another to jump into freezing water. I hate that video because it was taken the same day I recorded my own video of Eloise reciting a poem in assembly. She'd practised and practised; I'd arrived early with small Raff and smaller Jimmy to get good seats and poise the camera. Eloise was about three lines in when Jimmy toppled off his chair, split his head open, screamed blue murder and vomited on the carpet. I watched Hugh's video for the first time in the GP's treatment room, where Jimmy was being glued up and observed for concussion. There they were – Hugh and his friends being brave and admirable in their white, once-in-a-lifetime world – while Jimmy writhed and Raffy took the lids off about thirty sterile specimen jars. Meanwhile Eloise sat stoic and still, mutely refusing to admit disappointment, embarrassment or other emotions associated with having things dashed. I wanted to pluck Hugh out of his video, hold him up to my eyes and say, 'How very dare you.'

There's ~~probably~~ definitely been a splinter of ice in me ever since Hugh's Antarctic expedition, though I've tried to melt it. Must try harder. And I mustn't let my icy heart (or spleen) interfere with my resolve. Nor should I get too emotional (swallow throat lump). I shall remain businesslike and, as Ria suggested, just work at it. I will move systematically through all the Things That Might Make Hugh Properly Love Me Again.

Actually, I should probably get forensic and investigate our history too, for passion-reinvention strategies. And origins of decay. We certainly had passion once. Sometimes I catch a fleeting flash of it again, but for the most part, passion just seems to have fallen by the wayside, along with regular waxing and seeing films. (There are a lot of good things by the wayside, if only I could find where it is – somewhere near the too-hard basket, probably.)

Must cook dinner. I'll do some thinking while I work . . . Could we have cheese on toast if I give everyone a multivitamin?

THURSDAY 5th JANUARY

Hugh still hasn't been to work, which is ~~hard to believe~~ a positive. But I do get the feeling he is searching for things to do that don't involve family (me). He has fixed all the wear and tear in the plaster and painted over the mends. And then agreed to re-paint Eloise's bedroom. It's been clear for a long time that pale yellow with a birdy frieze is much too childish for a beanstalky secondary school girl with breast buds, God help us. (Senior school! How can this be?) She finally appealed to Hugh for deliverance from the nursery and he has obliged. I feel sad for the birds, but they probably don't want to share a room with an increasingly sullen prepubescent who has been ignoring them in favour of supernatural fiction for the better part of a decade. Not to mention her collection of sneakers and the incessant hauntings of Lana Del Rey. They've been through enough sorrow, those birdies . . .

But I shouldn't complain about Hugh's elsewhere focus. There are probably women everywhere who wish their husbands would do something handy for once and stop hanging about, getting in the way with their fawnings, their interest and their meaningful words. Hugh and I had a conversation about gravel today.

Oh, I know that it's unreasonable to expect that fluttery, in-love feeling all through marriage, and that there's every chance the butterfly-in-tummy thing isn't love at all, just a fleeting chemical response to heightened emotions. It wouldn't be normal to have them all the time. Howsoever, I don't want normal. Normal is too close to ordinary, which is too close to ornery, which I am rather too often these days.

Oh, for a few butterflies. Or one. They were there once. The first time I ever saw Hugh, I had a full-sized philharmonic orchestra of the bloody things in my stomach. A proper kaleidoscope of butterflies. And I couldn't take my eyes off him, I really couldn't. (Is that some sort of romantic music tinkling in my imagination; Elgar's 'Salut d'Amour' for viola?) And I've never been the same again . . .

University of Tasmania, 1992 (Oh, time, you speedy old bugger)
Ria and I had just started full-time at the Conservatorium of Music in Hobart – me to study viola while Ria chose piano among the fleet of instruments she'd already mastered. We'd barely even left school before Ria talked her way into a job for each of us at the university shop (or, rather, played her way in – she was a bit of a celebrity even then). We were hopeless with the cash register but quite good at stacking shelves and creating window displays. Our displays went down in University of Tasmania history. The shop manager had a thing for classical music and thought we were artistic geniuses, so gave us free rein. I even found a battered boutique mannequin at the tip shop, which we fixed up and named Caroline Smedley-Warren. Ria said this was the perfect name for a striking woman with good bone structure and a sense of humour. By the time our first orientation week came around, Caroline was in the window with a new perm,

a UTas-emblemed tracksuit, Wayfarers and a placard saying, 'Your future is so bright I have to wear shades.' It was from this window, at the end of O week, that I first encountered Hugh Parks.

I was arranging a pile of textbooks into a student desk tableau when I glanced out the window and saw a boy standing at the bus stop chatting in a group. He was wearing a blue T-shirt with red trim around his shapely upper arms. His hair was black and thick, and long enough to be wavy. Thick black wavy hair was, from where I stood with my wispy ~~red~~ auburn hair, the ultimate human plumage. And then I saw his eyes. Oh, those eyes! His hazel eyes in that particular light, with an autumny tree above him, were sort of amber. I stared at them and they reminded me of how tiny ancient insects get trapped and fossilised in amber; I wondered about what secrets might be hidden in those eyes. I'm not sure how long I stood there frozen, imagining his mysteries, when I realised the eyes were looking straight back at me! For an insane instant I considered staying frozen, to blend into the tableau with Caroline (who was by then dressed as a nerd and holding a sign saying, 'I bought my books last September, hurry up and get yours'), but he smiled at me and I jerked my gaze away. Then, realising how rude that was, I looked up at him again, smiled an awkward smile and did a little wave. He waved back, laughed and returned to his friends, leaving me with my embarrassment pulsing in my face.

I glanced at Caroline Smedley-Warren, as if she might offer me solace, but her expression was unforgiving. It said, 'You, my dear, are a prize berk, and for God's sake, put a comb in that baby fluff you call hair.' My traitorous eyes returned once more to the boy and he'd turned away, giving them licence to linger. *If he were mine,* I thought, looking at the dark curve of hair at the nape of his neck, *I'd never feel grumpy ever, ever again.*

Then Ria poked into the moment and said, 'I found a desk lamp,' which was quite apt given the light that had switched on inside me, but then she peered at my red cheeks and said, 'Jesus, Lobster Chops. What's happened? Did you wet yourself or something?'

'What?' I said. 'No. I don't know, bit hot in here. Good lamp. Very good lamp.' I busied myself with books while she studied me suspiciously, looked at Caroline and then back at me.

With narrow eyes she put the lamp on the table and backed away again. 'I have to get an extension cord; can I trust you two to behave?' I ignored her and used all my willpower not to look in the direction of the bus stop.

A minute or so later, I was buttoning Caroline's cardigan when there was a knock on the window. I turned with a start to find myself face to face with the amber-eyed boy. He was smiling again (I hate to think what my face was doing). He said something but I couldn't hear him through the thick glass.

'Pardon me?' I mouthed, with what I hoped was a friendly but cool look on my face.

He pointed towards my shoulder and mouthed, 'The bee. There's a bee,' in exaggerated fashion.

I swiped violently at my shoulder to brush away the offending bee, whacked Caroline in the jaw, lunged to catch her as she toppled over, lost balance myself, knocked the desk lamp and crashed to the floor in a pile of books, broken lamp, nerdy mannequin and utter, extreme mortification.

As the sounds of the shattered lamp died away, I peeked out from under Caroline's synthetic curls and wondered if I could possibly stay hidden there for the rest of my life.

Ria was first on the scene. 'Fucking hell, Susannah. Are you alive under there?'

I hoped I wasn't.

The amber-eyed boy was next. I could see the edge of his T-shirt and I knew it must be him because when he said, 'Are you okay? Here, I can help,' his voice was lovely, with a sort of clip unique to Tasmanians who surf. It matched his eyes and that unfairly sublime hair.

'I'm fine, I'm fine,' I said from under the rubble, then scrabbled about with Caroline to recover myself.

They lifted her off me; she was surprisingly heavy.

'What the hell happened?' asked Ria. 'I knew there was something going on with you and Caroline.'

'There was a bee,' I said. 'I'm allergic to them, and things went a bit . . .'

The boy started to laugh. I felt indignant and thought, *Of course, the handsome ones are always arseholes*. 'I can die from a bee sting,' I said. This was ~~a lie~~ an exaggeration. I just swell up a bit.

'I'm sorry,' he replied, 'but there wasn't a bee.'

'What? You said there was a bee. You pointed to my shoulder. That's why —'

'No,' he interrupted, not laughing now but wearing that infuriatingly wonderful smile. 'I was pointing at the sign. There should be a "b" in "September".'

The three of us looked at Caroline's sign. It said, *I bought my books last Septemer, hurry up and get yours.*

'I just didn't think a spelling mistake was in keeping with the whole geeky theme,' said the boy. Then he laughed again. 'I'm sorry. Susannah, was it? I'm Hugh.' And he shook my hand.

I can clearly remember (rememer) the feeling that shot up my arm from my hand when he touched it. 'There was a fizz right to my core,' I told Ria afterwards, once she'd got fed up with my dazed state and cross-examined me.

'A fizz right to your floor, more like it,' she said in disgust. 'Your pelvic floor. It's not love, you knob. It's lust. You can't love someone you don't know.' (How can someone so unromantic play 'Meine Freuden' with such feeling?)

'But it is,' I said, more to myself. 'It is love.'

She snorted, 'Look, he's gorgeous. I give you that. Definitely you should bonk him, but don't be dumb about it.'

But it was love, as it turned out. And absolutely I was dumb about it.

How do people make that feeling last? The butterflies, the fizzy core (and the fizzy floor)? Mum and Dad, for instance, have been married for over forty-five years and there is still obvious chemistry between them. Mum can be so infuriating sometimes but Dad's pride in her is evident. Sometimes he watches her for long moments before saying, 'Look at your mother. Isn't she lovely?'

Alison and Laurence have been married for longer still. (Gosh, is there a milestone coming up? Must check. Alison will be ~~incorrigible~~ furious if we forget.) And they have endured. At least Laurence has. On his birthday in December Alison gave a surprisingly tender speech and Laurence held her and kissed her head, then she gave him a butterfly kiss on the cheek. It was like a secret handshake imbued with deeply ingrained love. I shed a tear, perhaps because I realised even *they* still had life in their love while Hugh and I forget to touch for days and can't think of conversation in the car. I don't necessarily want the intensity of feeling I had in my uni days. I'd never get anything done. About the level of Isobel and Josh, perhaps, who look at each other's faces a lot, rest their arms on one another and spell 'healthy sex life' with their body language. From where does a marriage derive its stamina? Perhaps some research is required.

SATURDAY 7th JANUARY

It rained all day today so, after three games of Uno, one batch of brownies and Hugh trying to teach everyone to yo-yo, I suggested we go and see Mum and Dad. Hugh shuffled and said, 'Would you be able to drop me at the office, then? Just to check on things? I'll bring dinner home.'

I just knew he wouldn't get to Monday without going back to work. But, 'Sure!' I said brightly (because light in voice). 'Dad would just rope you into sorting out the sound system anyway.'

He chuckled (weakly) and said, 'Tell him I will next time.'

In the car on the way I compensated by turning up the radio and singing along to Lorde. Even Eloise looked up from her book long enough to appear impressed. At the office, Hugh got out of the car and said, 'Tell Frannie I'd love another jar of her relish.'

I said breezily, 'Will do, *byeeee*,' and drove away without turning down the music, checking if he had his keys or asking how he was getting home. In the rear-vision mirror I'm almost sure I saw Hugh gaze regretfully after us. Nonchalance is key to allure.

When we got to Mum and Dad's, we found Dad standing underneath the plum tree with a bucket of peaches. 'Before you say anything,' Dad said when he saw us, 'she insisted. And my hips are four years older than hers.'

'What?' I said, just as Jimmy yelled, 'Hello, Granny Frannie!' and waved into the tree at Mum's blue gumboots.

'Yoo-hoo,' came her voice from above the gumboots. 'Wonderful timing. The chookies have been on a laying rampage and I've made three egg and bacon pies.'

'The plums!' shouted Dad. 'Concentrate on the plums! One thing at a time, woman.' He looked at Mary-Lou and said, 'She's not right in the head, your grandmother. She's already been up the peach tree and before that she had a go on your swing.'

'You'll catch me if I fall, darling,' Mum called.

'Or you'll squash me flat and we'll both be dead,' said Dad. 'Fast-track your inheritance, Zannah. How are you, sweet pea?' He gave me a squeeze.

'Granny!' yelled Jim, always willing to help when there are new feats of balance to be attempted. 'Come down. I'll get up there for you.'

'I'm done, Jimmy, thank you,' she said and, on cue, a full bucket of plums whizzed down on a rope. 'Plum, anyone? They're delicious – all the nicest ones are up the top.'

When Mum had clambered down, Dad patted her bottom and said, 'Quite the nicest plum I've seen.'

Bottom pats annoy me. Too often they come unexpectedly with no chance to tighten gluteal muscles, so they turn into a wobbly bottom-fat pat. Much like those hugs-with-groin-thrust Hugh used to give me. They were annoying too. (*Why can't he just hug me without involving his penis?* I used to think.) But these days I'd quite welcome a thrusty hug.

Mum looked pleased with her bottom pat, though. She laughed in a flirty way. And I felt such a tug in my chest for all the familiar comfort of it all, along with a homesick sort of ache, as though all the good things are memories.

☆

Later, when the children were with Dad in the garage, playing their way through his record collection, and Mum and I were cutting yellow pictures out of her old magazines for a chair she wants to decoupage, I grasped a rare moment of silence, summoned an earnest voice and said, 'Mum?'

She took off her reading glasses, set down her scissors and said, 'Yes, I've had a little bit of botox in my frown lines; yes, it was expensive; no, I don't regret it – I feel terrific; and yes, your father knows.'

'What?'

'What?'

'You had botox?'

'What were you going to say?' She put her glasses back on and did a little hum.

'Gosh.' I peered at her face. 'You do look fresher.'

'Yes, and apparently there's a study somewhere that claims that facial expression is linked to the parts of the brain that control emotions, which means that if you freeze your frown, you freeze your grouch. Genius!'

'You've never been very frowny, though, Mum.'

'Not when I see you, darling. Now, what was it you were going to say?'

'I was going to ask how you and Dad have managed to stay happy for so long.'

'Oh.' She gave me a suspicious look.

'I just want to keep my marriage as strong as it is. Always.'

'Right. Good. Well, we love each other, so that's the principal requirement, I'm told. And we don't eat in front of the telly, we don't wear pyjamas and we don't keep secrets.'

'And botox?' I laughed.

'No, that's just a happy little addendum. There is one other thing, though.'

'What?'

'Terrence Squirrel.'

'Who?'

'He was a little crush I had once. A friend of Dad's who came to stay in 1986. Nothing ever came of it, just some heart flutters, nothing bedroomy. He's married and lives in France now but he still sends me gifts now and then. Keeps your dad on his toes.'

'Mum!' I was astounded. 'Dad knows about this?'

'Of course. That's the point. No secrets, remember.'

'He doesn't mind?'

'Well, he had a bit of a thing for the woman in the bakery so all's fair. I think it put a bit of vim in our relations, actually.' She left the kitchen to get more magazines, and I was happy to leave the discussion there.

SUNDAY 8th JANUARY

It's still raining, so today we fetched Valda over to watch *Chitty Chitty Bang Bang*. She didn't like my sandwiches and kept her trademark grumpy face firmly on, but she was tapping her foot through all of the songs so I know she enjoyed herself.

When the film was done and the fates of Truly and Caractacus were nicely entwined, I sighed loudly and asked her how she managed to stay married to Neville for sixty years. She said, 'Sixty-three years, eight months and four days.' And then she gazed up at the ceiling, as if Neville was watching, and her face shifted somehow, so that her eyes widened and seemed very blue. 'The trick to a lasting marriage is mutual respect, gentle handling, kindness and conversation.' Then she closed her eyes and a tear ran down her cheek.

'Oh, Valda,' I said. 'That's lovely. I'm sorry you don't have him any more.' And I put my hand on hers but she pulled away and said, 'Oh, he's still here.'

Raffy and Jim peered at the ceiling in alarm and Mary-Lou asked, 'Where do we go when we die? Where's Neville?' Her face was full of thinking; she rubbed her little freckly nose and I had one of those mothery pangs of love.

'He's someplace where there's no music and a lot of stout,' said Valda (which was a bit drab, I thought). 'Where will you go, Mary-Lou?'

'To somewhere with no spinach and a lot of puppies,' said Mary-Lou, before adding, 'and no stinky brothers.' Jimmy gave her a shove, she yelled and the moment was ruined. Children are so careless with moments. Adults are too, I suppose.

I knew Neville Bywaters was a kind man. Hugh wasn't so sure about him. He was always wary because once he saw Neville lose his temper with the wheelie bins. He was very well built, tall and imposing: a man of much presence but few words. But he was so attentive with his roses that I knew his heart had to be good. This confirms it. Respect, gentleness, kindness, communication. I will add them to the passion armoury. Some fruitful research (especially if you include Mum's plums and discount her Squirrel revelation; I don't think extramarital dalliances are the answer).

☆

WEDNESDAY 11th JANUARY

We're just home from two days at Opossum Bay. It was getting to that stage of the holidays when the children were starting to manhandle time in ways that drive me mad. I am a firm believer in boredom as an essential brain exercise, but there are limits. It's a rare phenomenon these days, boredom. It's probably about as outdated as the Jane Fonda workouts, but just as good for you. But when boredom leads to arguments, balls on the roof, defaced business documents, fridge gazing and the disappearance of the condensed milk, it's probably time I put something into their hours.

So we found a tiny house right on the water at Opossum Bay and I took the children there. What a gorgeous little town! As a special treat we got Hugh to drop us at Wrest Point and we took a water taxi over. How could I have ever missed going there when it's so close to Hobart? Makes me wonder how many little hamlets there are on this island that I've never visited.

In the spirit of sparkle, I gently asked Hugh whether he could get time off work to come with us, then when he gave us the inevitable no, I didn't make a fuss. I just made him a pot of chicken noodle soup and tidied a lot, so he wouldn't have to worry. Actually, to be honest, this was probably more about me trying to make him feel guilty, which is hardly kind, but it was for a good cause. I also spritzed my perfume around a bit so he'd return home to the scent of me and possibly feel some yearning. Nothing like a good old yearn to soften the heart.

Anyway, once we arrived at Opossum Bay and got over the initial arguments about who got the top bunk and whose fault it was that we forgot Barky's leash, it was all really lovely. The weather was perfect. There's a jetty to fish from and rock pools to explore and a sort of golden, nostalgic feel to the whole place. As if someone held a big seaside happiness festival there long ago and the air is still humming with it.

The Hadleys have a shack there! This is a thing in Tasmania – you and your neighbours leave the suburb and catch up again at the seaside, just with more gin and less rush. Their house was just four along from ours and it's not actually a shack, more a beach pavilion with an entertainment centre and a boating department. Mary-Lou looked less pleased with her bucket and spade when Thomas Hadley brought out his remote-controlled yacht. I felt much the same about my shorts when Isobel appeared in her bikini.

It turns out that Isobel is a professor of heart failure. A Professor of Medical Science, I mean, specialising in heart failure. She and Josh are both away a lot, giving papers at conferences and things. Sought-after sorts. Experts. I feel a bit lumpen beside them, especially in my bathers, but they are very nice. (Isobel and Josh, not the bathers; they are yellow and awful and have failed at boosting my boobs. It's tricky to boost boobs when there are no boobs to boost, I suppose.) I asked them about their research but mostly I was interested to know how they manage such high-flying lives.

'We work our calendars so that the children always have one of us home,' said Josh. 'It means we don't have all that much time together, but it's top-quality time, isn't it, honey?' At this point he put his hand on her neck.

Isobel smiled and said, 'Yes. We never run out of things to talk about.' They looked so interested in one another. Respect. Mutual.

They were also, like all the best people, very good at appearing interested in me. 'So you're a musician,' said Josh.

I gave them my standard response to this question: 'I studied music. Viola. I worked for the TSO for a bit, did some things for the

Australian Ballet and musical theatre. Then I had four children and Hugh's forensic work took off and, you know . . .'

They nodded sympathetically. 'Hugh's work sounds interesting,' said Josh, and on we talked about that for a bit. It's an old trick – throw them off the musical scent with a bit of forensic talk and everyone's distracted. It must be all those *CSI* programs on the telly.

Then Isobel said, 'And he told me he did a season in Antarctica; I'd love to go down there.'

'We could do that,' said Josh, his hand still on the back of her neck.

Then we joked about how their professions could get them to Antarctica. Seal infertility and heart failure in penguins and so on.

'Did you go too?' asked Isobel. 'Surely they need a violist down there?'

'Ah, no,' I said. 'Hugh went when we still had babies. I was pregnant with Mary-Lou so . . .' I tried not to sound piqued. 'I had a lot of help from the grandparents.'

'I hear the whole experience is pretty addictive,' said Josh. 'Will he go back?'

'Oh, you know what they say about ice,' I said. 'You never can better that first trip.'

Attempted wit is very good at covering up sore points. Apparently I have a few. Perhaps I should ask Isobel if too many sore points can lead to heart failure.

Later I saw Josh and Isobel swimming together. Actually, there was only a little bit of swimming and quite a lot of kissing. Passionate kissing. It went on for so long that I accidentally wondered whether he'd slipped his willy in. Then I had to look away because I give myself the creeps sometimes. But still I wonder . . . there were a lot of ripples.

Anyway, it was a nice few days. Did us good. And love is so much more than sex on the beach (I was reminded when we arrived home). The children leapt all over Hugh when they saw him. They bubbled with news and excitement as though they hadn't seen him for months. Even Raff seemed sparky. We were S Parks and all the little Sparks. We ate fish and chips around the island bench, Hugh told us about the case he's consulting on, Eloise displayed her Opossum Bay photos and Jimmy showed us how to do a sun salute (Isobel is a yoga buff, of course). Marriage is family, children, home. There are other ways to make love than having a shag in the sea.

I gave Hugh a proper hug and two kisses. He seemed genuinely pleased to have us back. Perhaps I should go away more often. Perhaps I should go to Antarctica.

NB: Hugh's case involves the collapse of an awning in Elizabeth Street. A pedestrian, a young man, lost his arm and had his spinal cord damaged. Puts things into perspective, really. Perhaps I should just thank my lucky stars and stop harping on about dwindling passion. Surely lucky stars have extra sparkle.

SATURDAY 14th JANUARY

How long is too long not to have sex? There was a period late last year when we didn't have sex for ~~six seven~~ nine weeks! It was that Novembery time of year when school has a fair and there are swimming carnivals and Grandparents Days. Eloise was huffy about me not letting her have some blonde put in her hair for the Year Six

Leavers' dinner. She's thirteen! And she never believes me that hair as fine as ours will not react well to chemical influences. Also red + blonde = pink. Mary-Lou had a ballet exam and there were an extortionate number of birthday parties. Then we had a school sex-education evening in which they said, 'Mum and Dad love each other enough to touch in loving ways' and I realised that it's been a very long time since 'intercourse' (terrible word), nor could I remember the last time I was touched in a loving way. Unless I counted the dog rubbing his eye-goop on my trousers.

So I went home and initiated sex that very evening and then in the middle of it, I accidentally thought about mouse poos, which can't be a good thing. It's just that I'd forgotten to sweep the mouse droppings from the bench by the toaster (I just can't bear to kill tiny animals with shiny little eyes so I'd been pretending they weren't there). I remembered them (the poos) just as my bottom was being caressed, and I had to concentrate very hard on getting my mind back to the job at hand. It's also probably not a good thing to call it a job, like it's chores, even though sometimes post-coital relaxation is more like job-done relief. Ticking a box, so to speak. Coital/coitus is another terrible word. Box isn't much better, when referring to the vagina (although getting it ticked can be very satisfying). Vagina is a pretty awful word too, actually. Sex needs a new vocabulary . . .

No, sex should only be 'work' if you happen to be a sex worker. For me it should be a pleasure. And it usually is, once we get into it. It's just that the getting-into-it part can all seem a bit effortful. Firstly, you have to just about book it in, much like a sex worker. Secondly, sinking into pillows and letting blessed sleep take me does often seem more sensible than tangling up the bedclothes and getting sweaty. Also, I'm much more inhibited about my body these days. My boobs are all saggy, having been so full of milk for approximately six years. It is the ultimate injustice – along with pimples on wrinkles – to have a flat chest that sags. Sagging chest skin. And they only get worse. I saw Valda's boobs once when she forgot to button up her nightdress and they looked like wind socks with no wind. I could have rolled them up and tucked them neatly into each other like an actual pair of socks.

(Valda's boobs remind me that I promised to take her a musical theatre CD; she said she'd like to get to know the musicals. Must fit that in.)

I wonder if it'd all be easier if I were paid for sex. I know someone who gave her husband a blow job every day for three months and got a new kitchen. I could ask for a Room of My Own. (Although even if I had one, I'd never use it; I'd always be coming out to see what everyone was up to. One of the conundrums of motherhood is that you want everyone to bugger off and leave you alone but then you worry about where they all are.)

So anyway, to go back to the original question – is nine weeks a proper drought or just a dry spell? There's a mother at school who quite openly says that she and her husband have sex every other day. Imagine being bold enough to say that at a trivia night. And having so much sex! She's one of those earthy women who appear quite ~~smelly~~ comfortable in their own skin. She's had her vulva moulded for that wall of plaster vulvas at Mona.

TUESDAY 17th JANUARY

It's the 17th already? Sparkle progress is slow, to say the least. Hugh and I are still just going about the business of being a family. Businesslike . . . I think I'm still reeling from the research phase, from which it's becoming all too clear just how much trouble Hugh and I might actually be in. Would I have been better off not probing the situation at all?

This morning I went to Valda's to drop off her musical theatre CD and found her telling Neville off about the plumbing. Even they're engaging with one another and he's been dead for two years. (I haven't received thanks for the CD but she's clearly enjoying it; we've had 'On My Own' from *Les Mis* blasting out of her windows this morning. She must be getting very deaf.)

WEDNESDAY 18th JANUARY

I decided to tell Hugh about the Sparkle Project. Communication is, after all, supposed to be the bedrock and cornerstone of a good relationship. It will seem all a bit random and suspicious if I just start executing passion measures without his informed involvement. He might think I'm having an affair, losing my mind or having a midlife crisis. Am I having a midlife crisis? Also I was hopeful he might be wildly enthusiastic about it and we could begin immediately. As a team.

So, in that sliver of time between all the children finally settling into bed and Hugh and I getting engrossed in the telly or falling asleep and not having sex, I said, 'Am I boring?'

Hugh moved his head towards me but his eyes stayed on the telly (*Indiana Jones*). 'Mm?'

'I worry that I'm boring.'

'You're not boring.' (Indy's winsome lady friend suddenly wields a shotgun and dispenses with an enemy.)

'I am,' I sigh. 'Part of my New Year's resolution is to not be boring.'

'Is it?'

'Yes. We're going to try a whole lot of new things.'

'Are we?' His fingernails tensely scratched the arm of the couch.

'Yes. I don't think there's enough, you know, *spark* between us.'

He looked at me then (quizzically or knowingly? Or irritably? Probably the last) so I added, 'What do you think?'

'Well, I don't think we can expect sunsets and roses at this stage of our lives, can we?' he said.

'I don't mean silly romance stuff,' I said. 'I mean passion. We used to be so . . . you know . . . passionate.'

He ran his fingers through his hair in that way he does when the children ask him to put the badminton net up. 'Zannah, I am passionate about you. I'm passionate about my family. Everything I do is for the family. We're busy. I don't think you'd find all that many couples head over heels all the time, let's be real.'

'Josh and Isobel seem quite head over.'

He laughed. 'Oh, why didn't you just say you'd like me to relentlessly ravage you in public?' He moved in next to me on the couch, slid a hand up my thigh and said, 'I've got a very snazzy car, a pool and a Rolf Lauren jacket. Please love me.' Then he sloppy-kissed my cheek and made a growly noise.

'It's Ralph Lauren, you idiot,' I said. Then one of us must have leaned on the remote control because the telly flicked over to a shot of ducks mating.

'Duck sparks!' Hugh shouted.

Raffy appeared, with his hair all pillow-rumpled. He rubbed his eyes and said, 'Is that duck murdering the other duck?'

'Yes,' said Hugh. 'It'll end badly. Go to bed.' Then he patted my leg and said, 'I'll take you to the Revolving Restaurant on Valentine's Day, how's that?' and then he left, ostensibly to put Raffy back to bed but really to avoid the issue. It was lucky he did, though, because after the ducks were some penguins, on ice. I quickly flicked it back to *Indiana Jones*. The last thing we need is for Hugh to be reminded how much more beautiful and interesting Antarctica is than me.

I got a bit cross when he returned. 'One – the Revolving Restaurant was exciting when I was seven,' I said, 'and that was because it was the first time I realised cauliflower could be delicious. Two – just now, right then, was the perfect opportunity for you to initiate, you know, lovemaking, and you're watching telly —'

'Well, it was lucky I didn't because Raffy would have witnessed something more disturbing than duck sex.'

'But before that you didn't. You just went all silly. There's no intensity any more, just silliness. Like friends or siblings.'

'Well, I thought about it,' he said, 'but you were on about romance and stuff, and I thought it wasn't appropriate because apparently men are always putting sex before romance.'

'I didn't say anything about romance. I said passion. You could have at least kissed me. On the lips.'

'Well, I'll kiss you now, then.'

'I don't want you to kiss me now. We've lost the window.'

'Well, sorry. The window was a little fogged up. I misread the signs.'

We sat huffily watching sparks fly out of Indiana's stupid lost ark. Then Hugh sighed and said, 'Don't overthink it, Susannah. Don't dream up problems. We're fine.'

☆

When he went to bed he didn't kiss me, on the lips or anywhere.

'Well, you won't mind if I keep on with my resolution?' I called after him.

'Go for it,' he said, but he had the same tone of voice as when I told him I was thinking about a permaculture course. I'll show him. I'll make our relationship so sustainable it will have its own ecosystem . . .

He's probably in bed awaiting the first sparkle experiment, but I'd prefer to be a bit more spontaneous. Also I haven't actually planned any experiments. And I'm tired . . . I'll just have a little rock in the chair . . . darkle, darkle . . .

He's always telling me not to overthink things. It so irritates him. But I can't very well help where my brain goes. I tried some mindfulness tapes once but the clock in the hallway seemed to tick louder and louder until it was virtually yelling at me that I was wasting precious time. So I went and cleaned the cutlery drawer.

Tomorrow, I will put thoughts into action and sort out my ~~marrage~~ marriage.

(Because the truth is, if I don't try something, anything, I don't know if Hugh and I can survive the rankles and the darkling. And I'm not sure I'll survive the not surviving.)

Allegro

TUESDAY 24th JANUARY

I am finally able to properly attend to the Sparkle Project because at last the children are back at school! So I'm all set up in the wardrobe with my diary (obviously), a very nice new pen (quite expensive, to aid quality of writings) and a cup of tea. I'm very keen to have a thorough rummage about in our back catalogues, when our (or at least my) sparkles were shimmering about all over the place . . .

The Ship Inn, Hobart, 1992

It was only a day or two after the 'bee' incident that I saw Hugh again, in the beer garden of a local pub where Ria and I were making a guest appearance with a band. They had a thing for Corrs covers and we were the Celtic bit. We'd dressed in kilts and frilled white shirts and I'd teased up my hair so the light would shine through it and make the most of its red. We were waiting off to the side of the stage when I noticed Hugh and his cool, swaggery engineering friends arrive.

'What's wrong?' Ria asked when she noticed I'd tried to shrink to fit into her shadow. (Impossible given my ungainly lank and her diminutive frame.)

'Nothing,' I squeaked. She looked around and spotted the group of blokes.

'A six-foot, dark-haired Hugh Parks sort of nothing?' She looked triumphant.

I wished desperately I hadn't made my love-strike so obvious, but then I could never hide anything from Ria anyway. By now we'd found out his name, who his friends were, what school he came from and what he was studying. She eyed him openly, taking rapid little sips from her Mercury cider. 'I still think we should be aiming for someone older, third year at least. Maybe even a lecturer. I see why you're smitten, though. He's vindaloo.'

Thankfully she had to stop scrutinising because we were motioned onto the stage, me with my viola, Ria with a piccolo. I managed to get through one and a half songs without looking in Hugh's direction, but then I noticed Ria raising eyebrows at me and I sneaked a look, to find that he was looking up at me. That smile, those eyes.

There were more butterflies, but they were swatted away by the person I'd become onstage, the one with a bit of cheek about her and a lot of front. She was never afraid to take a risk; she had her music to hide behind and could be, while not talented enough to be bumptious or insolent like Ria, quite confident. Stage-brave. Or was I just brave? (Is it still bravery if it's never occurred to you that something might go wrong? What is the opposite of brave? Terrified?)

Anyway, up there onstage I looked at Hugh along the length of my viola, found his gaze and held it with a lively and extended improvised instrumental bridge designed to claim attention. It left Ria and her piccolo far behind. When I'd finished, the bewildered band ended the song while Ria and I performed a small Irish jig that whipped people onto the dance floor. As I whirled I saw that Hugh had put his drink down to clap along. And that he was still watching.

Once the set was over and we left the stage, Ria said, 'That was some allegro, Susannah Mackay. You stole the show.' But the stage-brave me was rapidly disappearing, leaving Susannah to administer my tumult of feelings.

Hugh raised his stubbie at me and nodded from across the room. I gasped, did a small wave back, then, because that felt a bit dismissive, made the wave bigger, but then it was too big so I put my hand to my head and used it to twiddle my hair.

Ria snorted and said, 'Please tell me that's some sort of elaborate love signal the two of you have come up with. That or a serious nerve disorder.'

Hugh was still watching so I laughed very loudly as if Ria had said something properly funny and clever, then picked up my cider for a casual, grown-up sip. The top of the glass bottle connected painfully and loudly with my teeth.

Ria gasped. 'Jesus Christ. Are you okay?'

'Yes,' I said through gritted teeth. My eyes watered. 'Please just pretend that didn't happen.'

'But —'

'Please?'

And so she said, 'Have you sorted out your electives yet?' She stared at my mouth and added distractedly, 'I'm thinking about audio production.'

'Oh, production, of course. I'm thinking choir.' I tasted metal.

'Oh, choir, right.' Her eyes widened.

'I don't want to take on anything too hard.' My gum was throbbing.

'Umm . . .'

'There's blood, isn't there?' I said.

'Yes,' she said quietly.

'Bad?'

'Yes.'

'Shall we go?'

'Yes. Immediately.'

We hurried out. I didn't dare look back at Hugh. When we got out to the street and I found a car mirror to check myself in, I saw that my smile was filled with scary red teeth.

'It's a shame it's not Halloween,' said Ria, but she didn't laugh because my face was almost as red as my teeth and my eyes were full of despair – proper poetry despair, lovelorn and hopeless. I decided that I did indeed have a nervous disorder, a terminal one, and would need to confine myself to the windowless studios of the conservatorium for the rest of my undergraduate life.

Digging up this memory makes me wonder whether I might be able to reawaken those delicious first feelings, and hopefully improve on my general delivery, without the stage and the bloody teeth. I'll have time to have an actual try – out in the field, so to speak – now that the back-to-school flurry is over. Goodness me, *what* a flurry. Last week was swallowed up in a cloud of book-buying chaos and feeling anxious about too many activities or not enough and perhaps someone should be doing drama because Thingamie's mum said it worked wonders on his confidence and oh look I still haven't sorted through last year's art folders and soon it'll be September and we still haven't named the drink bottles let alone started anything new.

Anyway, they did indeed make it back to school. Eloise at her new school!!! She had an orientation day yesterday and we had a bit of a send-off breakfast with croissants, which I couldn't eat due to that swoony sort of feeling that comes with time rushing past your ears and turning your dear little kinder girl into a SECONDARY SCHOOL GIRL who doesn't care what colour her lunch box is.

Hugh did a breakfast fly-through before his court appearance this morning and called to Eloise, 'Go get 'em, darling.' To my watery eyes he said firmly, 'She'll be fine. Look at her, taking it in her stride.' Then he rubbed my shoulder, which was nice.

Ria attended our breakfast too – via FaceTime from London. It was evening over there so she had champagne and was all celebratory because she knew how misery bags I'd be.

'So, goddaughter of mine,' she said to Eloise, 'here's my advice: seek out the girls you'd most like to be friends with – the pretty, confident ones, the ones people are trying to impress – then go and make friends with someone else. Also, don't let Mum put hard-boiled eggs in your lunch box.'

I did not feel celebratory. I tried to be upbeat and brave, but Eloise looked so big and on the brink of things in her smart new uniform that of course I did a few sobs. She just patted me and said nothing. Then she let me do her hair. I resisted putting it in pigtails. St Catherine's has vastly improved its uniforms since I was there. A simple navy dress with white piping. Very tasteful. Goes well with Eloise's and my red hair.

'I had to wear brown gloves, a brown dress, beige knickers and a maroon beret,' I told the children. 'Imagine maroon with our hair!' They didn't believe me, so I showed them a photo. They screeched with laughter.

'Was that a hundred years ago?' Jimmy asked.

'Yes,' I said, because it nearly was, even though it was yesterday.

'You look like Eloise,' said Raffy. 'Same wafty hair.'

Poor Eloise. She will waste much time and money on hair-thickening gimmicks before she realises it's best to keep her wafty hair above her shoulders.

Eloise let me walk her into the classroom, which is the old science labs redone into a swish common room, a kitchenette and a variety of 'learning zones'. Her locker is right about where Ria and I had to dissect a frog and I decided once and for all that I would stick with the arts.

'Mum,' Eloise said after a moment or two of letting me have my faraway moment, 'you can go now.' And she gave me a kiss and a barely discernible push. A push! I left. On the way out I passed a globe of the world and I couldn't help pausing to spin it westwards, in case it turned back our years to a time when I could start all over again with Eloise. Do it all better.

Anyway, so I wallowed all day, which was unfair on the others, being their last day of holidays. It was the afternoon when I realised I should have taken them to the pictures or something. Instead I bribed them with jelly snakes to join me on a 'lovely walk' that happened to take us all the way back to St Catherine's by quarter past three. Eloise came bounding out ten minutes later, laughing with two other girls and looking very like my daughter but not quite.

'Mum, this is Mimi and Rebecca,' she said. 'We're in the same house group.'

'Hi, Mrs Parks,' said Rebecca, which made me laugh a bit. A small bit.

'How was your day, girls?' I asked in a bright'n'shiny voice.

'Yeah, great,' said Eloise, which had an element of 'durrr' about it. 'Hey, Mum, we're going to walk into town. I'll go to Dad's work at five and he'll bring me home. I already organised it with him.'

'Oh,' I said. My cosy idea of us walking home hand in hand (pausing for a hot choc, some insightful motherly advice and a little bondy hug) sloped off in dismay as the three girls trotted off towards the shops. The tug in my chest could have pulled an ocean liner.

'Told you she'd be fine,' said Raffy. 'She always is.'

I wonder if Eloise will ever need anyone.

So today I'm at home in an empty house. I can't help being ~~very~~ a bit pleased with the silence. Mary-Lou and Jimmy's arguments always escalate in January. The problem is they're so alike: far too good-looking, quite well mannered and charming but really stubborn and furiously competitive. The future with those two is concerning. Almost as concerning is Raffy's inertia, which has surely reached its peak. He takes relaxing to a whole new level, that boy. I'll have to entice him in the direction of something physical this term, an exhausting prospect. He's not overweight, just more solid than the rest of us. Anyway, I'm glad to hand them all over to the teachers; I did a tiny burnout outside their school gates this morning.

And so, empty house, wardrobe, diary, Sparkle Project. I will focus. Hugh must assume by now that I've lost interest – as I did with permaculture. And bread making. But he'd be wrong. I haven't felt this motivated since I learnt how to help Jimmy with his reading. I think I've even identified a Starting Point; I just need to be brave enough to implement it.

During some late-night research (note my dedication to the cause, although I did somehow rabbit-hole off into sheet thread counts too – it's amazing how quickly fitted sheets get threadbare, even without much friction), I stumbled on a definition of flirtation: 'behaviour that demonstrates a playful interest in someone', which is definitely what I was doing on that stage in the beer garden. The initial flirtation, or courtship, has the important function of accelerating the bond between two potential mates. It's seduction's first step.

There's no reason why I can't embark on a renewed courtship, is there? Every spark needs some sort of accelerator. I haven't really displayed my playful interest in Hugh for ages. I might have to look up 'How to flirt'. Or perhaps Ria is right and I should actually get my viola out . . .

Oh. So on that whim, I just picked up my viola to see if the brave, stage-version Susannah might stir. I haven't even opened the case since last year, when Mary-Lou started full-time school and my excuses not to play ran out. Now, with the memory of the beer garden spurring me on, I opened the case. The familiar smell of rosin floated out, and something else: cold, stale air? I touched the viola before picking it up, then brought it to my shoulder, but as I took up the bow I knew that nothing felt the same. Nothing felt. It was as if my hands weren't there at all. I didn't even try to play. With no hands, a nothing feeling would soon turn into a nothing note and a nothing piece of music and then a terrible, terrible pain.

I gave my hands to those who need them long ago. I gave my hands away . . .

WEDNESDAY 25th JANUARY

A quick note to say I'm in the wardrobe reading up on the machinations of flirting and doing some private practice of flirty manoeuvres in front of the mirror. There's a lot of talk about open stances and winks, but it's important to be subtle, methinks. As Ria said, don't be dumb about it.

FRIDAY 27th JANUARY

We had a very nice Australia Day holiday yesterday. It seems ridiculous to have a day off so soon after school went back but actually I quite liked having Eloise in my sights again, even though she spent the day with her book and a bevy of wraiths and phantoms.

She's loving school so much, which is terrific, of course, but I'm getting flashes of what it might feel like to have an empty nest. Ridiculously premature, I know. Sort of like getting the Sunday night feeling on Saturday morning, which I'm prone to at times.

We didn't have a raging Australia Day party or anything (invasion day after all) but Hugh stayed home and we did productive home things – sweeping the paths, washing the car, that sort of thing. Hugh even managed to re-pot the hydrangeas at long last. I love these sorts of home improvement days, when the sky is blue and I'm in my overalls and we're all where we're supposed to be. It feels like how things are meant to be after the romantic film ends. Content productivity. Hugh whistled while he was cleaning windows as though he'd quite forgotten he wasn't immersed in a groundbreaking case or having his breath taken away by the sun on an untouched ice field.

Valda was on her verandah with 'Tell Me on a Sunday'. Raffy sat with her and seemed pleased not to be asked to do anything energetic. The other children made her morning tea and she grumbled about it ('Everyone knows margarine is better') but had a sample of everything. ('That's a very dry chocolate ball.') She wouldn't let Raffy have seconds. 'You have spectacular eyelashes, Rafferty,' she said. 'But no one will notice them if you run to fat.' Only Valda can get away with saying that. I gave her a look but she ignored it. Raffy seemed unaffected and ate his chocolate ball anyway.

Hugh and I even cleaned the car. And while I was sitting in the front passenger seat trying to free a Lego man from the air vent, I found the perfect opportunity to put my flirting research into practice. Hugh turned up with a cloth and some spray and sat next to me in the passenger seat to clean the dash. We worked in silence for a moment and then I stopped what I was doing, turned to him and said, 'Hello, Hugh,' in a bright voice.

He glanced at me, bemused. I looked him straight in the eye. He said, 'Hello, Susannah,' then sprayed the windscreen.

I lowered my voice. 'I didn't realise how strong you are.' It sounded a bit stalky but, oh well, it got his attention. He looked at me again. I looked up at him through my eyelashes and moved my knees apart (open stance). He raised his eyebrows.

I coughed a bit, brought my voice closer to normal. 'The way you handled those hydrangeas. I never thought they'd come out. So root-bound, poor things.'

'They seem to be okay as long as you keep the water up to them,' he said.

We can't be talking about pot plants, I thought desperately. I rattled the arm of the Lego man and wondered what to say next.

'You need tweezers,' he said, looking sideways at me.

'Oh, do I?' My hand jumped to my face. I lifted my chin to the mirror and peered at it. 'Where?'

'No, you need tweezers to get that Lego out. Otherwise you might damage the vent.'

'Oh.' *Shit.* I blushed. 'There's this one hair that comes out just here sometimes . . . anyway . . .' *Bugger.*

He laughed (a proper laugh) and said, 'Are you blushing, Susannah?'

'No,' I said too quickly. Then, 'Yes.' I lowered my voice again. 'It's your dashing good looks.'

He laughed. 'Thanks. You're not so bad yourself, even in those daggy old overalls.'

I put my hand on his leg for a moment, sort of a long pat. The warmth of him always surprises me. He said, 'Are you creating sparks?'

'Trying to,' I said. 'How am I going?'

'I think I feel something.' He leaned in towards me and I prepared for a kiss but Eloise opened the boot and said, 'Mum, have you seen my sandshoes?' So Hugh scrubbed some foot scuffs on the glovebox and said he would need to get some Jif.

So there might be a little bit of groundwork laid at least. I'm about to go and join him on the couch to watch a film. Perhaps I'll snuggle in a bit. (I thought my overalls were kind of bohemian and sexy in a careless sort of way so there's some extra disappointment, albeit mild.)

LATER:

Reporting from the wardrobe! Flirty groundwork has paid off; we have movement on the sex front! A hand job! Should I recount in detail? Yes, bugger it. This is my private diary after all.

We didn't plan it; it happened mostly because the film we were watching turned out to be quite ~~horny~~ arousing. There was some very naturalistic sex happening in an alleyway.

Hugh said, 'I reckon they're actually . . .' and as we watched, I felt a stirring in my lower regions. He must have too because he ran his hand over my thigh a bit, then up to my stomach and back to my thigh, very lightly brushing the bits in between, still watching the television. On-screen, the very handsome man unbuttoned the front of the woman's dress and reached in to her ~~boobs bosoms~~ breasts. I wished I was wearing a dress too, or at least not those stupid overalls with their fumbly buttons. Hugh was pretty deft with the buttons, though, when he got to them. (Ugh, deft sounds sort of creepy, as though he goes around popping fly buttons all the time. There is probably such a thing as too much experience when it comes to sex.)

Anyway, he managed to somehow slip his hand into my knickers, just far enough to reach my little pink ~~clitoris gasp button~~ clitoris, which made me catch my breath. I reached for him then, and the hardness of him made me gasp again. I did the hand thing – up and down, up and down his ~~penis shaft manhood~~ penis, in time with the circular motion of his fingers on me – and within a few moments we were breathing heavily into one another's necks. When it arrived, his orgasm was so intense that it tipped me into my own. It was only when my muscles finally relaxed that I realised my arm was aching, as though I'd been blending butter and sugar until it was pale and smooth.

I shouldn't be likening sex to baking, though. Even if simultaneous orgasms are as satisfying as perfect cake batter. Although my satisfaction sank in the middle a bit when he said, 'Sorry, that was quick. It's been a while,' in a pointed tone, as if it's my fault. I don't see him making much sex efforts these days.

Maybe the tone wasn't pointed. My sensitivities may have sharpened it. I don't know.

Regardless, we have progress.

SUNDAY 29th JANUARY

Jimmy broke his arm today. Playing backyard cricket. So we've spent the whole afternoon and evening in the emergency department, waiting. Six hours and forty minutes of waiting for nurses and doctors and X-rays and more doctors until finally a consultant consulted and gave his instructions.

As it turns out, the instructions can't be carried out until tomorrow because Jimmy has a proper break, all the way through both bones in his forearm, and he's shifted the broken bit nastily to the right so that the whole thing needs pins and things to align it again. He's been very brave, dear little soldier. He screamed when it first happened, then hid his tears under his curls (must get his hair cut too) and remained stoic after that. Mary-Lou was in hysterics, which proves she does love him after all. So we're now waiting in the children's ward. I'm writing this by torchlight in a rollaway bed as he sleeps his codeine sleep. This writing is becoming a habit, isn't it? It's as if I need it to make sense of things . . . He looks so small in the bright-white bed. My handsome Jimmy. Oh, how we love them when they're poorly.

Hugh is home with the others and not here with me being flirty in my rollaway. This is how things should be, of course. Flirting seems silly from the bedside of my injured son, but will the Sparkle Project ever progress?

It's my fault for having four children. There is bound to be a constant stream of interruptions. 'How ridiculous. Don't you know how babies are made?' said Dad when I fell pregnant with Mary-Lou. 'And for goodness sake, give it a sensible name. Joan or Jill will do, or Dennis. No one uses good old Dennis nowadays.' I called her Mary-Lou in part to annoy Dad. But mostly because I looked at her when she was born and said, 'Hello, Mary-Lou,' without even thinking, and then Hugh sang that song by Ricky Nelson and that was that. Oh, that just-given-birth feeling. There's nothing at all like it in the world. Hugh and I so entirely together, creating miracles of life.

Poor Jim . . .

Perhaps this sparkle business is misguided and selfish. Perhaps a marriage should just be about the children. That's what created that incredible together feeling. Babies. Hugh and I could surely make it work if we just based our relationship on being a pair of people with the same children. That might be enough. I know we couldn't have prevented Jimmy breaking his arm, but I can be here and he can be there and it all works. We don't have to call in outside help and inconvenience others. We're a self-sufficient machine, even if we lack a little lubrication. Squeaks don't mean something will break or grind to a halt. They can be oiled later, when the kids don't need us so much. Or perhaps by then, if the squeaks are very bad, it won't be so terrible if it all falls apart.

My place is here, beside my little boy, so I can hold his hand and stroke his hair when he wakes up not knowing where he is.

It's quite nice here, actually. I had a meal brought to me and there's a telly above me and I have my book and no housework to do. And I'm where I'm meant to be.

LATER:

Bit restless. I think I've got myself worked up by the thought of Hugh and me living in a sparkle-free marriage. That won't do. That's giving up. I will not give up. The best thing I can do for my children is to raise them in a loving household. Actual love, where Mum and Dad are touching each other in loving ways.

So I might use this hospital downtime to continue rummaging through the past for clues. It's calming somehow, this note taking, as if I'm laminating fragile papers for safekeeping. Where was I? Oh, the bleeding teeth incident.

University of Tasmania, Hobart, 1992
Well, while I recatused myself from further social harm, Ria and her petite, pretty innocence shamelessly scavenged around campus for more Hugh facts.

'You're not doing choir,' she announced a few days after the beer garden episode. 'You already play the instrument closest to the human voice. You need to branch out.'

'What do you mean?' I asked nervously. Ria had a worryingly jubilant look in her eye. 'I'm not learning flute, Ria. I'm staying loyal to viola. You're the tarty multi-talented one.'

'No, you're doing astronomy.'

'What?'

She talked me into it, of course, after my initial and absolute rejection of the idea. 'You said you're worried about composition – no inspiration, you said – so here you go, what better inspiration than the whole fucking universe?'

I decided that she was right, even came up with the idea that I could compose a piece of music for viola inspired by the constellations. Actually, I initially said 'inspired by the star signs', which, I soon realised with a cringe, are covered by astrology, not astronomy, and that astronomy was offered by the physics department. This was apt, given my extreme physical reaction in the first class, when I realised that sitting a few rows ahead of me was none other than Hugh Parks. Ria had signed me up not to motivate my music, but to twiddle with my heartstrings.

He saw me in that first lecture, gave me a friendly but distant smiley-eyebrow greeting, which I pretended not to see. At the end he left straight away and I could breathe again. In subsequent lessons, I skulked in the far corner rows and tried to stop gazing at the back of his head.

Things stayed that way for months. Me noticing him, him not noticing me, me noticing him not noticing. It was a one-sided chemical reaction. His ionic structure remained static; he was clearly in class for the right reasons – to get enough units to complete his engineering degree, maybe even to get a better grasp of the Big Cosmic Picture. He was obviously very bright, though he never appeared to look askance at the scattering of my molecules or my cosmic vertigo, even when once the lecturer referred to my 'interesting idea' that reincarnation and other assorted higher orders probably shouldn't be ruled out. He never actually appeared to look at me at all.

As it turned out, I should have known better than to embark on any subject to do with science, no matter the chemistry. I thought we'd be gazing at stars but it was all singularity principles, gravitational collapse and black hole formation. The tutor, bewildered by a rogue music student stumbling her way through his cosmos, tried his best to bend my stubborn right-dominant brain around it all, but I was busy dreaming about Hugh gazing into my starry eyes (and perhaps at a later date inspecting my black hole).

Back then, let me think, what was it I found so compelling? That striking hair, worn slightly longer than most of the boys. Those eyes. That olive skin (now passed on to Raff, Jim and Mary-Lou; poor Eloise). There was something important about him, something more lit up than the rest of us. He didn't ever loiter like normal students do. He specialised in rapid departures, roaring away in a smart navy Mitsubishi the minute class was over, as if there were more important things than university when, for me, university was my life. The Con, the viola, Ria and Hugh. In bed at night I'd imagine a million different romantic scenarios that ended with Hugh taking me in his arms. All seemed as impossible as me getting a grip on planet classification. It was agony.

Then, in an unguarded moment during a lesson on the age of the universe, I sighed, thought, *Crikey, there's so little time to make a difference, isn't there? I'm a blip,* and then realised with horror that I'd spoken aloud, and that the whole class had heard me, including Hugh.

Our lecturer smiled and winked at me like he would a child. 'Puts it all into perspective, doesn't it?' It was a pat-pat comment, which just confirmed my insignificance. My cheeks fired up like a beacon, thwarting all efforts to turn invisible.

Afterwards, I was sidling out when a voice came from behind. 'We're all blips, you know. But also very unlikely, very lucky accidents.' I turned to see Hugh, walking quite close: close enough for me to smell his deodorant and feel wavery. I avoided his face and found myself looking at his crotch, then jerking my eyes away, then blushing again. I moved my viola case into the other hand and tried to hide behind it. He said, 'And you're a blip with a violin. That's something, Susannah.'

I looked at him then, right into his beautiful, mystery eyes. 'It's a viola. I'm a violist. But that's a common mistake so that's okay . . .'

'A violist. That's really something, then. See ya!' And he strode away towards the car park.

'He remembers my name!' I spouted to Ria as soon as I got back to the Con. 'He said I'm something, really something! He said "see ya". What do you think that means?'

'I think it means he wants to see ya bits' – Ria laughed – 'as soon as possible.'

'I hope I said "it's a viola" in a kind way, not a grumpy, don't-call-me-a-violinist way. He'll think I'm intense. People think all musicians are. Or angst-ridden.'

'You are angst-ridden. Just look at yourself,' Ria pointed out.

Gawd, I don't know how Ria put up with me, when I look back. She didn't have a father, had a mostly absent mother who worked herself to the bone, was expected to endure three occasionally delinquent older brothers while they tried their clumsy best with her formative years, and was then forced to wear all my petty longings.

It's no wonder she was a bit brusque with my full-of-Hugh heart every time I thrust it into her hands for regular examinations.

He was in my music too. Hugh. It went all anguished and *affannato*, no matter what piece I was playing. Max Bruch was my new best friend, because his compositions forced some romance upon the sometimes grumpy viola. And I took to playing music written for cello, which seemed to suit my mood, with its greater depth, even transposed for viola. My major composition piece, 'Starlit Sonata' was not, in the end (despite its name), inspired by the constellations. Instead it was a direct reflection of my aching heart and fevered imaginings. It was, Mum said, 'fit for the funeral of an infant duchess'. The piece afforded me a high distinction and an invitation to perform at the graduation ceremony. Meanwhile, the anguish was served by Hugh not speaking to me again for weeks and still rushing off after class while the rest of us idled, procrastinating about study and practice.

Then, a little way into trying to decipher how the Schwarzschild radius relates to black holes, I realised I was truly going to fail astronomy, and that I would have to repeat the unit or choose another elective, which would see me crawling back to the Con to do choir or a music analysis module or some other muso-wankery. I did an involuntary *hurrumph*.

'It's a bastard, isn't it – old Schwarzschild?' It was Hugh again, and his voice made me jump, which made me wince, then blush. (Seriously, there isn't a smidgen of cool in my DNA. If there was, I wouldn't have just used the word 'smidgen'.)

'I think he's probably onto something,' I said, in a strange whispery voice that didn't seem to come from me. 'Only I've no idea what. I don't understand a bit of it.'

'Can I help?'

I gaped at him and tried not to say aloud, *Yes, you could just give me a soft little kiss and tell me your secrets.*

'Let's make a deal.' He dragged his chair closer. 'I'll help you through Schwarzschild in the library if you do something for me?'

I fleetingly wondered if it had anything to do with me fiddling with his penis.

'This will sound weird, but I am wondering if you'd maybe play your viola for my grandmother. She's not well and she loves classical music and I don't know of anyone I can ask . . . It's just an idea. No obligations.'

I realised I hadn't made any semblance of a response. *Come on, Susannah. Do something.* 'Um. Okay. That should be fine. But you needn't help me with the black holes. I'm afraid it's all too late for that. I've barely passed an assignment. I should never have tried.'

But yes, I should, I thought. *If only for this moment of me being the centre of your attention, Hugh Parks.*

Holy God, I can only imagine the look of love in the trance-like gaze I cast over him. I can imagine my general thought processes too: he's gorgeous, and smart and thoughtful about old people; next he'll say he has a rescue dog and a part-time job in a bookshop.

'Well, let's work through some mock exam papers and get you at least sixty per cent. I have to do something in exchange.' He smiled.

Oh, that smile. I wanted to touch it, take it home.

'Is tomorrow okay, for Gran? We're not sure she's going to last much longer.'

'Yes,' I said, too quickly, then blushed. Again.

'Great. Thank you, Susannah. She's going to love it.' Then he touched my shoulder.

☆

'He touched my shoulder, he touched my shoulder,' I said to Ria later when I found her in my room rummaging in my wardrobe. 'There's a very good chance we'll be married soon,' and I sang a bit of 'This Is It' by Melba Moore and lay on the bed dreaming of being Hugh's girlfriend, hosting long lunch parties under trees with wine and marinated olives.

Ria put Beck's 'Loser' on the stereo and let herself out, wearing my denim skirt and espadrilles.

Later, though, she helped me decide on a piece for Hugh's grandmother: Bach's 'Suite Number Three', which we chose not to uplift an ailing woman or comfort her family, but to have a good old show-off. All the Bach cello suites are known to be technically demanding; it is widely assumed that if you can pull one off in an audition, you are home and hosed. 'That'll impress them,' said Ria. 'But don't get too caught up in it or your eyebrows will do that thing. Nothing more unattractive than overdeveloped musicality muscles of the face.'

Golly, Suite Number Three. My fingers can't remember what it's like to perform with such étude-like speed.

God, I've got so caught up in this remembering thing. It's almost midnight! Jimmy must be comfortable because he's only stirred once. Perhaps I should have got some of that Painstop stuff years ago when he thought playtime was at two a.m. every night for a year . . .

It is nice to think back to all those lovely loin-fizzy youthful feelings. How can I make them last? It's tricky when there are things like grubby ovens and superannuation forms. That's the problem with domestic life; things get so pedestrian so quickly. I don't want to be a pedestrian, dammit. I want to be a joy rider, a dancer, maybe even a hoon.

Pedestrians have awnings fall on them.

MONDAY 30th JANUARY

It's 1.56 a.m. and I CAN'T SLEEP IN HERE. Someone is rattling something at regular intervals and people keep pressing their stupid call buttons and it's so goddamn HOT. This is torture. Bloody cricket. If Hugh hadn't been so pushy about Jimmy getting some practice, this would never have happened. Well, okay, maybe Jimmy was always going to be sporty, but he gets that from Hugh. I should have married a tuba player. I suppose we wouldn't want Jimmy to be like Raffy – not interested in anything much at all.

Why don't they show some interest in safe things? Then I might be happy to drive them all over the bloody countryside AND no one would get a displaced fracture and end up in hospital with me having to toss and turn beside them. And then tomorrow I wouldn't have to pretend that sleeplessness is all part of the martyr-y motherhood deal along with a cobwebby vagina and having to use chocolate to get people to read books. I long for the days when parents thought Biggles was trash.

Actually, in Raffy's case, I'd be pleased if he had some interest in anything.

See, ornery old me is back. So soon into the Sparkle Project. Well, there you have it. That's why the spark up and snuffed. I'm a crabby old mole. And I've failed the project already. Didn't even get my first assignment in. By this time next week this journal will be stuffed into the pile of my other failures, somewhere near my dusty viola . . .

Just had a swig of Jimmy's Painstop. I need sleep to take me. If I fail to wake, this journal will be discovered and everyone will know that I am bonkers with wasted dreams. And a musty growler.

Gawd, no one's said 'growler' since 1997. I must be delirious.

THURSDAY 2nd FEBRUARY

You'd think fathers deserve a medal the way they carry on about everything being so easy on their own. And on the surface it looks as though everything's tickety-boo, until you move a cushion on the couch and find a scrunched-up school uniform and a cheese stick.

Jimmy and I are home, and the fallout from absent me is extensive. Eloise and Raffy told Mary-Lou ghost stories and now she refuses to sleep alone. No one fed the fish. Raffy is scruffier than ever (he has taken to wearing cut-off tracksuit bottoms) and his bookcase looks as though a vandal's been in. I am hopeful this means he might have read a book. I suspect it doesn't. He has a distinctly vacuous, over-screened expression on his smudged face.

They think Hugh's THE BEST because he doesn't try to get them to do things that stimulate their brains. He thinks driving them to the shops for the paper and a milkshake is his ticket to clock off from parenting and maybe sneak in a cheeky golf game while the children do whatever the bejesus they want. If I hadn't snuck broccoli into the muffins, there would have been no vitamins consumed in that house whatsoever. They ordered in pizza. With one of those horrible stuffed crusts. They'll never eat my homemade ones again.

So, okay, I didn't actually have to do much in the hospital (and the beetroot salad was surprisingly good – something to do with the sesame seeds?) but it was traumatic and hot and un-bloody-sleepable.

HURRUMPH.

Oh, dear . . . I should take my malodorous attitude away, give it some deep, fresh breaths and return in the flirty and open-stanced spirit of the Sparkle Project.

Passionato

WEDNESDAY 8th FEBRUARY

I'm at gymnastics and I'm supposed to be watching but I think that if I stay at the back and look up occasionally, I can get away with diary time. We're only here because Mary-Lou was all upset about not being able to do a cartwheel. Apparently cartwheels are quite the thing. If you can't do one, you're condemned to a life of library lunchtimes. So here we are in this unaccountably creepy (possibly built on a burial ground), smelly hall. I'm distracting myself with some progress notes – because there is progress!

This morning I sent Hugh some flirty text messages (!) i.e: *I had a rude dream about you last night.* There was no response for forty minutes, so I shunned the feeling of rebuff and sent another: *Shall I send you a picture of my boobs?* Then I waited. Nothing happened for another hour, so I thought, *bugger it, I'll send a photo anyway. He's had warning.* So I spent the next half an hour trying to take a boob selfie. Easier said than done, especially if you don't want any wrinkly face or crumply tummy in it. I ended up sending a blurry photo of one boob. I waited for a bit but there was still no reply. So I put my affront into some vigorous scrubbing of Barky, who hasn't had a bath since we took him to Opossum Bay, where he had a wrestle with a long-dead wallaby.

Three hours later I was in the supermarket queue with my basket of shopping when my phone went *ding!* I leapt on it because by then I'd started to feel quite queasy with regret about the blurry boob picture. It was indeed a message from Hugh! It said: *Where's the other?* Which had a slightly impatient, 'gimme your body' tone. Quite exciting. Except then it became apparent that I'd distractedly tipped the shopping basket because a cantaloupe, a tin of treacle and Valda's prunes fell out at my feet. The man in front of me bent to pick up the cantaloupe just as I reached for the treacle and we cracked heads. (I'd forgotten how much it hurts to bang your head.) We rubbed our respective bumps and the man said, 'Ohhhh, sorry. Are you okay?' at the same time as I did and then we laughed and he held out the cantaloupe and said, 'You've probably bruised both your melons,' and I almost choked because I thought he meant my boobs but of course he meant the cantaloupe and my head. Then he looked at the prunes and I blushed, because prunes, and he said, 'You don't see treacle much any more,' and I said, 'I put it in the compost bin to feed the microorganisms,' and he said, 'Ah.' Then there was a silence and I realised that he had a lovely round friendly face that made me think of sunny places so I lowered my voice a bit and said, 'I make a nice treacly gingerbread, though.'

I know! I flirted with a man in the supermarket! So it wasn't A-grade flirting but at least it was practice. And completely harmless (I mean, *gingerbread*). He and his sunny face had to pay for the groceries then, so I busied myself with my phone.

Later, I ended up sending Hugh a photo I found on the internet of some enormous boobs. He didn't reply. It's been a melon-y sort of day.

☆

PS It's Alison who makes the treacle gingerbread, not me. I lied. Imagine if Alison heard me use her gingerbread as a line for another man. I probably should have checked behind me in the queue. This is Tasmania after all. You're bound to be in a queue with your mother-in-law at some stage.

LATER:

I am in the wardrobe with a torch. Hugh is asleep. Or pretending to be. The good news is that we had some sex! He was home late and the children were eating dinner when he arrived so we didn't talk about my text messages. But when we went to bed he said, 'About those boobs,' and reached for me. So there we go, that's success.

Although there's a chance that the enormous boob picture I sent him had a lot to do with proceedings because he kissed me and I could already feel the swelling in his jeans. He ran his hand across my (no) breasts and I said, 'Oh my goodness, they must have popped,' and he laughed a bit. Then he wrestled with my nightie for a moment and knocked the books off the bedside table, which made the dog bark so we had to freeze for a minute and listen for awakened, incoming children. There were none, so I ~~straddled him mounted him~~ jumped up on him and turned so that I was facing the wall, looking over his feet. (I found the position in *Joy of Sex* – I know, it's positively vintage, but this stuff never dates, does it?) It surprised him. He gasped as I guided his hard, reaching flesh into ~~my . . . dammit, hole?~~ me. As I stared at the wall (bit weird) and moved my body up and down on his, I imagined that we were both twenty again, that my book hadn't just fallen on the floor and lost my page, and there were no children to stay quiet for. Hugh was still gasping, more so than usual. Encouraged, I moved faster. I took myself to a time when we were hungry for each other, when every moment alone together was a reason to touch. Then he grasped me around the waist and said, 'Zannah, can we please stop for a sec?'

That's the bad news. He wasn't trying to extend the pleasure, nor was he holding back for me to catch up. It was hurting him. He tried to play it down: 'Just too different. Good different, but a bit more pain than pleasure, you know. It's a fine line.'

We tried some more conventional positions, our usuals, and I had one of my quite-nice-without-blowing-my-mind orgasms. But he didn't. For the first time in all our years, Hugh didn't ~~come~~ climax. And I think he made some pain noises when we got to the rolling-over-to-go-to-sleep bit. I feel mortified; I think he's really hurt. I apologised and stroked his back until his 'It's really okay, Susannah' indicated irritation. He went to sleep and now I'm in the wardrobe.

Should I get him an icepack? A heat pack?

This is not ideal. I should have aimed for something more conventional. Just sex is an achievement in this potential ice age, never mind complicated new positions. Perhaps my expectations are too high. Is my beaver an overachiever?

That's not funny. Not funny at all.

Freddo ☆

SATURDAY 11th FEBRUARY

Speaking of Ice Age, Hugh and I had an argument today. On the back of a bent penis, this is not good.

We were all in the car on the way to Mum and Dad's when we got caught in traffic on the waterfront – there was some sort of charity fun run happening and we were trying to avoid it by taking a detour. We found ourselves stuck alongside the lairy red bulk of the Antarctic icebreaker *Aurora Australis*. Of course. As we inched along Castray Esplanade, Hugh watched a group of people on the deck. I tried to pretend it wasn't there.

'Dad!' yelled Mary-Lou. 'There's your big red boat!'

Hugh said, 'Yes, there she is. She's a beauty, isn't she?'

'Are you going back on there?' asked Jimmy.

'No, he's not,' said Raffy. 'Mum said he wouldn't leave us for that long again.'

'Probably,' Hugh said. 'If they needed me.'

'What's it like down there?' asked Jimmy, even though Hugh had described it in great detail many times before. And shown the photos.

'Like nothing you've ever known,' said Hugh. 'Magical.'

A wallop of jealousy hit me in the solar plexus, surprising me. I looked at one of the men on deck and felt unfairly cross with him.

We drove on a bit, then Mary-Lou said, 'Is Antarctica your favourite place in the world, Daddy?'

'Yes,' said Hugh. 'I think it is.'

'After home,' I said loudly, with an unbecoming amount of shrill.

Hugh looked at me and said, 'Yes, of course. After home.'

'I'm going to be an expeditioner like you, Dad,' said Jimmy.

'But you're not a 'speditioner any more, are you?' asked Mary-Lou.

'No, I'm not any more.'

And there was a silence, into which Mary-Lou put her little hand and patted Hugh on the shoulder. 'Don't be sad, Daddy,' she said.

'I'm not sad,' he said, 'I'll go back.'

'Not for a good ten years, surely,' I said. Then I tried to brighten my voice to add, 'I couldn't manage on my own without you again.' But the 'again' was heavy, and a bit sour.

'If there was an opening, I'd like to take it,' he said. 'They so rarely need my qualifications . . .'

I didn't trust myself to speak so I stayed quiet. He must have taken that as grump (which it was, really) because he said, 'It's natural to want to repeat one of the best times of your life, isn't it?'

'I'm pretty sure it's not natural to bugger off and leave your family for six months.'

'Five.'

'Five, then. Five months. Not natural.'

'It's okay to have things other than your family.'

'Yes, but nothing too much. That's too much. We have to sacrifice things.'

'Not everything. We don't all have to be as extreme as you, Susannah. We don't all have to —' he stopped short and swallowed his words.

'Have to what?' I could feel tears but willed them away. 'What, Hugh?'

He looked me straight in the eye and I realised too late that I didn't want to know. 'We don't all have to give up altogether.' It wasn't quite a shout, but his voice was raised and taut. There was a horrible silence. I was glad that Eloise had her earphones in.

After a moment, Mary-Lou said, 'Are you having a bicker?'

'No,' we both said shortly. And we were quiet all the way through the traffic to Taroona.

At lunch, Hugh was very quiet. I overcompensated with a lot of talk about the children: 'Mary-Lou's going to be a pumpkin in the ballet performance, Eloise probably needs braces, Raffy made a bottle opener in woodwork', etc.

Mum's eyes darted between Hugh and me. 'What's the matter, Hughie? You've barely touched your roulade.'

I thought about what would happen if I said, 'Well, the other night I almost broke his penis and now I've gone and broken his spirit.' But instead he said, 'Sorry, Frannie. I must have had one too many pancakes at breakfast.'

Re broken penis: it's back to normal, he tells me, but it must have been bad because he was walking gingerly and even cancelled squash. He never cancels squash. He never cancels anything. Did I squash his penis? Or wrench it? Graze it? I'm too embarrassed to ask, what with all that fervent riding and visualising old shaggy days while Hugh was gasping away in pain like a bride in the regency.

I am in a terrible mood. I shall take it with me to bed and put it to sleep. (That's if we fit, my mood and I, with Hugh and that great block of ice between us.)

☆

Bloody hell . . . I just turned off my torch too soon, slipped on Raffy's music book, crashed into the wardrobe and broke the hanging rail. I blame my ugg boots. No grip. These things wouldn't happen if I weren't such a lounge-wear fan. Must de-dag myself. A makeover? That would surely feed into the success of the resolution anyway. I'll pop it on the list. The wardrobe breakage was likely a timely reminder to update my wardrobe.

THINGS TO DO

- Have makeover (hair)
- Call wardrobe man (it's still under warranty so best not to let Hugh try fixing it)
- Find computer mouse
- Give Raffy his music folder (What is it doing in wardrobe?)

TUESDAY 14th FEBRUARY

I'm trying to see the funny side of things. It's not working very well.

Valentine's Day was heralded by a heart-wrenching soprano coming from Valda's house early this morning as I was making the lunches. A very moving love song – Berlioz, I think. It made me float expectantly about the kitchen before Hugh came in because *anyone with a beating heart cannot help but be affected by that*, I thought. But of course I was wrong. Jimmy and Mary-Lou were very busy trying to outdo one another's mosquito bites, Hugh was on the loo, and Eloise actually closed the window and said, 'Oh my God, is she joking? It's practically the middle of the night.' But I opened it again and said, 'It's Valentine's Day, you pile of wet blankets. Let the romance soak into your stony hearts.'

When Hugh did finally complete his morning ritual and join us in the kitchen, he said, 'Valda's into it early,' and closed the window again.

'It's Valentine's Day,' hissed Eloise and gave him a nudge.

'Oh. Happy Valentine's Day,' he said, opening the window again. He tried humming along for a bit, then gave up, kissed me on the forehead and reached for his coffee cup.

'Dad, you're meant to give roses and chocolates and stuff, aren't you?' said Eloise.

Yeah, I thought, in a whiny teenage voice.

'Commercial bollocks,' said Hugh. 'Mum and I've never worried about Valentine's Day.' He's right, we never have. Only this year, I am worried about it. This is the trouble with resolutions. Expectations soar. 'That's right,' I said. 'I'm never bothered. I only got you a card.' And I pulled a large envelope from my handbag. He did look worried then. The card had sparkles all over it and inside it said:

> *We might have seen debacle,*
> *And a bit of argle bargle,*
> *But I am very partial*
> *To Hugh.*
> *When I have lost my marbles,*
> *And have swollen metacarpals,*
> *I won't have lost my sparkle*
> *For you.*

Hugh laughed a proper Hugh laugh. Making him laugh, I realise, is one of my favourite things. I looked at the laugh crinkles and the dashing silver flecks in his hair and felt a flurry behind my sternum. A butterfly?

'Josh gave Isobel a diamond tennis bracelet on Valentine's Day last year,' said Eloise.

Hugh stopped laughing and frowned at her. 'Mum doesn't need a tennis bracelet,' he said. 'What's a tennis bracelet?'

'Dad gave Mum a pot of chalk paint last year,' I added with a sigh. 'In her favourite blue.'

Hugh put up a hand and said, 'All right, all right. I'll come up with something by this afternoon.' He grabbed his computer and an apple, kissed me and said, 'Thanks. Good card,' then left before anyone could ask him for anything else.

'So we're not going to the Revolving Restaurant, then?' I called after him.

'Thought you didn't like the cauliflower!' he called back with a smile.

I did a hammed-up 'Oh, you' face that turned into real dismay when he'd gone. 'Actually, it was the cauliflower that I liked,' I said to myself. 'If you'd only pay attention to my details.' He's so brilliant with engineering details . . .

I shouldn't be thingy. He has to rush to work so someone can get him a proper coffee. Also he must be stressed from having to find some socks and a tie. Poor love.

I'm being a grouch because herein began one of those nightmare school mornings. Valda's Valentine soundtrack became an underscore to chaos of unprecedented proportions. Soon after Hugh left I realised that Raffy hadn't even got out of bed yet, and that our scheduled departure was mere moments away if we wanted to make it to Eloise's bus in time.

'Rafferty!' I shouted at the lump in his bed. 'GET UP. What are you doing? It's seven thirty. Oh my GOD.'

'I'm listening to the music,' said the lump in muffled tones.

'Well, listen with skates on. HURRY!'

'But you're still in your nightie,' he said, his tousled black hair emerging from the bedclothes. And so I was. *Bugger*, I thought.

Seventeen minutes later I'd stuffed my nightie into a pair of shorts, broken up an argument between Mary-Lou and Jimmy about whether green jellybeans are apple-flavoured or lime, fished Raff's sports uniform out of the dirty wash pile and flapped it out the bedroom window to freshen it up, taped up the grip on Eloise's tennis racquet, signed Mary-Lou's excursion slip, found Raffy's laptop charger, eaten a small beetle that I thought was a sultana from the muesli, sponged yoghurt from Jimmy's shirt, given Barky his arthritis medicine and found Eloise's bus pass, which wasn't in the washing pile but in her blazer pocket all along.

'Mum, I'll just go to the bus stop alone. Then you won't be in such a rush,' Eloise said.

'No, no, we're ready,' I said. 'Nearly.'

She looked at my hair. 'Please just let me walk myself. I'll be fine.'

'I know that,' I said, locating a substantial but quite delicate bird's nest at the back of my head. 'I like the walk. It's important chat time.'

This isn't true. Ever since Eloise was born I've had to find ways to distract my brain from visualising all the terrible things that could happen to her. The other children feature in my nightmares as well, but mostly Eloise. She's the one my brain harps on about the most. An oft-repeated refrain, I suppose: a tune so familiar you don't even know you're whistling it. It's worse since she started catching the bus to St Catherine's. Sometimes at night I have to get up and look at recipe books to stop myself thinking about bus crashes, pervy men, etc. It's the only time I look at recipe books.

When everyone was finally ready we were still behind time, so I abandoned the walk-to-school idea and hurried everyone into the car, a feat that was hampered by the discovery of a dead kitten on the nature strip.

'Mum!' gasped Jimmy.

'Oh, dear,' I said, catching Jimmy's arm and steering him towards the car, hoping that the rest of us might sail past without noticing. But Mary-Lou was on our heels. She saw the kitten, stopped in her tracks, opened her mouth and screamed.

'Oh, darling. It's all right. Poor little pussy cat.' I crushed her face to my middle, mostly to muffle the din. 'Please calm down. It's the way of the world.' But she wailed on.

'Shouldn't we do something?' asked Jimmy, through tears of his own.

'But it's dead,' said Eloise.

'And we're late,' I said. 'Come on.'

'Don't leeeaavvve himmmmm,' wailed Mary-Lou, stomping her feet on the grass.

'We can't just leave him there,' said Jimmy in despair.

'Oh, for God's sake,' I said, pulling a plastic bag from my pocket (kept there for Barky's messes). 'Get in the car.'

I gathered the (very cold, bit stiff) kitten into the bag and got in the car with it on my lap, then popped it into the compartment inside the door next to my drink bottle.

We drove on, Mary-Lou still sobbing, Eloise in the front seat, looking like she needed to be put in foster care with a normal family.

When I got home again (forty-five minutes later because Mary-Lou blubbered to the teacher and I had to convince them that she didn't need the school counsellor), Isobel was jogging past as I was moving from car to house with kitten. I had to put it in my handbag.

She stopped and did a bit of small talk before asking, 'Are you going out for a lovely Valentine's dinner or anything?' And I said, 'Oh, no. We don't worry too much about Valentine's Day. You know. All a bit much.' I looked on her wrist for a tennis bracelet but there wasn't one. Replaced by a yacht this year, probably.

'Oh, fantastic,' she said. 'Would you mind having Ava and Thomas for a few hours tonight? I wouldn't ask but our sitter is having her wisdom teeth done . . .'

'Of course!' I said quickly because the rule is you don't pause for too long when asked to have other people's children or you get a reputation for being stand-offish. Also, I was trying to get away because dead cat in handbag.

'Oh, thank you. Great. We won't be late. Josh is taking me to the Revolving Restaurant.'

Later (once I'd buried the kitten in the garden) Isobel phoned and said, 'Would you mind having one more? My friends are doing Valentine's too and they don't have a babysitter either.' I think Hugh and I are the only people not 'doing Valentine's'. Alison and Laurence are eating at the Astor Grill and Mum's watching *Singin' in the Rain* on Netflix and 'snuggling-in' with Dad.

So anyway, fast-forward to five o'clock this afternoon and there are seven children in the house. Mary-Lou was beside herself with joy to have newcomers.

Eloise said, 'Can't we go to Ava's for a swim instead?' And then, 'What are we all going to have for dinner?'

I realised she was embarrassed. I'd got a bit carried away with the whole neighbourhood-mama thing and made fruit sticks and honey joys. I also set up the badminton net (bit wonky – there seems to be a piece missing) and cleaned the bird poo off the trampoline (*I feel so neighbourly*, I thought. *Soon people will be putting me down as the support person on their school enrolment forms*). I should have just stuck with the honey joys.

Barky was also displeased with our visitors. Ava brought an enormous pink teddy bear with her that Mary-Lou was instantly smitten with.

'His name is Strawberry-Baby,' she said. 'Ava got him for Christmas and she's getting another one next week even though it's not Christmas or her birthday.' She hugged it and patted it and spoke to it in the voice she reserves for Barky. He was very put out (dog, not bear).

Jude (Ava and Thomas's friend, Jimmy's age) was the only one to show any interest in badminton, so I insisted Jimmy go and play too. *I wonder why they're not friends*, I thought. *Jude seems like Jimmy's sort of boy.*

'You have a strong arm, Jude,' I said. 'Do you play cricket with Jimmy?'

Jude said, 'No.'

Then Mary-Lou, Raffy and Ava declared that they were going to make slime. 'Okay,' I said. 'That sounds fun,' and off they went to get the ingredients. *How very resourceful*, I thought when I saw Raffy looking up a recipe and lining up ingredients.

Twenty minutes later there was glitter everywhere. EVERY-WHERE. And a sticky sort of dough that dried to the taps, the sink, the cupboard knobs and the benchtops. At this point Ava declared slime-making a failure and they ran off to jump on the badminton net, leaving Barky behind, licking up the glitter. I shut him in Mary-Lou's room so I could clean up. Failed slime is IMPOSSIBLE to clean. As well as the glitter, it apparently has glue in it, food colouring, icing sugar and my entire bottle of contact lens solution. Honestly.

Soon after that, there was a horrific scream from Mary-Lou's bedroom and we all rushed in to find Ava standing amid piles and piles of polyester stuffing. Barky was shaking the skin of her eviscerated Strawberry-Baby.

'Barky!' I barked, and he looked at me and ran out of the room with a final, snorty grumble. I shut him outside. Ava was inconsolable. I offered her another honey joy but she only howled more. She refused to come out of Mary-Lou's room until I promised to buy her another Strawberry-Baby.

'They come from Teddies Galore and there's a blue one to match my bedroom,' said Mary-Lou.

At dinnertime, everyone played with their food instead of eating it because I'd made spinach pie and 'Spinach has grubs in it and makes your wee green,' said Thomas. I ate mine, Mary-Lou's and some of Ava's. Then Hugh came home and said, 'Well, hello. Looks like I'm in time for the party,' and was all hilarious and not at all tense. I cleaned up while he pretended to eat the grubs in the spinach pie and did a little farewell toast for Strawberry-Baby that even Ava enjoyed.

Jude helped me clear some dishes from the table and said, 'Thank you for dinner, Mrs Parks,' and I said, 'Oh, thank you, Jude. You're a good boy.' He blushed a bit and scurried back to the table. There was a funny sort of silence then, and Raffy came over to whisper, 'Mum, Jude's a girl.'

When everyone was finally collected by loved-up, Valentiney Josh and Isobel and I'd given my mortified apologies (most sincerely to Jude, who is such a lovely child, oh God), I went to retrieve the disgraced Barky from the garden. He was under the holly tree looking altogether pleased with himself, a dug-up kitten at his feet. I had to sit on the garden bench for a long moment and think about how strange life can be, and about the chances of a normal family fostering me, to teach me their ways. Then I had to get Hugh.

He patted me on the arm and said, 'Ah, well, at least the children missed this little epilogue.' But mostly he laughed. Then he bagged up the kitten again, said, 'The Lord hath given, the Lord hath taken away,' and popped it gently in the wheelie bin. I was too wrung out to feel guilty.

Later he gave me my Valentine's Day surprise: a bunch of flowers from the servo (yellow gerberas, pink patterned cellophane) and a packet of Fruit Tingles. For God's sake. Tingles are pretty close to sparkles, though, I suppose. I wonder what would happen if you popped a Fruit Tingle in your fanny.

Barky has come into the wardrobe, gazing at me with his head on his paws. I can't look at him. The furry little arsehole.

Triste

WEDNESDAY 15th FEBRUARY

Oh. Oh, dear.

The wardrobe man turned up today and he's very, very handsome. He is also about twelve (well, maybe thirty), tall, blond, tanned and blue-eyed with some sort of hypersexual European accent. And perhaps I imagined it, but I think I've just been on the receiving end of some first-class flirting!

Does this sort of thing happen all the time to middle-aged women with red bird's nest fluff for hair and 'please want me' in their eyes? I mean, there we were, Wednesday morning, dead flies in the hallway, cereal bowls in the bathroom, Strawberry-Baby tufts on the carpets, *Middlemarch* audiobook on the stereo and me in my loungewear, when he looked at me. I mean, he really looked at me. I was brewing some tea for us and we'd run out of pleasantries so there was silence and he looked through my eyes and possibly through the muddled-up wiring behind them and into my throat and down, down into my chest, which is where I think perhaps the soul might be. He looked into my soul.

I know this sounds ridiculous but that's what it felt like. As though, in that moment of complete silence, he sang to me. In the distance, 'Once You Lose Your Heart' drifted from Valda's window (a capella – such a touching interpretation, must ask her who produced it).

I don't know what my face was doing, but I think I spoke first. I think I said, 'Anyway . . .' as though someone had spoken off topic, but no one had, except I'm pretty sure we'd slipped into some sort of unspoken aside. And then I said, 'We should have paid for the better model. That rail shouldn't have broken, should it?' And the moment broke too.

If wardrobe man did look into my soul, I wonder what he saw . . .

Anyway, he took his tea into the wardrobe and started fixing the rail. There was that awkward moment when you're not sure if you should hang around watching what he is doing or leave him to it. I ended up leaving, then fiddled about in the kitchen like a normal person might. I ditched the usual Thursday night pesto (jar) pasta (instant) plans and decided to make my own fettuccine.

I shouldn't even be thinking about this – let alone writing about it – but the thing is, I felt a spark! And given that this is all about sparks, the Wardrobe Man deserves a mention. And perhaps that spark does something towards explaining what happened next.

I went back into the wardrobe to make sure all was going as planned (also perhaps to make sure I hadn't conjured him up altogether like some kind of hopeful mid-drought mirage). He'd replaced the broken rail and was rubbing his hands on a hand towel while staring absently at my viola.

'Oh, you're done already,' I said, and he jumped. 'Oh, sorry. Didn't mean to sneak up.' I tried a direct stare into his eyes.

'Yes, all done. No troubles,' he said, then nodded towards the viola case. 'Your viola?'

'Yes!' I said, surprised that he hadn't mixed it up with a violin. Also surprised that he looked properly interested. I haven't been interesting for years. And Ria is right, being interesting is very nice;

transformative even. So I smiled and sent an interested look right back at his.

He gestured to the viola case and said, 'May I?' and, looking through my eyelashes, I nodded.

So he opened the case and said, 'Oh, it is beautiful,' and I saw that it really was. All elegant curves and rich brown. He picked it up gently and said, 'They're works of art, aren't they? I wish I could make these instead of wardrobes. I used to do a lot of classical dancing.'

(The beautiful boy is a ballet dancer!!! I couldn't help but cast my mind to images of him in tights, *avec* substantial package.)

Then he held the viola out to me and said, 'Please.' The instrument's curlicued eyes looked up at me, hopeful and sad. I reached out towards it just for an instant before I felt a faint fizz in my hands. I recoiled abruptly. So abruptly that he said, 'Are you all right?'

'Yes,' I said. 'Yes.' But in the far distance I could see things I hadn't looked at for a long time, and I didn't feel all right at all. I clenched my nothing hands and said, 'Could you put it back please? I feel a bit funny and I wouldn't want to drop it.'

So he put the viola back in its case and said, 'Do you need to sit down?'

'No, thank you. Sorry, too much coffee, I think. Or something. I'll just go and . . .' I left the wardrobe because at that kind of proximity he could easily see the holes in my soul.

He left after that and now, from where I sit (back in the wardrobe), I see that he probably didn't look into my soul at all, that he was probably just a really nice bloke.

☆

I overstepped things. Badly. Far, far worse than any potential tingle in my nethers was the fizz in my hands. I almost played my viola for the first time in eleven years to a man I don't know. Hugh's recital. The promise I've given to him all the times he's asked me to play for him again. 'One day I will,' I kept saying, 'I promise.' He has, I suppose, given up asking, but still. He used to proudly tell dinner guests about my music . . . One day, one day . . .

Will our love life head this way too? 'One day we might again, one day . . .' until one of us gives it to someone else?

It's terrible, the sound of your own deterioration, with an accompaniment of betrayal. I will not be picking up the viola again. At least I know that for sure.

THURSDAY 16th FEBRUARY

If I could let this Wardrobe Man experience inform the Sparkle Project (which might negate some of this searing shame), I could say that I have received a very important lesson: genuine and keen interest in a person and their endeavours really can lead to heightened attraction. Does this mean I should ask Hugh questions about golf? Get him to demonstrate his swing? Ask him to show me his Antarctic photos? Show some renewed (gentle) interest in his penis? A blow job? They say a moist environment is best for healing.

MONDAY 20th FEBRUARY

Holy God, the Wardrobe Man just sent me a text:

> Hello dear Susannah, I hope everything is functioning
> well again in your wardrobe. Please let me know

if you have any further problems. It was very nice
meeting you. Yours, Max (Wonderobes)

Perhaps he really does have a crush. I mean, he said 'dear'. Is that an
English-as-a-second-language thing or is that some swoony romance
right there? And 'yours' – is he reading an eighteenth-century book
on English Letter Writing? Also, 'Max' is an inexplicably sexy name
(although he'd be sexy even if he'd said 'Yours, Darryl').

I have deleted it without replying, so that should be the end of the
affair (not an actual affair, obviously, although the viola thing could
have been just as disloyal).

TUESDAY 21st FEBRUARY

Just to exacerbate feelings of guilt, Hugh has finished the awning
case and is having one of his attentive patches. He phoned from
work this morning to suggest he leave early and we pick up the
smaller children together so that he can see their new classrooms
and teachers. This is good; Jimmy's been banging on for two weeks
about Hugh going in and seeing a robot he's had a hand in building.
But it's also discomforting. At least when he's being all important
and distracted, I might be able to justify at least part of the Wardrobe
Man incident.

There's a slim chance he's feeling sorry for me after the penis
injury, the Antarctica argument and the Valentine's Day debacle. But
it's more likely he's just had a satisfactory conclusion to some hard
work and is feeling good. Hugh never dwells on things. I dwell on
my misgivings for so long I could build houses and grow oak trees
on them.

☆

I went into the office to collect him and he was at his desk, all capable in his suit with the gold tie that brings out his eyes. He smiled at me and his wedding band shone and I thought, *How can I truly have any misgivings?* Honestly. And at the same time, I remembered the feeling in my hands when the Wardrobe Man held out my viola. The guilt went *twang* . . .

While Hugh was gathering his things and leaving instructions for people, I had the wild idea that I could mitigate my guilt with a sort of confession. So once we were in the car I said, 'The man who came to fix the wardrobe was very nice.'

'Oh, I forgot about that,' said Hugh. 'Is it all sorted?'

'Yep.'

'Good-o.'

I took a breath. 'I think he took a bit of a shine to me.'

'Did he?' said Hugh with a little chuckle and nary a hint of concern.

And then I said (because I think I wanted him to be jealous), 'He was quite flirty. He told me he was a classical dancer. I think he wanted to dance with me.' (Little bit of embroidery.)

Hugh wasn't jealous. He laughed and said, 'Oh, come on. Give me a break. What added extras was he trying to sell?'

'None!' I said, but this wasn't true. He had offered to come back and retrofit a jewellery drawer. Hugh's right, of course. I realise now that Max mightn't be a nice bloke at all. He's a salesman, a very good one. Charm is in his training manual. 'Are you saying he wouldn't want to dance with me?' I asked with some mock (and genuine) affront.

'No, that's not what I'm saying,' Hugh said. 'A woman like you? Of course he'd want to dance with you.'

We pulled up outside school and got out of the car and I asked, 'Would you want to dance with me?' And Hugh said, 'Most certainly,' in a silly voice. Then he looked around furtively, took me for a little waltz on the footpath and honked my boobs as though they were old-fashioned car horns, which they are nearly, except flat.

It wasn't all that romantic. Just a small flaring of ye olde warmth. Potential passion. I shouldn't mess with that by telling him the viola part of the story. I mean, relationships can't really be built on honest communication. Honesty is not bricks, and if I told Hugh that I nearly gave my first recital in years to a wardrobe salesman, he would be understandably upset and our building could well sustain some nasty cracks.

Or worse, he might not be upset at all.

Diplomacy and compromise are the other foundations of a relationship, aren't they? And if you think about it, they are often mired in dishonesty. There's much to be said for leaving things unsaid. Letting it pass. It usually does. Like a gallstone. We all have to bite our tongues and grit our teeth throughout our lives. Old people's tongues are quite pock-marked if you care to look . . .

In other news, Hugh said all the right things about Jimmy's robot and Jimmy was well pleased. Raffy's teacher showed us the stars he's received for helping in music. Raffy's never mentioned those. He won't even practise the recorder (not such a bad thing). I wish he'd agree to piano lessons.

WEDNESDAY 22nd FEBRUARY

Warmth snuffed. The *Aurora Australis* is all over the news for rescuing some French scientists from their trapped boat. Hugh's gone all quiet. I know he's imagining himself in the thick of the excitement.

☆

School called. We have six lost library books. For goodness sake. How did I end up spending my life searching for sundries, washing undies and trying to get out of cooking?

SUNDAY 26th FEBRUARY

This afternoon was one of those wistful golden ones: still and yellow and warm with birdsong and bare skin. And a little glass of gin, even though it was a school night. I opened up the kitchen doors to let the last of the sun in (this is the time of year when Tasmanians start clinging desperately to sunbeams) and folded the washing while everyone played cricket on the lawn. I would have joined in but my ongoing viola/wardrobe man thoughts had me ironing underwear.

Through the open door came gleeful shouts and having-fun laughter. And behind that came a little breeze that slipped in and stroked my face, like Mum might have done when I was very small, being lectured and forgiven for some mischief. It stopped me, that breeze, made me gasp. *This is what makes me,* I thought. *This life, those people, this dear old house. All part of me. Without them, there'd be nothing left of me at all.*

There was another thought, worried by the breeze: *what if everything really does fall to pieces?*

When they all came in, we ate, we put the children to bed, we sat in front of the telly. I thought about being interested and asked Hugh how things were going at work and he said, 'Very well, thank you,' as though I was an elderly aunt asking how he's liking Geography.

'What have you got on this week?' I asked.

'Well, we're starting the interviews tomorrow,' he said. 'They'll take a day or two, I reckon.'

'Interviews for what?' I asked.

He looked uncomfortable, shifted towards me and said, 'For the new roles.' His toes waggled. 'I told you about that, didn't I?'

'No,' I said.

'I must have.'

'No, you certainly didn't.'

'Oh,' he said and sighed. 'I want to put on an electrical engineer. We're getting a lot of electrical enquiries. And we need an office manager.'

'Oh, right,' I said, trying to channel nonchalance but failing. 'But I could come and do the office manager thing. Didn't we talk about that once?'

'We need someone full-time, though. You can't manage that.'

'No, I suppose not.' I was suddenly very conscious of the over-flowing newspaper basket and the threads of spider web hanging from the ceiling.

Then he patted my head and said goodnight and I lingered, irritating myself by sighing a lot and being altogether pointless. Then I swept the hearth, because even Cinderella didn't just sit around being pathetic.

But one day I'd like to be taken to the ball.

♫

A Battuta ☆

♡

WEDNESDAY 1st MARCH

Little to report. Sparkle is scarce. If I could just fetch it back –
some of it at least – but it's so hard to hold. Just a little puff and it
blows away. I need to discipline myself, concentrate and stick to my
resolve. *A battuta*. Strictly in tempo. Going back in time in search of
sparkle . . .

Hobart, 1992

The day I went to play my viola for Hugh's grandmother, he drove me
from uni to the Wintergreen Eldercare Home in his very grown-up
car. It smelled like new carpet and had no McDonald's chip boxes on
the floor. I felt like a dignitary. I tried not to act impressed because
materialism doesn't suit enigmatic musicians, but I was impressed –
very. I'd only just managed to scrape up enough busking coinage for
a dodgy bike. I tried to arrange my thoughts around an intelligent
but not nerdy conversation topic and failed.

(When not wearing my stage make-up, I was very shy. I was a
violist, after all – eternal dark-horsey third fiddle with gangly arms,
big ugly hands and a natural instinct to stay safely within the lim-
ited repertoire available to violists. Violinists had much more actual
confidence than me. Ria and I told ourselves that violins were shrill
and common, the blackbirds of the musical world.)

Hugh fiddled with the radio knobs and said, 'What sort of music do you listen to?'

And I said, 'Oh, whatever. Lemonheads or Madonna or something,' which was a lie, but I was terrified of being too classically musical. Ria and I both hated the general Conservatorium attitude that classical musicians were on a higher plane than the rest of the human race: elite athletes with more class and less sweat. Her brothers had taught us very early on that we were nothing special, and we wholeheartedly believed them. As a result, we made friends with the contemporary rock students and joined a darts club. I dreamed of elevating the enigmatic viola from the shadowy recesses of the orchestra pit to the stadium stage. Really, when I think back, I was just elevating my twattage level a few notches above the others and securing my status as a person who never properly fit in.

Thankfully Wintergreen wasn't too far away, because Hugh was a Lemonheads fan and I only knew 'Mrs Robinson'. The home was one of those flash ones, with tasteful box hedging and no soup smell. Hugh's grandmother was tiny, her skin almost transparent over her bones. A papery white phantom. There was family gathered: Alison, Laurence, Hugh's sisters and brother, all tired-looking, some with bloodshot eyes. With a pang I realised I'd been invited to perform at a death vigil.

Shit, I thought, and went cold. I wished desperately I'd worn something other than fisherman's pants and thongs. Hugh introduced me to his family. I don't remember my first impressions beyond 'upper middle class' because the second person I met was 'my girlfriend, Hannah'.

She was gorgeous: blonde, glossy and flawless. She had a purse that I just knew would clip perfectly shut on her hand mirror, non-supermarket lipstick and spare hair slide. It matched her shoes (heels) and her belt. And when she stood beside Hugh and smiled her dazzly breath-mint smile at me, I realised that the two of them were also perfectly matched. H&H.

Memory is wobbly after that, but I guess Hugh introduced my performance somehow, and I'm hoping my default settings included pleasantries and compassion. If I'd been more mindful of the moment, I might have switched the Bach piece to something more tributey and stirring. Heavenly bells and downy angels, etc. But I had departed the scene and fallen into the deep pit of unrequited love. Black holes, it turned out, were not formed by the death of a star but by the final *poof* of hope.

When I got my viola out of its case, it must have been like clutching the hand of an old, cahooty friend. 'It's us against the beautiful people,' it might have said to me. 'Phooey to them. And phooey to physics, restraint, happy endings and that perfect damn Hannah. And Bach,' because without really thinking about it I was – down in my black hole – playing the bejesus out of a brooding, pissed-off viola solo I'd studied for my entrance exam.

I can only imagine what I would have looked like; demonic possession comes to mind. Anger blended with fierce jealousy and a proper nothing-will-ever-come-to-any-good broken heart. It was so inappropriate that I ought to have been marched from the scene like a lion from a butterfly house. The silence, when the heart-wrenching frenzy drew to a close, was excruciating. Hugh's mum was actually gaping. Hannah had a hand over her mouth like I'd committed a violence. And in a way I had. If music could kill, they'd all be dead as stone, never mind old age.

I cast the viola-weapon back into its case and shut the lid on it, then stole a glance at the figure on the bed. She was looking directly at me and her pale, pale eyes were wide and sort of flashing. (Anger? Adrenaline? Agony?)

And she spoke. It was hard to believe that the clear, direct voice came from her. She looked so half-there, yet her voice was whole. 'Tchaikovsky,' it said firmly. '"Aveu passionné". And what *passionné*, Susannah. What *passionné*.'

I wished them all well and left pretty quickly after that. Despite the apparent affirmation from Gran, there were some very intense dear-God-get-her-out-of-here vibes crackling around the room. I didn't care about that, though (which amazes me, really; these days I'm so fearful of putting a foot wrong that I barely put either of them anywhere). I just cared about all the pieces of dashed hopes messing up the room and the fact that Hannah smelled suspiciously of Chanel No. 5. I brushed off Hugh's offer of a lift, wished them well and caught the bus back to college with my viola on my knee. I cried a bit (buses are very good places for shedding lonely tears), but I also patted the viola case and whispered, 'Go us.' With my viola I wasn't really lonely at all.

Ria was only a slight comfort when eventually I found my way back to my room. She plied me with bourbon and cigarettes. (I never smoked, but it sort of fitted with the whole being-a-bit-beside-myself thing. They were Alpines, which Ria said were like a breath of fresh air.) Once she'd managed to prise the story out of me, she said something like, 'Jesus, I wish I'd been there. When Tchaikovsky talks serious, he has every person in the room sucker-punched with his *passionné*. You're a wild bird, Susannah Mackay; no one is safe from your singing hands.'

Later (after more wine) I said, 'There's every chance I finished off poor Granny.'

'Oh, well,' said Ria. 'What a way to go. Exactly what I'd choose – you and your hypersensitive viola. And, anyway, if she's dead, she won't let on to Hugh what the title means; "Passion Confession" is a dead giveaway.'

I didn't go to any more Astronomy. Stargazing was no longer on my agenda. I wanted instead to forget about Hugh and the planets and the whole experience – I was being tortured enough by my own brain conjuring up endless visions of Hugh and Hannah eating our marinated olives with our clever and attractive friends. Besides, Astronomy didn't need me and I had surely failed it, dismally.

But about a fortnight later I ran into Hugh in the computer lab (funny to think that no one had their own computer back then). Anyway, there he was, in a pale blue jumper and with those eyes. My knees wobbled. He jumped up from his desk, said my name and put his hands on my shoulders.

'Susannah! The exam's next week and I haven't seen you. We have work to do.'

'But it's over between me and astronomy,' I said. *And us.*

'But you've done okay on your assignments, haven't you? A pass is really possible and besides, repeating your elective unit would be madness when you should be focusing on that gift of yours.'

He said *gift.* I swayed for a minute. 'Is your granny okay? I think I was a bit . . .' I didn't know how to apologise for such a ~~bonkers~~ vehement performance.

'She died. She was really old, ready to go. The funeral went well.'

I must have looked horrified. 'Oh, God. I'm so sorry, Hugh, I'm so . . . I should never . . . I was really . . .'

Hugh rescued me. 'She loved your music, she really did. She wished you'd stayed for more.'

'Really?'

'Of course. You were kind of intense, but jeez, really bloody amazing. She loved it so much that she wrote you a thank you letter. Here . . .' He rummaged in his bag and pulled out an envelope, sealed, with my name on the front in tiny, wobbly letters. 'I don't know what the handwriting's like but her brain was in good shape . . . Anyway, let's meet in the library tomorrow for Astronomy cram, okay? I need it too; you'll be doing me a favour.'

I told him I would, then spent the next almost-hour sitting in front of him on my allocated computer, trying to concentrate on my assignment and wondering whether I was meant to open the letter while he was there or wait until later. I could also feel the heat from Hugh behind me and wondered whether he might be noticing the knots in the back of my hair, or the splay of my bottom on the chair, and whether he could see that I was getting nowhere with my assignment. It was torment, finally ending when Hugh's computer time blessedly ran out and he had to leave. He waved me see-you-later and once I was sure he'd gone, I opened the letter.

And here (deciphered as best I can from the shakiest of handwritings) is what it said:

Dear Susannah,

I must thank you for your music. I am very pleased to have it now among my milestone memories. I've had a long life of music and this, from you at the end, was an unexpected bounty.

I do hope that you can continue on. It would be a terrible shame if you didn't. You need to make sure those big, clever hands of yours are kept warm by someone, so they can fly

like that always. May I misquote my old friend ST Coleridge and say, he who loveth best, playeth best?
Yours, Coralie Parks

PS I have always found dear Hugh to be a very warm fellow. Perhaps, simply tell him, do you think? Time is precious.

PPS And try to remember that what seems like love is just the beginning of love.

Oh, I haven't read this for years. How right she was about time being precious. I mean, I believed her then, I think, but I didn't actually feel it. Back then, my future was so very far away and nothing seemed a rush. Little did I know that before too long I'd give my time to another person and then a decade to babies and when eventually I raised my eyes to the horizon I discovered that my future had arrived while I was testing the bathwater and pureeing chicken. It was upon me like a large woolly blanket: comforting and warm but slightly cloying, too close to see any pleasing design, and sometimes a little itchy. Coralie forgot to say that the state of one's hands might be improved by not having babies. Women can't, after all, 'have it all'. Something always goes wrong. Didn't Jane Austen jump out a window to escape a betrothed, a life spread too thin and the traumatic fallout of too much juggling?

I've kept the letter ever since and never showed anyone, not even Hugh. Or Ria. It seemed too sacred. Hugh has never asked to see it, possibly not even wondered over it. I wondered over it for years and years. And now as I ponder it again, I realise that I don't remember when the beginning of love ended or whether we had a middle. I think, though, that I might have glimpsed the end . . .

THURSDAY 2nd MARCH

The digging for sparkle must have worked because after I left the wardrobe last night I went to switch off the telly in the sitting room and there was an ad on for Blundstone boots. A gorgeously grubbied jillaroo pulled on a pair of old boots, jumped from a shearer's quarters verandah into a huge-skied morning and said, right in my face, 'Get up and put ya boots on, Austraya.'

Come on, Austraya, I thought. *Put ya boots on.* And then, *There will be no endings here. This is still the middle of things.*

I gave my stupid self a shake, waltzed to the bedroom (*Come on, Austraya*) and jumped on my husband.

He sat bolt upright – taking me with him – and yelled, 'What?' His fists were clenched and for a horrible moment I thought he might throw a punch. That or pick me up and toss me off the bed.

'Sorry. Oh, sorry.' I shooshed into his ear and stroked his hair until he lay back down and relaxed again. 'I just thought we might have a snuggle.'

He put a sleepy hand on my back. Under the sheets, he was so warm. I kissed his chest and he sighed a good sort of sigh so I moved up to his face and kissed him hard on the mouth. I kissed his neck and breathed into his ears and wondered whether I should whisper his name. (I've never done that talking-during-sex thing. If I started now, it would seem weird, wouldn't it?) I stayed silent and instead just breathed a little more heavily and guided his hand to my ~~boobs~~ chest. He massaged gently and with a little groan (groan or moan? Which is less negative? Grunt?) he ran his other hand to my bottom and then onto my clitoris. Those little nubs really can charge you up, can't they? It's as though Hugh's pressing on it loosened the ligaments in my hips. I felt all pliable, my thighs fell apart and I pulled him onto me. I was really surprised by how wet I was, and by how quickly his thrusts brought me to a sudden, intense orgasm. It fired along my fibres, switched on my muscles and held me clenched for a long, shuddering moment. When it finally passed, I pressed my head to his chest and let his heartbeat almost put me to sleep.

But he hadn't climaxed yet so there had to be a bit of rousing myself. It went on for ~~ages~~ quite a bit, actually, and after a while, it all got a bit, um, frictious. Okay, dry. I had to concentrate extra hard. I thought about that younger, lust-worthy astronomy Hugh, the one in the pale blue jumper. And (eek) a tiny (really, really tiny) flash of Max the Wardrobe Man.

We made love for over an hour, all told, which is a bloody long time when you're fifteen years married and forty-three years old with crazy hair to think about. But it was all worth it in the end, because when Hugh climaxed he held me just tight enough to make him seem a little bit possessive and me a little bit loved. *Perhaps I do have something to give,* I thought, *even if it's just a slippery(ish) hole and some pleasure.*

Anyway, I'm feeling better about it all. This lovemaking business does actually make love. I just need to focus and stop being so erratic. More erotica, less erratica. My new catchphrase?

SUNDAY 5th MARCH

I have a bladder infection. I am writing this from the after-hours doctor's surgery. The one where you can't make an appointment but just have to sit among the germs and wait. They are playing

Dolly Parton in the waiting room. She is twanging on about eating apples and fishing, which is probably what everyone's doing with their Sunday, for God's sake. In the meantime I need to wee but not wee ALL THE TIME and I wish she'd SHUT UP. *Shut UP, Dolly Parton.* The romance is not here. It's curled up to die in my bladder and leaves only an afterburn when I wee.

. . . I've been waiting for so long that I'm going to have to call home and ask Hugh to get the washing in before the dew gets it. It's really hot in here. I'm starting to feel woozy and I want to go home.

WEDNESDAY 8th MARCH

Gosh, I was really sick. I had to have intravenous antibiotics.

Ria thought it was hysterical when I phoned to tell her that I'd recovered and not to drop everything and fly in. 'Sparkle Project going swimmingly, then,' she said, laughing.

'It's not funny. I probably could have died.'

'God, you'd hate that. Death by wee infection is so unromantic, Helen Burns.'

(Once, when we were about eleven, I made Ria be Jane Eyre while I was the saintly Helen Burns. She had to cry over my dead body. She's never let me live it down.)

'At least you'd leave a very useful legacy – always do wees after intercourse and never wipe from back bottom to front bottom. They could announce it at your funeral. You'd be your grandchildren's cautionary tale. Hilaire Belloc could write the eulogy.'

'Shut up, please.'

'Sorry, Helen. Helen Fanny Burns.'

Anyway, in light of a near fatal kidney infection, a bent-back penis and a close encounter with a wardrobe man, I think I can safely say that the early phase of the Sparkle Project has been a total FLOP.

Time to get serious and spark the heck up.

♪♪

Capriccio

WEDNESDAY 15th MARCH

I've decided to give my interior a complete makeover. I just read that back and it sounds as though I'm getting a colon cleanse. Or a douche (silly word). No, I mean that I will improve my inner self; I will shiny myself up into a selfless, patient and generally better person. A pillar and a role model. In doing so, I might start to LOVE MYSELF. There is only so much self-respect to be generated by yelling at children, keeping biros in your ponytail and finding a jar of pasta sauce with no preservatives.

I don't hate myself. I think I'm okay. If I saw me walking down the street one day, I might even smile and say hello (after all, there is nothing awe-strikingly unapproachable about me). But there is definitely a regular 'you could do better' spike in my self-awareness charts. I feel inferior to most people in our circles. I'm never as confident or skilful, thoughtful or patient, brave or brainy as anyone else. Or as stylish, but that's an issue for another day.

As previously noted, I need some brave without the stage. Real confidence that manifests as real action. Actual doings. Not a bunch of invisible crotchets and quavers floating around in the air like dust motes. Dust notes.

The dusty smell of the theatre used to bolster my courage too, I think: dust and paint and leather. Theatres and music studios don't have windows, but this never once bothered me; there seemed to be no better place. I probably didn't look outwards enough. I never thought about all the terrible things that can happen . . .

Anyway, during my week or so of ~~relaxation~~ kidney recovery and reflection, I had a think about my current motivations and they really are, as observed by Ria, very narrow. They are: to keep my family safe, healthy and happy, the household running smoothly and Barky out of trouble. How boring. Also how unhealthy. There's no consideration of community in my current scope. And no consideration of myself. And I'm probably smothering instead of mothering. No one wins.

Any potential moments I could spend enjoying my own company or contributing to the wider community get squandered on thoughts of disaster or worry for my family's welfare. For instance, this morning I had the chance to enjoy a bit of pottering time in town while looking for a birthday present for Alison, but instead I got all jumpy because Eloise hadn't messaged me to say where her tennis lesson had been moved to. She wasn't trapped under a fallen bookcase – she just didn't get around to it until after lunch – but I couldn't help worrying. Eloise and silence have never been a comfortable pairing. Mum always says, 'It's no wonder you catastrophise, darling. You've had a trauma. You are post-traumatic,' in her best tragic voice, but jeez, it was twelve years ago and I wasn't in the war.

So, yes, time for a shift in attitude. I will be interested, look further afield for motivation and do for others. I will be so inner-glowy that I won't need a stage or any limelight for people to notice me. I will positively sparkle. Hugh will be unable to resist me. Compassion equals passion.

☆

(I just checked the mirror for glow. None yet. No twinkle in the eyes. More like an extra fanny between my eyebrows from all the frowning I do. I'm more of an irritant than anything. Hugh was irritated this morning when I said, 'Lightbulbs can't go in the recycling.')

THURSDAY 16th MARCH

I have been very busy sorting through everyone's clothes, bagging up things for St Vinnie's and doing Hugh's filing. And I will NOT get huffy when no one notices.

I feel quite glowy already.

Is it selfish to do selfless acts in order to feel selfless?

LATER:

Eloise is annoyed with me for giving away her unicorn crop top. Just when she's pinned a Matisse print above her bed and started saying no to cake, she reminds you that she hasn't yet exited childhood. So confusing. She refuses to play Guess Who? with Raffy these days, their favourite thing. He said he doesn't really mind because 'Every day is a game of Guess Who? with Eloise in the house.'

He has a good brain, Raffy. I wonder when he might start to exert it slightly. People sometimes ask – I think because he doesn't like sport and looks so like Hugh – whether Raffy might follow the engineering path. I don't think he's too concerned about finding any path. Jim, on the other hand, discovers a different one every week. This week it's the Olympic Water Polo Team Path. I don't want to be a squasher of dreams but, for goodness sake, handball in a pool? On a Friday night? I think I prefer the Circus Path.

Meanwhile Hugh is huffing and puffing about not being able to find the phone number for the man who does the gutter thingos. Seems I cleaned it up. No thanks for that hour's work. He can do his own filing in future.

I'm not supposed to expect thanks either, am I? Right.

SUNDAY 19th MARCH

Today we took Valda to Henry's gorgeous new shop. I've neglected both of them, Valda and Henry. Poor Valda. Despite her general grump, she is deserving of some selfless acts. She doesn't have any family that I know of, no children, no Neville. And even if she did, neighbourly caregiving should be habitual and involuntary. Like a morning wee.

I knew Valda would enjoy Lettercello. Henry has a few antiques as well as books, and Valda and Neville were quite into history. At least I'm guessing they were; there are old maps framed on Valda's sitting room walls and a dusty old stuffed owl on the mantelpiece. I think Valda feels a bit tentative about taking herself anywhere these days. She's pretty wobbly and needs a wheelchair for longer outings.

I was a bit alarmed at the sight of the wheelchair. And I'd bumped her into the doorframe and run over her coat before we even got in the car. The children were looking wide-eyed from the car windows in a 'this is not a good idea' sort of way. I thought about taking her back inside and saying, 'Well, wasn't that lovely. How about all those books!' and letting her think the dementia has her. But I didn't, because that is evil and would have rendered me irreversibly selfish forevermore, my confidence mortally wounded and my marriage down the gurgler, doomed.

☆

So I took on the persona of one of those sturdy British nurses in Hyde Park and got her in the car (bit jumbly when you're not sure which arm to support, etc.) and even got the chair folded up and into the boot. *And off we go*, I thought. *Jolly good*.

In the car, Valda sniffed and said, 'Could we open a window? Either someone's passed wind or there's fruit under the seat. I think probably fruit. These sorts of cars always have something under the seat.' *These sorts of cars*.

The children sniggered in the back because wind passing is not something people do these days; everyone lets one rip or pops off. Farting should just be farting, in my book.

So I opened the window and turned up the radio slightly to block out further sniggers (or farts) and Valda said, 'Good God. There's a midget,' because we happened to drive past a dwarf/little person. And then Mary-Lou said, 'What's a midget?' so I turned the radio up a bit more and Valda said, 'Everything has to be so loud these days,' so I turned it down again.

Two minutes later we pulled up outside Henry's shop and Mary-Lou said, 'I thought you said we were going to a museum.'

'This is Henry's shop. It's like a museum,' I said. 'You want to see Henry, don't you?'

'I told Dad we were going to a museum,' she said with a sniffle. 'I want to see the map of Antarctica made of ice and the husky dogs.'

Of course you do, I thought.

'I think Henry has birds,' I said.

'Dead birds?' Jimmy frowned. He loves birds.

Valda raised her eyebrows and said, 'We could go to the museum afterwards. I'd like to do a brass rubbing.'

And I said, 'Let's see how we go,' which is mother for 'No'.

Outside the car I couldn't get the wheelchair to fold back out. It was cold but I worked up a sweat. And then I jammed my finger and some tears came and I was cross with myself for being pathetic.

Valda said, 'We could have been through the museum and having a scone by now.'

Jimmy got it in the end. It clicked smoothly into place for him. Valda patted his head and said, 'Thankfully someone has some sense,' and I noticed for the first time that Valda has a small wart on her nose.

Oh, Henry's shop! It's a dream! I want to move in. (*'Helloooo, Henry. Where can I pop my sleeping bundle?'*) Of course it's beautiful, with Henry's taste. He has antiques trips to France – ooh la la. Just being in a bookshop makes me feel good about the world. And antiques smell like wisdom. He plans to play his cello there some Sundays, along with other musicians.

Lettercello is housed in a dear little stone building in the shadow of St Brigid's Church. It has a shingled roof and a village green, walls of books, Henry's priceless clock collection on display, 'Where's the Playground Susie' on the record player and a huge bamboo cage with budgerigars of the most perfect blue. And a Henry, who is the only cellist in the world with a passion for country music. He wishes he'd been like Glen Campbell and picked up a guitar at four instead of a cello. Every morning he gets up at five a.m. and does an hour of cello practice, then half an hour of guitar.

I do a cold sweat when I think of the hours and hours that his fingers have danced the fingerboard, while mine have all stiffened and jellied. I told him once that I thought my hands wouldn't recover. 'Nonsense,' Henry said in his quiet way. 'You'll have strength back in no time. If you practise.' He keeps sending me links to finger rehabilitation exercises and new compositions. We haven't talked much about why I stopped, although he knows. His heart is too soft for such hard things.

Sometimes the envy I feel for Henry's unhurried, gentle life is so strong I could chew on it. Even more so now he has Lettercello, I realise. I'm the same about Ria's glamorous, high-profile life too, sometimes. Without my small/enormous attachments (i.e. fruit of loins) and Hugh's trousers to wash, I could be as gentle and calming as Henry, couldn't I? I could change my name to Serene, carry an attractive air of mystery. As I am, my heart's mostly on my sleeve, along with the morning's eggs and some dishwater.

Anyway, today we found Henry presiding over his small but exquisite shipment of French antiques, carefully cleaning a gramaphone with a beautiful blue painted horn. His hired 'indispensable barista-slash-bookworm' Charmian (oh my goodness, she is just like a young Barbra Streisand – all up-do and swishy eyeliner) was seeing to customers in the books section. It was like entering another, older world. Even the children kept a respectful, wide-eyed silence. I wished I'd put them in pinnies. (Raffy was wearing a shrunken T-shirt that showed his belly, Jimmy was in his boardshorts and Mary-Lou had put on her most frothy frills. I must pay more attention to weekend outfits.)

Henry was thrilled to see us. 'Susannah! And some little Susannahs. What a delight!'

He greeted Valda fondly, asked if she'd warmed to Waylon Jennings yet, then made us tea. Valda was disarmed of her grumpy mood (or 'Henried' as we used to say in the orchestra) and asked whether something could go on the gramophone. So Henry gave her a box of vinyl records, from which she selected a recording of Dame Joan Sutherland singing Bellini.

We all listened, Henry and Charmian attending to things and Valda apparently somewhere else in the folds of time. Raffy came in and leaned on me and listened to Dame Joan too. 'Who was that singing?' he asked when the music finished.

'That was Dame Joan Sutherland,' said Valda, 'my dear friend.' Which is a lovely way to describe your favourite music.

'Mum's best friend, Ria, is a very famous pianist,' said Raffy. 'She is Ria Mirrin.'

Charmian gasped. 'Ria Mirrin! My God, I love her film work. She's your friend?'

'Yes,' said Raffy. 'They had scholarships to the same school and they grew up together in each other's houses because Ria was like an orphan. Then they played music together a lot. Mum has her viola in the wardrobe for when she's finished raising us.'

'You play viola?' breathed Charmian. 'With Ria Mirrin?'

'Mum was the best student at the Con,' said Raffy and I discovered that I was blushing with pride. I am proud of me, I suppose. Of *that* me at least. Also, I wasn't aware that Raffy could take in so much detail. And recount it. He should be doing better in history.

'Ria told him that,' I said. 'She exaggerates.'

'No, it was Dad who told me that. He said you were dazzling.'

'And he's right,' added Henry. 'Dazzling. She has absolute pitch. Perfect pitch. We all hated her and loved her for it.'

Charmian gasped and said, 'But isn't perfect pitch, like, one in a million?'

'One in ten thousand,' said Raffy. *How does he know that?*

I sort of mumbled and blushed a bit more and then Henry said, 'How *is* that beautiful viola of yours?'

Charmian sighed. 'Yes, your viola. It must have stories and stories.'

☆

It does have stories and stories, my viola. It was made by Baldwin Malcolmson in Scotland in 1837, from sycamore. Inside there's an inscription that says, *Made especially for Miss Eloise Driscoll.* I bought it in 1992 with the money I won in a youth orchestra competition. My playing was good enough without Eloise Driscoll, but infinitely better with. So pure and sensitive were her notes that if there was any love or mischief or grizzle in me, out it would come in the music. There's a similar instrument called a viola d'amore, distinct for its sympathetic or resonant strings, which are an underlying choir of finer strings played indirectly through resonance. My viola didn't have actual resonant strings, but they were most definitely sympathetic. I was forced to moderate my moods for fear of extraneous and inappropriate influences (the Coralie incident is a prime example). In that way, I guess, for me, playing was a sort of meditation, mindfulness: the stuff that everyone bangs on about as being key to better life control. Oh . . .

It was Ria who suggested I name my first baby Eloise. When I was pregnant with her and still playing, I imagined her tiny listening ears and her little hands reaching for the sound. Sometimes I thought I could hear her baby cries in the notes; other times the loving, patient, slightly worried tones of the future, new-mother me. As it happened, those ones outdid the music in the end. And I rarely heard Eloise cry at all.

I told Charmian and Henry about Eloise Driscoll, and a bit about the Coralie story. They listened, enraptured . . . my most avid listeners since Max the Wardrobe Man. I forgot that Valda was listening too, until she said, 'The story isn't finished yet, though, is it? That's to say, why aren't you still playing?'

I swallowed.

'You could play here one Sunday?' suggested Charmian in a voice so open and unguarded that for a moment I thought I could. But then my heart took a nervous dive.

'No, I couldn't.'

'Oh, please do,' said Charmian. 'We're calling it The Goodtime Hour, only it'll go all afternoon. All sorts of music.'

'What a lovely idea. But no, I'm sorry. I haven't played for ten years.' I looked at my hands. *Eleven and a half.*

'Leave her be,' Henry said in his gentle voice, his hand on my shoulder. Then he said, 'Is it really ten years? You haven't picked it up at all?'

'Not really,' I whispered.

He shook his head sadly and said, 'I would give away all my clocks to turn back the time, Susannah.' His eyes shone.

Valda was watching us suspiciously. 'Why can't you play?' she asked sharply.

I tried to laugh. 'I'm so busy and I hate to not give it everything.'

'What rot,' said Valda. 'If you are given a talent, it is your duty to make the most of it.'

'No, it's my duty to be with my children,' I said, my voice wobbling.

'You should use your parenthood,' said Valda, 'In fact, you must, in the interests of visibility – art and literature has more dogs than babies. And more abortions.'

'It's all too mundane,' I said.

'Oh!' said Charmian. 'But artists use mundane things all the time – look at still life, all jugs and eggplants. Just promise us you'll bring the viola in for a visit one day, at least? You don't have to play it . . .' She trailed off because there were some tears in my eyes.

I sniffed and said, 'Sorry, it's not a happy story,' but Valda cut in with, 'The trouble with your generation is you have too many choices.' She looked as though she might spit at my feet. God, that woman would make a dead horse gallop.

I nodded weakly and Henry said, 'I'm mixing brandies.' Then he looked at me so sadly that I smiled and said, 'I'll play again one day.' The old lie felt easy and familiar.

Valda was sick of the subject anyway. 'Now, show me these birds, Jimmy,' she said curtly. 'I'll have to be getting home soon. I have a mind to find my old records, and Neville will be in a mood.'

I never can tell where Valda sits on the dementia spectrum; one minute she's all ghost and wobble and forget, the next she's the poster girl for insight. I was glad for her shortness for once. It spared me from further questioning.

If I allow myself to think about it, I can't see the music in parenthood. It's just white noise, with no space. No room of one's own.

Charmian is not Tasmanian. (She told me when the others were looking at the birds.) I already knew that without actually knowing it, as we do. She's from the mainland and has spent the last ten years travelling the world. 'I've never been good at sitting still,' she told me. 'I moved around a lot as a child so I'm good at goodbyes.'

'I'm trying to entice her to stay,' said Henry with a sigh. 'I'm spiking her tea with dreams. But she'll up and disappear one day.'

'I don't follow dreams. I follow travel plans,' said Charmian.

'You don't have dreams?' I asked, because it seemed an encouraging idea.

'I do. I just don't know they're dreams until I'm looking at them.'

That seems like wisdom to me. I should have emptied my head of dreams and expectations years and years ago. No dreams, no disappointments.

Or perhaps I should have up and disappeared while I had the chance.

Henry gave Valda the Joan Sutherland.

Then, despite me not fumbling with the wheelchair again and Valda looking very pleased with the outing, I left feeling all mixed. Delighted by Lettercello and dear Henry and the striking Charmian, but hollow somehow, as though a shiny steam train had passed by without me on it. I read somewhere that the Greek word for 'return' is *nostos*; *algos* means suffering. So *nostosalgos* or nostalgia is the suffering caused by never returning . . .

But there's something else too. I'm ashamed to say it: for a minute there, I felt admired. It was a nice feeling, but then it was gone. Imagine being admired by people like Henry and Charmian, with all their style and perfectly formed raisin d'être.

Later, when I was home jabbing at the s-bend with a coathanger, I wondered if Lettercello was all just a figment of my imagination.

Contemporary life is so miscellaneous.

LATER:

I just sat on the chair in Eloise's room for a very long time. She still has that dearest little snore. I had to sit on my hands to stop myself from touching her face, patting her back, tucking in her bedclothes. Once I would have hopped in and curled around her like a parenthesis, keeping in the trust and turning out the hurt. Can't do that now. Her legs are so long. And she might be cross with me. Last time I sat in there – probably over a year ago – I did pat her and she woke up a bit. She whispered, 'Hi, Mum,' without even looking. She's so used to me.

Long legs, short years. I realise that I miss the very basic care-giving things. When they needed me to wash them and dry them and dress them and spoonfeed them, my hands were full and useful and making amends. Atonement by ablution. No one needs me to wipe their bottom any more. No more stools of repentance.

I mustn't forget to back up my photos.

TUESDAY 21st MARCH

!!!!!!!!!!!!I had a VERY exciting early morning phone call from Ria today!!!!!!!!!!!!!

'HELEN?! If you're wearing socks, prepare to have them knocked off.'

'You found Caroline Smedley-Warren?'

'No.'

'Princess Di is alive and living in your spare flat?'

'Yes, but it's not that.'

'You met a man?'

'Fuck no. Ewww.' (Ria had one long-term, disastrous relation-ship and has since sworn off boyfriends forever. And girlfriends, although she had a lovely one for a minute in 1999. No, Ria is a self-proclaimed *partita* – a short solo piece with her own harmonic structure.)

'You've taken up the tuba?'

'No. On my list, though.'

'I give up, then. Nothing can be as exciting as Caroline or the tuba.'

Ria took a dramatic intake of breath. 'It has to do with a certain three-movement sonata, circa 1992.'

'What sonata?'

Ria hummed into the phone: a faraway, familiar tune. I listened for a minute, then interrupted. 'Wrong key.'

She ignored me. 'Your brilliant, agonising, astronomy-inspired "Starlit Sonata" could be making a comeback.'

'What do you mean?' My voice was chilly with suspicion.

'Settle down, sunshine. You don't have to touch a string, but I might have slipped on a banana peel and accidentally revised your sonata for piano. In G major.'

I scoff-snorted. 'And?'

'Annnd . . .' The rest came out in a rush. 'I have a big production company interested in it for a major motion picture.'

'Are you joking?'

'I wouldn't joke about this, you dick. Give me some credit.'

'In G major?'

'Oh, for fuck's sake. Your composition might be hitting the mainstream big time and you're worried about the key. You bloody nerd.'

'Oh my God.' I went to the mirror and looked into my wide eyes. To share the moment with myself? Check it was real? 'Oh. My. God.'

'I stole your music. Are you pissed off? If it happens, you'll get all the composition credit. And cash. Lots of cash. Of course. Do you mind?'

'No,' I said without thinking. 'I don't think I do. It's written. It might as well be shared.' I winked at myself and I thought I saw an eye twinkle.

'Jesus, what's going on?' Ria asked. 'I thought I'd have a tantrum on my hands.'

'I'm not saying I'll perform it.'

'Are you kidding? It's a happy kids' film, not a weepy biopic.'

'Right,' I said doubtfully.

'Of course, you can perform if you want to.'

'I don't want to.'

'Thought as much.' There was silence, then, 'One day I'll have a tantrum about that but not now because fucking hooray for Susannah Mackay's "Starlit Sonata". I always said you were a genius.'

'What's the film?' I asked when she'd calmed down.

'*Pollyanna*.'

Good old astronomy, eh? Finally I can justify the time and expense of my presence in the physics department to Mum and Dad. It would have been more apt to name it the 'I Want Hugh Parks to Love Me Sonata'. It's still probably my best composition, not that I did much more composition: too busy with paid work. Anyway, go astronomy, possibly paying its little way. Ria sent me the new recording, in the new key; it's perfect for *Pollyanna*, not so lovelorn. I was unerringly, agonisingly lovestruck back then . . .

Hobart, 1992

I did meet Hugh in the library for cram sessions. This was when I actually got to know him and realised he was a genuinely nice bloke. Sometimes I forgot that I wanted him to shut up and press against me in the stacks. And I wasn't so flustered. We talked about real stuff, like how rubber bands are made and which country we'd most like to live in when we left Tasmania. We made each other laugh, sometimes uncontrollably. We had a game called 'What's my thesis?' in which we had to match library patrons with their likely thesis topic: 'Ego-driven Architecture', 'Farts in Modern Poetry' and so on. Hugh liked to observe the students in the poetry section most of all. 'Look at all those poetry people,' he'd say. 'It's like they all know something we don't.' Sometimes he'd take a book of poems off the shelf and recite a bit in a silly voice. *'The fair breeze blew, the white foam flew, The furrow followed free . . .'* and so on.

Things we didn't talk about included my frenzied recital at the nursing home and his girlfriend, Hannah. Sometimes I could almost convince myself that our study sessions were not at all about studying. But he never lingered and always, once the session was done, made purposefully for the car park. I pictured Hannah waiting for him somewhere with those white teeth and one of those focaccia sandwiches that were so trendy at the time. *'Here's your lunch, darling.'*

On the day of the exam we met half an hour before so I could recite my answers to him in a last-ditch attempt to make them stick. As we walked in, he squeezed my arm, which very nearly made my precarious learnings stream out into the ether. I am sure I walked into the room with the posture of a Guatemalan woman with the month's victuals on my head.

When the exam was over, Hugh and I had a short debrief and then he said, 'See you soon,' and made for his car in the usual manner. I watched him go and felt myself deflate, as hopes, dreams and physics facts poured out of the toppling basket on my head to the concrete at my feet. Coralie's words fluttered around my heart – *Perhaps, simply tell him, do you think?* – and for a heart-flipping moment I teetered, so thoroughly muddled by fatigue and the breathless, unfamiliar notion of doing something properly brave and real. And then he was gone and it was too late and there was only the dull expanse of summer and, beyond that, university semesters without Hugh in them.

Later I realised that, unrequited love aside, the big yawning feeling I had in my chest was there because I'd let a true-proper friend get away. I missed the laughs already.

Despite the extra effort, I failed Astronomy. Rightly so, really. I still can't explain the speed of light or the formation of stars, but then sometimes I can't remember what I did yesterday or what my dreams are, so . . .

I was too full of unrequited fervour to worry about failing the class. I had choir to fall on as my repeat elective, which would keep me safely inside the Con and not take too much time away from the more intense second year. I had 'Starlit Sonata' to think about too, which I spent the summer tweaking and refining (while pining) for the graduation ceremony in February. And, of course, I still had true-proper Ria, who patiently listened to my heart-wrenchings and then flicked each one wryly into her large pile of things not to 'give a red rooster's wrinkled arsehole' about. She reasoned that the only things we should worry about were:

1) Our carefully curated (snobby and obscure) collection of music
2) Our instruments and playing them
3) Sticky date pudding
4) Cheap champagne
5) Ways to get out of Tasmania.

Number five took up most of our spare time because, of course, no one worth anything ever stayed on in backwatery old Tasmania. This was fuelled by a lot of number one, and even more number four.

I still have trouble believing that I haven't lived anywhere but this island. I had dreamed about Places Far Away ever since I saw Aled Jones on the telly singing Christmas carols to the Queen in 1984. I remember holding tight to my viola case and whispering that one day it would sing in ancient cathedrals and theatres too . . .

☆

I'm writing this from the gymnastics hall. I'm here for two hours on a Tuesday now because Raff has decided to give it a try and I fear that if I display anything but encouragement, he will enter adulthood all bent up in a couch shape. I give him and gymnastics four weeks at the most. Mary-Lou is swinging on a handrail with her friends. I'm scared she'll fall on her head and break her neck but no one else's mother is jumping up and telling them to stop. Risk-taking is vital for human development, a psychologist once told me. So should I sit here and hope that some other catastrophist mother will go and tell the little girls to stop swinging on the handrails? I'll bet if I do that, someone will fracture a skull. This wiry carpet is laid straight over a concrete floor, I can tell.

Right, I'm back. The little girls are now playing duck, duck, goose in the space between the café and the bench seats. My suggestion. Two of the girls protested and a small group of parents looked a bit miffed about me bossing their children. They whispered to each other and tilted their chins in my direction, but I don't care. I'm going with my gut, and we all know a mother's intuition should not be ignored. And if only they knew what terrible things can happen when we're distracted . . .

Anyway, the girls look as though they're enjoying their game. And I can record a bit more history. I love this retelling; it puts me back there, when Hugh was all mystery and intrigue with dreamed-up bits. The Hugh whose skin I'd never touched and ~~whose poos I'd never caught a whiff of~~ who was unspoilt by the basics. He is lovely. I see other women thinking he's lovely. They flutter and giggle and things, tell him he's funny. They must wonder what he's doing with me.

I want to go home and have a good look at him, see if I can see *that* Hugh again. I'd be amazed all over again that he's mine.

I shouldn't get my hopes up, though. He's likely to ask whether

I've found the BAS statements or noticed that the dog's rego's expired. A child will wail. Someone will sneak a biscuit before dinner and I will yell.

I wonder if he ever sees *that* me. Probably not, I've only glimpsed her a handful of times myself so . . .

Hobart, February 1993

The graduation ceremony performance was my biggest audience yet. I knew my music inside and out but I was still nervous – tripping up stairs or having my dress tucked into my knickers were things that happened to me. Mum bought me a simple black dress and paid for my hair to be professionally tamed. We put it all together with respectable results. Mum teared up and Ria said, 'Holy shit. You'll be ditching me for the beautiful people soon.'

It went pretty well, considering two things: 1) I was introduced as 'one of the university's most promising instrumentalists', which set the expectations fearfully high. And (much more unnerving) 2) I spotted Hugh in the audience: the muse to my starry-night melancholia. He was right at the front and smiling up at me. I smiled back, then blushed and looked at my mum. She nodded encouragingly and mimed doing some deep breaths. Ria was at the piano as my accompanist, her eyebrows and one corner of her mouth going up in a distinct 'you're a moron' expression. My bottom clenched in embarrassment.

I took some of Mum's deep breaths, tried to blank my mind but couldn't, remembered the *passionné* of the nursing home and decided to let a bit of that feeling take over again. I lifted my viola, held my breath and played. In it all went, all the heart-aching, middle-night waking, all the wist and wanting and wasted wishments. The composition didn't sound much like mine any more. It was sort of distant and otherworldly, like it was something private between it and my viola. I didn't feel all that involved.

The applause, when it came, didn't seem as though it was for me either. I even did a few little claps on my leg as if to join in. Mum was out of her seat, and so were a few others, then a few more and then most of the hall. Hugh was not clapping or standing but just looking up at me, with a nod and a big smile. I smiled back and felt, for the first time ever, very proud to be me.

It is, like Coralie said, a milestone memory.

Afterwards, I even forgot that Hugh was there somewhere, until he touched me on the shoulder, smiled, kissed me on the cheek and said, 'Wow. Really, Susannah. Wow. You're a star. And not an exploding ball of gas sort of star.'

It felt like the best thing anyone had ever said to me. I might have put my hand to the spot on my cheek where the kiss had been and gazed up at him like a child before a cupcake. 'Why are you here?' was all I could think of to say. *Rude.*

He looked momentarily uncomfortable, unusual for him. 'I heard you were performing.'

'Really? You came to see me?'

'Well, I was kind of literally blown away the first time. I was curious to see more.'

I remember I let out a ridiculous giggle, blushed and said, 'Well, we could meet in the library again and I could teach you about music and stuff.'

He laughed and said, 'We could.' Then, much to my embarrassment, he rushed off.

Ria was in hysterics later when we were debriefing over champagne in my room. 'That is the best pick-up line ever!' This level of glee from Ria was not a good sign.

'I wasn't meaning it like that. I was referring to our astronomy lessons. And I was caught off guard. I don't know what to do with compliments. I should have told him about failing astronomy.'

'He knows.'

'What? How?'

'I told him.'

'Did you? When?'

'When I told him you'd written a piece about stars and gave him a ticket to the graduation show.'

'What? What else did you tell him?' I was panic-stricken.

'Calm your arse. I didn't tell him about your heart being lost in the minor third.'

'So why did you ask him to come?'

'I'd had about enough of my best friend moping about like a Mopey McNohope. And I've never ever heard you play like that – it was completely excoriated, agonising beauty. He needed to see the business he's silent partnered: his co-creation. It's like you two had a perfect baby together and he didn't know.'

My panic eased slightly. 'You promise you didn't tell him anything else?'

'I didn't need to. The music sorted that out. It wasn't a lament, Susannah. It was a serenade.'

I said there was a strong chance I might wallop her in the cake hole so she should probably leave, but instead she said, 'Oh, but the romance of composing a song for one's beloved,' and broke out in a sleazy rendition of Neil Sedaka's 'Star Crossed Lovers'.

I didn't find it remotely funny. Instead I lost my temper. I'd never, since we'd met at Junior Strings in 1984, had cause to be angry with Ria before; she'd never been able to put a foot wrong. She was the sage to my monkey. When I first set eyes on her she was playing a half-sized cello and I thought she was exquisite and demure. She turned out to be nothing of the sort. Exquisite to look at, yes, fairy-like even, with chestnut plaits as thick as her arms. But a more determined, potty-mouthed, lion-hearted girl-woman has never lived. She was heralded as a prodigy at age nine and went on to learn everything she could about music with absolute dedication. She plays seven instruments, three at a professional standard, and is these days properly up in lights. Piano seems to be her lasting love, but one never knows with Ria. She'll probably take up the bassoon at age seventy and blow everyone away. When one day I was made to cry by our scary music teacher, she directed that fierce heart my way and has never wavered. I owe her pretty much everything, actually. (And now a film score.)

Ria watched me lose my temper. She munched on my Savoury Shapes and listened as I yelled about it being none of her business – ridiculous because I'd well and truly made the whole Hugh (un) affair her business by pouring out my riddled heart to her every day for almost a year. When I'd run out of things to yell, she said, 'Look, it was your viola who spilled the love beans, not me, sunshine. And he was fascinated. I saw it in his eyes.' She threw her hands in the air and yelled, '*Tu nescio quam fulgentes estis!*' which she tried to tell me means 'Bog off, you silly cow,' but later admitted the true translation: 'You don't know how brilliant you are.'

Ria loves Latin. She and I memorised a heap of Latin insults. Very useful for throwing at snooty teachers or know-it-all mature-age students. It was nasty, but we felt good about ourselves for keeping a dying language alive. '*Bliteus belua es!*' (You're a beastly idiot!) Ria would exclaim while giving hearty applause after a pompous performance. '*Quis est haec simia?*' (Who is this monkey?)

After the graduation concert, I tried my best to put Hugh out of my mind and enjoy what remained of the summer. I even had a little forget-him fling with a gorgeous surfie at the beach who kissed me by the light of the beach fire, told me I was beautiful and made me wish I had a guitar and a poncho. But I didn't mind when a week later I spotted him on the jetty cuddling the prettiest girl in town.

Back at uni, when summer had spat me out into second year, Ria signed us up for touch football and dragged me along. Hugh was the coach. He winked at us from under his cap and beautiful summer tan. There is no end to Ria's wile.

Hark, I hear the grumble of gymnastics finished. Home. I'm going to put on my glowiest smile and see if I can get a wink out of Hugh. My Hugh.

♪♪ Rallentando ♪♪

WEDNESDAY 22nd MARCH

When we got home after gymnastics, Hugh wasn't there. I'd forgotten he had that Women in Engineering thingo to go to. He's appointed a woman electrical engineer! I shouldn't have put an exclamation mark there; why shouldn't he appoint a woman? 'She was the best candidate by far,' he said. But still, I'm proud of him for being progressive. Her name's April. She's Canadian but went to uni here and then did an extra electrical specialty, a doctorate. I met her last week. Very nice, so young (twenty-six), strange laugh, nods a lot. Not Hugh's type at all, so those particular butterflies can rest. Hugh says she has a lot of zeal. I think that's why she nods, all the zeal.

When Hugh eventually got home, he said that April gave a very impressive talk and that she's been the director of the Women in Engineering Tasmania branch since she graduated. That *is* impressive. We were eating our late dinner of meatballs, which were a bit cold in the middle and distinctly grey, so I said, 'My Starlit Sonata's being looked at by a production company in England for one of their films.'

He was shocked at first, then thrilled. Genuinely thrilled. He gave me a kiss and said, 'That's amazing, Zannah. Really amazing.' And he looked at me in an old way and I felt warm, but soon he was saying, 'There you are, see? People want your music. That's what you should be doing, Zannah.' And I had to say, 'Thank you,' and clear the dishes. He sighed and walked away.

Once he would have tried to fix things; suggest I go and see Henry, talk to an expert, watch the orchestra play, listen to my old recordings, anything to 'get the music back'. I've long given up trying to make him understand about being too injured to play any more. About my cold, gone-away hands.

Once we were in bed he said, 'We should have everyone from work over for dinner, now that we have April and Katrina.' (Katrina is the new office manager; she's fifty-something and looks as though she could organise a gay wedding in Southern Somalia. I can see that the office is far better off in her very capable hands.) I did not feel excited by the prospect of hosting a work dinner. Not because I don't like them – I do – just because I'm *terrible* at entertaining. But in the spirit of others (and inner glow), I said, 'That would be lovely. When?'

SATURDAY 25th MARCH

Two bad things happened today:

     1) Jimmy scratched his name into the side of my car.

It's not huge, just a playing card–sized 'Jim' on the front passenger door. That's the door all three older children argue over every time we drive anywhere, no matter how many times I try enforcing a front-seat roster. Sometimes there are tears over a drive to the milk bar, for goodness sake. Etching his claim over the front seat was Jimmy's instant demotion to the back seat for the foreseeable future.

'What did you do?' I heard Hugh roar from the garage while Mary-Lou and I were making breakfast yesterday morning. 'Why would you do that? Are you brain dead?'

I've never heard him shout like that, not ever. I dropped the butter knife and ran. I found Hugh, red-faced and sort of increased in size, looming over Jimmy. Mary-Lou came in behind me and leaned in, peeking around my bottom.

'It wasn't my fault,' Jimmy said in a whine. 'Eloise said she'd give me the front seat yesterday if I —'

'It is your fault, it is!' Hugh shouted. 'Look at it. You think we can wash that off? That'll cost hundreds and hundreds to fix.' He was pointing at the car. I looked. Jimmy's carved letters twinkled silver at me. I gasped.

'It's not my fault.' Jimmy's voice was a whisper. I realised, despite his capable nature and his bravado, that Jimmy is very small for his age. I looked at his knobbly, slightly grubby knees, his tousled curls, and tried not to intervene. 'It was my turn in the front,' Jimmy said feebly.

'Stop saying that,' Hugh yelled, his face now close to Jimmy's. The smaller face crumpled.

'You come with me.' Hugh grabbed Jimmy by the arm and took him inside. I followed. 'I'm sick of you kids wrecking things, I'm sick of you fighting and I'm sick of you blaming everyone but yourselves. DON'T DO IT!' He tossed Jimmy into his room and pulled the door shut with a bang. With a wild glance my way that I didn't recognise, he stomped off down the hallway to the study. Jimmy wailed. The whole scene even brought Raffy and Eloise out of bed. And no one looked pleased to be the one not in trouble.

Jimmy was hysterical for ages. 'I'm so stupid, Dad hates me, take all my money from the bank,' etc. etc. It took me an hour to calm him down to just sniffs. But still he refused pancakes and lay on his bed facing the wall, tears on his pillow.

Eventually I went to the study. 'Hugh?' I asked.

He didn't turn to look at me. 'Sorry, I just lost it, just – lost it.'

'It's okay. I do it all the time,' I said. It's true. I just don't have the same kind of earthquake impact.

'Yeah, but I don't,' he said. 'That's not me.' I couldn't help feeling stung: so I'm the loony shouty one? 'I'm tired. Work's full on,' he said, sighing. 'I'm a bit . . . I'll go and talk to him.'

'Can I help?' I said. 'With work? I could file and make coffees and things.'

'No,' he said. (Too quickly?) 'Thanks.'

They've sorted it out. Jimmy will work for extra pocket money until he can pay for at least some of the repair. He's stopped crying. But I can tell he's shaken. He won't forget that in a hurry. I hate the thought of our children being afraid of us.

Eloise, on the other hand, who did indeed renege on her promise to Jimmy that the front seat was his if he took the rubbish out for her, doesn't appear to have the slightest bit of remorse regarding her role in the affair. 'What a dumb thing to do, but, jeez, Dad didn't have to bust a valve over it.' I wish I had her oaken hide.

Could I ease Hugh's workload by working in the office, alongside scary Katrina? (Which reminds me, I need to set a date for the work dinner party.) I know so little about the inner workings of Parks Forensic Engineering. It's probably time I learnt. I could turn into one of those 'what did we ever do without you' indispensables. I like that idea. But Jimmy's general woe should be addressed first.

☆

2) We got attacked by wasps.

Valda had taken Raffy to her garage to show him Neville's car (immaculate old Valiant, pale blue, gorgeous) and they popped open the bonnet to release a huge swarm of outraged wasps. They billowed out around Raffy, he instinctively ran and then, realising Valda couldn't, went back. He yelled, 'Mum! Dad! MUUUUUU-UUUUM,' and by the time I got to them, he'd got her outside but was yelling and swatting and swiping so madly that I thought all of them – Raff, Valda, walking frame and sundry wasps – were going to end up in a writhing heap on the floor. I went in to help but Hugh dodged past me with, 'Not you, Zannnah. You're allergic to stings', collected Valda up into his arms and moved swiftly into the house with her, Raff and I, and the wasps, on their heels.

Raffy has nineteen wasp bites, mostly on his head because they'd got caught up in his waves of hair. Valda has eleven, Hugh four and me one. Actually none, but I turned a day-old garden prickle into a wasp bite because I felt a bit left out. So stupid. I have given everyone (except me – I didn't take the idiot sham any further) antihistamines and have them on close anaphylaxis watch. They have Vicks on their bites. No one would let me call an ambulance or take them to a doctor, so I had to monitor their airways regularly. Valda got very impatient with me about my frequent observation visits to her house. (She wouldn't hear of staying in our spare room.) For the evening check I crept in in case she was asleep in front of the telly. She wasn't. She was sitting bolt upright with her phone in her hand, her wasp spots glowing in the telly light – an alarming red with a menthol blue sheen.

'You keep sneaking around and I'll call the police. And I'll close your airway up if you don't stop fussing. Never seen such a fusser. I'm perfectly fine.'

'Right.' I turned to go. 'I'll call a pest man tomorrow, to sort out the car.'

'Don't bother, I've called a detailer. He said he'd deal with the nest and clean the car up for sale.'

'For sale?' I couldn't believe it. Neville's Valiant. It was his pride and joy, more so than his roses.

'Yes. It's high time.' Her words were forced into a firm shape, but still a little rickety. 'High time,' she said again, this time to the ceiling, with resolve.

So everyone's a bit rattled and tender. (Well, most of us. Eloise is never rattled.) How can I and my inner glow un-rattle them? Will think (and try not to think about how bad things are supposed to happen in threes).

MONDAY 27th MARCH

OH MY GOOOOOOOOOD!!!! Many Hands Pictures in England are going to pay me £37 000 for 'Starlit Sonata'. POUNDS! I just looked it up. That's $66 492!! They're going to pay Ria in the next few days and she'll transfer it to me. She says I should open my own account. (Should I?) This is an incredible feeling. That would have covered my uni fees well and truly, never mind one physics unit.

I could surprise Hugh with a trip away. It's our anniversary next week! We could go somewhere lovely, just the two of us. What a boost for the Sparkle Project! Could we go to that beautiful manor house up near Stanley? It's exorbitant, apparently. High-functioning marriages all over the place seem to have regular weekends away with no children. Alison has been offering to have the children to stay for ages and I've not taken her up on it.

Or I could take the whole family away for a properly bonding, cheer-up experience. That expensive guided walk at Cradle Mountain? I've always wanted to do that.

On a slightly more superficial note, I could buy myself some outer glow and confidence in the form of hairdressing and beauty therapy things without worrying about expense. I could get some new clothes – if I could just figure out my particular style. I'd ride my bike again if I had a flowered dress and some espadrilles. Also if my hair was thicker and shinier. (*Give Barky an egg; his coat is looking dull.)

I won't tell Hugh about the money yet. Must order thoughts.

The manor house is called Brynkirra and it has a river, a bathing house and a butler. I just looked it up. I could take the whole family. Kate Winslet stayed there once . . . Oh, sod it. Why not. Everyone needs a good cheer-up. They're worth it, my family. (And I'm worth $66 492 . . .)

Just booked it for two nights the weekend after Easter! $6100 for two nights and three days, oh my Goddy God. It'll be an unforgettable family holiday. AND I booked it for the weekend of Raffy's tenth birthday, which is perfect because I was very stuck for birthday party ideas. Raffy says he doesn't mind what he does, which is good of him but unhelpful, and usually leads to me organising nothing, then feeling guilty and saying yes to dinner at an all-you-can-eat place with unlimited soft serve and fizzy beetroot.

Gosh, how lovely to be able to throw some money at self-improvement and familial happiness. Brynkirra wouldn't dream of a fizzy beetroot.

Flourishes ☆

☆

TUESDAY 28th MARCH

So I went and got my hair done at this swanky new hair salon, the sort where they pop your feet into a foot spa and get you a glass of champagne and you think *eeek, how much is this all going to cost?*

It took hours. And they didn't chat much – *waaaay* too sophisticated for that. It was all elegant silence and fringed chandeliers and uber-cool ripped tees. It made me miss my usual hairdresser, Paul in Lenah Valley, with his shameless, snippy gossip and his raggedy magazines. I felt guilty too. Paul would be sad if he saw me in the new place. I wonder whether beauticians these days can laser away guilt. Probably not. They'd be run off their feet. Mine would be the stubborn kind anyway, the sort that keeps coming back. My guilt is an everlasting gobstopper.

I did leave feeling expensive and swishy, though, with my new layered-bob-with-long-fringe look. AND I had some colour! Just a few streaks of blonde and a lightening rinse. They said the colours are all natural and won't make my fine hair break off into fluffy wisps, like when I was seventeen and tried straight peroxide. So I'm a tiny bit more strawberry blonde than red. A very tiny bit apparently, as no one in the family has yet noticed the change. Anyway I was so excited to get out of the salon and have a good look at my new self.

Until I peeked in the car mirror and saw that my face didn't match my glossy new, tiny-bit-blonde hairdo. It's like when you snazzy up the garden and it makes the pavers look tired.

So I made a spur of the moment booking at the only beauty parlour that could fit me in. It's called Beauty Madgic – a dubious name that rang small alarm bells. They went erroneously unheeded. Madge, the beautician herself, immediately scrutinised my eyebrows with an expression of alarm, said I looked weary under the weight of my 'heavy pelmets', proclaimed herself Queen of Brows and led me into the depths of her parlour.

On the upside, Madge was right about the brows. After peering at mine through a magnifying glass for ages while she 'diagnosed' the problems and noted them down on a card (such attention to detail!), she whipped them into the shape of their lives. Madgic was weaved. To think the remedy to my wearied face has been right above my eyes all this time.

Then it was time for Madge to attend to Lower Forestville. For the sake of the Sparkle Project, I'd booked my first ever Brazilian. Madge made a small dismay noise when she lifted the sheet. I prayed she wouldn't get out the magnifying glass. She didn't. I suppose we were working on more of a macro level.

'Have you taken paracetamol?' she asked. At this point I should have put my knickers back on and galloped off into the day.

Instead I made some daft comment about being toughened by four rounds of labour and ignored the tugging in my abdomen. *Gut feelings, Susannah Parks, should never be ignored; have you not learnt your lesson?*

It was agony. I mean, there were hairs removed that have been there since puberty. AND I had no idea that a Brazilian means having your bottomhole waxed. What? Why do we need hair-free bumholes to feel sexy? It's another example of world gone mad. I was beginning to wonder whether Madge wasn't some ageing dominatrix. I sucked in my tummy, now swollen with urgent instinct. But that wasn't the worst of it.

Once I was flipped over again to get at the bulk of the hair, something happened to the wax. It stopped coming away in one merciful piece and instead broke up, so that each fingertip-sized piece had to be ripped out, one searing bit at a time. I sweated and gasped and flinched; tears came to my eyes and finally I said, 'Madge, this is not right, is it? We're going to have to stop.'

'Hmm,' she said. 'You should probably have trimmed before you arrived. It's always much more painful when it's so long.' I mean, she made it sound like I had a mons pubis full of dreadlocks. And that the wax malfunction was my fault. Halfway through the torturous job is not the time to suggest I trim, either. So unreasonable, but of course I'm a cravenly moron when it comes to standing up for my rights and I tried to get all humorous from beneath my temper. 'I can't possibly go on without an epidural,' I said, getting up off the trolley and fishing my knickers from my bag. She protested, citing my asymmetrical, sticky nethers, and I mumbled something about trimming and coming back to finish off. That was a lie. I am NEVER going back into that evil Madgician's lair. She only let me pay for the brows, which is a bald (!) admission of wax guilt if ever I've seen one.

I had to rush into a chemist for a home waxing kit before school pick-up, and then we had to get to gymnastics, and in the hall loos I weed in my knickers because they were stuck to my wax clumps and I couldn't get them down in time.

☆

I'm still now too frightened to inspect myself closely for fear that part of my vulva has been ripped off and left behind in Madge's rubbish bin. But I've got to go and finish the waxing as best I can while everyone's asleep, and on the slim chance that Hugh gets amorous (and stuck to my bits). Tra-la-la.

SATURDAY 1st APRIL

This morning I woke up to screaming and thought immediately that we'd been hit by the Third Bad Thing. But it was just that Eloise had drawn a very realistic-looking spider on the loo roll for April Fools' Day. Mary-Lou was her unfortunate victim. It took me ages to calm her down and there's every chance she won't trust toilet rolls ever again. As an apology, Eloise gave her a hug and all the apricot delights from her lunch box.

So I'm thinking that the Madge Debacle must have been the other bad thing.

MONDAY 3rd APRIL

Today I brought in a 'Wardrobe Editor', which is a person you pay to sort out your style. (I was hoping she'd just assign me one but it doesn't work that way, apparently.) Her name is Ellie and she's responsible for Isobel's style, which is quite mesmerising. So I was hoping for striking at the very least.

When she arrived (looking amazing in animal-print pants, no less), Ellie told me, 'The essence of my business is to help people pull together complete outfits from their existing pieces (clothes) with only the addition of a few key items.'

But as it turned out I think I might have tainted her essence, because she didn't seem to be able to find much in the way of outfit-forming pieces. She did a lot of culling at first but then had to go back to the cull pile because there was hardly anything left. Then she said, tellingly, 'We may need to buy a bit more than those key pieces. It'll be more like a style shop. Next level. How does that sit with you?'

'Fine,' I said, thinking of my Starlit money. 'Great.' Gosh, it felt good not to have to worry. Or suggest Target women's department.

'Good,' she said, peering at the housecoat I made when Eloise turned two. (Useful, with a doily sewn onto the pocket. I wear it when the children are sick in bed and I'm squeezing lemons and boiling a chicken carcass and being altogether nurturing and lovely.)

Other casualties of Cyclone Ellie included six pairs of jeans (apparently 501s will not be making a comeback unless they're 'reconditioned' to ease their tummy-cutting propensity), my Japanese silk pyjamas, my black orchestra skirts and a fringed suede jacket. She let me keep a few of the shirts, jeans and jumpers that are my current uniform. She said they are very 'shabby chic' but I'm pretty sure she was hard-pressed for compliments. Shabby chic peaked a decade ago. And I'm not an overstuffed white couch.

'Okay, how about Thursday for the style shop?' she asked. 'Can you manage until then?'

'Of course,' I said. 'I usually wear the same thing all week anyway.'

She looked worried so I added, 'I do a wash on Wednesdays.'

'Well, just pop on some activewear for Thursday if you like. Easy for the change rooms.'

'Okay,' I said, making a mental note to buy some activewear before Thursday.

Then as a thank you for being her 'guinea pig' (but probably more as a 'sorry I couldn't help you') she gave me a cosmetic gift voucher, along with the advice, 'Go for full-coverage natural, with plumpers.' (WTF?) 'And make sure they don't give you a pink lip. Browns are your tones.'

Since when did lipstick become 'lip' and pants 'a pant'? I have funny visions of me with a brown lip and a missing trouser leg.

It's no wonder style-y people like Ellie think I'm odd. (They say cute and quirky, but they mean odd.)

And now I'm sitting in the much-emptier wardrobe wondering what will fill the space vacated by Susannah the Violist's clothes. This is a ~~scary~~ VERY EXCITING thought. Blank canvases, uncolonised lands, etc. Surely it's the perfect opportunity for exciting and passionate reinventions, the start of something new.

I do feel a bit sort of empty, though. Beige. Hurry up, Thursday. Ooh, but I hope the money drops into my account before then. Might have to use the credit card.

WEDNESDAY 5th APRIL

It was our wedding anniversary yesterday. I was trying not to make too big a thing about it in case it detracted from the Brynkirra surprise. Also it's sixteen years, so not a particularly significant number. And because poor old Tuesday is probably the most unromantic day of the week. I was just going to do a slightly posher version of my roast chicken to honour the occasion but Hugh sailed triumphantly into breakfast and said, 'Happy anniversary, my dear wife. I don't have a present but I'm taking us all out to dinner tonight.'

'All of us?' said Eloise with a wrinkled nose.

'Of course. Why not?'

Instead of 'Because romance', I said, 'Where are we going?' and then hoped it wouldn't be somewhere fancy on account of having nothing left to wear, not even a featureless black skirt.

'What about the old Traveller's Rest?' Hugh said. 'Show the children one of our old haunts.' This was a nice thought except that the Traveller's Rest is where I got fanny-grabbed by an acquaintance of Hugh's who thought he was magnificent and handed out sexual violations like party favours. Hugh pushed him and called him a cockhead so the bouncers threw us all out. I never felt the same about the Traveller's Rest after that.

'Hmmm,' I said.

'Oh, I know!' said Hugh with glee. 'How about the Ball and Chain?' which was a little bit funny but mostly not.

But the Ball and Chain is happily casual and their steaks never disappoint so along we went. We shouldn't have bothered, as it turns out, because Mary-Lou lost her temper with Jimmy for taking the last of the corn chips at the salad bar and upset his plate all over the carpet. Hugh dragged her screaming through the restaurant to the counter to apologise and she spent the rest of the meal facing the wall. We were home by quarter to eight.

Once the children were in bed, I leaned on Hugh, sighed and said, 'Ah, family life.'

'Never mind,' he said. 'There'll be another anniversary next year, and we'll leave the little arseholes at home.' Then we had a bit of a laugh and a moment with some warmth in it and I made him a cappuccino with a wobbly heart in the top but he stirred it without looking and it disappeared . . .

I thought about following up the warmth with some anniversary seduction but Mary-Lou tiptoed in with a letter that said, *'I love you*

Mum and Dad and sorry sorry and sorry.' It had a picture of our family with hills and flowers and a giant sun in the corner. She cried a bit and I had to put her to bed and remind her that we love her even when we're cross. That took a while so that when I finally got to bed it seemed more appropriate for Hugh and me to give one another a little pat of solidarity and drift off to sleep.

It was a school night, after all. We can have belated anniversary sex at Brynkirra.

THURSDAY 6th APRIL

The third bad thing happened. I should have known. Ria phoned about *Pollyanna.*

'The fuckwits have canned the film,' she said. 'The co-producers had a massive barney. It's the talk of London. Dammit, I thought it was a definite.'

'But weren't they in production?' I tried to keep my voice from sounding desperate. 'All that work.'

'I'm sorry, Helen. These things fall over at the eleventh hour all the time.'

'Maybe my music's cursed,' I said.

There was a static huff through the phone, then, 'Yeah, I reckon you're right. The actress playing Pollyanna will probably fall off London Bridge tomorrow; I'd better warn them.'

I sniffed.

'Cheer up,' she said. 'There are better places for "Starlit". It's an elegy, not a nocturne. I'll put it back in a minor scale and sell it to Tim Burton.'

☆

Thankfully she called well before my shopping appointment with Ellie, so I hadn't yet belted the credit card and caused untold damage. I phoned Ellie to cancel.

'I just need a bit more time to think about what sort of message I want to send with my look,' I said, which probably isn't a lie.

'Yes,' she said. 'Very important to do some self-analysis. I can help with this too so we can fit a conscious reflection appointment in before the style shop.'

For goodness sake. I should have just told her I'm in a period of sudden financial stress. I should have cancelled Brynkirra too but I can't bear to just yet. All those sumptuous figments of us running through the woods and skipping down staircases. Thank goodness I'd kept it all a surprise. No one need ever know.

LATER:

I've cancelled Brynkirra. I'm so steeped in disappointment that my toes hurt. I tried to cheer myself up with a spot of op-shopping. People are passionate about op-shopping so I was hopeful I could be too. I'm not. But I did find a *Joan Sutherland Sings Bellini* album for Valda and a leopard-print dress, which I bought as a sort of nod to Ellie and her efforts.

I gave up then and went to help with Easter craft in Jimmy's class. 'Easter is about new beginnings,' the teacher said, which felt hopeful. I cut out a pile of rabbit ears and blew some eggs and felt much cheerier. A little flaring of inner glow. Also, blowing eggs is very satisfying.

Further disappointment lies in the fact that Hugh still hasn't noticed my hair, despite the distinct tempering of the red and the bloodcurdling cost of it. The children noticed my other hair, though.

This morning Mary-Lou barged into the bathroom and yelled, 'MUM! Where's your woof-woof gone?' (*Woof-woof* meaning furry patch between legs that could be mistaken for a small hairy dog, according to Eloise when she was three.) Mary-Lou, on this occasion, yelled out to the rest of the family, 'Come and see, come and see. Mum has a boiled (bald) woof-woof!'

Eloise popped her head around the corner and gasped in what can only be described as horror. 'Oh my God. Can't be unseen, can't be unseen,' she said, as if she wasn't the little girl who only about six months ago didn't bat an eyelid if any of us were in the nude. Thankfully Hugh had already left for work and Raff and Jimmy knew full well they didn't want the slightest glimpse of my boiled woof-woof.

Valda noticed my hair (head hair, obviously). Raffy brought her over for afternoon tea and she looked at me and said, 'Are you going for a job in a bank?'

FRIDAY 7th APRIL (GOOD FRIDAY)

Valda sold the Valiant. The detailer evidently fell in love with it and within moments the deal was done. I stood with Valda on her verandah as the car drove out of her driveway, venetians winking in the sun. She sighed deeply and, to my surprise, put her hand on my arm and left it there. After a long moment, she said, 'There we are, then,' went back to her chair and picked up her book. I gently offered a cup of tea and she barked a 'No' that was harsh even for her. I left her to it. I'll send Raff in the morning with an Easter bun. I made them this afternoon for the Hadleys as an Eastery love-thy-neighbour gesture (glowy glow glow).

☆

SUNDAY 9th APRIL

We had an Easter lunch with Mum and Dad today. Mum made a trifle with hot cross buns (it had far too much cinnamon but points for creativity). Soon after we arrived Mum took me aside and, with a mysterious smile, showed me a little box filled with chocolate hearts wrapped in pink foil.

'An Easter gift from Terrence,' she said. Her cheeks were as pink as the foil.

'Terrence?' I asked.

'Terrence. Terrence Squirrel,' she said. 'They're from La Maison Dujardin in Paris. Exquisite.'

I didn't like her whispery tones. 'Mum, please don't involve me in your secret squirrel love affair.'

'It's not an affair. And there's no secret, I told you that. Dad loves these. They have absinthe in them.'

'Absinthe? Doesn't that make you hallucinate?'

'Yes, the green fairy! Just one of these innocent little hearts will have you galloping about humping the furniture in no time.'

'Oh, Mum, please be sensible.' I laughed, though.

'Darling, as Eloise says, lighten up. We don't all feel the need to get about in hair shirts. Be done with this guilt, darling, please. It's very depleting. No wonder you get shoulder pain, carrying that guilt around all these years. Throw it in a box, lock it up and throw away the key. Actually, throw away the box. Good for nothing.' And she unwrapped a heart, popped it in my mouth and said, 'Absinthe makes the heart grow fonder.'

Later, when I was helping Dad retrieve pumpkins from the garage (we'll all be orange-hued by next week – must find that rosemary pumpkin bread recipe), I said to him, 'So, Dad, Terrence Squirrel...'

I watched for a reaction but he continued with his pumpkin selection. 'Mum told me about him.'

'Mmm,' said Dad when he realised I was waiting for him to contribute, 'Mr Squirrel.'

'You don't like him?' I asked.

'Yes, I like him. He's an old friend,' said Dad.

'It seems that Mum likes him very much,' I said.

'Seems so,' he said, then put a butternut and two sugar pie pumpkins into a box. 'Beauties,' he muttered.

'You don't mind?'

'No, got plenty. We always overdo the pumpkins.'

'I mean Terrence Squirrel, Dad.' Being deliberately obtuse is one of his favourite things. 'Him sending Mum presents, et cetera.'

'There's no et cetera. He just sends presents and a bit of a card now and then.'

'You don't mind?'

'Nope.'

'I feel as though I might.'

Dad sighed and gave me a weary smile. 'Look, I'll let you in on a bit of a secret – there is no Terrence Squirrel. Well, there is, but we haven't heard peep from him since the eighties.'

'What? So who sent the absinthe chocolates?'

'I did.'

'You're Terrence Squirrel?!'

'Yes.'

'Why?'

'You can see how pleased she is today. Does her good. She'll be cheery for weeks.'

'Why can't *you* just give her the chocolates?'

'Well, that'd be too strange. I've never been one for romance and other exotic things. I'm just the home paddock. But I do like to see her so chuffed.'

'How do you do it?'

'My friend Louis in the post office has a mail order catalogue, a Paris postmarker and a nice copperplate.'

'And the woman in the bakery? Did you have a thing for her?'

'Ah, Rosa Bianchi. No. Just for her vanilla slices. Doesn't hurt your mum to think otherwise, though.'

'Jeepers, Dad. What tangled webs we weave.'

'We've got to play the game, Zannah-doo.'

On the way home in the car I thought about playing the game, concocted a plan to pose as a penpal from the South Pole, scrapped the plan and just said to Hugh, 'If you really want to go back to Antarctica, you should.'

And he said, 'It's okay. I can't now.'

'Why not?'

He stayed silent so I tried to be light. 'Do they have a cut-off age?'

'No.' He laughed but his eyes didn't crinkle.

'Too busy at work?'

'Something like that,' he said, with an underside of char.

'What do you mean, Hugh?' I felt the prickly onset of anger.

He tapped his fingers on the handbrake and said, 'They asked me for this coming season. And I declined.'

'What?' I couldn't believe it. 'You didn't say. You should have talked to me.'

'You've made it pretty clear how you feel about it so I didn't think it was worth ploughing it all up again.' Then he turned the radio up and said, 'Hey, Jim, this is the perfect rev-up song for footy.' And I was dismissed in favour of 'Eye of the Tiger'.

I will have to find out more about this Antarctica offer at a later date, sans children.

Hugh and Jimmy cooked dinner tonight: Hugh's suggestion. They made hamburgers. Hugh's still making up for the car-yelling incident. I wish he'd just yell at me over the Antarctic thing. He might be compelled to try harder with me. Perhaps I should scratch 'I hate Antarctica' on the driver's door and we can just have a yelling match and be done with it.

If I was a truly selfless person, I would play Dad's game and make Hugh go off to the South Pole. Or dammit, if I had that money, I could buy him a flight to Antarctica for a few days, just so he could scratch his itch. Ice is good on a mozzie bite. And other associated ineffectual thoughts.

FRIDAY 14th APRIL

I was just rocking the wardrobe chair so vigorously that it banged into the wall and made a small dent. So now there's a new dent in here. This wardrobe is certainly seeing some changes . . . I've made some changes . . . For instance, we are going to Brynkirra – the whole family, including Barky. I fixed things. Here's what happened:

I spent the early part of the week trying to make people feel happy, trying to shiny myself up, shed my grief, etc. Then on Wednesday, just as I was trimming the parsley and trying to visualise what my guilt box looked like, school phoned to say that Mary-Lou had had a bump on the head, that she was fine but they were obliged to let me know, and she'd like to talk to me.

'Mummy?' Mary-Lou's phone voice was very small. It felt a long, long way away. My heart gave a little kick.

'Are you all right, Mary-Lou?'

'Yes, thank you.' But her voice wobbled.

'Brave girl. You don't need me to come and get you, do you?'

'No.'

'Okay,' I said. But I lingered.

'My head aches,' she said, 'and I want to show you my bump.' Her little faraway voice made a sob.

And so I collected Mary-Lou, rubbed her bump and put her to bed with the telly. She perched herself up among the pillows and looked thoroughly content. Then I felt worried that I'd overreacted and been too coddly and that she'll be wailing for her mother every time she gets a paper cut.

'For HEAVEN'S SAKE,' I said aloud. 'Now my guilt is making me feel guilty.'

My eyes rested on my viola case, on its shelf, sealed and locked. *My box of guilt.* I gave it a little poke. I wanted it to react. In the glasspaper silence there was an image of Eloise as a baby, lying awake in her cot, looking blankly at the ceiling.

'Mummy?' came a voice from the door. Mary-Lou. 'Can we do something?'

'Yes,' I said. 'Yes, we can.' And I picked up the viola, found my keys, took her hand and marched us out the door.

Charmian was at the counter when we got to Lettercello. She gasped when she saw the viola case and clapped her hands.

'Promised I'd bring it in to show you,' I said, putting the case on the counter.

Henry appeared from a back room, with a cobweb in his hair. 'Ah, there she is,' he said to the viola. To me he said, 'Susannah, your hair! So sun-kissed and swishy.' And to Mary-Lou, 'Hello, Fairy-Mary. Would you like a marshmallow?'

'It's beautiful,' said Charmian once I'd opened the viola case. 'Can I touch it?'

'Of course,' I said, and she caressed the old wood. I wondered whether the instrument felt a stirring of hope. Those smooth hands.

'I read a book once,' she said, 'about how they're made. Such craftsmanship. It must be worth a fortune.'

'I don't know, really,' I said. 'It cost me everything I had when I bought it, but I'm not sure these days. Henry, I was wondering if you'd get it valued, actually. And sell it for me too?'

He said, 'Absolutely not. This is your voice.'

'Did I say that?' I said. 'God, I can be such a twat.'

'No, I'm saying that.' He swiped some invisible dust from the bench.

'Oh.'

'You should hear, Charmian, the things Susannah can say with that instrument. Such *cantando* in her hands.'

'But please, Henry, this is the first very important decision I've made in a long time. Can you help me?'

He shook his head. 'No.' And he turned his attention to some bookwork.

I wasn't giving up. 'It's part of a grand plan of self-expression. Voice lessons, of a sort. Please, Henry, this viola is wasted on me.' *And I'm wasting away with it here.* I felt a wobble of tears.

He looked at me, softened. 'Look, how about you leave it here for the weekend? I'll soap the pegs for you, give her some TLC. She can stay with my cello in the sitting room. They'll have a lovely time. You can see how you feel without it, come back and collect it whenever. But I won't put it up for sale.' He nodded a firm full stop.

Then this morning, Henry phoned. 'Susannah?' His voice was serious.

'Henry?' I asked.

'I am obliged to tell you this but I know it won't matter either way.'

'Tell me what?'

'Someone has offered $40 000 for your viola.'

'What?' My heart did an enormous leap, right up to my throat.

'I told them no, of course, but there are a few things I should tell you. Firstly, they want it very badly.'

'Oh my God. Obviously. Why?'

'That's the other thing; the buyer is Mr Elliot Driscoll, Eloise Driscoll's grandson.'

And because he knew it was all a bit much to take in without the comforts of his shop and a cup of peppermint tea, he said I should probably come back over.

It turns out that Elliot Driscoll is the friend of the local priest, Father Graham, who is a Lettercello regular. Father Graham saw the viola, and the name on it, and phoned his friend immediately. Elliot paid a visit and couldn't believe his eyes.

'He was in raptures,' said Henry. 'You should have seen him. It was like a reunion.'

'It made me cry,' sighed Charmian, with a dramatic swoon.

'Don't mind her,' said Henry. 'She's fallen in love. Again. It's the plumber's apprentice this time. I blame the romance section.'

And so I said, 'Right, then. It should probably go back to where it belongs.'

'No,' said Henry. But he looked at me and said no more. Decisiveness must be striking in an indecisive person. 'I can't take all that money, though,' I said. 'Too much.' *I can't charge anyone to take away my remorse.*

'Apparently Elliot is super wealthy,' said Charmian. 'I think he'd pay a lot more.'

'I certainly don't want more.'

'Right,' said Henry, who knew he was defeated. Because with that, everything seemed, in very slow motion, to click into place.

So, Brynkirra is re-booked and we're back on our cheery-up track. Raffy gets his special birthday, the children will all be doing ripping, outdoorsy things and everything will be utterly Pollyanna. Also there's a swanky restaurant in Stanley so Hugh and I can still have a just-the-two-of-us dinner. Also we can have our own wing, away from the children and animals, so sex is more than possible. And I still have (slightly) better hair and smooth pubic bits. I've instructed everyone to pack but they don't know where we're going yet. I feel very, very excited, and so light! This ol' rocking chair must be loving the loss of such weight. And beside me there's a viola-shaped space on the shelf where my guilt used to be.

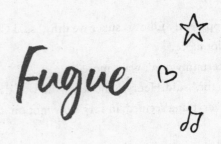

Fugue

SATURDAY 15th APRIL

We are in Ross, on the way to Brynkirra. Hugh and I, Eloise, Raffy, Jimmy, Mary-Lou and Barky. And Valda.

Valda was a last-minute addition. She was miserable when I went to say goodbye. She wasn't on the verandah but all hunched up in the sitting room, looking like Mary-Lou when she's coming down with something. I couldn't just leave her.

'Are you all right, Valda?' I asked. 'We'll be back on Monday.'

'Yes. Have a good time.' But she seemed sort of shrouded in something heavy.

'Would you like to come?' I asked without really thinking. 'We're going to Stanley.'

I expected her to prod me out with orders not to fuss, but there was a pause. She looked at me. 'Yes. I like Stanley,' she said. 'And I need to get out of this house. Neville is furious about the Valiant. I knew he loved that thing more than me.'

'Come on, then,' I said, not wanting to delve into any dementics and also trying to swallow the idea of Valda on our family holiday. 'There are plenty of rooms, we might as well use them.' *Thirty-one of them*, I thought, *to be precise.*

☆

All the way up the Midlands Highway I've been seeing lovely things I've never noticed before. The unlikely dash of a proud pencil pine against the sparse hills, an arch of autumn leaves, a pretty laced verandah . . . Valda wanted to pop into the Ross Village Bakery because she'd heard that they have good eclairs. And the children were clamouring for a hot chocolate. The Ross Bakery has brilliant vanilla slices. I must tell Dad. Perhaps Rosa Bianchi works there. Actually, I should have just asked Mum and Dad to come. But then I'd have had to ask Alison and Laurence and we can't have that.

Hugh isn't entirely rapturous about an unscheduled long weekend. I heard him say on the phone to the office, 'I won't be in on Monday. I have to go to Stanley,' as though he had to attend a trigonometry convention. He'll change his tune when he sees our manor house. Perhaps I should have asked his parents. He often hints that we should make more effort with them.

FIFTEEN MINUTES LATER:

I phoned them all. Mum, Dad, Alison and Laurence. They're all coming. Might as well. I mean, thirty-one rooms and a butler.

Look at me go, putting the sun in everyone's corner.

MUCH LATER:

This place is truly incredible. Like a house in a colonial drama, except renovated: all the trimmings. 'Displaying consummate taste and finest of luxuries' said the website, 'a garden like a poem'. Everyone is completely blown away. Thank God. All that panic and angst and convoluted rearrangements have paid off in shovels and spades. This was meant to be!

It *is* like a poem. Or a symphony. That's it, a symphony. (I've had two glasses of French champagne. Is it obvious?) There's a pool, a games room, a gym, an enormous kitchen, nine bedrooms, a tennis court, a ballroom, a croquet lawn, a dining room and six reception rooms. We should be receiving people!

And, oh, the children's faces when we drove along the driveway! Priceless.

'How the hell can we afford this?' Hugh said in amazement after we were greeted by a softly spoken, impeccably polite uniformed man and shown in. 'Did you rob someone?'

'No.' I laughed.

'Jesus, you didn't take Valda's Valiant money, did you?'

'No!' I didn't laugh; he looked serious. 'You can't really think I'd do that?'

'Well, she might have offered. You never know with her.' He tapped his head.

The children were ahead of us with the polite man (Rodney the butler!!) and Valda. They were pacing silently along the hallways, stunned. I suppose grandeur like this would elicit good behaviour in anyone. The house is a bit like a scary grandfather. (One who is quite soft-hearted and likes a bit of poetry in his garden.) We caught up with them and Valda, who said, 'It's all a bit showy. Don't think we'll be having Gravox with our lamb.'

'It's chicken on tonight's menu,' said Rodney. 'And ice cream. And for you' – he paused and smiled down at Barky – 'kangaroo stew, I believe.' Barky looked at me as if to make sure it was all right to be pleased.

'I'd like to read up on the history of this place,' Hugh stated.

'There are historical records in the library,' said Rodney. (The library!) 'And I am happy to answer questions.'

'The owners, are they gamblers?' asked Valda.

'Ah, no,' he said with a smile. 'Wool.'

'Same thing,' said Valda. 'I should have known. Graziers love their shoes shiny and their carpets plush.'

'The family brought the first sheep into Tasmania,' Rodney went on.

'Are they still here?' asked Jimmy.

'Well, the sheep are certainly still here,' said Rodney. 'On a smaller scale. The family, no. They sold the house and land to a group of investors.'

'Foreign ownership,' said Valda crossly.

'It's an Australian consortium,' said Rodney kindly. 'New South Wales, I believe.'

'Like I said,' Valda snapped. 'Foreign.' Rodney remained neutral. There must be butler schools that teach that. I tried to think of something else to say but Valda added, 'And I'd say the family *are* still here. Places like this hold them in the walls.' She tapped a solid wall. 'They won't have gone far.'

Barky made a small growly noise. My skin prickled. Raffy's eyes widened. Eloise looked thrilled. Mary-Lou, who hadn't been listening, tugged at Rodney's sleeve and said, 'Are you the only slave?'

'Ah!' said Hugh later when the children's excitement had overrun their awe and sent them flying around, choosing bedrooms. 'You got the film money, didn't you! Did Ria send you a sneaky cheque?'

I smiled.

'I knew it! See what your music is capable of!' And he pushed open the door to the most opulent bedroom I've ever seen.

I didn't lie. It's almost the truth. It was my music, in a way. The viola was my music . . . Anyway, there's a flower room where someone arranges bouquets! The window dressings look like something out of the Theatre Royal. There's a curtained window seat in the bedrooms – a reading nook? And a huge four-poster bed that made me want to sing 'I Could Have Danced All Night'. And Hugh isn't cross that I haven't saved the money for school uniforms or garden mulch. This is the best! Hugh and me on our own for three days might have been too much anyway. What would we have talked about all that time? I feel all unbridled and gallopy. Frisky. Just as well there are no chandeliers in our bedroom. There are four in the ballroom, though.

Mum and Dad drove Alison and Laurence up. Alison had to go and have a lie-down immediately because she said that Dad's driving made her carsick. She was trying to be impassive to all the splendour, as though she was entirely used to it, but I know she was taken; I saw her rub the chintz on the chaise longue.

Mum's been running about with the children, pretending to be a ghost. (Valda told her about the ancestors in the walls theory.) Mum's expert at giving frights. Once when I was little Mum hid in the box that the washing machine came in and burst out of it when I arrived home from school. I screamed blue murder; she laughed about it for years.

It's late. I might hop into our huge feathery bed. Should I wake my husband and seduce him? There's a romantic colonial feel to this room. But Hugh was so exhausted that he was asleep by nine-thirty. I think I'll save seduction for our romantic evening tomorrow. Sigh.

What was that sigh? Sex drive still on low setting, methinks. Also, there was a fight over the blue room because it has gold curtains, Mary-Lou wouldn't eat her chicken and Barky left grubby marks on a cushion. Even in a palace, there are the same old things.

SUNDAY 16th APRIL

We've had the most lovely, active, rosy-cheeked, Raffy's birthday day. The discovery of the river and the bathhouse was a revelation. There's a clinker dinghy! And in the bathhouse are fishing rods and kites and other wholesome delights (and poetry everywhere). The garden has a folly! I'm not sure what you do with a folly but I sat in it for a minute. There's a love seat. I sat on that too, with Valda and Mum. (Hugh was busy baiting up fishing lines.)

We had a moment with Eloise, who was cross there aren't any ponies. 'But you've never liked ponies,' I told her.

'Well, I've read the whole 'Shadow Horse' series,' she said.

'I like ponies,' said Mary-Lou proudly. 'I'm getting one for my birthday.' This is what happens when you place children in a luxury mansion, I suppose, they ~~turn into pompous little pricks~~ get highfalutin ideas.

There was another moment with Raffy, who was a bit disappointed that he got books for his birthday. 'Come on, Raff,' Hugh said. 'This whole thing is your birthday present.'

Raffy looked around at the magnificence and said, 'Thomas got a phone for his birthday.'

For Christ's sake. But we bit our tongues and Rodney saved the day with an incredible birthday bundt. 'Bundts,' he said, deadpan, 'are my specialty.'

'Well, that's a triumphant bundt,' I said and Hugh laughed.

☆

Rodney has had an amazing effect on Laurence, because they both dabble in watercolour painting. Rodney set up some easels and paints and Laurence produced a very nice picture of the children flying a kite by the river. Mary-Lou painted Rodney and said she'd like to marry him one day (so would I a little bit, such a Renaissance man). I coerced Hugh into painting me while I painted him (I saw them do this in a film once. It was very romantic). Portraits are very hard. I tried to exaggerate Hugh's lovely twinkly, smile-crinkled eyes, but he just looked wild and weather-beaten. He said, 'Jesus,' then showed the picture of me, only it wasn't me at all but a bird, flying over the ocean.

'That's a very nice painting,' said Laurence, which got everyone's attention because it's about the longest sentence he's ever uttered. People gathered around.

'Mum's not a seagull, silly Daddy,' said Mary-Lou.

'But she's not a bad bird,' quipped Dad with a wink at me.

'It's not a seagull,' said Hugh. 'It's an albatross.' And then he smiled in a shy sort of way at me and added a stroke of blue to the sea. I felt a warm sort of feeling. But later when I showed Alison the painting she said with glee, 'Ah, Coleridge's albatross! "Instead of the cross, the Albatross about my neck was hung".' I felt cold again. 'Hugh's always been good at art,' she added. 'He won the art prize in secondary school.'

And Mum, who'd been trying to enthuse Raffy with the kites and was late to the scene, said, 'What have you painted, darling? A demented farmer?'

In the end we gave up trying to engage the birthday boy with the great outdoors and Valda took him into the music room, where they found a cupboard full of CDs. The others turned the croquet mallets upside down and used them as crutches so they could hobble about and be tragic with English accents. They called the game 'cripples'. They renamed Barky 'Rover'. Barky seemed put out.

'At least they're using their imaginations,' I said to Hugh, who was untangling a kite string and looking quite relaxed. I realised I hadn't seen him that way in a while and it took me a moment to work out what was different.

Anyway, I've left them all out there to come in early and prepare for The Date. It's been blissful. Everyone is occupied, so no interruptions. The bath is huge, the floor is heated, everything smells like fresh linen, the little bottles of shampoo, etc. are by Crabtree & Evelyn. There's a vanity kit with cotton buds and tweezers in it. So I've been indulging in some vanity.

I've done all my nails (there were flecks of toenail polish still there from when Eloise painted them at Christmas time), curled my hair, applied glowy body lotion, put on some sort of lengthening mascara with fibres (bit cloggy but effective), even whitened my teeth. The latter didn't go quite as planned as I left the mouthguard in for too long and now have a blister on my gum – not too noticeable if I don't smile too widely, which is best for my crow's-feet and eye bags anyway. The box said 'two shades whiter in ten minutes', so I thought I'd go for four shades in twenty. A mistake, but I'm not going to let it bother me. Hopefully it won't hamper any heated kissing manoeuvres.

I'm wearing the op-shop leopard-print dress, which actually looks okay, I think. As long as I don't overdo the make-up, I think it could be considered stylish. Leopard print does tread a fine line between chic and cheap, doesn't it? I've taken a photo of myself and sent it to Ria, and she gave me her tick of approval:

> Helen! Don't you look smart (growl). You don't
> look a day older than the night H took you to
> McDonald's for your first date. Is that where you're
> headed tonight?!!

She had to bring that up . . . When I'm lamenting the fact that I didn't marry a man who knows ballroom dancing and quite likes a rollneck, I add the McDonald's memory to my regrettables and berate myself for not heeding my alarm bells and running for far-away pastures. But it wasn't really a first date. Was it?

Hobart, 1993

It happened on one of those terrible Hobart days when winter has decided to put on its best show, complete with hail, sleet and a wind that will freeze your eyeballs and cut you clean in half. 'You've got three chances of getting me to touch footy training today,' Ria had told me. 'Buckley's, Fuckley's and none.' This meant that I had to bundle off to training on my own because a strong risk of exposure wasn't about to keep me from my weekly sighting of Hugh. 'You've been totally brained by love, haven't you, you poor old fucking twit?' Ria said as I set off. 'It's horrible to watch.'

When I got to training, no one was there. I jigged about on the uni oval for about five minutes and then decided that I was indeed a twit. But then Hugh's car drove in and I mentally high-fived myself. 'Now, that's commitment,' he said when he'd got out of the car. 'I wasn't even going to come but then I thought I'd better drop in in case . . .' he trailed off.

'In case some idiot shows up.'

He laughed. 'Yes. You idiot, get in the car. I'll give you a lift.'

'But I have my bike. I'll be right.'

'No, you won't. I'll put it in the back. Come on. You'll freeze your arse off. It's my job as coach to look after the team.'

So we manoeuvred the bike into the back of the car and jumped in just as another squall came off the mountain and tumbled with a gust of frigid wind from the sea. Even the yachts in the Derwent Sailing Squadron looked tucked up and unwilling. I smiled smugly at them from the girlfriend seat.

Hugh and I bantered a bit as he drove up towards college, had a laugh probably, I don't remember. And then he said, 'You know, I don't feel all that comfortable having you and Ria on the team. I worry that something might happen to your arms or your hands. You can't play your music without your hands.'

'Well, you can't very well engineer things without yours, can you?' I said. 'You should worry about your own hands.'

'Look at yours, though. They're perfect.' And he picked one up then and examined it, turned it over. 'They're cold too. Would you like to get some dinner?'

It was such an unexpected question. I'm not sure what I did with my face but it must have looked astonished. 'I would. I really would. I'd really like that,' I sort of whispered. Then I blushed, and something in the close atmosphere shifted.

'I mean, I'm hungry,' he added awkwardly. 'And it might warm us up a bit. There's a cosy place in Magnet Court. I'm always hungry when it's cold. Why is that?'

I don't know if I answered, I just remember thinking how adorable Hugh was when he felt awkward. There was a bit of silence then, so Hugh turned on the radio. It was Boyz II Men singing 'I'll Make Love to You', which he quickly switched over. Belinda Carlisle trilled out 'Mad About You' and he switched it off. Then there was silence, with a large bumbling elephant in it. I cursed myself for treating his dinner suggestion like a proposal and tried to think of things to say that could steer us back to safety.

But then he made a sudden turn into the McDonald's drive-through and said, 'Actually, I really feel like a Big Mac. That okay?' We bought two burgers and then he dropped me back to college. The whole experience (later labelled 'The McDonald's Incident'), was, I believed, a clear 'friend-zone' manoeuvre. I cried myself to sleep that night.

(He flung his gherkin out in disgust. I'd already eaten mine. *People who love gherkins*, I thought, *can never expect to win the heart of people who don't*. Perhaps I should have paid that more heed.)

Where on earth is Hugh? He said he'd meet me here for pre-dinner drinks. I've already had two. Three. He'll be here any minute, surely. Perhaps he's lost in the house, gone to the wrong wing. I'll phone him.

Found him. He's on his way. He was playing Roar with the children and forgot the time. This is a very good sign. I can't remember the last time they played Roar. It's a game invented by Hugh. He hides, they look for him and if they don't see him and say 'roar' in time, he can leap out with a giant ROOOAAAAARRR, catch them and squeeze their knees on that sensitive reflex spot. Sometimes, in unlikely places like at the theatre or at school speech night, he'll whisper 'roar'. I love that man.

MONDAY 17th APRIL

Oh, dear GOD, I have a terrible, terrible hangover. And a horrible feeling that any inner glow I might have had has been extinguished by champagne. And gin. We are home, and I have banished myself to the wardrobe to face my music and accurately report the events of our dinner date.

I could blame Hugh for being late. Twenty-five minutes isn't that long, except by then I'd reached that squiffy stage when every new drink seems like the best idea ever because they are causing SUCH FUN! When he finally entered the room, I leapt out from the reading nook and yelled, 'ROOOAAAAARRRRR!'

He yelled, 'FUUUCK!' because I really scared him. Must have been the leopard dress. I thought it was hilarious. When he'd composed himself a bit, Hugh said, 'Hey, look at you! You're so . . . wow.' Compliments are apparently fraught with danger. I tried to give him an encouraging smile but he was looking at all the strewn-about evidence of my vanity. I'd forgotten to pack it up. Blame the gin. 'What's all this?' he asked.

'All this,' I said, 'is you and I going on a date, just the two of us. And you, my darling,' I lowered my voice and opened my stance, 'are in big trouble.'

I never call him Darling.

I'd booked us into Nost, a restaurant in Stanley that keeps getting rave reviews everywhere. It turned out to be *waaaaay* too hipster for us.

We arrived at the restaurant twenty minutes past our allocated time but the laconic, man-bunned maître d' appeared unperturbed. Or on dope. He said, 'All good hey, Thursey,' which I took to be some sort of New-Age greeting. I was contemplating giving a peace sign when I heard, 'Hey, Fezzle,' from behind me and a bloke with a long beard – presumably Thursey – came past. He was wearing bright green skinny jeans and an Ansett T-shirt.

'Mazza pumping?' asked Fezzle.

'Midtown. Rippy. Sat out the back and watched the kooks.'

'Niiiice.'

I gave Hugh a bewildered look. He smiled and sipped some water from what looked like a small Vegemite jar.

'Thank you, Fezzle,' said Hugh seriously. I held in a laugh.

'What were they saying, do you think?' I asked once Fezzle had resumed his post at the front door. 'Who's Mazza?'

'Mazza's a beach, I'd say,' said Hugh. 'A surf break. Marrawah, maybe? The beard bloke's been there but the surf wasn't great. There were rips, and novice surfers probably from out of town.'

'Listen to you!' I was amazed. 'How can you decode that exchange?'

'Spent a bit of time with a surfy bloke at Davis Station. We all used to imitate him. It was great.' He smiled broadly at the memory. The old Hugh smile. Not for me.

'Oh.' There was a pause with something crackling in it. Not sparks. I felt very midtown.

'Honeyed bespoke pilsner?' I waved the craft beer list at him.

He smiled and said, 'Sweet, that'd be mint.'

I tried a laugh. And choked. Possibly on a chia seed.

The coughing and spluttering went on for a long time. I had tears streaming and people staring. Even the laid-back Fezzle seemed a bit concerned, Hugh said later. I had to stand up, thus causing something of a scene. Hugh stood up too. I clutched his arm. He looked embarrassed and I wondered whether he'd quite like me to get on and stop breathing to end the noisy leopard-printed drama. *That would probably be the most exciting thing to happen in Stanley since Kate Winslet was here*, I thought. I finally caught my breath before anyone felt the need to administer the Heimlich manoeuvre (thank goodness, they would have encountered my shapewear) and, after some worried hand pats from Hugh and me not being able to talk for a good ten minutes, normality resumed. An extreme way to avoid Antarctic awkwardness but it worked. Chia really is a superfood.

Dinner arrived – spirulina-infused beef with harissa kale chips for Hugh, confit of organic duck with Bloody Mary jus for me. Hugh tried his best to rid his face of its blatant WTF expression but failed. We laughed again and reflected on the near-death choking experience and what to do if I died. (Spend nothing on coffin but lots on large marble statue of weeping angel; ensure children brush teeth, etc.) Then the conversation turned to children and our vacuum cleaner. (Too cumbersome, bit crappy suction-wise despite relative newness. Should we write a letter to manufacturer and should we get a non-shedding dog next time, blah blah blah.) See the problem? We had arrived at Boring Point and it was time to rip off our inhibitions, jump off and go skinny dipping. I closed my mouth over whatever bit of tedium was coming next, stared down at my blurred reflection amid the remnants of celery syllabub and felt suddenly VERY CROSS about being altogether blurry and never ever brave.

I took a glug of champagne and a very deep breath and said, 'Why did they want you back at Davis?'

He put down his fork. 'Not Davis this time. Mawson. Just for three months. There's a new supervising engineer who's very keen to have all the structures checked out. Nothing's gone wrong, they're just pre-empting things. There's such a turnover of staff that old knowledge can go missing. And they wanted someone who'd been before. I know the rosters, how the kitchen operates, you know.'

I'll put you on a goddamn roster here if you like, I thought, *in a place where there are small people who look like you and a kitchen that you don't know how to operate.* But I swallowed the words down and said, 'And you really said no?'

'Yep.'

An apology popped into my head and stopped there, because I wasn't sorry at all. Then I thought *thanks*, but I didn't say that either because how pathetic. Instead I thought about how I'm meant to show interest in his passions, and I said, 'What does the Aurora Australis look like from Antarctica? The southern light show, I mean, not the boat.'

He looked at me but through me and said, 'I was trying to tell April about this the other day and the best I can come up with, I think, is that it's as though you're watching the very, very best that nature can offer. It's kind of crucial, as though if you look away or even breathe, you might miss something. And when it's gone you feel like you've met an almighty presence.' His eyes connected with me. 'Does that make any sense?'

'Yes,' I said. 'It's as if someone's told you an important secret, only you can't quite decipher it.'

'Yes!' His eyes caught the shine of the industrial-style lights above us. 'Have you seen it?'

'Yes, briefly, once.'

'You've never said.'

'No,' I said, stepping cautiously. 'I was a bit pissed off with the whole subject, I suppose.' His eyes cast down, so (*no no, stay with me*) I swigged at my champagne again and went on, hurriedly. 'It was years ago, when I was at school. I was with Ria. She made me sneak out of the house and go to a party. I was so terrified we'd get found out but she bribed me with a Crowded House CD. We had to walk about four kilometres to get to the party, so we only stayed an hour and walked home again. We'd just got to the turn-off into my street when Ria stopped and gasped. There, in the southern sky, were streaks of vivid light, purples and pinks, beaming upwards through the wires of someone's clothesline. We were silent for a bit, then Ria whispered, "Aurora Australis, licking the corners of the sky," because we had this English teacher who was obsessed with TS Eliot's Prufrock so we'd learnt it by heart. Is this boring?'

Hugh smiled, leaned in a bit and said, 'Not at all.'

I went on, gushily. 'We couldn't believe our luck. It was cold and we could see our breaths in the air, and Ria said she wanted to put them in a jar so she could keep our happy aurora sighs forever.'

Hugh laughed. 'You weirdos.' This is how he used to talk to me. Fond. Proud of my peculiarities.

'I was so grateful to Hobart City Council for buggering up the lighting on Seaview Avenue, and to Ria for getting me outside in the dark when I was so scared.'

And Hugh said, 'Rare solar winds and magnificent universe disturbances can happen when we are brave.'

Then all those gulps of champagne must have set in because I remember feeling a sort of head whorl, mistaking it for bravery and thinking, I'm going to damn well disturb the universe. I took Hugh's hand, leaned forward and whispered, 'Perhaps we could go to Antarctica together. Then we could make passionate love among the penguin colonies. Could they bear to have a woman among the brave frontiersmen?'

'Well, April's going,' he said.

The playfulness in the air went 'poof!' leaving me hanging like a giggle at a funeral.

'Is she? When?'

'September,' he said. 'I suggested they take her instead of me. She's really bloody impressive, Zannah. I think we're lucky to have her. If she can add Antarctic Expeditioner to her CV, then that's great.'

He continued to enthuse (perhaps, I wonder now, to soothe his own regret) but I wasn't really listening. My impressions of the earthy

April were glitching around with images of a young Jane Goodall – all adorable focus and unheeded beauty. The upward-tilted chin of someone who'd never dream of setting down their camera or packing up their drafting desk because their painfully divided heart insisted they go to watch their children in their school cross-country event.

A young couple glided past our table and I wished I could stand, take the girl by the shoulders and say, 'Look out, beware! Hazards ahead! Relentless emotional labour with invisible results! Don't be fooled by apple pies and dancing. They turn out to be fish fingers and drudgery. You won't be able to glide anywhere any more. Run, run, take your unrumpled face skin and go and build a building, paint a picture, save a whale, close the door, keep safe your hands and your whole, light heart.'

But I didn't stand. Some things are just ineffable, especially with alcohol added. So I said, 'Oh, that's terrific for April,' in a voice that reminded me of an old Fisher-Price phone we had once, bright and plastic.

'It is.' And then – after a beat – he raised his glass. 'Here's to you, Susannah, for "Starlit Sonata" and *Pollyanna* and bringing us all here – thank you.' It felt like an end point and for a lucid moment it seemed like a very good idea to just go back to our sumptuous manor house, watch a film and see if lovemaking happened before sleep. Like the normal Susannah and Hugh would. But the woman in the leopard-print dress thought, *You are so predictably half-hearted, Susannah*, had another drink and asked Hugh to list his sexual fantasies.

Half an hour later I was reciting more TS Eliot (something about forcing moments to their crises). Forty-five minutes later I was asking Fezzle and Thursey back to Brynkirra for a castle party. ('We have Pringles. So much better than your horrible discomfit of orgasmic virgin Mary duck.') Fifty minutes later Hugh was trying to get me home amid slurred protests. ('But we never did get to the bottom of your sexual fantasies – oh, wait, perhaps bottoms are your sexual fantasies. They don't call it DATE night for nothing!')

An hour later I was being sick in a wheelie bin.

Hugh had to pretty much carry me back to Brynkirra, where we were greeted in the entrance hall by a silent and shrouded figure. I screamed. The apparition laughed.

'Hello, Frannie,' Hugh said.

Mum and her flannel nightie appeared from under the sheet. 'We've been having a lovely time with Eloise and Valda's ghost stories,' she said. At that moment, two small giggling ghosts scuttled past us, along with a bounding Barky, who hasn't bounded for years and was clearly having a brilliant time. Then Valda wheeled her chair along the corridor wearing an armoured helmet. She said, 'Woooooooo'. From somewhere in the house there was a clattering noise and a child's scream.

'Laurence is being a poltergeist,' said Mum, her eyes twinkling. 'He's really come out of his shell this weekend. We've been doing quite a bit of haunting in Alison's general direction. That's what you get when you opt for an early night. Susannah, you look a bit tipped up, darling.'

'You look like mutton dressed up as a leopard,' said Valda.

'Mummy, have you had a lot of beers?' asked Mary-Lou, peeking out from under her sheet.

'You should be in bed,' I said slurrily.

'Rubbish,' said Mum. 'It's not ten yet and Rodney's coming over for a midnight feast. He's bringing Iced VoVos.'

Then (because of course) Alison appeared with a glass of water and an expression of disdain. She pointed the expression at me, laughed and said, 'Oh, dear dear dear.' Which was probably justified, but I was suddenly hot with fed-uppery so I spat back, 'Alison, how is it that you've kept your heart so HARD all these years? Do you mix cement in with your porridge?' And then suddenly my feet were taking me wonkily along the hallway towards the stairs. Perhaps they were marching me deservedly to bed, or perhaps they realised before I did that I was going to be sick. Because I was. Into a large marble urn on a plinth.

The next morning, there was another strange apparition looking back at me from the mirror. It was like a newly evolved species of human, complete with stained lips, black-rimmed, bloodshot eyes, matted hair that seemed redder than it should (it was probably embarrassed) and the imprint of a waffle blanket on its cheek. *Homo regretto-mortifi*: she stared at me from the toilet with a startled expression. (Why they put full-length mirrors right in front of the loo I'll never understand.) I groaned, gave myself the bird and put my ruined face in my hands.

Hugh was watching from the bedroom. The bathroom was partitioned by glass, but it was transparent unless you chose to press a button to make it opaque. What kind of gimmicky, interior-stylist bullshittery is that? In a manor house? Even the most passionately hot and horny couple need a spontaneous private wee. Don't they? Or do they just wee on one another? Sigh, I have so much to learn.

'You right, Zannah?' he called out, because I guess it was pretty bloody CRYSTAL clear that I wasn't.

'Not really,' I said. 'Not by a very long shot.' And then I found the stupid opaque button and poked it grumpily. And then I suppose Hugh watched the apparition go misty and disappear.

'I'll give you five minutes and then I'm coming in,' he said, which was sweet, I suppose, given he'd glimpsed what I'd become. I had to negotiate fifteen, though, as my bowels had started to rumble and I needed time to deal with that. Hotel rooms aren't always as romantic as one hopes.

Hugh ran me a huge bath, helped me into it, sat on the edge and informed me that the children spooked themselves so much they had to sleep in our bed. Even Eloise.

'So let me get this straight,' I said. 'We rented this magnificent, eight-bedroom house, went on a romantic date and ended up sleeping with all of our children?'

'Nope,' said Hugh. 'Barky and I slept down the hall a bit. Not enough room for us.'

I went under the water for a moment, then came up again, spluttered and said, 'I hate myself.' He gave me a washer and squeezed my foot. 'Just very socially excited. You had a very good time.'

We were quiet for a minute while I washed trashy Susannah away. A clock chimed. He got me Panadol and a glass of water and went for the door. 'I'll go down and make sure there's Vegemite toast.'

'Thanks,' I called, then covered my face with the washer.

'And Zannah?'

I peeked out as Hugh's face came back around the door. It was, I realised, disturbingly fresh. 'Yes?'

'Nice wax job.'

He left again and I laughed, then blushed.

Sometimes it's hard to move between functional partnership to friends to lovers. And back. Confusing. Would it be easier to let the sparkles go and just be friends?

Some eyelash fibres were floating in the bath.

At breakfast, I whispered an apology to Rodney for being sick in the urn. He just nodded as if I'd said something about the toast.

Mary-Lou said, 'Mummy ate some bad things at the restaurant. She bomited in a wheelie bin too.'

'We don't talk about disgusting things at the dinner table, thank you, Mary-Lou,' said Alison, briefly side-eyeing me.

Mum came in, looked at me and said, 'Oh, dear. Someone won't want a banana smoothie this morning.'

And Valda laughed and said, 'Rodney, I think Susannah would like sardines on her toast, please.'

'We've all been there,' said Laurence. 'Everybody leave her alone.' And his words were so unexpected that everybody did. (The Laurence shell is indeed open, or at least ajar; the weekend evidently wasn't a complete failure.)

Rodney quietly brought me a glass of lemon barley water.

I am very pleased to be home. Even without reading nooks and gold curtains. No ghosts here. Even Eloise Driscoll is gone.

FRIDAY 21st APRIL

I talked to Ria today. 'How are you?' I asked and she said, 'Tits deep in a new commission – the musical version of *I Capture the Castle*.'

'Oh my GOD. Tell me you're not joking. How perfect.'

'Come over and help. It's killing me.'

'I can hear Cassandra's Midsummer's Eve song already.'

'Pack your bags. I'll book the flight.'

'You'd have to bring in some panpipes for the beautiful, enigmatic Topaz. I love her. And I love that you're giving these characters a musical adaptation, they truly deserve it. Some don't, you know – some characters.'

'I'm very serious, Helen. I'll fetch you over myself if I have to. I haven't slept properly for weeks, I need you. And *you, your character* needs a musical adaptation. Another one. Come *on*.'

'Stop, Ria. Please . . .'

'But just think,' said Ria in an exaggerated English accent, 'what Cassandra could do for you. She said it, didn't she? If you make yourself write, you might find out what is wrong with you. We could do *Jane Eyre* too one day.'

'Shut up, Gloria, or I'll tell everyone your real name.'

To distract her, I told Ria all about the Brynkirra trip. About Fezzle and Thursey and elderly ghosts and Rodney and the painted albatross. She laughed her head off and said, 'I bloody love Tasmania. This sort of shit doesn't happen anywhere else in the world. Hilarious.'

'It's not hilarious,' I said grumpily.

'Oh, come on, Helen. It sounds like a brilliant extended family holiday. I'm so bummed I wasn't there too. Think of the memories. And you got depicted as an albatross! That's all romance.'

'Ria, an albatross is a metaphor for burden or a curse. I looked it up. Coleridge.'

'Bollocks,' she said. 'It's a beautiful soaring beast of flight, over the sparkling sea. That's what he meant. Hugh doesn't know the first thing about Coleridge.'

Except I'm almost sure he does. All those times when Hugh and I were meant to be studying in the library, he was quite fascinated with the poetry section, and Coleridge was there, wasn't he? I could be wrong; I was very busy pretending not to be impressed.

Anyway, the albatross thing has prompted me to delve back into our story again, so I'm here in the wardrobe again . . . And thinking back, it was, despite my yearnings and pretending, actually very nice being just friends with Hugh . . .

Hobart, 1993

Ria and I discovered quickly that we weren't at all intriguing or unusual on the touch footy field. Everyone had something interesting to offer, from all sorts of backgrounds. I perhaps stood out more than others because I was utterly hopeless (very long limbs are easy to get tangled up in) so any awe I inspired in Hugh via music was quickly neutralised by my bumbles on the oval. His good-humoured coaching style just gave me a new dimension to adore, but I had Ria close by to keep me grounded and, anyway, I was having way too much fun to get too bogged down in heartache.

After a while, Hugh stopped hurrying off after training or lectures and would hang around a bit more. He teased us incessantly. He and Ria squabbled like siblings. I mostly laughed. By the time second semester rolled around and the touch footy season ended, we were studying together, eating together and drinking together. Hannah sometimes joined us but she was mostly too busy with her advertising job to hang with us, which suited me perfectly. To her credit, she didn't appear cross, and she could have. I suppose she didn't feel threatened; she was attractive and together and secure in Hugh's love for her. Ria and I ate Wizz Fizz and laughed at farts. They were proper sweethearts, had grown up together, knew everything there was to know about one another. That's what she used to tell me. Sometimes I had terrible urges to smoosh strawberries into her perfect face or throw her shoes over fences. These were unfair. She was always kind. That was the year Ria's mum died. Hannah was so grown-up about it. She was the one who knew all about funeral arrangements and who to call to find two of Ria's brothers in the WA mines. I was the one who checked Ria's face for breakages so often that she had to tell me to 'please fuck off, for the love of God'. Yes, poor Hannah, she tried to be our friend, but she bored us and we irritated her, so it never really worked. I didn't like myself much when she was around.

It was fun, but it was also very hard work. I had to be carefree and lighthearted all the time and pretend that Hugh's opinions didn't matter that much, that his touch didn't burn my skin and his casual, see-you-when-I'm-looking-at-you goodbyes didn't have my heart sinking back to its usual lowly position in my chest. Sometimes at night I would sob, and then have a look in the mirror to see what limerence and heartache looked like. The friendship without the yearning love would have been even more fun.

Oh, but sometimes I yearn to yearn. These days I'm either harried or weary; neither are emotions, just physical effects. I must sleep. It takes me a whole week to recover from hangovers these days.

SUNDAY 23rd APRIL

I'm very down in the dumps. Post-holiday blues? Bound to happen when there's a butler involved.

I've just hung the washing on the line and had to unroll Hugh's work-shirtsleeves so they'd dry properly, then noticed that I'd hung the shirt next to the expensive silky stockings I wore on our date. ('You can't skimp on hosiery,' said Ellie.) I felt suddenly very pointless. *When did I last roll up my shirtsleeves?* I thought. *I pretend I'm productive and hardworking because I'm raising four children, but in all honesty I'm pathetic. Women through the ages have raised children AND handwashed the sheets, ironed* everything, grown their own food, ground their own grains, made their own clothes and so forth. I never roll up my shirtsleeves. I make gravy from a packet and complain about having to move the wheelie bins.

And then, *I sold my viola for vanity and luxury. I sold my viola.*

And there under the clothesline, my pointlessness got underlined. The weight of my recent indulgences fell down on me: while Hugh was sleeves-up and providing, I was spending money on bullshit. Hairdressery, teeth whitening, hosiery bullshit. I am ashamed.

The billowing sheets snapped me on the thighs, fresh and flirty. The scream of the mundane was loud and suggestive.

What am I doing with my life? Mary-Lou is well into Grade One. It's time I got a job. Or at least joined the Country Women's Association. Apparently in Tasmania you don't have to live in the country to join, and they are a veritable hive of industry. A HIVE. (Mustn't forget honey – apparently a spoonful before bed wards off viruses.)

SATURDAY 29th APRIL

Hugh is cross with me. Very cross. He knows about me selling the viola. Everything seems blunted when he's so annoyed: no point in anything.

Rafferty noticed that the viola was missing from the wardrobe, and I was forced to tell. (I've been working up to it; there just hasn't been a good time.)

Hugh was aghast. 'You did what?'

'You can't have,' said Raff incredulously.

'It was mine to sell,' I said, 'and I was sick of not being able to afford anything for the family. I want to contribute. Everyone was so sad or upset or stressed, and the viola was just sitting there reminding me of things. The film fell through and Pollyanna couldn't pay for our holiday so . . . well, it's quite a nice story actually . . .' I stopped. Hugh's face was thunderous. My voice turned cold. 'It was mine. My viola, my choice. No one was angry with Valda for selling the Valiant.'

Raffy said, 'Who's Pollyanna?' and burst into tears. I've never known Raffy to be so sensitive. He's usually so busy in Rafferty World. Perhaps turning ten has switched something on. I hope this means he might grow a bit faster. He's starting to look quite, um, nuggety. At least he won't have my unwieldy build.

I told them about the Elliot–Eloise Driscoll connection. They were very unimpressed. I tried to dress it up in romantics. 'Who knows, perhaps Eloise Driscoll was forced to sell the viola, and now that it's back with its rightful family, she can rest in peace.'

'Yes,' said Hugh. 'There were probably very good reasons to give away vocations in those days.'

'Oh, come on, Hugh. Music isn't something I'm duty-bound to do. I wasn't called to it. No one's called to anything. We don't have fates; you are the biggest believer of that. I did astronomy, remember? We're all here because of a one-in-a-trillion accident. The death of a chancy little star.' It was the angriest I've ever been with him in front of the children. He looked sort of disgusted.

Eloise watched us, then said, 'Whoa.'

Raffy poked out his bottom lip and said, 'Well, I hope Idiot Driscoll knows to wash his hands before handling the bow.'

I won't let them make me feel guilty. NO MORE GUILT. It's layering up so much that it'll surely smother me soon.

Valda got heaps of wheelchair practice, we all got to row a clinker dinghy, Hugh played Roar, Laurence came out of his shell, Raffy had a nice birthday, Eloise smiled a lot, looked up from her books and put us all in one of her ghost stories. It was worth it. Wasn't it?

THURSDAY 4th MAY

For goodness sake, Hugh is still grumpy. So is Raffy. They can't all expect me to push four people out of my vagina hole, scrub their shirt collars and not make my own decisions.

And now they're all playing snakes and ladders. Raffy is all snuggled into Hugh, which is rare. I feel very sorrowful and left out, like when Shelly Howard from Grade Three suddenly declared she wouldn't be my friend any more and ran off with Dearne Wells, who had thick ringlets and a teacup poodle. I'm calling Mum and Dad. They will support me . . .

LATER:

Mum and Dad are furious too. Here's how that went:

'So, Dad, remember when I was fifteen and I accidentally bought a four-thousand-dollar bed over the phone?'

'Yes,' he said.

'And you know how you still have that bed and you and Mum love it because it has all those bells and whistles you can no longer do without?'

'Yes.'

'Well, I've done something similar in that it might appear stupid but will, in the long run, work out best for everyone.'

'Did you get one of those massage chairs? Wally got one; said it was a waste of money and he should have bought a machine for beef jerky instead.'

'They're such ugly chairs too!' Mum yelled from the background.

'Am I on speaker phone?'

'Yes.'

'Right. Well, I sold my viola.'

There was lots of rustling and commotion and then Mum came on. 'You sold your viola and bought a massage chair? Oh, darling, how could you?'

'No, Mum. No, I sold it and I'm saving the money. Most of it. Perhaps for the children's education. Something not so selfish as a valuable viola gathering dust. I got forty thousand for it.'

There was a bit of silence, some muffly phone-to-chest noises and then Mum came back, yelling this time. 'That's not the selfish thing.' More rustling, something muffled. 'You never played for the children —'

'Wait, Mum, but listen, it was meant to be . . .' I told her the Elliot Driscoll bit, adding my theory about Eloise probably being forced to give it up. She listened in silence and when I'd finished, she said, 'Oh, Susannah, I can't speak to you. You silly girl.'

Then she hung up.

A minute later, she phoned back. 'Let me tell you something, Susannah. If Eloise Driscoll could have kept playing her viola, she would have. She would NOT have dicked about wondering whether she was WORTHY. She would say, "You spoilt, spoilt woman, with all your CHOICES. Spoilt by your choices." And she would box your ears, just as I would if I were there and not on the end of a phone line. Goodbye.'

☆

Mum always used to say that she'd box my ears. She never did. What does it even mean?

Also, she said 'dick'!

LATER:

A text from Ria! A slightly supportive one. Well, it wasn't actual support, but she wasn't angry at least. I'm so sick of angry. I sent her a very long email explaining why I sold the viola and that I didn't need any more fury directed my way, thank you. She replied with this:

> No fury here. Looks like you've well and truly
> justified your actions. Move on, get a new one.
> Cut out old wood. Good-o. Can't write more,
> busy with 'I Capture the Castle' etc. R x

Ouch. But she's right. Move on. I read her text aloud to Hugh (leaving out the 'get a new one' bit). Not sure I like my viola being referred to as 'old wood' but oh well, moving on.

LATER STILL:

Another text from Ria with links to violas for sale, no note. Not even a kiss. She's trying to shake my sentimental bones. I can tell she's cross.

Bloody hell, I'm cross too. And I WILL NOT get sentimental and what-iffy. My music is MINE. I'll show them all that I have made a brilliant decision that will make room for all sorts of shiny bells and new whistles. What is happening around here? Why am I the baddie?

☆

I think Hugh's fallen asleep in Raff's room, which has never happened before, so that's that, then. The beginning of the end? Separate rooms, separate gonads, separate lives, probably. Where were we in the Sparkle Project? Oh, that's right, the Very Happy Family Holiday phase. Well, what if there isn't a happy family?

Oh, God. What if there really isn't? I don't know what the next phase of the Sparkle Project is, but I'm moving into it immediately.

Interlude

WEDNESDAY 10th MAY

Not quite ready to move into next phase. Call this a necessary interval, perhaps? Because, life, you old bastard, I can NOT believe the way you can kick me in the self-esteems right when they're reaching their lowest ebb. Here's what happened today, holy GOD:

Eloise was playing singles against a young girl who reminded me of a gazelle and had a serve like a paper cut. The girl's mother arrived a little way into the match and I glanced at her just long enough to see that she was very attractive and beautifully dressed. I tried not to look too openly but, let's face it, a woman with style is infinitely fascinating to other women.

Anyway, the thing is . . . it was Hannah!!!!! The mother of the gazelle was HANNAH. Hugh's ex, Hannah. Hannah of clippy heels and very healthy hair. And she was just as perfect as ever, if not more. In the instant before my memory registered her properly, I sort of waved in a 'hello, I know you' kind of way, then I faltered and froze. *Ah, there you are,* I thought. *Of course you're here, come to join us in the confoundry of blinding disappointments.* She looked over. 'Susannah?'

'Hannah?' And for the first time I noticed how similar our names are, which is probably another sign of scurrilous happenstance.

'I should have known,' she said. 'Your daughter is the image of you. She's gorgeous.'

She was so genuine and warm that I felt suddenly like I might cry. A thief atoned? Or something. I went all garbly. 'Hannah, oh my goodness, you look lovely. It's been so long. Is this your daughter?'

'Yes. We've moved back here from Singapore.'

'Oh, well done. She's lovely and what a backhand!' I waffled. 'I've always wanted a backhand like that. Mine is awful, on account of me not playing tennis much at all. Ever. I'm so busy all the time – I have a baby still. Well, she's six, so not really a baby. I should have time for tennis. Singapore! How exotic. I hope Tassie isn't too boring for you . . .' I went on like that, dear God.

Then Eloise smashed a ball straight into the Gazelle-girl's beautiful face and my rattling train of a mouth was brought to a blessed, terrible screeching halt.

We rushed towards her daughter, who was on her knees with her hands covering her nose. Eloise looked horrified. 'Oh, no. I'm so sorry, I'm so . . .'

'Show me, Em. Let me see. Oh, darling,' Hannah was saying, and Em moved her hands. Blood flowed out. We gasped. Em's eyes rolled, she fell onto me, a dead weight. I lowered her to the ground.

'Emily?' Hannah was saying. 'Em?'

I grappled around in my bag for my phone and called an ambulance. 'Eloise, get someone from the club,' I said. She ran.

'Oh, God. Emmy?' Hannah whispered.

I put my ear to Em's pale lips. 'She's okay, Hannah,' I said in a panicky voice. 'She's not dead.'

'I know she's not dead, Susannah,' said Hannah in a much calmer voice. 'Jesus.'

'Sorry. I mean, she's just fainted, I think. You'll be okay, Em.' I turned her onto her side. Hannah pulled some tissues from her bag and put them to Emily's face. They were soaked in seconds so I took off my cardigan and put it in their place. Em gave a whimper, opened her eyes and tried to push the cardigan away.

'Leave it, darling. You're bleeding,' said Hannah.

'Em,' I said, 'can you see us?'

She nodded.

'Can you tell me what day it is?'

'Wednesday.'

'Can you tell me your mum's name?'

'Hannah de Montagu.'

De Montagu. I gulped and said, 'What?' like an idiot. The poor girl had to repeat it.

'Yes, that's right,' said Hannah de Montagu. 'Darling, can you remember everything that happened?'

'Yes,' snapped Em. 'She hit me in the nose.'

It was a petulant teenage voice. Normal. Relief! No apparent head injury. Also, she had a beautiful English accent. I was fascinated. *Am I in the presence of nobility?* I thought. *Is this blue blood coming from Em's nose?*

Eloise came back with a tennis coach and a first-aid kit. She moved to apply ice. 'Don't touch,' Em said acidly. Eloise jumped back, stung. I ached for her.

'Darling, you fainted,' said Hannah. 'We're getting an ambulance, okay.'

Emily turned and vomited a bloody mess into my cardigan and onto the court. Eloise gasped and said, 'Oh, no. I'm so sorry.' Hannah stroked Emily's hair.

There was silence then, while we waited for the ambulance.

I thought about making conversation ('So, what've you been up to since I last saw you?') but it didn't seem right. 'You must have a killer serve,' said the coach to Eloise, which didn't seem right either.

Eloise and I stood aside while the paramedics loaded Emily onto a trolley and into the ambulance. I offered to follow them to hospital but Hannah said, 'No, please don't worry.'

'We could bring you in some dinner or something?' I offered.

'No, really. We'll be fine.'

'I could call your husband to get your car?'

'No, Susannah. Honestly, we'll manage.' She put up a hand. It said, leave us alone.

'Okay. So sorry.' But I thought of something else. 'Hannah, could I just get your number? So we can check how —'

'No, Susannah, please . . .'

'Okay, yep, sorry, not the time,' I stammered.

'I'm really, really sorry,' said Eloise, stricken.

Hannah came back and touched her shoulder. 'It was an accident, Eloise. She'll be fine, I promise.' And then they whizzed off, sirens blaring.

Eloise watched them long after the ambulance had disappeared. She's now gone to bed early. I've never seen her so bothered.

I'm a bit shaken myself. Apart from the drama, I was reminded that Hannah was actually always very nice. I just wanted her not to be. And Hannah de Montagu seemed just as nice. And even more effortlessly chic. Dammit. She would die before she wore leopard print and her elegant mind would never wander to stuff like whether heated car seats cause thrush.

I've had to phone Ria for possibly the biggest debrief since she performed for the Queen. We drank gin. (On a Wednesday, because calamity control. Also gin is not a drink-drink. It's got botanicals, which are essentially greens.)

'She was entirely different to how I remember her,' I said. 'Or was she? Did we shape her into a villain for convenience?'

'We never made her a villain,' Ria said. 'We just highlighted her boringness because we were so fun.'

'Perhaps she was just mature?'

'You can be mature and fun, though. Apparently.'

'We were unnecessarily nasty, weren't we? We thought we were extraordinary and she was ordinary.'

'We are extraordinary.'

'You are, with your groundbreaking musicals. My major achievement this week is defining "pert" for Jimmy without referring to nipples.'

'You are raising the good people of the future. Have you bought a new viola yet?'

I was silent, so she added, 'She dented three panels of Hugh's car, don't forget. Boring *and* psycho.'

'I stole her sweetheart, don't forget.'

'They would never have lasted. Why does Jimmy need to know "pert"?'

'Imagine how beautiful their children would have been.'

Ria sighed. 'You're right. Yours have been beaten half to death by the ugly stick. I don't know how you can be seen with them.'

'She's probably a baroness,' I said wistfully. 'Her car has a pearly sheen.'

'Oh, for fuck's sake, Susannah. Go and find your senses. You've left them somewhere. I've no time for this bullshit.'

'Nor do I,' I said. 'I'm off to grow four humans and do my bit for world peace.'

'That's the spirit.'

UPSIDES:

We got home early-ish for once. I am terrible at the getting home after school bit. Those few hours in which to fit dinner and homework, plant-watering, emergency dog-washing and getting Matchbox cars untangled from someone's hair, etc. The epitome of the rushing years. And me at my most fractious.

Eloise and I had a bondy moment brought on by mutual mortification. I blurted out who Hannah is. 'Seriously?' she said, with teenage dramatic voice. 'I just pelted a tennis ball into the nose of the daughter of the woman you stole Dad from? Oh. My. God. Literally ohmygod.'

'Oh. My. Goddy. God,' I said, because teen drama seemed, for once, entirely appropriate. 'You soooo would have won.'

Sigh. I really love my children. Sometimes the love punches you in the stomach and slaps your silly face. Love is a violence, really.

SUNDAY 14th MAY

I think Eloise is a bit disturbed by the tennis thing. Well, perhaps not disturbed. Discomposed. This is unusual for her; she's usually so restrained. Is it awful to say there's a part of me that's pleased to see some wavering? Unwavering composure is just not normal for a thirteen-year-old girl. She didn't even cry when she dislocated her finger in a netball game when she was seven. Or when Barky went missing after Mary-Lou was born (one too many rivals, apparently). She's tough is Eloise. But is she really? Sometimes I'm not convinced.

We wish we could send flowers and a card, but we don't know where Hannah and Emily live. I tried ~~an extensive~~ a small online search but only found de Montagus living in Monaco. Most likely relatives, for goodness sake.

I've just been in to watch Eloise sleeping. Hugh found me in her room. He came in, put his arm around me and stayed there for a minute. It reminded me of that night when I sat on the floor of Eloise's room when she was nineteen months old. He held me while I sobbed. He cried too. It felt like our burden then. But it wasn't long before he didn't seem to feel it any more and the burden seemed squarely mine. In her room today it felt like he joined me for a minute, under the weight. I wish he'd come there more often, not to fix, just to sit.

He's a sorter-outer. A problem solver, a fixer. I know how much effort he puts into trying to fix things, fix me. He gets frustrated when things won't go back together. Even so, I'm surprised he's been so cross about me selling the viola. It's the first bit of underthinky fixing I've done.

WEDNESDAY 17th MAY

This afternoon, Raff and I made a Good Plain Cake from *The 21st Birthday Cookery Book of the Country Women's Association in Tasmania*. He was actually mildly enthused, which is nice, and less grumpy about the viola. He's going to take some cake over to Valda. He's spending a lot of time with her lately – was there for hours the other day. So there's that, I suppose.

There should be more 'cookery'. And more good plain things . . . Am I too hung up on being extraordinary? Is this why I get frustrated with Raffy, because he's heading along the ordinary path? There's really nothing wrong with ordinary. Lots of people love Good Plain Cake, because it's good. Perhaps good and plain is what I should be striving for? Perhaps then I'd remember people's birthdays and stop talking to the goldfish. I should probably aim a bit lower in the bedroom department as well. Nothing wrong with good plain sex, is there? At least it's sex. I can't bear to calculate how many days it's been since Hugh and I had any, plain or otherwise.

And here's another thing: I told Hugh about the Hannah incident and how she might have married into aristocracy and moved back here from Singapore, and HE ALREADY KNEW. 'Yeah, I heard she's about. Her husband's English. They bought that big house in Hampden Road – the one that famous colonial architect built. Spending a shitload on it, apparently.'

What? Shouldn't Hugh and I have had a good old gossip about this when he first knew? I asked why he hadn't told me and he said he forgot. He forgot?!

'Are the de Montagus some sort of royalty?' I ~~demanded~~ asked and he said, 'Settle down. I don't know.'

I hate being told to settle down.

Surely he must feel at least a faint whispering of Hannah de Montagu regret.

FRIDAY 19th MAY
SEX HAPPENED!!!

☆

I don't think I need to go into too much detail. It wasn't anything startling. Done is better than passionate, though. Those Country Women's Association ladies wouldn't worry too much about complicated methods or decorations. As long as things are sufficiently moist. Good plain sex.

LATER:
That Good Plain Cake that Raffy and I made? It's already very stale. It's probably time I attended properly to the Sparkle Project.

Decelerando ♭

SUNDAY 21st MAY

The boys and I walked all the way down to Lettercello this morning. It was one of those Hobart days when the sky is clear as bells and the air is cold and shiny. The sort of day that makes you have another look at things and wish for the milk-bar days. Mr Ng on the corner was asleep in his hammock and the young couple next to him were out painting their fence. Most of the houses in West Hobart look well kept and tasteful these days. Other than Ron and Myrtle's, and we wouldn't have them any other way. Hectic purple houses will likely be all the rage one day. 'Ron and Myrtle's is my favourite,' said Jimmy as we passed. I'm not sure whether he was being serious. He probably was. His favourite shoes are bright orange high-tops.

I took them the Hampden Road way so that I could drop a card in the letterbox of Hannah's house. A little message from Eloise to Emily (plus a note from me with my phone number so ~~I can see whether Hannah hates me~~ we can hear how Emily's nose is). It was also a chance to gaze for a moment at the splendour of the place and feel a little dizzy. It has a historical significance plaque. West Hobart is not nearly as crowded and touristy as Battery Point, so . . . why am I being so rivalrous? I'm behaving like Jimmy.

☆

We went to Lettercello because Jimmy had been pestering to see Henry's birds again and Raff has been asking about the gramophone. And because Henry's been worriedly phoning in to check on my post-viola state. I thought he could inspect me in person and see that my wounds aren't open and raw.

We found Henry and Charmian stacking some beautiful vellum suitcases and listening to Emmylou Harris. 'Ah,' he said. 'Not in pieces, Susannah. That's good to see.'

'I think I'm all here,' I said, giving him a peck on the cheek and my best happy face.

'I'll make coffee,' said Charmian.

'Helloooo,' came a voice from behind us. It was a grey-haired man with a clerical collar, an enormous smile and a large box of books. 'Hellooooo,' he called again. 'How are our purveyors of fine wares? Here I am, to lower the tone.' He put the box down on a little wrought-iron table.

'Hello, Father Graham,' said Henry. 'I have your crystal snifters.'

'Henry,' said Father Graham, shaking Henry's hand. 'And hello, Charmian-of-the-books!'

'Tea, Father Graham?' called Charmian from somewhere muffled.

'Yes, please; I have a minute before the next onslaught.' He smiled at me. 'Bit of a dispute over plots in the graveyard, in the midst of the masses.' He rolled his twinkling eyes at me.

'Father Graham,' said Henry. 'Meet my friends, Susannah, Rafferty and Jim.'

'Ah, the viola player!' said Father Graham. 'Elliot Driscoll is thrilled. You've made his year, so thank you for that.' I felt Henry's eyes on me; my smile was perfectly steady. Father Graham went on. 'I am enjoying having Henry here. It's perked the old place up nicely. He's not a believer, of course, but it is my job to convert him. Not today, though.' He gave his brow a theatrical swipe. 'Keep the snifters here, Henry. I might have to pop over later for a little snort. Do you have Russian Caravan, Charmian? That was lovely last time.' He leaned down to Jimmy and said, 'It's a special smoky tea. Would you like one too?'

That's really how it went! Those little pockets of English telly charm actually do exist. It's of course where Henry's always belonged. No wonder he's sleeping well.

'Here are the promised books, Henry,' said Father Graham, nodding at the box of books. 'They don't look like much but you never know. The church would appreciate a small percentage but don't worry too much. Not sure what's in there. Let's have a rummage, shall we?'

So that's how we ended up spending the morning getting to know Father Graham (who is more full of beans than anyone I've ever met) and sorting old books. Father Graham was right, the collection was patchy. I was hoping to find another copy of *I Capture the Castle*, which is my favourite book of all time. I have six editions in total. I didn't find another – just a Georgette Heyer omnibus AND a book called *Sustaining Sexual Intimacy*! It's not that old and is written by a serious-sounding fellow called Dr Russell Folds. Actually, that doesn't sound serious at all now that I've written it down. Folds, in the wrong context (such as a book about sexual intimacy) could be riddled with connotation. Or am I just being grubby-minded? Rustly folds. Oh, dear. Will I be able to take Dr Folds seriously now?

I've had a brief flick through but I haven't read anything properly yet. I shall start from the beginning and avidly read every word. And I should get some index cards, so I can write down important points and then put them in a box alphabetically so as to refer to them when needed. I can keep them in my bedside table cupboard. I'll be so conscientious. No more trying random things I've seen in films. Just proven, expert, doctorly advice. From one fold to another.

I bought the Heyer too; I had to hide Dr Folds behind it, and anyway I can never resist a little historical romance. Speaking of historical romance, I've grown some good old-fashioned pubes back. And I'm keeping them, even if my folds rustle.

TUESDAY 23rd MAY

I love Georgette Heyer! Ohhh, for the Regency days of having to be escorted and not being able to show ankles, and the inevitable, agonising restraint with its wonderfully torturous sexual tension. Think of that first fevered encounter after a long courtship. Perhaps that's what's wrong with us all now – we don't hold enough back.

Even in marriage there's probably too much letting all our privacies hang out. My boobs, for instance, lost all their dignity once they were used as feeding vessels and are now often exposed and hanging/drooping around. No one gives them a second look, perhaps not even a first. I should be more modest.

Bedrooms were separate too. This idea has some merit. Conjugal visits (knock before entering) and a bit of fevered sneaking about while the rest of the time you can close your door, sleep without disturbance and not hold in your farts. Oh, wait. Hugh never holds in his farts. And I don't always either, to be completely honest. Dr Folds has other ideas, though. Not about farts, but quite shocking. For instance, there's quite a lot of – *eeeeek* – tasting oneself. And he is quite free with the word *fuck*, something that would have my Regency personages calling for smelling salts.

Luckily there is other Dr Folds advice. Will find quote . . . (Dear God, it's just occurred to me that this large book is second-hand, possibly third- or fourth-hand. Think of what it might have witnessed from the bedside tables. And think of the bodily substances with which it may be smote from said hands. Eeeeeek, I'm stepping away from the book . . . Oh, but there was something I wanted to quote. I'm getting the rubber gloves. And the Glen 20.)

I'm back. Here's the quote: *Intimate sex is not a human instinct, it's not natural. It's a potential: something that needs thought, discussion and planning for that potential to be reached.* Aha! See, I *should* be overthinking the passion stuff.

Now that I have permission to continue my work (and Hugh will be asleep enough for me to take Dr Folds to bed), I am retiring to the bedroom to read up on the next phase. With gloves . . .

FRIDAY 26th MAY

Well, I've read and read and, holy moly, Dr Russell Folds makes my overthinking look like mere thought flits. I feel positively beleaguered. The good news is that he strongly advocates for searching through the history of a relationship to identify the deepest connections, so I'm ahead on that front. I mean, I haven't actually got to the bottom of the connections but at least I've made a start. He does ask some quite blunt questions, such as 'Are your connections sketchy?'

Hmmm . . . I do worry that we don't like the same things any more, except our children, and even them not all of the time. Sometimes I wonder if we ever did like the same things. Does anyone really know that the person they fell in love with is the right person? Does anyone really know their own true selves when they are that young? Do lasting sparks come from proper, soulmatey, kindred connections? Is this what Coralie meant? Are these the things we need for the bit after the beginning of love?

We're the best of friends, though, aren't we . . .? Are we? Why, if he's my friend, do I feel as though we're tiptoeing around one another? Why are there fewer moments of warmth? Why do my fantasies involve things like time alone to have cheese and bickies for dinner, lick the icing off the Boston bun and steam my pores?

Oh, dear. I've just realised that when it comes to sexual fantasies, I don't actually have any. Aren't we all meant to have at least one? I do wish that sex would get easier, that I'd want it more often and know what to do, and that there wouldn't be a white elephant in the room every time the children are asleep and the dishes are done and Hugh yawns. Could this be classified as a sexual fantasy? To be better at it?

Oh, my goodness. Dr Folds appears to have opened a can of worms.

(Bugger! I've just remembered that Jimmy was itching his bottom the other day and I forgot to ask him if it was hole or cheek. Praying for cheek.)

SATURDAY 27th MAY

I think I need to acknowledge that Hugh and I are not actually all that compatible. And that I don't have any fantastical sexual desires. These are big-ticket items, which could well degrade the outcome of the Sparkle Project unless addressed. Oh, Dr Folds, you wily old bugger. I should have known the problems might run deeper than my folds. Of course they do.

So with that in mind, here are the Things Hugh and I Have in Common:

- The children
- Barky
- The house and all our possessions
- Ria
- Henry
- Neither of us like peas. Or balloons.

We don't like the same foods or many of the same movies or the same television. He can't stand the theatre; I don't like the footy. He's a morning person, I'm a night owl. He's native trees and beer, I'm oaks and gin. I'm beach, he's mountains . . . I believe in reincarnation; he believes in steak. Let's call the whole thing off.

We're not opposites either, as in 'opposites attract' opposites. We had similar, normal-ish upbringings with plenty of love in them. So perhaps we've never been right together; it's just that there was lust and a wedding and babies and domesticities to cloud the view. But we were friends first, and it was him I knew and loved, not an idea of him. Wasn't it? I didn't wake up next to him one morning after we were married asking myself, 'Who is this man?' He doesn't annoy me or repel me; I like him coming home; I don't want to be with anyone else – although I do wonder sometimes whether it wouldn't be easier being married to a woman. A wife would be handy – someone who knows which time of the month not to ask for computer advice; someone who could empathetically contribute to my one-pot recipe collection.

So many things to ponder. Sigh. I'll try to work through them, but in the meantime I might go and seduce my husband. It's been a while, and a man is always compatible with a woman who is attentive to his penis.

SUNDAY 28th MAY

Penis attending turned out quite well. I think. I say 'I think' because something a bit weird happened . . .

I was actually quite horny when it came to it, which surprised me. For a close, breathless moment I noticed that he was solely focused and that there was apparently nothing swaying his amber eyes from me. Then he kissed me with some quite deliberate firmness, as though testing for sparks. I felt memory stir, felt his tongue on mine, which is another thing that hasn't happened in a while. Tongue kissing. It sent ripples through me; there was a sudden wetness between my legs and on the sheets beneath me.

And this is where things went a bit peculiar. The 'wetness', instead of adding to things in a lubricating kind of way, made subsequent penile-vaginal contact a little, er, squeaky. Suddenly it was like we were trying to have sex in the bath – watery. But aren't vaginal secretions during sex supposed to have a viscosity that reduces friction? How did water get down there? I can only deduce that a bit of wee came out. Quite a lot of wee. I'd put off doing wees pre-sex because after my bladder infection I am conscious that a wee is essential as soon as possible post-sex in order to flush out potential bladder bugs. So I might have had quite a full bladder.

Hugh was evidently pleased with the wee. His breathing got raspy and his movements more pressing. Thankfully, because I think I got aroused again and produced some moisture of the appropriate texture, we were able to move beyond the squeakiness to orgasm, both of us. But still, as I sat on the loo afterwards for the flush-out wee, I did feel very discomfited.

This morning I stripped the bed and before I put the sheets in the machine I sniffed them for wee smells. I couldn't find any, but my investigations were cut short by Eloise walking in and seeing me sniffing the sheets. 'What are you doing, Mum?' she asked. Fair question. I told her I thought we'd been eating too many curries lately and that I could smell them on the sheets. 'It's the garam masala. It comes out of your skin,' I said, like a bonkers person. She looked at me as such and walked on.

I'm very glad I didn't say it was the cumin.

So what do I do about this, then? The wee thing? Just hope it doesn't happen again? Write to Dr Folds? *Dear Dr Folds, is it okay to use wee as a vaginal lubricant?*

Maybe it wasn't wee. Maybe one's natural lubricants get thinner with age, much like the skin on the back of one's hand. Another sexual mystery. Will they ever cease?

WEDNESDAY 31st MAY

No time for Dr Folds or sex, or writing about not having sex; week from hell upon me. No time for anything but bills and chores and bores and getting things that were on top of me off me (not Hugh, obviously). I feel all fuzzy in the head with my Too Much Things to Do List. ('Mummy, you have too much things to do,' said Mary-Lou when I was talking to myself in the car this morning.) It would be quicker to get through a Things NOT to Do List.

All of Hugh's work crew are coming to dinner on Friday, along with Expeditioner April and Scary Katrina. I've also asked some extra friends of ours. I'm serving chicken from the CWA cookery book. People love those old-fashioned classic recipes. *Mustn't forget ground ginger.

SATURDAY 3rd JUNE

Oh, God, the dinner party was *terrrrrrible*. I was terrible. I just couldn't enjoy myself. It was as though I was on the outside, peering in at things, and everything looked plastic and pretend. I couldn't think of items to contribute to the conversation, I was overly worried about the food, I felt dowdy and fussy and dumb and embarrassing. The CWA ladies would be ashamed.

I mean, it went just like any normal dinner party – laughs, gossip, politics, talk of pink salt and schools and broken washing machines; someone drinking too much and getting shouty about the council. Everyone was so excited about the new electrical direction of Parks Forensic Engineering. But I wasn't on the inside with them all and their excitement. I was out, sullen and grumpled like someone's crabby old aunt.

I was tired, I think; it's been a long week. The women had offered to bring things and I declined but they still did. There was an heirloom carrot salad with truffle oil, for God's sake. 'Oh, I just whipped it up from leftovers in the fridge.' It made my jubilee chicken look like chicken à la frump. And how did I miss the ankle boot memo? Even April had them on, and she's meant to be the outdoorsy type. I've only ever seen her in those terrible sports sandals. Also, she joined in on the discussion about pepper grinders, so she's normal as well as forging all sorts of pathways for women.

I know I'm showing my insecurities but all I could think was how ridiculous we are. Women pound their linens in the Ganges and milk their house cows while we grizzle about inefficient appliances and gush over cherry blossom print. People create vaccines and prosthetic limbs while we're worrying about how to cook quail eggs. It's just bullshit. I wish Ria had been there; she would have marched in and applied acid to everyone's veneers, and Hugh might have seen through them all and they would have left in their huffs and the three of us could have got pissed and laughed our heads off like we used to.

But Hugh was on the inside with all of them, looking like he fitted right in, and he does. He always fits. I, with my blurred edges and raggedy nails, just don't. I wore spotty tights. Have I changed, or has he? Am I just calling bullshit on myself while everyone goes on being genuine? I mean, they are making the world a safer place by identifying errors and ensuring they don't happen again. I spent an hour and a half trying to get a fairy wren out of the house yesterday.

Why am I feeling like this? Why did my eyes sting when at one a.m. Hugh put the placemats away and said, 'She's a really top bird, that Amanda. I like her.' Amanda is the mechanical engineer's wife and she is the very essence of what we all avoided like the plague at uni. She has plumped-up lips and wears skinny jeans like they're tracksuit bottoms. She was the one on about cherry print and quail. Which are normal things to talk about, I suppose.

Tristan and Isolde is raging at me from Valda's house. Perhaps I should assign Wagnerian leitmotifs to my daily rituals. I might find myself less muddled. I blame Dr Folds and the Sparkle Project. It's made me overanalyse things. For God's sake, it's meant to be about love and sex and passion and fun. I haven't even properly put any specific strategies into practice.

I'll feel better tomorrow; I think I just need a good sleep.

PS I just got my period – I'M NOT MENTAL!! JUST HORMONAL. Thank God for that and how can PMS go for a whole week? How unfair is it that we have to suffer such severe emotional flux for the sake of a bit of uterine lining. Absolute design fault that should by now have evolved the hell away.

☆

PPS Amanda mentioned that April, Hugh's new electrical engineer, is possibly gay. Amanda is the sort of person who feels the need to mention these things. I'm pointing it out only because I was actually a tiny bit worried that with April being so brilliant and all, Hugh might develop a thing for her. So perhaps there are no worries there. He wouldn't have a thing for her, though; with all that overzealous nodding she does. So irritating. And she wears culottes. She also wears an iron ring on her little finger, which is what Canadian engineers do when they graduate, as a reminder to put integrity before ego as they work. Interesting fact.

TUESDAY 6th JUNE

Such bad timing, that dinner party. Just when I was already tied up in knots over whether or not Hugh and I are truly compatible. Not to mention the second-worst case of PMS in history. (The first is that British woman who murdered her mother and had her sentence reduced to manslaughter due to raging PMS.)

What a difference a few days make to hormone levels. Today, without oestrogen clouding my view, I can see that Hugh and I of course have differences – normal ones, reconcilable ones. There was something called the Pauli Exclusion Principle in astronomy – certain particles cannot be at the same place at the same time with the same energy, or else things would go crashing through floors. We are necessarily different. (And how I managed to keep that in my brain all these years *and* extract it now I'll never know.)

I'm going to take us back to our beginnings again. The present (at present) is frankly not as pleasant. Where were we? Ah, friends.

☆

Hobart, 1994

The friends thing took a turn when Hugh and I were eating lunch in the cafeteria. There was a student – an older bloke, mature age – sitting at the table next to us on his own, talking to himself. I don't remember us acknowledging him; there were all sorts around uni, we didn't judge. But after a little while, his talking turned to shouts and he stood up. He was wearing a long dark coat, much like the scary student from *The Breakfast Club*. Judd Nelson? We watched. He wasn't arguing with anyone – perhaps just himself – but he started throwing stuff around the room: drink bottles, plates, chairs. People were ducking out of the way. The throwing things was accompanied by a primal sort of roar. That's what chilled me most; there was anger and despair in that roar, of the kind that can't be contained. I'd heard it in music before but this was upscale, *forte* and very, very live.

In an alarmingly quiet fashion, because I was still registering that this was a dangerous situation, Hugh took my hand. He took my hand! But I felt only a millisecond of rush because at the very same moment, I was hit in the face by a glass. It smashed on impact. To add insult to injury, quite literally, I tried to dodge the blow and smacked my head into the wall. I don't remember the next bit but Hugh tells me that he picked me up and made for the door, then ran (I hope he was carrying me like a princess and not a sack of spuds) until he found us a place to hide. My memory has that place as a bit of hedged garden, with a lawn, trees and perhaps roses. But he says it was a bit of cleared pine bark and some ferns. Anyway, in the garden he laid me down and I looked at him. There was blood on his shirt and for a horrible moment I thought he was hurt. I gasped and put my hand on the large patch of blood. 'It's okay,' he said, pulling his handkerchief out of his pocket and pressing it gently to my cheek. I hadn't even realised that the skin was broken. 'Not too bad.' His dear face was lined with worry. 'What's my name?' he asked.

'Hugh Parks,' I said.

'And yours?'

'Susannah Parks. I mean, Susannah Mackay.' Ooooooops. *Rewind, rewind*, I thought, mortification outdoing fear of facial disfigurement or further harm from psychopath still at large.

Hugh smiled. 'That'll do,' he said and kissed my head, stroked my hair, kissed my lips, then kissed them again. I felt a tear come then, which might have been a fear-tear or a relief-tear but most likely a happy-tear. It was followed by a silly little whimper. He cradled my head and kissed me again, whispering, 'It's okay. You're safe. We're safe.'

I clutched at his arms and held them and felt dizzy with the overwhelm of it all.

My nose has got that pre-tears fizz about it. The man in the long coat injured eight people that day. One of them was hit over the head with a chair. It took three security men and four police with guns to stop his rampage. We could hear people screaming. But even so, there in the shrubbery with my head in Hugh's hands and his beautiful eyes wide for me, I have never felt so safe.

And then I lost consciousness, which is SUCH a shame because I completely missed the most poignant moment of my life.

The next bit I remember was waking in a hospital bed to find my parents beside me and no Hugh and I was breathless with having been cheated of my happy ending. They said I had lost consciousness due to concussion but I knew better. It was the over-beat of a desperate heart. Percussion concussion.

Hugh had apparently travelled with me in the ambulance and then gone home. He came back to visit the following day. Hannah came with him. She brought flowers, said that the word for flower in Japanese is 'hana' and then there was one of those awkward silences that come before people say they should go when they don't have to. I couldn't look at Hugh but the monitor showed my heart-rate increase. And we all knew. Except Dad, but that doesn't mean anything – he once didn't notice that Mum had left him for a morning until she came back at lunchtime with her suitcase in her hand. Hannah and Hugh's visit lasted about four minutes. Mum eyeballed me as they left and then said, 'Goodness, Zannah. The air is thick with feeling. I can barely breathe.'

Dad said, 'You muppet,' to the footy on the telly, and Mum said, 'Exactly.'

Later she gave me a lecture about being assertive, the same one I'd heard time and time again since I was capable of memories. She suggested I ask him out. I said, 'But he's with Hannah. That would be mean. And I wouldn't know what to wear.'

She responded with, 'No knickers.'

Dad heard that bit. The two of them laughed all the way through the final quarter.

I was out of hospital by that afternoon, my cheek stitched up, my head mildly aching, and my heart in agony. I never found out what provoked the man in the long coat's fury and despair, but Ria and I imagined up theories.

'He probably just calculated his uni debt,' said Ria. 'Or a computer lost his thesis.'

'Or perhaps he lost his ultimate heart's desire.' I sighed. 'Perhaps he'd been dreaming about it forever and had a tantalising taste of it, then had it taken away again.'

Ria got under the bed and said, 'Go on, throw chairs. I'm safe.'

☆

Five days later, Hugh knocked on my door and politely asked if he could come in. I'd been trying to phone him in a normal sort of friendly way – ostensibly to thank him for saving me from a madman but really to pop a gauge on the wall of the 'friendship' and try to fill the torment of silence. His asking permission to come in was not normal. Usually he would just rock on in with a 'Hey-ho' (We're talking early nineties here; 'yolo' wasn't a thing then) so we were back in strange territory. I think I offered him a hot drink. He declined. And then he said, 'Hannah and I have broken up.' I resisted the urge to change my offer to champagne (and wet my knickers) and sort of just stared. He looked back with concern and said, 'How's your face?'

'Stitches out tomorrow. How's your heart?' Something had steeled in me; I felt braver.

'No stitches required,' he said and then with a husky half-sigh, he walked towards me and was kissing me with such tenderness I thought I might cry again, only there wasn't time because the tenderness turned quickly into something very effervescent and over-flowing and we were trying to stem its current, which meant that even breathing seemed an imposition.

If Coralie were commentating (bit of a creepy thought given that she's Hugh's [dead] grandmother), she might have said that this moment marked the end of the beginning of love. She might have said that from here on in was the middle part, when all the hard work really starts. And I might have reassured the man in the long coat that there are longer, more enduring hardships than the slippery-quick loss of something you didn't really know.

But Coralie's not here, and for the sake of the Sparkle Project and my historical recordings, I'm going to recount that Very First Time:

His arms were wrapped around me and his hands were under

my clothes, in my hair, on my thighs. I felt a sway in my legs but his arms kept me upright. His kisses were gentle but fierce and even better than I'd imagined countless times. He paused for a moment, one hand cupping my face and the other low on my back, and looked into my eyes, searching left then right, left then right, because he was close enough to tell. There seemed to be something he wanted to say, but I kissed it away because I was afraid that words might tarnish the shine, and because I wanted him so terribly and it was time not to wait.

He let me take him into the bedroom, where I unbuttoned his shirt, and where I couldn't decide whether to gaze at him or kiss him. So I did both, and the relief of not hiding, and finally fixing my eyes on him openly, was huge. He slipped my T-shirt over my head and took a moment to brush my stitched cheek. He whispered, 'I'm sorry you got hurt. I'll stop anyone hurting you again,' and he touched away a tear that I didn't know was there. He kissed my smile and breathed my sighs and felt my tongue with his. I swayed again, and this time he fell with me onto the bed. The smell of him that close was more than familiar; it was comfort. Soap and warmth and that mystery smell of a late summer afternoon. And a hint of home. We kept our eyes open and watched one another.

(Dr Folds would approve. He is a strong advocate for keeping eyes open during sex. At what point, I wonder, did we stop wanting to look at each other while making love? Was it when bits of our bodies started getting a bit wobbly? Or does he still watch and I don't want to watch him watching the wobbles?)

He let me take the lead but he didn't let me rush, which is what I wanted to do. He took some of the moments to take my hand, to brush the frenzy from my hair, to slow me down. He smiled at me and I was shy again, so I buried my face in his chest. He kissed my neck and whispered, 'Susannah, don't hide,' then louder, 'Susannah.' So I looked up at him and he said, 'I love your face.' And then he kissed my face and my heart pounded again because he said the word 'love' and I was frantically searching for whether 'I love your face' meant the same thing as 'I love you', and because I had to bite my lips from saying, 'Oh, but I love you, all of you,' and other things that might have frightened him away. Thankfully the next kiss was on my mouth and by then I was no longer in control of my lips or my actions, because without thinking I had his jeans unbuttoned and my hand on his boxer shorts where I found his penis, heated and straining against the cotton.

(Dammit, that word is so mood destroying. But we can't have cock, knob or stiffy et al.)

He slipped my shorts down then. My knickers went with them and soon we were both naked. Excruciatingly, he slowed me down again; rolled me beneath him and traced my skin with his fingers. From my lips, my neck, my breasts to my ~~tummy~~ stomach. Everything hummed with sensation. All this time I could feel the pressure of him on my thigh and had noted that his penis was substantial. My heart raced faster, matched by a steady thrill ~~in my vagina~~ between my legs. I took him in my hand and the hardness shocked me. He breathed into my neck, kissed my ~~boobs~~ breasts. I bit him lightly on the shoulder in a last-ditch attempt to resist, then guided him quickly to that slippery, wanting part of me that took him easily inside.

(Goodness, is this really us? Is my memory distorted by time, or by the contrast of current gloom?)

For a few long seconds I stopped breathing and time seemed to gather up on itself and falter because there was nothing but us, nothing but the bliss of him and the wonderful thing we were doing together. I held him and pulled him into me again and again and again until both of us cried out. The release was like a pain; my sighs had sobs in them and his hands on my hair were both a giving of thanks and a long-awaited hello.

That was it, then, really. We weren't apart again. I mean, we were, obviously, geographically apart, but that was the binding seal. He stopped rushing off all the time; said that was the thing he did when he was having adulterous thoughts about me. 'I knew that if you and I had too much alone time, I'd step over the boundary fence,' he said. 'I just don't do that kind of thing. Hannah and I had headed in different directions, but she didn't deserve that.' I loved that about him, his loyalty. I love that about him.

Hugh maintains that he turned up that day with intentions to tell me he'd broken up with Hannah, and that it would be best to stay away from one another for a time, until Hannah's heart was somewhat mended (it was shattered, she had said, 'Shattered, you moron!') and she'd stopped wanting to hurt him and his property. But then he saw me in my towelling shorts and Bambi T-shirt and decided that he couldn't do without me. Hmm, I wonder if anyone sells towelling shorts these days? Actually, perhaps he was being ironic?? Maybe he didn't think I was adorable and just thought, *Dear God, let's get her out of those hideous clothes.*

He's mine, though, despite towelling shorts. Really mine. It took me ages to realise that; for so long I felt like a thief, that he might be taken back, reclaimed. Even after we were engaged to be married. It might have even taken babies to make me think I was safe.

Oh, gosh, I've written right into the night and I must go to bed. Next to My Hugh. Mine. I might find it difficult not to jump on him and tell him I love his face. Oh, wait! Tomorrow I'm helping with Healthy Choices breakfast at school and I have to be up by five. So sleep.

****Dear Susannah of the Future,
Refer back to this page for evidence that he is your one.****

♫

Minuet ☆ ♡

FRIDAY 9th JUNE

I just kissed Hugh – a passionate kiss with tongue, etc. – with my eyes open. I was a bit terrified he might have his open too and we'd be eye to eye and awkward. But his were closed. And blurred by proximity. That's about it. Then I realised that it's supposed to be both of us, that we need to be locking eyes, so to speak. This will be harder than I thought.

Speaking of eyes, I should get Jimmy's tested. He said the other day that the board is a bit blurry.

SATURDAY 10th JUNE

Three more eyes-open kisses. Have been hoping that his might flicker open and catch mine, but I don't think they have. It's a bit hard to tell that close up. At any rate, I'm starting to like the extreme close-up view of Hugh. When he does come into focus (it takes approximately four seconds for my eyes to adjust), I really do love his face. And there's something quite fun about staring at someone right under their nose without them knowing. None of this is particularly sexy, though, just interesting (and probably weird).

Anyway, what I've discovered is that most of the time my husband kisses with his eyes closed. This is a good thing. It would be uncomfortable to know that he's been peering at me up close all this time. Or maybe he did once, but stopped when things started to look a bit alarmingly creased.

He's very suspicious, though. After the last one he looked at me and said, 'So is all this kissing about your sparkle thing or is this to make up for selling the viola? If it's the viola, it's okay. I'm not angry any more. I can see that you need to move on. You can find a new one whenever you're ready.'

He must have been talking to Ria because they've both tried the new viola tack. I nodded and smiled, playing the game, but it hurts that the two closest people to me just don't get it.

I wonder, could I write them both an official letter spelling it out? (I am getting quite accustomed to putting thoughts and feelings into writings.) What would I say . . .?

Dear Hugh and Ria,

Bless you for your encouragements but honestly I am fine with not playing the viola, composing pieces or making further contributions to the field of music.

We can reflect all we want on what went wrong (and have, ad nauseam), but it won't fix things. I know, because subsequent site testing shows the damage to me is irreversible, and that further rusting and scouring has only compounded the problem. Therefore, it must be concluded that those parts of me given to music should now be boxed, memorialised and archived. Or discarded.

I have learnt to accept this, but your failure to do so, along with your persistent bringing up of the possibility of my

return to music, only serves to weaken my remaining
supports and hinder the chances of recovery, or at least
functional repair.

As you well know from your work, Hugh, we can learn
from disasters, but we can't undo them.
Yours very faithfully,
Susannah

Hmm, would I ever send that? Perhaps I'll sit on it a while.

For now, the next step: eyes wide open during actual sex. After all this kissing, the opportunity will arise very soon, I should think. It will be good for a change of sexual tone, says Dr Folds. Speaking of tone, I should probably get into some sort of exercise routine. If I'm going to encourage eyes-open sex, I'd rather not have jiggly bits. Everyone I know has an exercise routine. Even I did once, before sleep became a scarcity. I was once quite good at Zumba. This is my problem. I'm all enthused about something and then get distracted by the next thing – like Jimmy not knowing what a fraction is, or people coming for dinner, or Eloise's knotty hair (Isobel recommends hair masks; I wish she'd just get it cut), and so on and on and on . . . Anyway, presently it's our sexual tone that needs tightening.

Eyes-open sex shouldn't be that hard, but it is, it really is. I'm nervous. I was never this nervous on the stage. Perhaps because you can't really see the immediate audience reaction. The lights, the distance. Can you do eyes-wide-open sex with lights off?

I'm not making myself feel any better; I just need to not think and go and play Monopoly with Mary-Lou, who's been hovering with the thimble and the dog the whole time I've been writing this. She'll want to be the dog. I'm always the bloody thimble.

But tonight should be the night . . .

SUNDAY 11th JUNE

I did it! I altered our sexual tone. I am so proud of myself.

I didn't start all that admirably, though. I thought I should quell the nerves and work myself up to it a bit. So I snuck a look at some porn. I know – actual XXX porn, not the R stuff, which I'm told has pink bits covered. I've listened to extrovert friends talking openly about their porn habits and it appears to be a normal part of some marriages. Nothing at all to be ashamed of. And besides, I thought I might observe from afar how eyes-wide-open sex plays out.

I saw the Monopoly game through 'til the end, then made sure all and sundry were occupied, shut myself in the study, said I was attending to bills and googled 'porn'. It's incredible how quickly you can find it – I mean, there's nothing clandestine about XXX-rated sex videos, apparently. A whole string of porn sites popped up for me to click on. I went for one simply called porn.net because at least it had the class to tell it like it is. Did I just use 'class' and 'porn' in the same sentence?

I don't want to dwell on this too long but OH. MY. GOLLY. GOSH. Immediately there were images of penises and vaginas, penises in vaginas, penises in mouths, penises in bottom holes, two penises in vaginas at the same time and what looked like a penis in one woman's vagina and another in her bottom hole. 'Is that one man with two penises?' I asked myself. But most disturbing of all was that every woman I saw was being pushed about, ordered to their knees or having their hair pulled.

I didn't feel aroused, I just felt ANGRY. And then a bit scared about being tracked by the government and finding myself named and shamed in the local paper tomorrow morning. I shut the site down, only to find one of those pop-up thingies with a picture of a woman with huge boobs and a telephone saying, *I'm Gillian. I'm only five minutes from you and I'm seriously horny.* I shrieked, pulled the power plug out of the wall and checked out the window for horny Gillian. The computer stopped whirring and blacked out. 'Mum, you can't do that,' came a stern voice from behind me. I shrieked again and turned to find that Mary-Lou had come into the room. 'You have to shut it down properly,' she clucked, clearly imitating me.

I couldn't very well ask her whether she'd seen anything. ('Darling, did you happen to see a bottom with a doodle in it?') She didn't appear disturbed, though, just triumphant that she'd found me 'wuining the computer'. So that's it between me and porn. I still feel grubby about it, and I'll be checking Mary-Lou for signs of disturbance for the rest of my life. That stuff can't be unseen . . . I washed my hands and had a large glass of water.

But then later the anger had sort of developed into a kind of asser-tive determination, and I got into bed beside him, held his penis, opened my eyes wide and looked at him. And I mean right at his eyes, not at his shoulder or his chest or the bit above his eyes, and at that moment he opened his eyes too. It was only perhaps a bit longer than an instant – a few frames. Any longer and one of us might have said, 'Do I have a booger or something?' I preferred it to seem like an accidental meeting of the eyes, so I kissed his shoulder in order to hide. Isn't it amazing how giveaway our eyes are? Little big windows. And is it surprising that even after years and years together, when everything is supposedly shared, we still feel compelled to hide them?

But then I remembered the potential excitement of a renewed sexual tone and I (clenching my bottom muscles) lifted my hips towards him and looked unswervingly into his face. I must have looked like a possum in the headlights because he did a sort of double take, then gave a chuckly sort of 'Hello there', which could have easily been followed by 'you creepy weirdo'. To give myself some credit, I didn't cower away into shut-eyed safety; I held my gaze, but at the same time I realised that the intensity of it was a bit much and that it perhaps needed softening. So I un-widened my eyes a little, and then there was the inevitable awkward bit about how to hold my face at such intimate (penetration) moments. (The sex face, I think it's termed. God knows what mine is. I hate to think.) But then things actually did get tonally interesting . . .

I stopped thinking about the peculiarity of the moment and looked at him properly. My gaze softened naturally as my eyes brushed his mouth, his warm skin, the creases in the corners of his eyes; they might be marks of the years we've been together. Without trying I started to move slower, with a sort of curious intent. He responded, his expression turning from puzzled amusement to interest. He watched me watch him, and there was such an attraction in his eyes that I almost gasped in surprise at it. It was an expression I hadn't seen in a very long time. It looked a bit like proper old 'til-death-do-us-part love. Then it occurred to me that I mightn't have seen this expression simply because I hadn't looked.

We do still have some spark. And I had butterflies too.

I didn't manage to keep my eyes open during the climax. Actually, come to think of it, I'm not even sure that I did climax. He did, but did I? It didn't matter either way; just having extreme fizzy bits and a very fuzzy heart was evidently enough.

Good ol' Dr Folds, eh.

PS I tried to sustain the feeling into the day but we had Laurence and Alison over so it was a bit awkward. Alison held Hugh's face and said, 'You look tired, darling. Are you overdoing things? I hope you're getting fed properly. There are some very good supplements out there now. What are your thoughts on apple cider vinegar?'

I wondered about saying, 'He's tired because we shagged all night. What are your thoughts on that, Alison?'

MONDAY 12th JUNE

We had morning sex. Monday morning sex! It was a bit, um, forced, and Hugh stopped me for a minute and said, 'Resolution going well, then?' so I was a bit embarrassed. Then he said, 'Susannah, we don't have to —' but I kissed away his words because his penis was saying we definitely should. (In hindsight, could it have been a morning wee erection?)

I didn't do the Eyes Wide Open thing, mainly because morning light is harsh on wobbly bits. As it happened, Mary-Lou waltzed in mere moments after we'd finished. I knew there was an argument against morning sex beyond stale breath. We were still a bit puffed, but

Mary-Lou didn't appear to notice anything unusual, unless 'Mum and Dad, do you know that not all monkeys eat bananas?' is some kind of cryptic code for 'Oh, my lord, Daddy's been poking Mummy with his banana.' I mean, seriously. What child gets up at six to make revelations about monkeys?

Some monkeys prefer nuts, apparently.

Could this be a SEX WEEK? This is another of Dr Folds' suggestions. I scoffed at the idea when I first read it, but we're well on our way so perhaps I should press on?

*Buy cranberry juice.

TUESDAY 13th JUNE

It's very late, but I'm just checking in to say we just had some more sex, so that's four times in three days! He was asleep when I came to bed, and I admit I was ~~completely~~ a little cold on the idea of a sex week in light of the fact that today had nothing remotely sexy in it – we've started swimming lessons on Tuesday mornings. I do dread swimming lessons. All those chlorine particles and wart germs and battling children to get in the pool and battling them to get out and knickers rolling up and socks not going on. But if you don't take your children to swimming lessons, you'll be marked as a bad parent because they might one day drown as a result. We live on an island, after all.

Anyway, I was lying there thinking, *Let's forget sex week,* and longing for sleep, but then I realised that sex week really only just kicked off, and that it's been a long time since I actually finished any project that I started. So I woke him up with a little massage and it went on from there, longer than expected. (I guess the sperm isn't so close to the surface, having been expelled at regular intervals lately.) So now it's almost midnight. I have to sleep so I won't go into too much steamy detail but suffice to say, we had sex. Sort of run-of-the-mill sex. I mean, it was fine, but fine is what you say when you're talking about the weather, or when you're not happy but don't want to say.

He fell instantly back to sleep again, crunched right up against me. So I can't sleep.

Sex week is overrated.

WEDNESDAY 14th JUNE

Is there such a thing as too much sex? I don't know, but I'm buggered . . . Buggered as in tired, not buggered as in poked up bottom, God forbid.

Speaking of bottoms, I had to buy some incontinence pads for Valda. The care person who does her shopping didn't get the right ones so Valda asked me. In the chemist, I had a sudden wave of fondness for her and spent $29.90 on a pair of lace-trimmed 'Contidance leak-proof panties, reassurance with style'. I thought they looked much more dignified than those enormous rustly paper pads. And the chemist woman was so enthusiastic about them. 'Our oldies deserve a bit of sass,' she said. I'm not sure I'd describe the knickers as sassy. But the lace had a rose pattern like Valda's curtains so I thought they'd please her. They didn't. She said, 'Well, thank you, Susannah. Those will be very useful when I next go to a dance with my lover and show him my briefs. Will you wash them when I crap myself?'

I couldn't believe she said 'crap' and I nearly laughed. But she said it in an angry-sad sort of way, then looked at her hands and moved her fingers as though she couldn't quite believe they were so aged. So I didn't laugh. I just said, 'Yes. Yes, I'll wash them.' And she looked at me for a moment that went for so long I got all awkward and said, 'Don't worry. I shat myself in the supermarket last year. Gastro.' And she laughed. She has a lovely laugh. Like bells. We played some *Phantom of the Opera* and sat for a bit before I had to get to school.

THURSDAY 15th JUNE

I'm calling it. Sex week is over. Quantity over quality is never a good idea. Tonight, it was clear that neither of us was at all into it. Well, his penis was but I've learnt that that doesn't mean much. I'm pretty sure I heard him sigh. Not a passionate sort of sigh but an impatient one, of the sort one might do when waiting for the children to put on their seatbelts. And me? Well, let's just say it's lucky I knew where to find the Vaseline.

And then almost immediately afterwards we were having a near-argument about who'd misplaced the wi-fi password. Shouldn't lots of sex send its charge well into next week, smudging out all mundane domestic events? Instead, any drifts of ecstasy and love evaporated even before I'd got my breath back. (Just realised that all this sex is probably as effective as a bi-weekly Zumba class, so there's one less thing I need to feel guilty about.)

So, here's my theory: there appears to be a sort of saturation point when sex becomes just another thing in the day, not a special, thrilling treat like it might be when you have it only once a week or once every few months. I mean, I don't want ice cream every day. I don't want sunny days or sherbet or packages in the mail every day, because they wouldn't mean as much. Sexual abstinence, or refusal, is possibly imperative to a fresh and sparkly sex life.

Hugh would probably only refuse sex under extreme circumstances (such as a traumatised penis). He'd fear that it would signal for me to pack up my libido, buy some Horlicks and take up knitting. So even if he doesn't feel like sex, he will push on. Or his penis will.

So the upshot is that I don't think we should have sex tomorrow. The novelty's worn off. Five days is a working week, so we did sort of have a sex week. It was quite a bit of work. I'm prescribing a sex break.

In other news, after school drop-off I was running back to the car when the school principal stopped me and asked whether I would please think about playing my viola for next year's school musical production. I got all flustered and on-the-spot, and I think I might have said yes. Now I'll have to work up to a no. Must do it soon; nos are like cheese. They get harder the longer you leave them.

MONDAY 19th JUNE

Three reasons why it's ironic (or is it paradoxical, I never know) that I should have prescribed a sex break:

1) We have been known to go for fifty days without sex, so a sex break is not breaking new ground.

2) I have a cold. A proper, snotty cold, with a proper not-now-darling headache. And a fever. I should be in bed probably, but I've had to defuse a violent dispute between Jimmy and Mary-Lou over pencil cases. And Raffy needs collecting from choir (his latest whim).

3) Hugh has announced that he has to go to Melbourne tomorrow. For up to a fortnight. A pedestrian overpass

collapsed in a university. Two people died and there's a clamour for answers. Terrible. Those poor people. I'll be suspicious of overpasses now. Another thing to worry about.

So a sex break seems, now that it's thrust upon me, not such a good idea. Apparently vaginal atrophy is a thing. I know because I saw some vaginal atrophy cream in the supermarket. What the hell? It was between the feminine hygiene products and the nappies, as if to say, 'Women, deal with your baby's excrement, keep your vaginas clean and don't let them waste away.' Why wouldn't they put the nappies next to the men's shaving creams?

Atrophy sounds quite restful, actually. Vaginal retirement.

THURSDAY 22nd JUNE

The cold didn't end up moving to my chest and causing mild pneumonia, which is a bit of a shame. I did get increasingly delirious, though, and had a horny dream about the school principal. Oh, dear.

Hugh didn't delay his trip for the sake of my health. I'm trying not to feel begrudgey about that. Nor about the ease with which men can truck in and out of the house, with very little luggage and no flurry over who's taking what shoes and where are all the hairbrushes? 'I have to go to Melbourne,' they say, and then they do. No agonising over babysitters or travel wipes or making casseroles to freeze. No phoning sports coaches or turning down invitations or writing down phone numbers. No guilt. All safe in the knowledge that the house's noggins are suitably fortified by me, the reinforcing girder.

I wasn't all that ill, really. But I would have liked someone to spoon me some broth or something. I still did the school runs. And Hugh has gone. I tried to do a very casual, 'see you when I'm looking at you' goodbye and not be needy. If I wasn't in my jarmies with a cold, I might have left before him and gone for a nonchalant jog.

It might do us good to be apart.

SUNDAY 25th JUNE

The children are all over at Valda's watching old films. They got bored by my frenzied tidying of the garden. I'm trying to arrange things so that when Hugh gets home he'll be taken aback by how independent and capable I can be.

So, too busy to write. Trust me, there'll be butterflies in our stomachs and fondness in our hearts after all this absence.

LATER:

Mum popped in this afternoon and found me up a ladder ruthlessly clipping the wisteria from the pencil pine. She peered up at me, and at the freshly weeded garden beds, and said, 'Are you pregnant?'

'What?'

'When I was pregnant with you, I was suddenly offended by the honeysuckle vine over the terrace. I pulled it all out. I still miss the smell, and the finches never forgave me.'

I came down off the ladder and said, 'No, I'd just like Hugh to come home and see how well I can manage without him.'

'Well, don't manage too well,' she said. 'He mightn't feel needed enough. Always best to be a bit helpless without them. We should get Dad to tighten the lids on all your jars – men love being asked to open a lid.'

'I don't want to be helpless, though, Mum. I want to be capable.'

'You don't have to be completely useless, just a little in need of some masculine support. I never mowed the lawn, for instance, though I can, of course. Nothing like an unkempt lawn for keeping a husband at home.'

Is she right? When Hugh was in Antarctica I went to enormous pains to make everything immaculate for his return, even painted the skirting boards and had his suits dry-cleaned. He never knew that, a week prior, I was crying on the floor of the kitchen because there was an ant plague in the pantry, a dead rat in the ceiling and a fault in the chest freezer that had ruined all my preserved peaches.

Perhaps I'll throw a few ants in the sugar.

MONDAY 26th JUNE

My wedding rings smell funny. Smelly wedding rings are NOT a sign of anything, Susannah, so stop before you start. Other than questionable hygiene. I am taking them off now and putting them in soda water.

Hugh just called: he is distant. Distant *and* distant. No fizz, no butterflies. I might need to put myself in soda water too.

TUESDAY 27th JUNE

I'm listening to old music and missing Hugh. Missing is good for passion, so I'm working on increasing it by going back in time again. I found all our old CDs on Raffy's bookcase. (How is it that

children can't seem to handle CDs without breaking all the covers?)
Eloise tells me I am the only person in the world to still buy CDs
and that all of my music is embarrassing and ancient. This is not
true. One day she'll understand that music doesn't have to be cool.
Van Morrison's 'Sweet Thing' was Hugh's and my 'song'. Not
cool by today's standards, but I still love it. Hugh played it on the
stereo when we moved into our first house, back when I still had
champagne eyes.

Hobart, 1995–1999

After the towelling shorts day, it wasn't all happily ever after. Hugh
still had commitments. Hugh's family, I discovered, had so many
family traditions, events and dinners, picnics and lunches, all with
their particular and complicated conventions that ensured they were
almost impenetrable to outsiders. Alison is the sort of person who
books the polo every year and expects everyone there with shined
shoes, a plate of chicken sandwiches (with chives and white pepper), two bottles of French champagne, a carnation in their lapel
and a medium-sized hat. As an only child, whose family traditions
extended as far as dinner on our knees with *Rumpole* on a Sunday
night, I was all at sea. I once went to the Dawn Service in a yellow
polar fleece, with a hangover and no rosemary. Alison asked that
I stand at the back 'in case your fleece frightens the horses'. Hugh's
sisters looked very pleased with my disgrace. Laurence gave me a
sympathetic smile. Hugh was completely oblivious.

There were moments of perfect happiness, though – like the hot
midsummer's night we left a Christmas party to go skinny-dipping
in Lake Meadowbank. Or the time I took him to the Theatre Royal
to hear the Southern Singers perform the *Messiah*. He couldn't
believe how much it moved him. Those moments came between

times of wondering when he would do the natural thing and move on to someone normal. He was never a doting boyfriend but he was adventurous, loving, easygoing, gentle, never jealous . . . always casual about things.

I was far from casual. I analysed everything. Birthday cards and presents were scrutinised for commitment clues. Once he gave me a Huon pine, which take up to five hundred years to grow to full height. I was in raptures over that present. ('We are definitely growing old together now, definitely . . .') I had to give the tree to Dad, on account of share houses and no permanent address. He killed it with too much Magic Gro. And still hanging over me was the enormous question of whether Hugh loving my face was the same thing as loving me.

'No way,' said Ria bluntly a few months into Hugh and me being together. 'He just said he loved your face so you wouldn't feel bad about your madman scar. It's much too soon for I love you.'

'Is it?' I said with a miles-away face. *I love you* had been on the tip of my tongue so many times.

'Don't you dare, Susannah.' Ria had read my expression. 'You tell him that now and he'll quit the Susannah popsicle stand in a heartbeat. Didn't you learn anything from *Sweet Valley High*?'

So I didn't tell him I loved him. I mostly mooned around, waiting for the next meeting, while he was off seeing his friends and family. Also, he landed a part-time internship with AbelTas Constructions so he was juggling that with studies and family and me. I tried very hard not to mind.

The sex, when it happened (a lot – two or three times a week seemed utterly drought-stricken back then), was incredible. All that sexual tension. Is that what's missing? Not sex but sexual tension? Are we both too available? Is it too easy? Some of the best sex we've had was when we were staying at Mum and Dad's and had to refrain entirely on account of our small house and the proximity of parental ears. Oh, the ecstasy of holding back! Once, the build-up was so great that we hid in a cleaning cupboard in the Engineering department and had sex among the brooms. I can't think too hard about that now on account of Hugh being away and wasting valuable horniness.

La-li-la.

The effect of these emotional shifts on my music was pretty incredible too. I worked extremely hard, not just because I was trying to think about things other than Hugh, but because I really loved it. I really did, didn't I? I did.

I wrote a career-launching song with viola riffs for Alison Mills, a contemporary singing student. She lives in Nashville now, making fortunes, her name changed to Albright. She still sends me Christmas cards. I got invited to collaborate with the Conservatorium's head of strings. We wrote some really good pieces . . . It was probably the height of my career, actually. Which is pathetic given I was still at uni . . . I can't think about that either.

I never quite believed that Hugh would stay with me forever. Even after the time I forgot my bike and accidentally walked to uni wearing my bike helmet and he said, 'Oh, Susannah. I love you.' For a moment I felt a surge of joy, except that he looked a bit stricken, as if it was a fatal slip of the tongue. So I just did a laugh and pretended he'd said, 'Oh, Susannah. You're such a loser,' which seemed more apt.

'Well, you never know when you need protection from something accidentally falling on your head,' I said, blushing.

Then there was some awkward silence and I looked at the sky in case there might be something falling, or at least something I could use for a bit of indifferent conversation, when he took my face in his hands and said, 'Or for when you accidentally fall head over heels – in love.'

'No,' I said. 'Then helmets can't save you. Nothing can.'

'Well, good,' he said. 'Because I don't want to be saved. I love you, Zannah.'

'I love you too.'

'He said he loved me, he said he loved me, oh my God he loves me,' I yelped at Ria later.

'Oh, God,' said Ria, peering suspiciously at my glee. 'Tell me you didn't get all gaspy and say it right back. There's so much more rooting in broom cupboards before that.' (There wasn't much I kept from Ria.)

'Ummm,' I said, remembering the breathy 'I love you too' that I'd posted into Hugh's ear.

'Fucken oath, Susannah,' she sighed. 'We discussed this. Upper hand.' She raised a beautiful piano hand. 'Up. Per. Hand.'

I've never had the upper hand. I did manage to relax a bit, though. I stopped wishing I could be small enough to ride around in his pocket every minute of the day. We settled into what we and all our friends accepted as a 'long-term relationship'. Mine was an uneasy settlement on account of lower hand. Mum and Dad adored him, to the point that I'd pop in to visit them and find Hugh under the car with Dad, or having a cup of tea and sharing dirty jokes with Mum. 'I think they love you more than me,' I said to him and he took me in his arms and said, 'Can't blame them, really, but don't worry. I love you more than me.'

Meanwhile I carved myself a niche in Hugh's family as 'the

hopeless one' and they all (minus Alison, whose disdain has a very long shelf life) started doing exaggerated eye rolls and calling me cute. I didn't mind. Alison eventually gave up asking us to all the things, and that suited us – we were so busy . . . I probably hammed up the role, really: made myself clumsier, my cooking more disastrous, my clothes less stylish. Did I? And if I did, when did that caricature turn into reality? How long does a method actor immerse herself in a role before she occupies it completely?

It was three years before we had our first proper argument. Ria was in Sydney by then, having been offered a scholarship at the Sydney Conservatorium of Music. I was doing my honours in composition and working casually for the TSO; Hugh was finishing his degree. I was happy, if a little diminished by Ria's absence. (I was always braver with her on hand.) I moved my things from college into a crumbling, crazy share house in Davey Street that we named Bedlamshire. It was home to a fine arts student who painted boots, a reluctant law student who left branches of marijuana on the windowsills to dry, a geologist we'd never actually seen and a fisherman who brought impossibly huge shells home and left them stinking in the courtyard. And me, sometimes, when I wasn't at Hugh's.

My music was quieter, lighter, more experimental; a lot of off-string bowing and whispery *sul tasto*. I was all about showing what the viola could do beyond doubling a bassline, taking the middle voice or wrenching hearts. And getting Hugh and me a double pass off the island. My thesis was titled 'New Frontiers'. Hugh and I secretly subtitled it 'Get Me Outta Here'.

I missed Ria terribly and was very unsettled by the fact that she had achieved our goal of leaving Tasmania well before me. But she was studying under a madly brilliant piano virtuoso, moving from strength to strength and sharing all her achievements with me via phone calls and letters and emails. Hugh and I spent quite a few weekends in her tiny Surry Hills flat, where we drank beer and dreamed of one day living and working abroad. At least I thought that's what we were all dreaming of.

One evening I got back to Bedlamshire to find Hugh had packed up my things into boxes. 'What's going on?' I asked. 'Are we being evicted?' I was thinking of the smelly shells.

'Nope,' Hugh said with a mysterious smile.

I narrowed my eyes at him.

'I'm getting you outta here.'

'What? But I'm not nearly finished my thesis.' Already my thoughts were flying over Bass Strait. 'And these guys need the rent.'

'I found someone for your room. She's a comedian. They'll love her.' Then he held up a set of keys. 'And I bought us a house.'

'You what? Where?'

'Newtown.'

'Newtown, Sydney?'

'No. Newtown, Hobart, you dill.'

'Oh.' I felt my face fall. I picked it up again. 'Well, that's a good place for an investment. How can you afford it?'

'Coralie. She left me enough for a decent deposit, and AbelTas have offered me a job on their design team as soon as uni finishes. So I just sort of jumped in.'

'But we haven't left yet, Hugh. We're meant to go off and find ourselves in Central Park or in grimy London flats. We'll come back one day probably, but we can't just not leave.'

'Why not? This is home. Everything's here. Our families, work, your orchestra. We can have holidays away.'

'But we can find work on the mainland, overseas. This is what we dreamed about.'

'You dreamed about it, Zannah. You and Ria.'

'You were there too, Hugh, in those dreams.' I felt desperate. 'Rent the house out and we'll come back to it in a few years.'

'Live there with me for a few years and we'll rethink then.'

'Rent it out for one year.'

'Live with me for one year.' He took my hands. 'Come on, Susannah. I'll never get these responsibilities anywhere else. Being in a small state is an advantage, and I can't afford a three-bedroom house in Sydney. It's sensible.'

'Did you get yourself some slippers and a La-Z-Boy too?' I was getting shouty. 'I don't want to be sensible. I want to be young! How dare you just pack up all my things and assume my life away as though I'm your kept woman.' I started wildly unpacking boxes.

He put his palms up. 'Zannah —'

'What if I say no?' I yelled. 'What if I say I got a job with the SSO? Would you come with me?'

'Have you got a job with the SSO?'

'No, but what if I did?'

His face hardened. 'I wouldn't shout about it.'

'Where have you put all my music books?'

He spoke calmly. 'I've put them in the house already. It has a music room. That's what sold me in the end.'

I eventually agreed to a year. And then the TSO offered me part-time permanency, Hugh got a promotion, musical theatre productions picked up in Hobart and I had more work than I needed. We tumbled into what I think must have been the bit before the middle of love.

☆

And now he's the one kicking career goals on the mainland while I'm in a West Hobart wardrobe rocking myself to sleep. He's only called twice. Once was to check I'd paid the water bill. I'm going to stop calling him. Upper hand.

I am miffed. Miff, I realise, is on my shoulder so often these days that I hardly notice it. It's probably left a permanent chip.

FRIDAY 30th JUNE

Eloise and I took Valda a new lipstick. I made the mistake of calling out, 'Yoo-hooo?'

'I do dislike yoo-hooing,' came a voice from the bedroom. Valda appeared behind it.

'Oh, Valda,' I said. 'Look at you go with that frame. Well done. That's terrific!'

She eyed me for a moment and said, 'It's not terrific, not one bit.'

'Sorry,' I said. 'I know.'

'How can you know? I don't see your frame.'

There was silence, then Eloise said, 'Right. Good chat,' and I said, 'It's a lovely day.'

'It's not,' said Valda. 'It's cold. I prefer the cloudy days in winter, keeps the heat in.'

'We have a present for you, Valda.'

'I don't want any more Vivaldi; he's for twits, Neville says. That solo violin birdsong . . .' She screwed up her face.

'No, it's a new lipstick.' I held the little package out to her. 'We – Eloise and I – thought you might like a new colour.'

She didn't look at it. 'I have plenty of lipstick, thank you very much. I bought Myer out of my colour years ago and it'll see me to the grave. Neville didn't like me in anything else. Once I changed to pink for a tennis party and he flirted with Lurlene Wallace all day to spite me. He was much better tempered with me in coral lipstick.'

'It is a coral shade,' said Eloise. 'Just a bit darker than yours.'

'But Valda,' I said as gently as I could, 'he's not here any more. And I don't think he'd mind if you let him go.'

'Yes, he would. Very much mind. What do you know?'

And so I was quiet. After a minute I went to the CD player, found the Vivaldi I'd lent to Valda the other day and slipped it into the player. His Goldfinch flute concerto piped in on the morning. I made tea, poured her a cup and then left.

'Susannah?' she called before I'd got to the front door.

I stopped. 'Yes, Valda?'

'Turn it up, please.'

'Okay.'

'And leave the lipstick.'

Oh, Neville, you old sod. I thought he'd been worn thin by Valda. Perhaps not. The lipstick is called 'Coralie'! Hugh would like that. (I phoned him. He sounds so animated he'll probably come back as Astro Boy. I'm taking care to be excited with him; this case could change building standards for the better of all. And he's found something to stimulate him other than Antarctica and blow jobs.)

I'm reading *Danny, the Champion of the World* to Jimmy and Mary-Lou. I love Roald Dahl. I will miss reading him to the children when they're all grown. Sometimes I don't want things to change at all; sometimes I wish for time to stop so I can read Roald Dahl at my children's bedside every night forever. There'd be time to collect pine cones, find shapes in the clouds and teach them all French. The rush of the years takes my breath away sometimes. No wonder anxiety is always in the media.

We're halfway through the year but sparkle is scarce.

SATURDAY 1st JULY

Oops, had a horny dream about Danny the Champion of the World's dad. It's not surprising, really. Such a patient and gentle man (apart from the killing pheasants). So engaged with his son . . . God, listen to bonkers me. At least it was a fictional character this time and not the children's principal. Damnations. I still haven't talked to him about the school musical.

Which reminds me, Raffy wants to do a project and a presentation about the viola now, featuring me and Eloise Driscoll. He seems moderately enthusiastic, which for Raffy is about a point eight on the Richter Scale. Major. He says he can even get Elliot Driscoll to bring the viola in; he's already mentioned it to Father Graham! I am astounded by such initiative, in a child who still thinks setting the table is fetching a pile of forks. I'm trying to steer him towards the piano and Ria's work. The promotional material is out for *I Capture The Castle – The Musical*! It opens next March and is booking out already. He could talk about all that. Far more interesting than the story of a promising career derailed. Although I suppose it could be a cautionary tale about not putting all your eggs in one basket because all sorts of things out of your control could upset it, make a nasty mess and leave a lot of eggshells for everyone to walk on forevermore.

Also, I don't think I'd cope with seeing it again, the viola. The empty shelf in the wardrobe is bad enough. There's little point in sitting in there for the quiet because it's not quiet. It's humming with gone. I remembered that I left a scribbled composition in the case pocket, so perhaps I could ask Elliot Driscoll for it back. Or not. Perhaps it belongs to the viola. I don't know. Will put it on my list of Things to Think About. Or on the list of Things Not to Think About . . . The piece was called 'Lullaby for Eloise'.

Eloise is at Oatlands today, at a friend's farm. It's only an hour's drive but the Midlands, with its rickety windmills and wobbly sheds, seems a world away. She's staying the night. If she gets homesick, I'll drive up. I can't help hoping she'll get homesick, or display some other emotional light and dark. She won't. The other three are in the garden with Ava and Thomas. Josh and Isobel have had to go out, probably to lunch for two in a butterfly house, or to give a paper at a team-parenting seminar.

LATER:
That's two horny dreams about other people in less than a week. Am I obsessed?

Doubt it. Probably just my atrophied vaginal baroreceptors sending neglected signals. Or the absence of Hugh. I haven't felt much like sending flirty text messages or boob shots. It seems a bit desperate. I can't compete with the drama of the courtroom and all those future lifesaving overpass improvements. *Oh, shut up, Susannah, for goodness sake. Where's your benevolence?*

TUESDAY 4th JULY
This is probably a good time to knock a few items off my list of Things to Do. The things unrelated to love and romance, which is

most things. (Children, washing, letter-writing, current events, entertaining, clock batteries, smoke alarms, garden weeds, pest man, mending, odd-sock amnesty, fish tank, car service, photo albums and exercise, just to name a few.) I can store current sparkle progress in my sexual muscle memory and draw on it later. Actually, there really hasn't been much progress . . .

The word 'exercise' looks so hopeful and perky. I feel sorry for it already.

Bit teary today. I'm on the couch with my list and there's a thing on the telly about how pegs are made that Hugh and I could watch together. I will note it down to talk about when he gets home.

THURSDAY 6th JULY

Hugh came home unexpectedly yesterday afternoon but he's gone again today. For another fortnight. 'I'm sorry, Zannah,' he said. 'It's taking so much longer than anyone thought. There's more technical detail than we bargained on; this incident is a result of at least four separate oversights. Such a freak event. Anyway, I know you can manage. Everything's looking smicko here.' (I'd been redefining the edges of the garden beds, but suddenly wished I hadn't. Mum might have been right.)

I felt instantly cross and said, 'God, I hate it when terrible things are referred to as "incidents". There is nothing incidental about negligent behaviour resulting in terrible injury.'

If he wore glasses, he would have looked at me over them. He said, 'Do we need to talk?' And I said, 'No,' and remembered again how he'd never wanted to leave Hobart. I had to chew up a little ball of something bitter, swallow it down. *Think of it as one of those raw food energy balls*, I thought, then gave a bright, energetic smile and said, 'Could you change the batteries in the smoke alarms?' Then I had another little think and added, 'And tell me all about the oversights.'

He looks different. It's as if he's come back from the tropics with a tan, only he hasn't got a tan. He just looks, I don't know, healthier? Glowing? If he were a woman, I'd think he might be pregnant. He's just lit up with industry, I suppose. No wonder the Antarctic Division wanted him back.

He told me all about the case. It does sound interesting.

'This matter is really instrumental, Zannah,' he said, then explained how the overpass's box girders didn't have enough stiffeners and the members were overburdened. I refrained from distasteful innuendo that might reflect unfavourably on our relations, but the parallels weren't lost on me. He's taking April back with him this time to see how the process of giving expert evidence works.

'Well, I'll be here ready to wash your blackened shirts from all your time at the coalface,' I said, which was meant to be lighthearted but came out covered in grump.

I gave my selfless bone a hefty nudge and listened properly, even asked some pertinent questions and got so interested that he must have had one of those waves of fondness because he said, 'But tell me about you. What's been happening here?' And I couldn't think of anything beyond Mary-Lou getting a certificate for being helpful, so I kissed him. And he kissed me back with unexpected passion, which I think allows me to say HE INITIATED SEX! We kissed and kissed until I got distracted by the smell of my armpits (if I'd known he was coming home, I would have showered after weeding), then he pulled a twig out of my hair and I said, 'I'll meet you in the bedroom. I'll just have a quick shower.'

It wasn't as quick as I'd meant it to be because hair wash, emergency eyebrow plucking and leg shave, so by the time I got to bed he was fast asleep. I didn't wake him. It must be exhausting being so instrumental.

Sometimes one's most useful orifices are the earholes. I will phone him more this time.

Sex break untainted.

♩♩

Cadenza ☆
♩♩

MONDAY 10th JULY

I've had an idea. With Hugh away, now might be the time to get in touch with myself; myself meaning my vulva. I've never been particularly big on masturbation. Actually, I've never done it at all, so I'm not sure where to start but it might have to be with some raunchy material. Not computer porn, as I'm terrified randy Gillian will pop up again. And not *The Joy of Sex* – I'm over that. (That beardy man in the illustrations gives me the heebies.)

There's a chance that this is the missing element of our sex life. (Masturbation, not Gillian. Or the beardy man.) Apparently women who know their own vaginas and masturbate regularly are 'more balanced, more confident and less stressed'. Similar results to butler school, I imagine.

Hugh just called. It was brief.

'How're things?' I asked.

'Great. Slow. We're hearing victim impact statements – hard work.'

'Oh, no. What sort of things?'

'I'll tell you later, bit much on.'

'How's April faring?'

'Fine, I think. She's staying with friends so I haven't seen her much. How're the kids?'

'Very well. Eloise made a candle holder in metal work.'

'She does metal work?'

'Yes,' I said with a bit too much 'you should know that' inflection. Perhaps a bit of 'why shouldn't she?' too. How much loading can one small word take before the girders of a conversation come crashing down?

'Nice. Well, I'll call them all before bed. I gotta go.'

THURSDAY 13th JULY

So I found a book with quite a bit of raunch. It's mostly lesbian, admittedly, but I think I got a bit of a lower stirring from it last time I read it. Is there a chance that I have a smidgen of gay about me? How very chic.

Anyway, after re-reading some heated lesbian sex scenes that involved a large leather dildo, I found myself quite drawn to my clitoris. And my clitoris, in turn, seemed very happy with the attention. If handled in the right way, those little buttons can take quite a bit of pressure, can't they? It was very quick. I felt a bit silly at first, and kept thinking that someone might catch me, but there was no one home except Barky and he was asleep in the washing.

After a minute of rubbing that little raised triangle of flesh, I forgot about anything else. The effect was instantaneous, my muscles all at once relaxing and tensing. There was a loosening of the legs and an edging apart of the knees. I put my head back onto the cushion behind me and it was like my fingers were encouraged by the movement of my hips, slight at first, then more pronounced. It wasn't much more than a minute before I brought myself to a shuddery, gasping orgasm, with an aftershock of small involuntary muscle clenches deep within that I'd never felt before. The feeling was intense: familiar but altogether different.

And it was nice. Really, really nice. I was left feeling amazed but also guilty that I could reach such heights in so short a time, with no Hugh. It was only quite a bit later that I realised I had completely ignored my vagina (as in the actual hole) and this made me feel a bit guilty too. It was all clitoris. When it comes to sexual pleasure, I'm wondering, do we even need the hole? Do we need penetration? Do we need men? We certainly don't need too many more babies coming out of the holes. The population explosion is the biggest threat to mankind. Goodness me, could the clitoris be the dear little pink solution to all the world's problems?

Valda asked me for a good book the other day. I think I'll lend her the lesbian one. I'm feeling cheeky.

SATURDAY 15th JULY

Oh my GOD. I just fell off the stool in the kitchen while inspecting my clitoris. It's a bit sore so I thought I'd have a quick look over my pre-dawn coffee. Barky walked in and gave me such a guilty fright that I fell off and the stool fell on my foot and I yelled and woke all the children. Even Raffy and Eloise got out of bed. My foot has a bruise. So does my dignity.

The dog scampered away, possibly embarrassed. Thank God for elastic-waisted pyjamas or I might have been on the floor with my trousers down. The children only think I'm clumsy, not depraved and clumsy.

My clitoris smarts. This is probably why masturbation was once declared a sin, because they thought one might wear one's clitoris off altogether and riddle marriage and passion with even more problems. Imagine wearing off your clitoris early on and then not having it to make sparks and ardour and orgasm so much more attainable?

It's ~~very~~ a bit addictive, this masturbation thing. I can't imagine why I didn't get into it sooner. As in, twenty-five years ago. I blame my viola and all the time I spent fiddling with that. Just look where I can focus that vibrato practice now that the viola's gone.

The viola's gone. I just shed a tear. I don't miss it but I do. I suppose there was a little bit of hope in that box of guilt.

I did play my music for Eloise. Quite a lot when she was a tiny baby. A very sketchy rendition of 'Lullaby for Eloise' was the last thing I played for her. By then, sincerity had been replaced by guilt. The resonance of guilt is a strong and ugly sound, with too much reverb. And a buzz, as if a seam has lifted. I got the bow re-haired and replaced the strings before they were due; I crumpled up the lullaby and tried other things, but it was still there, that buzz . . .

I've been very tolerant of the children since I've discovered self-arousal. Perhaps it's a form of mindfulness. I haven't raised my voice once since Hugh left, not even when I found Jimmy eating my activated almonds. (I don't know what those things are meant to do but they're really expensive and sound as though they'll have me leaping tall buildings in a single bound.) It's as though I respect my body too much to put it through the stress of irritation. My feet shouldn't be stomped and my vocal cords shouldn't be strummed. My body is a temple, with a fun button.

☆

THURSDAY 20th JULY

Things are somehow simpler without Hugh. Dinners, for instance, have mostly been soup. Once from a can. Hugh thinks soup is an entrée. There's also been eggs and bacon, chicken sandwiches (with avocado – avocados evidently have every nutrient you ever need) and one night we all had muesli. (Nothing wrong with a brekkie for dinner, is there? There were seeds.) I haven't ironed a thing, nor have I had to soak any white business shirts. I've read a whole book, caught up on phone calls owed, skyped Ria. She doesn't look well.

'Have you lost weight?' I said, then actually touched the screen where her cheek was. 'Or does the screen take weight off?'

'I don't think so,' she said. 'Might have; working too much. We have Cassandra auditions next week and I'm still rewriting parts. Plus I've started on another musical idea that won't leave me alone. I'm buggered. I have one of those twitches in my eye that makes the lyricist think I'm winking at him. I'm not. He's a knob.'

'Use Latin on him. That'll make you feel better.'

'I did, but it's not the same without you sniggering at my elbow. That reminds me, I have to show you something . . .' She walked me through her apartment to a corner of the room, where a striking mannequin with very familiar bone structure stood.

I gasped, 'Is that . . . is that Caroline Smedley-Warren's sister? Oh my god!'

'I know. Can you believe it? She's just the same. I found her in the costume department and begged and begged for her. She's living with me now. We're very happy together. What shall we call her?'

'Deborah, of course.'

'Deborah. Perfect.'

Ria's new musical is called *The Boy with No Dreams*. She hasn't said, but I've an inkling that Raffy is her muse. I told her about Charmian only realising her dreams are her dreams when she's looking at them. She's inspired to include that in a song. I hope she doesn't overdo the modulations: such a cliché. (I'd never tell her that, though. She'd be thrilled by my interest and probably suggest a collaboration.)

Mostly, though, while Hugh's been away I've had such silence, with time to sit in it.

We think we need to catch up on filing and calls and emails and cleaning grout, when actually I think we need to catch up on silence. I'm breathing again. I haven't, I realise, been breathing so well with Hugh here. So much cold fog, elephants and eggshells.

. . . . See? Thinking and thinking and thinking time.

Ooh, I've been able to sprawl out in the bed too, except for last night when Mary-Lou hopped in and snuggled up like she used to before kindergarten took my baby from me.

I promise I didn't go anywhere near myself with her there! Haven't for two nights, actually, as things are still a bit raw. I'm thinking about perhaps getting myself some sort of vibrator – partly to spare my clitoris but also because I'm curious now. Shouldn't I be buying something like that with my husband, though? Something we investigate together? I mean, if poor Hugh comes home and finds me shacked up with a shiny new vibrator (who merely needs a battery or two periodically and doesn't need its trousers washed or its steak medium-rare), wouldn't he feel a little left out? I think I would.

I'll sleep on it.

FRIDAY 21st JULY

I spoke to Hugh. He said, 'Can you look in the filing cabinet for the superannuation certificates?' and 'Did you keep the fuel receipts?' and nothing about missing us because 'I have to go. I'll call you later.' And I was left with an empty phone, into which I said, 'Yes, I'm keeping the children wonderfully alive, thank you very much. Oh, darling, I love you too. No, don't you dare send me flowers. I've had more than enough, and no need to organise a surprise adventure. It's only a month since you took me to Paris and rented that amazing apartment in Cuba. And thank you for talking to the children about not being complete little arseholes in the car. Love you. Bye.' Then I gave the phone the middle finger. And the dog, who looked a bit judgey for my liking. Then I opened a jar of gherkins.

Oh, I know he's busy. I shouldn't be cross. I am stopping this nonsense and going back to record sparklier times.

Speaking of gherkins . . .

Hobart, 2002

We'd been in the Newtown house for three years and had multiple (keep Susannah happy) trips to the mainland (none overseas) when I sort of gave up on the idea of a marriage proposal. I mean, if it didn't happen on the Barrier Reef or on Cable Beach or by the Sydney Opera House (celebrating Ria's first big guest appearance), then it was unlikely to happen at all. I didn't pester him (still terrified I might frighten him off with adoration) but he must have known how much I wanted it. At weddings, as we stood side by side in churches watching people declare their forevers, there was a palpable frisson of want emanating from me. But the wedding seasons came and went and we did up the house a bit, and supported one another in our blossoming careers. We laughed a lot and talked about how we were the only normal people in a world full of weirdos, and that seemed like enough.

Then one night we went to a fancy-dress birthday party held by Hugh's fancy new clients. We were riding the wave of a windfall; it was a big, lucrative, exciting job – the Hobart Museum renovation. The concept drawings looked amazing, like nothing Hobart had seen before. (This was way before Mona blew anything remotely avant-garde right out of the cool waters of the Derwent.)

'Someone in Europe is bound to snap you up after this,' I told him. 'Brave, young, dashing engineer.'

'It's a team effort, though,' he said humbly. 'And we're not doing this to get into a coffee table book. It's just a great thing for Hobart.'

'Yes,' I said, but thought, *Bugger Hobart. What about me?*

The fancy-dress party was for Garrett Green, the museum manager. We were asked to go as something starting with G. I overthought it and decided that museum people wouldn't be the superficial types who'd dress as glamour girls or Goldilocks. I dressed Hugh as a garden gnome and myself as a gherkin.

On the way in we passed a golfer, a goddess, some gypsies, a genie and Goldie Hawn. Everyone looked very Glamorous. I felt ugly and hot and got a bit drunk. I told Greta Garbo a very dirty joke about brussels sprouts, knocked over a plate of meatballs and tripped down a small flight of steps onto Grizabella the cat, whose tail was ripped off in the kerfuffle. Later, after I'd hit the dance floor with Gisele Bündchen, Ginger Rogers and a governess (and felt happily confident in my execution of the Macarena), it became evident that I wasn't the life of the party, but the laugh of the party. There were people asking me for jokes, challenging me to the chicken dance and sniggering behind their hands. It was very (literally) sobering, and one of the first times I'd felt like a proper misfit. I suddenly wanted my mum. And Ria.

With a furious blush flaring under my green make-up, I went in search of Hugh and found him in the sitting room with his gnome hat off, talking to an impossibly tall female gladiator in a leather bikini. I ventured up to say hello but lost the last of my confidence and tried instead to sink into a couch. But my costume wouldn't bend and I slid off onto the floor with quite a thud.

'Oh my God,' I heard the gladiator say. 'How embarrassing. That gherkin is really pickled.' Then she laughed hysterically at her own joke and added, 'I've never seen the point of pickling cucumbers – so revolting.'

'Oh, that's a shame,' said Hugh, coming over to help me up. 'We can't be friends, then, because gherkins are my favourite. Especially this one.'

'Oh, she's your friend,' said the gladiator. 'She's adorable.'

'Yes, I adore her,' said Hugh. 'But she's not my friend. She's my wife. At least she's going to be, if she'll have me.' He looked at my stunned face and said, 'Will you have me?'

I gaped at him, tried to speak and he said, 'Wait, sorry, don't answer, hang on . . .' and he pulled me by the hand, away from the gaping gladiator, through the party and out the front door. Outside, he manoeuvred me around the garden to a lit-up marble fountain of a boy with a harp. There, he went down on one knee and said, 'Susannah Mackay, will you be my wife. Please?' And with that, most likely for the first time in the history of the universe, a gherkin leapt into the arms of a garden gnome, kissed him all over his rosy-cheeked face and shrieked, 'Yes!'

As we left, the garden gnome high-fived the harp boy.

☆

It's a very silly story, but at least it's memorable. The children love to relate the tale. Mary-Lou has drawn pictures of me as a gherkin and told her class for show and tell. I should be proud . . .

I feel much more amiable. Just sent Hugh a goodnight text, with 'Miss you' and 'OXOXOXO'. Well done me.

LATER:

As a little reward for summoning benevolence, I have ordered a vibrator online, express post in discreet packaging. It's pink with pearls inside that are meant to stimulate you right to your very core. Also, it comes with a pair of free Ben Wa balls, whatever they are.

TUESDAY 25th JULY

A discreet package arrived today. I am too frightened to open it.

THURSDAY 27th JULY

The package is still at the back of my cupboard, where I put it yesterday in the hopes that its presence would fade and stop signalling out to me like a scary beacon.

I must distract myself with noble pursuits until Hugh gets back. Then I'll lob the package into the nearest St Vinnie's Bin. It'll give those people who spend their days sorting through other people's unwanteds a bit of a laugh at least.

Feeling a bit low today. Can't blame PMS because it's not that time. Am I lonely? Hugh's been away for sixteen days and every time I speak it's to remind children to use commas or manners or floss.

Sometimes I lie awake thinking about bits of caught kiwi-fruit skin eating into their teeth.

I thought about inviting all the neighbours over for early dinner but Ava said that Josh is away. I was going to phone Isobel, but then I lost my temper this morning and felt further depleted. Really lost it. This is mostly why I'm so low now. The guilt of it, and the physical low after an explosive fight-or-flight response. Why such a tantrum?

We were late. My fault. I got in a flap about what clothes to wear, and then cross because I don't have a high-flying job with clear and stylish workwear requirements. My grump just snowballed from there, really:

- Mary-Lou wailed about no time for plaits. How do some mums manage elaborate braids, etc. every day? Do they rise with the birds? Mine are lucky to get a comb wafted in their direction, which is not ideal for the small ones, with their curls.
- Eloise (who has given up entirely on her hair and taken to stuffing it into a bun as if it doesn't deserve to exist) was huffing about not seeing bus-stop friends, and she didn't offer to tidy the breakfast things.
- Raffy had tissue fluff all over his windcheater.
- I found another grey pube.
- In the car, Jimmy leaned forward to change the radio and snapped the lid off the compartment between the front seats. A snapped front compartment lid is like a grey pube – a proper devaluer, and irreversible.
- Mary-Lou declared that last week, Jimmy dropped his box of sultanas in the car and many of them went down the seat cracks.

- Jimmy switched the radio from an interesting conversation about China's terracotta soldiers to a Justin Bieber song and I felt affronted, which means I am a grumpy old lady.
- Justin Bieber is undeniably sexy. And he would never dream of looking twice at me. Because I am clearly a dirty old woman.

It was too much. I shrieked at Jimmy to get back in his seat and that shriek was like a pressure release valve on a demented balloon. I was awful. Danny the Champion's dad would be shocked and embarrassed.

Then, from the passenger seat, Eloise reached over and patted my thigh. She didn't look at me, or say anything, just patted. My snippy little big girl, the one with the deodorant and the sullen silences. And with that pat, I sobbed and sorried all the rest of the way to school, told them I didn't deserve such lovely children and I should go and sit in the naughty spot for a good few hours. Their silence implied agreement.

I stopped crying only because we were nearly at school and there's that really chirpy lollipop lady who looks like she's never even once lost her shit and also that mother whose name I can't remember but is the one who takes care of crises. You know those ones? Rock-like women with listening ears and glistening eyes and strong, waterproof shoulders who are very busy gathering donations for the school fair and writing newsletters and might, deep down, be thrilled to know the business of others. If she saw my tear-stained face, she'd drag me off for a cup of tea and a chat, which would be intolerable because I'd have to make something up that isn't anything to do with Justin Bieber or sultanas.

(I hasten to add that Justin Bieber is over eighteen, so I'm not all that creepy. I also have a tiny crush on Taylor Swift. I might as well get that off my chest while I'm here in these murky depths.)

Anyway, I collected myself enough to get the children the rest of the way and myself into town. But I couldn't collect my dignity. It was back on the side of the road with the broken bits of lid. (I threw them out the window.) It's a terrible thing to lose your dignity in front of your children, not to mention the littering.

Do I need some sort of mood stabiliser? Butler school? Vitamin D is meant to be good. So is a trip to Paris in the spring. So is masturbating. I should take it up again. *The package, the package!*

In town, where I was to catch up on birthday presents (two godchildren in the last week, both Hugh's – why is this part of my work?), there was a woman pushing her babies along in a pram with packages hanging off the handlebars and I cried again because mine don't need a pram any more. They have gone off to school with their sense of purpose intact and mine shredded up like the washed tissue bits on Raffy's jumper. Linty old used-up purpose. Then I cried some more because I found those pram days stifling and I was perpetually irritated when I should have been squeezing every drop of meaning from every precious moment and revelling in my plump and juicy raisin d'etre. Oh, wait, is it rai*son* d'etre? I can't even get that right.

Then I had to sign some papers in the health insurance place and my signature looked suddenly pathetic and feeble, like a person resigned to the fact that they will never amount to anything much. When I married Hugh, I practised my new signature a bit, but not all that much, because I was so married and mature, and practising signatures was for flitty little girls. *Oh, that'll do. Understated elegance, like I'll soon be*, I thought smugly. Well, bugger that. I should have created an autograph, not a boring signature fit only for school diaries and dentist claim forms. No wonder S Parks has never achieved anything other than a stretched vagina, four future delinquents and no actual sparks.

(By the way, the delinquents seemed fine this afternoon, especially after I took them on a guilt trip to the sweet shop after school. Mary-Lou chose a large electric blue lollipop shaped like a diamond ring. I hate to think what they use to make that blue. Vitriol? I've let them watch telly again: *Anne of Green Gables*. I'll go and join them soon, I think. Sometimes a dose of Anne is just the ticket.)

I think if I had that time again, I'd never have changed my name at all. Susannah Mackay was doing quite well for herself, thank you very much. It was even a bit groovy to keep one's maiden name when we were married. All the cool people were doing it (although clearly I'm not cool because I just used the word groovy). I claimed that it would be confusing for children, etc. but really I was just so in love, I wanted everything of Hugh, especially his name. I was proud to be rebranded as a Parks. If there was a Parks uniform, I would have gladly worn it. Pathetic. Susannah Parks is just someone's mum's name. A parent. A transparent, because I'm almost invisible, like an empty glass vase.

If Hugh and I divorced, would I go back to my maiden name? Sometimes I envy divorced people. Every second week free of children and duty and fights over the computer. I wouldn't be lonely, and if I were, I'd revel in the loneliness, positively swizzle about in it like Cleopatra in her milk. I could get a little solid brick house with no creaks that never needs painting, put some daisies in the vase . . .

☆

Now I'm fantasising about divorce!! I think I need to go and dig out that package. It's probably just what I need, to get my pecker up.

That probably wasn't the most timely use of the word 'pecker'.

. . . No package. Instead I'm joining in on *Anne of Green Gables*. Anne would understand my wayward brain. I too love dimpled elbows. My elbows are really wrinkly, like scrotums. Sometimes the children pull at them. Another random irritant.

SATURDAY 29th JULY

I've just read back over my thoughts over the last few days and am wondering whether all that twiddling with my clitoris has increased oestrogen production. I'm all over the place. Maybe I've fiddled my way into hormonal dementia . . . I should definitely *not* open the package. Instead I'm going to make a zucchini slice and take the children to the beach. The beach in winter is enchanting and moody.

LATER:

Went to beach. It was cold. Now there is sand all over the floors. I am going to ignore it and phone Ria.

LATER STILL:

Ria is coming over to stay!!! She said, 'It's high time I checked in on you before the Sparkle Project comes together and you no longer have the vaguest of interest in me.' Really it's because she wangled some sort of promotional gig here so that her agent has let her escape home. She'll be here in a week and HOORAY!!!

SUNDAY 30th JULY

Late last night, I opened the package. By God did I open the package.

After three gin and tonics (two while talking to Ria), I emptied my mind, steeled myself with affirmation of real-life bravery and homed in on the box in the wardrobe. There, amid a blizzard of those white squishy packaging peanuts, was a resplendent, lavender-coloured vibrator. The lavender almost stopped me. *Why not skin colour? Why does everything for women have to be pinkish and pastelly?* And then I thought, *Well, actually, penises are sort of pinkish and pastelly, and some probably go quite lavender at times.* But still, it was all pearlised and ditzy. Looking at it, I felt the same as when I peer into a showbag. Trashy, guilty and disgusted. And the thing actually smelled like showbags – you know, that sweet plastic, manufactured smell. (And, yes, I did sniff the vibrator. I don't know why. I guess you should thoroughly assess anything you are thinking about putting inside yourself, but it does seem a very strange thing to do.) But soon enough I managed to look past the sickly presentation and see the object for what it was – a toy, in lieu of my husband (who has been away for thirty-eight DAYS): just another item in the Sparkle toolkit. Based on that, I had a go.

It did at first seem seedy. I couldn't help imagining what teenage Susannah – the one with no thoughts beyond a music room and a viola bow – would think of me brandishing a vibrator. And then I turned the thing on. And, well, it turned me on. I'm still too ashamed/embarrassed to share too much but in mere minutes I was gasping like a trout on a riverbank and it was all over. Intense. Efficient. Could be dangerously addictive. Ria says she sometimes pops home for a little whiz. I can see why.

What concerns me is that after all this self-sufficiency and efficiency (economy of time and energy, no mess, no emotional involvement, guaranteed outcome), I might not want to bother with anything more complex, like a penis and a man. Will Hugh's penis be pink and pearly enough?

I think I need my husband to come back.

TUESDAY 1st AUGUST

Hugh will be home tomorrow night. Ria arrives on Thursday. This is very, very good news. I am so looking forward to seeing both of them, I really am.

I mean, I am, but there are several misgivings, if I'm to be totally honest:

1) I have got entirely used to the few hours after the children are in bed when I am alone, with the history channel to watch and the internet to browse. (I've developed an interest in 1940s fashion. And sloths.) Sometimes I might search my legs for ingrown hairs. Or have a spoonful of that instant frosting you can buy in little tubs for when birthday cakes are all too much, for Christ's sake.

2) Will Ria finally see how pathetic my existence is? (Must tidy up bathroom cabinet. It's a shrine to anti-ageing fads and desperation.)

3) I have told Ria waaaaay too much about the Sparkle Project and now she'll be on constant lookout for evidence of marital atrophy. I can't keep things from her even if I'm keeping them from her.

4) No more regular clitoris/vibrator dates.

Other than that, I can't wait to see them both. I'm sick of myself. And I'm sick of the kids too – it's only Tuesday and I'm sure it should be Thursday at least. Jimmy's lost another tooth and the tooth fairy is three days late.

WEDNESDAY 2nd AUGUST

The tooth fairy came. She slipped on a book, knocked over a lamp and woke two of the children. For God's sake. Can I get anything right?

I must get the house in order. It's markedly more disordered than usual on account of me not bothering for a while. Just shows that most of my cleaning is done for the sake of Hugh. I would analyse that further but the fridge smells funny, the fireplace is choked up with ash and Barky has eaten a balloon. Last time he did that I had to check his poos. I'm tempted to pretend I didn't see him eating it. Dog poo surveillance was never a life goal. Also, when the heck do single parents find the time to change bedsheets?

And I haven't seen Valda since Sunday. I'll make her an egg sandwich and pop over for lunch. She loves an egg sandwich. With curry powder. I wonder if she's read the lesbian book??

8.30 – He's home!! He's in seeing the children. They will never go to sleep now. Whipped into a frenzy; their squeals of delight are delightful. Might not be a bad thing if we don't get around to sex tonight; I'll have time to ~~reopen the hornbag~~ reawaken the old razzle dazzle. And I'm exhausted from razzle-dazzling the house. I got EVERYTHING done; the house is sparkling, even if I'm not. Valda came over, ate my egg sandwiches and barked orders from the couch. That woman should author a shiny-house-in-no-time book.

She'd make a fortune. (I asked her whether she'd read the lesbian book and she said, 'Yes, it was quite boring.'!!!!)

12.30 – No lovemaking. The children hooliganed around until almost ten and then Hugh showered and by the time I'd pottered about (that time between ten and really late goes so fast), Hugh was almost asleep. He patted my leg with his foot.

And now I'm sleepless and trying not to think about my Lavender Friend in the sock drawer.

I need to get myself out of this solo phase, for goodness sake. This must be the heralding of a new phase, with a team . . .

Trio ♪♪ ♪♪

THURSDAY 3rd AUGUST

RIA IS HERE!!!! I collected her and her enormous suitcase from the airport this morning. She really does look tired. Her hair isn't as buoyant as usual and her beautiful olive skin looks sort of tarnished – she'll do well for a break. But her quicksilver wit isn't at all tarnished. We've been talking and talking. There is always so much to tell her, even in my low-flying life. Hugh has just been pouring us wine, chuckling and getting his own dinner.

About Hugh. We haven't yet had the romantic 'how-lovely-to-have-you-home' talk or any of my planned passionate kisses or anything remotely sexual. He went off to work this morning and I drove the children to school and everything is back to ho-hum normal on that front. There are trousers in the wash basket and I've remembered about the precision-timed dance that we do every morning to ensure our bathroom times don't clash and we can avoid disturbing sights or smelly smells.

Men take up a lot of room . . .

But Hugh and Ria were so thrilled to see each other again; it was lovely to watch. The Best. They hugged for ages. It was far more moving than Hugh's and my reunion.

Off I go. Must tend to poor exhausted Ria.

TUESDAY 8th AUGUST

I can't describe how lovely it is to have Ria here. It's a bit like having you, dear diary, come to life, insofar as nothing's sacred. I've realised that while Hugh is my best friend in some ways, there are some things you can't tell a husband. Such as most of my thoughts. 'Sorry, Hugh darling, no sex tonight. I've had a long day with my vibrator and I'm actually a bit distracted because I have a crush on Danny the Champion of the World's dad and really just want to lie quietly in bed and daydream about divorce.' Honesty can be foolhardy.

Ria and I have imagined up a trip for me to go on my own to visit her in London for the premiere of *I Capture the Castle*. Nice to dream. I'll never do it; we both know that. Ria said, 'Ah, well. One day when the last of the children is married and living in a gated community with CCTV linked to your laptop.' I wish I could prove her wrong.

It surprises me that Ria is so tolerant of my children given that she has none of her own. She's lovely with them. They find her instantly disarming and hilarious. They want to be near her all the time, as opposed to behind their closed bedroom doors (Eloise).

'Hello hello hello,' she said when she came with me to collect them from school. 'You all look old enough for me to say bloody, bugger, ballbag, bollocks and bum trumpets. But not old enough for arse bandit.' They screamed with laughter, a sound that makes me smile right from my toes.

We're all having a lovely time together. It's like the old days when I was trying not to tell Hugh that I loved him and we were all wonderful, platonic-ish friends. This morning Hugh said, 'I love seeing you laugh so much.' Do I not laugh enough? Must add laughing to my list of Things to Do.

SATURDAY 12th AUGUST

Today we went for a bushwalk . . . and herein begins a Very Long Story. I could just sigh, say, 'It's a very long story,' and move on for the sake of my dignity but it's somehow pertinent to issues of passion.

When I took Ria her tea this morning, she said, 'I would kill for some proper Australian air. You know, the fresh kind, not the kind with people in it.' I suppose London air is full of people's judgements and sorrows and burps and wishes. Here we have unprocessed, wildflower air. 'We're so lucky to be Tasmanian,' she said, and sighed a very sentimental sigh. So unlike gritty old Ria.

So we decided on a bushwalk. Hugh made us a hearty breakfast of eggs and mushrooms and toast while Ria and I bossed the children about rucksacks and laughed about vibrators (I told her about my brave new frontier, *bzz bzz*). I also mentioned the little balls that came free with the vibrator, which I'd shoved in the sock drawer in my haste to get to the business. Ben Wa balls. Ria insisted I fetch them out.

'They're love eggs,' she said gleefully. 'You pop them up your muff as you go about your day. The ultimate multi-tasking tool.'

'You mean, I can fold washing and get horny at the same time?'

'Well, you won't be tearing your clothes off but it's a mild sort of stimulant. Coffee for the cunt.' She knows I hate that word with a passion. I can't believe I just smote my diary with it. I gave her a little shove and said, 'End of conversation.'

But she was on a roll. 'It'd certainly spice up a family bushwalk.'

'Ria, you're a disgrace.'

'I thought you wanted to be braver.'

'God, did I tell you that too? Must step away from the gin when we talk.'

'Calm waters don't put wind in your sails, Susannah – just ask the ancient mariner.'

'I'm leaving. Can you please bag up the scroggin?'

'Bag up the scroggin!' She snorted through the wall. 'Make some waves, Helen Fanny Burns. Life's far too short.'

We all went to Collins Bonnet in the end, where there was a tiny bit of snow for extra refreshment. To distract trudgy old Raff and Mary-Lou's little legs from the hills, we pretended to be the Secret Seven. Ria said there was orangeade in the drink bottles and said 'jolly' in a perfect English accent. Even Eloise was laughing and asking what kippers are. She didn't laugh when I tried on the English accent, though. I'll never be cool like Ria. If we really were the Secret Seven, I'd be Pam, the pathetic one who cries a lot, trips on the tree roots and wishes she was more knowing like Janet and Peter.

I never know anything about anything, I thought. *I know how to cut ribbons so they don't fray and to keep the stems of cut hydrangeas very long and that's about it.* Ria must have noticed a slight downcast in my demeanour because she sidled up alongside me and said, 'I brought the Ben Wa balls; just saying.'

Which is how, somewhere in the transformative air and amid the myrtle trees, I moved from Pathetic Pam to Daring Desiree. It's a wonder there wasn't a spontaneous daylight aurora.

The fact that I had two metal balls on a string in my vagina while in the company of my children and best friend in the wholesome scrogginey setting of a mountainside does leave me feeling a bit uncomfortable. But I must emphasise that the insertion was done discreetly, behind a tree. And the actual wearing of them is subtle. Ish.

The first sensation is of cold. The second is that you need to tense everything up to stop them falling out. Suddenly I had more to worry about than tripping over roots. So I walked strangely at first. 'Mum, did you shit yourself?' asked Jimmy, which made Ria spit water everywhere and Hugh shout, 'Oi.' After that I tried relaxing a bit and found that they weren't going to fall out. It wasn't actually arousing as such, but it made me very aware of my vagina (as if I haven't been aware of it enough lately) and when I sat down on a rock to eat I definitely felt a thrill and a sudden urge to sit on Hugh. (I didn't, though. My boundaries haven't eroded completely.)

'You're glowing, Zannah. I knew the fresh air would do us all good,' said Ria pointedly. I glared at her and said, 'Would you like some cake to put in that cake hole?'

And then things got weird(er). From nowhere, an emu appeared. 'Look, Mum, an ostrich!' yelled Mary-Lou (which just goes to show she's been watching too much American telly) and we all oohed and ahhed and then we didn't because the emu was making an ominous thumping sound from somewhere deep in its throat and then it ran, straight for us!

For a moment I stood between it and the children and did a silly sort of kung-fu stance but as it got closer, I decided that was a very bad idea and just as I was thinking that, Hugh yelled, 'Get out of the way!' and herded Ria and the children up onto a rocky outcrop. Meanwhile I panicked and ran the other way, with the emu in hot pursuit. I ran and ran, all the time hearing that horrible thumping sound and imagining that at any moment I would be opened up from neck to bottom by one of those horrible leathery talons. It was just like *Jurassic Park*, really. And then, when I couldn't run any more, I scrambled up a she-oak tree, scraped my hand and tried not to expire from fear and unfitness. The emu stopped running (he didn't even puff, the bastard) and just kind of waited.

'I'm okay!' I yelled out between tearing breaths, because I could hear Raffy screeching, 'Mum!'

'I'm okay!' I yelled again. 'But HEEEEEELLLLLLP!' And with that, *plop!* My Ben Wa balls fell neatly into my knickers. I suppose ye olde pelvic floor doesn't come into play amid the fight-or-flight response. I did what any besieged human would do. I plucked them out and threw them at the emu. And missed. The emu didn't flinch.

Then Hugh arrived on the scene with a muesli bar, which proved to be the perfect weapon. He held it out to the emu, who sniffed the air and stepped closer. Hugh threw the muesli bar. The emu went after it, I climbed down from my perch and together Hugh and I beat a hasty retreat, hand in hand. It would have been really romantic had I not been all sweaty and puffed. And in a bit of a state about Hugh not seeing the shiny balls lying on the rocks.

And that, dear diary, is how, when we are far beyond the Anthropocene epoch and aliens are picking through plastic to analyse the geological history of the Earth, they will find my love eggs in the unlikeliest of places.

Later I said, 'Does anyone buy the idea that I was acting as a very brave decoy and that me running saved all your lives?'

And Ria said, 'No.'

Hugh rubbed my back.

On the way home I tripped on a lot of roots, but I also laughed. And laughed and laughed. Ria imitated my kung-fu pose.

None of us thought to question why there was a solitary emu poking about on Collins Bonnet. They're not native to Tasmania, are they? I've worried about the poor thing since. A bird that can't fly, alone up there with all the wallabies. It must watch the cockatoos and fret terribly about its identity. I hope there's a native hen or two up there so there are at least a few other birds whose wings don't work. They need to stick together.

I must add that when we got to the top, the view was INCREDIBLE. Once we'd stopped our puffing, there was that glorious silence that happens when something is so lovely that it takes away words as well as breath. They're not needed because the picture before you is calmly painting the words. Silence. Like this: . . . .
. . . .
. . . .
. . . .
. . . .
. . . .
. . . .
. . . .
. . . .
. . . .

Silence truly is golden when there are oft-grumbly children partaking in it, and when you can see all the way to the sea. When the silence was broken, it was by Raff remarking on the unusual call of a bird. And then Jimmy asked Ria to put the bird call in her music, to which Ria said, 'That's the best idea any seven-year-old bloke has ever had in the history of the world.' And Jimmy beamed.

'What are the birds saying?' asked Jimmy and we all had a guess. Hugh's was, 'Who wants a bit of nookie?' which was eerily significant, and Ria said, 'I think they're saying that everything's all right.' So we all shut up and listened again and Jimmy – my second-least snuggly child – snuggled into her and said, 'I like that. We can just listen to the birds when we feel sad.'

It was the sort of moment you'd put on Instagram and everyone would feel a bit miffed that they hadn't taken their children walking up a mountain and put them in a moment in which bird calls were a thing. Bird calls would rarely register with the youth of today. Unless they were tweets.

Once the children had got bored with the silence they built cairns while Hugh and I prepared lunch. Hugh said, 'Well, this is nice.' Ria had a little snooze. It was. So nice. When we got down we saw fit to stop at a corner shop and get a bag of mixed sweeties each. They were the ones with teeth and pineapples, racing cars and milk bottles, etc. Eighties treats. No one minded that they weren't all that soft. I dropped mine and lost a couple to the gutter so Mary-Lou gave me a pat and one of her honey bears. I've never liked honey bears but I was so touched I cried. Happy tears. Really happy ones.

'I love having you here,' I said to Ria and she said, 'Oh, for fuck's sake,' but she squeezed my hand and looked a bit watery in the eye department too. Hugh just smiled at us.

Then we came home and I could let the children watch telly without any qualms about them not being active enough, so Hugh and Ria and I could drink wine and eat French sticks and cheese.

It was a lovely day.

Everyone's in bed now. I said I'd tidy up. I haven't. I've clattered a few pots, written these words and finished the last of the wine. Must sleep. Ria's doing her concert tomorrow night. I can't be a complete wreck.

PS The 'love eggs' didn't lead to passionate sex. And I know there is not much in the way of relevant sparky points lately, but there is contentment, lots of it. I think I look different next to Ria. Less blurry, perhaps? Less sick of myself. Anyway, contentment could spark romance, which sparks lust. Not tonight, though. Bit achy in the hip region.

PPS A few days ago I was fantasising about being without Hugh; that divorce would be freeing and spacey. Today, Hugh is an anchor and the thought of floating aimlessly away without him, with the likelihood of wreckage, is anything but freeing. Gosh, such mood swings. Are my hormones, since I passed forty, controlling my brain?

SUNDAY 13th AUGUST

It must be said that alcohol, in quantities that take you to the 'love youse all' level but not a drop beyond, is a powerful spark tool. The trick is to make sure you stay balanced on the level of high self-confidence and euphoria, without falling into staggery skankville. Last night, it appears that I nailed it.

Before I went to bed, I removed every stitch of clothing and sort of slunk about in front of the mirror, tried on some heels, took off heels (naked with heels is not my thing, especially because my only heels are Mary Janes with a thick heel – I looked like a librarian who'd forgotten to get dressed) and flipped my hair from its usual side parting to the other side, as though I was shedding an old self.

In the bedroom, I stood above Hugh and gently stroked his shoulder. He opened his eyes and squinted up at my silhouette. (I left the wardrobe light on for a bit of mild illumination.) I slipped in under the covers and on top of him. He gasped (possibly because of my raw sexuality but more likely because I'd been posing in front of the mirror for so long that I'd got a bit cold). I kissed his chest, his neck, his lips, then took his arms above his head and pinned them down. His groan was both a sound of pleasure and a question: who are you? So I showed him who I could be. Daring Desiree. All the commanding, searching, touching, thrusting, knowing parts of her. He was powerless. He shuddered and gasped and tried to hold back but in the end succumbed to the wave of his climax. When it was over he lay washed up on the sheets and I stroked his hair until he fell back to sleep.

I didn't mind that there wasn't time for my own orgasm. I knew exactly how to manage that, with the minimum of fuss.

I actually woke up this morning feeling a little embarrassed, in case my memories of the liaison were distorted by alcohol, but Hugh tipped up on one elbow beside me and said, 'Wow,' and then again, with a sort of disbelieving laugh, 'Wo-ow.' So I'm thinking I was totally *en pointe*. Then he said, 'But you didn't get to . . .' (Clears throat, eyebrow waggle – bit hard to say 'come' in the harsh light of day.) 'Would you like me to sort that out for you now?'

Without thinking I told him that I'd sorted the problem out for myself, which made me blush because I'd forgotten that he knows nothing of my solo efforts while he was away. He looked surprised, then impressed and said, 'I'd like to see that.'

'If you're very good,' I said from under the covers where I was finishing my blush. When I emerged, I think he was looking at me differently.

WE HAVE PROGRESS! Must try to figure out how to do that without the bottle of wine.

Anyway, Hugh's taken the boys to Jimmy's end-of-footy-season sausage sizzle and left the girls here with me. His smile sparkled at me when he left. Ria's had to go and get organised for her performance tonight. She's previewing some of the *Capture* songs; I can't wait.

The girls are bickering. None of the children argue with Ria. Because she plays with them, I suppose. I avoid playing because it disappoints me. Everything I like – books, puzzles, word games, card making – is too BO-RING for them. Not enough action. It's a side effect of all those stupid devices and instant entertainment. Delayed gratification is a thing of the past. They have each other to play with anyway, and they'll never know how to make their own fun if I'm constantly making it for them. Fun is like sandwiches. You have to learn to make your own or some bastard will add too much onion.

LATER:

The girls and I have been preparing for Ria's concert. We've had a little celebratory tea party and Eloise has kindly applied an egg and lemon mixture to my face. 'It brightens and tightens the skin,' she said. 'I saw it on YouTube.' Tightens is right. I could barely open my mouth to pop the fairy bread in. Mary-Lou has done my hair; she has done a heap of little plaits and used about thirty clips and ties of varying styles. I look like a merry-go-round. A tight-lipped merry-go-round, with hundreds and thousands stuck to my lemon-juice face.

We're all going to Ria's performance – Valda, Mum, Dad, Henry and Charmian too. Even Mary-Lou, which is such a rare treat for her given that the show starts at eight-thirty. Mary-Lou claims she's never seen the stars, a suggestion I sort of laughed off but there's a chance she's right. What sort of mother never shows her child the stars? Anyway, the show is a Very Big Deal. I know because Ria's personal assistant, Joseph, called here to make sure I thought Ria was in a good frame of mind.

'Has she been looking after herself, do you think?' he asked.

'Well,' I said, 'she's had a lot of fresh air, quite a bit of wine, lots of home-cooked meals and a good core workout from all the laughing. I'd definitely vouch for her preparedness.'

'Oh, that's good to hear.' Joseph sounded genuinely relieved. 'She's not nervous?'

'Are you joking? Ria's never been nervous in her life.' I must have sounded incredulous because Joseph said hurriedly, 'Oh, I know, it's just that she didn't want me to come with her and there's press everywhere down there and I was worried.'

'It's okay, Joseph. We're looking after her. And, honestly, she's not nervous. She's never seen performance as performance, just as a wondrous sharing.'

Joseph didn't sound placated. 'Okay, thank you. Could you just make sure she has her warm water and pineapple juice? And could you tell her that I've watered her cyclamen and postponed her meeting with Richard Curtis.'

Sometimes I forget just how famous Ria Mirrin is. Our little Gloria.

We're going out to dinner before the show, a treat from Ria for being her biggest fans and indispensable entourage (actually, she said, 'hangiest hangers-on and smelliest smells' but the restaurant was very posh so we know she meant 'thank you'). Ooh la la. I'm not sure how to break it to Mary-Lou that I can't possibly keep all her little plaits in, although Ria would probably get a good laugh out of them. She seems to really need our laughs, soaking them up as though she hasn't had any for a while.

I realise too that *I* have laughed more with Ria in the last week than I have all year. I wish she would stay for good. I think Hugh does as well. I think he feels less responsible for me when Ria's here. Or is it that Ria makes my difference seem more variant and less aberrant? She would never move back here, though. Her home is in London now. 'Everything sounds tinny here,' she said. 'It's probably the lack of wallpaper.' She's leaving in four days. Oh.

Going to shower.

Might wallpaper the bedrooms soon.

MONDAY 14th AUGUST

Oh, the concert! When there are people like Ria Mirrin, my Ria, who can take a piece of music and put it through their instrument and out into people's souls, where it thrums at the heartstrings and makes marks in memory and says all the best things about music and performance and art; when there are those people, it's okay for me to never play music again. Music has good hands; it doesn't need my useless ones. And I say that in complete honesty, without a trace of bitter feeling or regret. I don't need to play any more. Selling my viola was most definitely the right thing.

Tomorrow I will march straight to the principal's office and finally say, 'No, I won't be playing for the school. I'm sorry, but perhaps I could make sushi in the canteen once in a while?' I don't know how to make sushi but I can learn. I can learn anything. What shall I learn? See, look at all these doors opening now that the big old heavy creaky one is finally closed for good.

Ria. She was breathtaking. We all adored it. The whole full-house concert hall adored it. She got the complete silence, gasp, standing ovation, the cheers and whistles, the shakes of the head, the tears.

All of it. And she cried!!! Tough, old, don't-blubber Ria cried and blew kisses and stayed onstage for a bit, when her trademark ending is to nod to the audience and walk straight off. I couldn't believe my eyes. Wish I'd filmed that bit. Great for future blackmail. I've teased her already but she's actually a little touchy, not quite teasable.

Hugh whistled, clapped his loudest and looked very moved, Raffy seemed entirely overcome, Jimmy cheered and Mary-Lou cried along with me and Ria. Actually, I sobbed. Noisily. Sobs are the best way to describe what it's like to hear your best friend turn your favourite book into songs. I don't have words. Eloise was her usual unmoveable self (which made me cry a bit more), but she smiled a lot and was clearly impressed.

At the dinner beforehand, Ria popped in unexpectedly from her pre-concert rituals with a birthday cake for me! It's not my birthday until Wednesday, but how lovely!

Also, Hannah was at the concert! She must have spotted us in the foyer because she came up and said hello, and it was all a bit awkward for a minute because Hugh said, 'Hannah!' and looked thrilled and Hannah kissed his cheek and they did a sort of hug, and then Hannah gave me a plastic bag and said, 'Thank you, Susannah, for this and for the card. I washed all the blood out.' And for a weird minute I didn't know what she was talking about but then I looked in the bag and saw my cardie.

Eloise asked, 'How's Emily?' like the sensible girl she is and we talked about how fine Emily is and then the bells rang and we were ushered in to our VIP seats at the front of the dress circle while Hannah de Montagu went up to the gods and I tried not to feel smug.

I loved today.

TUESDAY 15th AUGUST

It's late. I can't sleep. Today I foolishly told Ria about being asked to play viola at school and inadvertently opened some kind of floodgate. Oh My Lordy. At first she was just typical Ria. 'If you say no, I will shit in an envelope and post it to you from London.' But then she made a completely startling speech; it went like this:

'The combination of being very tired, quite emotional, you turning forty-four tomorrow and me leaving again leads me to say some things I vowed I wouldn't say. One: I love you very much, so use that to brace yourself for this. Two: something happened to you in childbirth to make your skull VERY THICK because you can't seem to understand that everyone is waiting for you to play again, everyone – Eloise needs to hear you play again. And the other children who have never heard you play. But mostly your husband, who fell in love with that show-off with the viola. She's still there, Susannah, but only just. Only just. And if thickheaded Susannah Wash-house Parks keeps smothering Susannah Genius Mackay until she stops breathing altogether, I will never forgive her. Never. Three: I said Genius. Ge.Ni.Us. You didn't even have to TRY at being a brilliant musician. You just are. I spent my life practising while you floated around with your perfect pitch, studying the stars and occasionally picking up your instrument to blow everyone's socks off. It killed me, Susannah, to see it come so easily to you. But not as much as seeing that brilliance go down the gurgler with the baby's fucking bathwater. And four: please refer back to one. I love you.'

Then she wiped her snotty nose because incredibly she was crying again, hugged me so tightly I couldn't breathe, and went to bed.

☆

I can't believe it. Me, a genius? And did she say she was jealous of me? Inadequate, distracted me? She was wrong about lots of things. For one, I was always thickheaded. It wasn't an accident of childbirth. I just am. From school I only remember useless things like what the floral emblem of South Australia is (Sturt's Desert Pea). Also, I used to practise A LOT. Didn't I? She's the genius. Ask anyone. And the world doesn't need my music. I still firmly believe that. It's getting along perfectly without it, for fuck's sake.

I'm cross. Ria was altogether harsh. But I shouldn't swear, even though Ria does. All the time. She can't say all those things just before my birthday, dammit. Before she leaves the country. It's nearly my birthday now. I won't sleep and tomorrow will show every one of my forty-four years.

WEDNESDAY 16th AUGUST

It's six a.m. It's my birthday. No one is awake yet. I got to sleep in the end, but only after I resolved to forgive Ria her outburst. She's never had good reason to let anything conflict with her music. She's not a mother, she's never had a traumatic experience, so how could I expect her to understand?

Today is going to be a lovely day for both of us. Ria and I are going to send the children off to school and Hugh off to work and go to Mona for lunch. Mona is so un-Tasmanian. All the staff look like they fly-in, fly-out from Coolville. I can pretend I actually did leave the island. Also, now that I'm better acquainted with my vulva, I can have another look at the wall of vaginas and see where I sit on the dangly lab spectrum. The first time I saw the vulvas (Ria says it's disrespectful not to give the work its actual name, which is *Cunts and Other Conversations*, but I know it's just so she can hear me say that word), I thought it was some kind of ancient fossil display. Hopefully the Sparkle Project will save my vagina from an ancient fossil fate. Will birthday sex happen, I wonder?

LATER:

SPEECHLESS. What words must speak things should say can't think oh dear me and oh.

LATER STILL:

I'm in bed. Under covers. Still in shock. Birthday sex won't be happening. Can't say why. Oh.

SATURDAY 19th AUGUST

So about my birthday. I think I'm sufficiently recovered to recount . . .

Mona was terrific as always. Ria and I got swept up in the intrigue of it and didn't talk about violas. She was in a very caution-to-the-wind mood. We ate salted caramel cheesecake and truffles, and Ria bought a bottle of Henschke Hill of Grace, which cost a fortune and tasted like a castle with intricate wood panelling and a lot of basement. She said, 'If this, your forty-fourth birthday, was your last day on earth, how would you spend it?'

And I answered, 'With you and a bottle of extortionate wine, thank you very much. And maybe Keanu Reeves if he was about. And Hugh, of course. And the children. And Barky.'

And I realised I meant it (~~especially~~ not Keanu).

We bounced on the enormous trampoline and sang Madonna songs in the Madonna room and got told off for touching the

Fat Car. We laughed and laughed. I wished Hugh could've come. It was lovely.

But.

When we got home, Mum and Dad were there. Mum had collected the children from school for me. I was surprised to see Dad, though. Mum noticed me being surprised.

'Dad wanted to come and see the children's school,' she said in a stilted voice, looking hard at Ria. 'He was very pleased with Jimmy's drawing of a capsicum. And the fort. They've taken forts away from schools on the mainland. Apparently they encourage warfare – ridiculous. Mrs Grubb was lovely. Is she from Launceston? I know some Launceston Grubbs.'

I eyed her suspiciously. I looked at Dad, who was reading the newspaper. 'You liked the capsicum picture, Dad?'

'Yes, please,' said Dad to the paper. Mum cleared her throat and he looked up. 'What?'

'We met Eloise at her bus stop, didn't we, Jack?' Mum went on. 'We've all had some cantaloupe. Quite a nice one for this time of year.'

'Hugh here yet?' asked Dad.

'What's going on?' I asked, looking at Ria. There was a knock at the door and a 'Yooo-hooo!' It was Henry.

'Come in, Henry!' called Ria. She looked at me and sang 'Happy birthday to you' in a light voice.

'But I've had a birthday cake already,' I said. 'And lots of happy birthdays. And lunch today. That's enough. I just want some cheese on toast now.'

But then Raffy turned up with Valda, and Mary-Lou said, 'There is something very important soon,' but got violently nudged by Jim and burst into tears.

Ria brought out some drinks and nibbles. Hugh arrived home.

'Sorry.' He was a bit breathless. 'Am I late?'

'Not that I'm aware of,' I said. 'But apparently I wouldn't know.'

'Everyone's here,' said Ria.

'It's time!' shouted Raffy. His cheeks were flushed with excitement. Then Hugh disappeared from the room for a minute and there was a bit of silence, into which Mum said, 'Just think, exactly forty-four years ago I was having my woo-woo sewn up by that darling Dr Johns.' Raffy gasped; Eloise squeaked and clapped a hand over her eyes. Mum looked at them and said, 'Darlings, it's completely normal to develop a crush on your obstetrician.'

Then Hugh came back in carrying a huge box, the children did a synchronised 'Tada!' and Hugh laid the box at my feet. 'Happy birthday, dear wife,' he said and kissed me.

'Thank you,' I mumbled.

'You must have been wondering why you didn't get any presents when you woke up,' said Jimmy.

'It's from everyone,' said Hugh. 'Mostly Ria.'

'From everyone,' said Ria. 'Raff put his pocket money in.' Raffy beamed.

'Open it and open it and open it,' yelled Mary-Lou until Dad grabbed her and tucked her onto his knee. So open it I did.

Inside the box was a silver-wrapped parcel of a very familiar shape. *My viola. They've bought back my viola,* I thought, and then to my surprise, *Thank God.*

And as I tore back the silver paper, my heart beat again, double time, only I wished it wouldn't. I wished it to stop altogether because what I was looking at was indeed a viola case, but it was new and shiny and definitely not mine.

I think back now to their dear expectant faces . . . I can see them as though I'd run outside to peek in through the window. Look at them – having plotted and gathered and bated their breath for me – now putting their joy and pride backstage to wait behind wide eyes for the cue. Fists clasped and held to breasts, happy little pause squeaks and Hugh (oh, Hugh) looking at my face, utterly terrified.

And there's me, opening the case, peering ashen-faced at the glossy new instrument (I'd always wondered whether colour could really drain from people's faces but, yes, look, there it goes from mine) and trying to smile but failing terribly.

I said 'thank you' and 'wow' and 'it's beautiful', and then, while everyone waited for me to pick it up, I added, 'I'm overcome.' And then had a few minutes in the wardrobe in which I tried to catch my breath and think of what to say but couldn't. So I went back out and peeked at it again, looked away and (because it seemed right) said, 'Is it from England?'

'Wales,' said Ria, who by this stage had recognised my ~~horror misgivings~~ horror and began babbling to the rest of the room. 'Grumpy old bugger, the luthier. Very bitter about the perfection of the violin and the neglect of the viola. But everyone who's anyone recommended him. He says it's a developing instrument and that he is the only one in the world who recognises that. Everyone else just copies old ones. Something like that.'

We all looked down at the instrument, as if waiting for it to pop up and say hello. It shined its dreadful gloss at me. The wood had a reddish-brown. It was mottled. Ugly. I've never, thanks to my hair, liked anything that warms to red.

'He needed to know everything about you, Zannah,' said Hugh. 'We sent him your playing history, your style.'

'I played him your recordings,' added Ria, with a hint of urgency. 'He's got it right. He only has the best tonewoods. Apparently he has piles of really old spruce and maple from all over the world and he taps bits of it until he hears the magic. Yours is from Switzerland and Canada.' She widened her eyes at me. 'It's called the Susannah Viola and he said it's a triumph.'

'Gosh,' I said, in a voice that sounded suddenly like Mum's. 'It must have been very expensive.'

'It was,' said Valda, who was looking pointedly at me. More silence.

'Yes, it was,' piped Mary-Lou. 'Dad said I'm not ever allowed to touch it because of all the money. Aren't you allowed to touch it either, Mummy?'

No, I thought. *No, I'm not.* But I smiled and said, 'Yes, I think I'm allowed to touch it, darling. But at the moment I just want to look at it. It's so beautiful. Thank you, everyone.' I did a stupid little show of blowing kisses.

'The bow is Pernambuco – the best wood for bows,' said Raffy. 'And Mongolian horsehair. Henry found it.'

'Oh, so you're all in on this, then?' I said with solarium brightness.

Another silence, then Mum spoke. 'Well, plenty of time for you and Susannah Viola to get to know one another. I'm sure it's something you want to do alone. Let's have another drink, shall we?' She held up her empty glass. Mum hardly drinks any more so this was a bad sign. *Come on, Susannah. Lift your heavy spirits.*

But Valda, who'd been watching me closely, said, 'The viola plays the inner voice of the strings section. I, for one, would like to hear what your inner voice has to say. Or else I'll go back to my television.'

I made an unattractive nasal laugh noise and said, 'Oh, no one wants to hear my inner voice, do they?'

'I do,' said Hugh. But I crumpled up the silver paper and took it into the kitchen, calling, 'Who wants more bickies and dip?'

Later, when everyone had gone and the children were in bed, Ria, Hugh and I were cleaning up and I said, 'Thank you. I know how much effort you put into that gift. And the expense! It's too much.'

And Ria said, 'Fuck that, Susannah. We can see how pissed off you are. Come on, out with it. Inner voice and all.' Her eyebrows challenged me. 'Come on. Let us have it.'

'It's a very personal thing, choosing an instrument,' I suggested tentatively.

'We had your arm measurements,' said Hugh. 'Sent the specs of your old viola off. This is a better fit.'

'We know you personally,' said Ria, 'better than you know yourself, probably.'

'But you don't,' I said. 'You think you do, but you don't. You don't understand.'

'Look, Susannah,' Ria said gently. 'This terrible thing happened. It was fucked up, but it wasn't your fault. Everyone's told you that a thousand times because it's true. And it certainly wasn't the fault of a bit of shaped-up, polished wood with strings.'

My hands trembled. I looked at them. Hugh covered them with his and said, 'There's no rush, but just sit with it for a while. You without a viola just isn't right. You'll see. But in your own time.'

Ria leaned in on us and said, 'And just bear in mind that music isn't —' but I pushed through them to stand and said, 'Please stop talking. I closed this door such a long time ago. Please, please don't open it again.' And with the measured steps of someone likely to fall, I quietly went to bed.

Ria flew out the next day. Thursday. She cried again when she left, which is highly unusual. Probably because the farewell was cordial. We're never cordial. Usually she says, 'Bugger off, then,' and I say, 'See you when I'm looking at you.' This time she held me in a bear hug, put some tears on my shoulder and said, 'Love you, Helen Burns. Sorry to be so crotchety.' Which is a clever musical pun but neither of us laughed.

It's not a bad thing she's gone. Too much spruce and maple-glossed tension in the air. I've been so very sad, though, since my birthday. Heavy. This is what happens when people insist on opening the wrong door. I have a huge sense of something not done, like when you leave the supermarket with the feeling of having forgotten something for tonight's curry and arrive home without coconut milk. I hate that feeling. I've tried to phone her twice but no answer yet. I remembered to unplug her phone charger and put it in her hand bag so it can't be that . . .

MONDAY 21st AUGUST

Four things:

1) Hugh is being exceptionally kind. I think he knows how raw I am after the birthday and Ria leaving. I don't feel I deserve his kindness because I'm still feeling crabby about that viola. I can't help it. He put it on the same shelf as Eloise Driscoll.

But I don't want him to be cross either, so clearly he can't
win. No wonder he wanted to run away to the South Pole.
The ice caps are melting down there but here, the glaciers are
resolute and inching ahead.

2) No word from Ria yet.

3) I removed my cardigan from the bag that Hannah had given
   me at the concert and there was a card with it. It said:

Dear Susannah and Eloise,

   *Emily is back to normal again. Thank you for your help
that day and please remember that it was an accident. I was
very short that day. I'd had a shock. I'm sorry. We would love
to have you over for lunch soon. We don't know all that many
people here any more and it would be great to see you all.*
Love, Hannah, Charlie, Emily and Nell. X

Her writing is so neat it looks like a font. And she left her phone
number. I texted her straight away:

Dear Hannah,
Thank you for your note. We would love to see
you all, but it must be at our house. It's the least
we can do for you all, and Emily's nose.
Love, Susannah

I toyed with the idea of a 'x' but in the end left it off. I was in a brutal
kind of mood because:

4) I ate five rescue remedy lozenges and went to see the school
   principal. I just said, 'I'm sorry, but I have the name of a
   wonderful cellist friend of mine who is very happy to play

for the musical in exchange for putting something in the
newsletter about his bookshop.'

He said, 'What a shame. It would have been nice for your children
to see their mother perform. Eloise's class is doing a unit on female
role models.'

Of course they are.

Anyway, I did it, I said no. Lettercello will get a little publicity
kick and Ria can shit in an envelope and post it.

We all miss Ria, but in some ways it's nice to just be us again. I sat
next to Hugh in front of the telly once the children were (pretending
to be) tucked into bed and he put his arm around the bit of couch
that I was sitting on and said of the man presenting the show, 'What's
going on with that bloke's hair?' And it felt nice to be us again. I've
put a blanket over the viola and hopefully that'll stop any serious
talk about me. I don't want to be me; I want to be us. I thought
about thanking him again for the viola, in case I hadn't been grateful
enough. But I thought better of it.

Things can swing so easily. Best not to push.

I have taken the batteries out of the vibrator and put them in my
book light.

♩♩

Rondo ♡

MONDAY 4th SEPTEMBER

Our wedding photo fell off the wall this morning. It didn't break.
This could be a sign of strength, but what if the falling off the wall bit
was the sign? No one knocked it, and unless the house itself gave it a
pointed nudge, it just unaccountably fell. Weird. Especially because
Hugh is back in Melbourne. Some kind of hiccup on the overpass
case. There's no denying he is pleased about this development,
even though he made a play of it being a thorn in his side. I know
better. And as the original thorn, I do know. He was so buoyant this
morning he could have floated across Bass Strait.

Valda is broadcasting some sort of Baroque opera music out her
windows and I'm not in the mood. Handel?

I looked for a long time at the wedding photo and realised that
I'm horribly jealous of that bride, all flushed with love and possibility.
And I'm terrified that I'll never feel those whirligig, hammering-heart
feelings ever again. They're like touchpaper, those feelings, setting
things ablaze. A fire, by nature, does die down without fuel and
attention. It's easy to let it go out completely while you're cleaning
the oven . . . but fires need oxygen too, I suppose. Like children.
Must try not to smother.

We can't realistically be in full wedding day love all of the time,
can we? Everyone must be a little bit out of love with their spouse

on occasions. Such as when they leave a skid mark in the loo, or when they choose a continent of ice over a family . . . or when they turn out to be nothing like the brave, clever person you thought they were . . . Wait, this is not a good train of thought. I'll go back again, to our wedding day. The right feelings were there. Hugh says it's one of his most favourite memories.

Taroona, Hobart, 4th April 2003

I insisted that we have a really understated and simple wedding: no bells, whistles or drama. This was what I imagined Hugh would want. It was what I wanted myself to want. I rolled my eyes at expensive photographers and chandeliers hanging from trees and sentimental trinkets. I laughed at neurotic and demanding brides who cried over the shade of their fuchsias. I shrugged off offers of dress-hunting trips and wedding planners and videography.

I booked the church near Mum and Dad's and the golf club down the road for the reception. Convenient, not a sniff of pretension. Hugh was concerned. 'Come on, Zannah. This is your day. You need a bit of fluff and ribbon. Ask more people, get a string quartet in, hire some swans. You only get one chance.'

I laughed him off and said in a poetic fashion, 'Our love will fill the vases and adorn the archways.'

When the day arrived, I woke up early in my parents' house, looked out at the sun rising on my monumental day and pranced out into it for a solitary bridal walk. *I must be glowing,* I thought. *People will know I'm a bride.* But no one gave me a second glance, except perhaps to look askance at my expectant expression. I felt put out. By ten o'clock, with no bridesmaids ironing my silkens or putting cucumber on my eyes, I was a picture of unattractive snively-miff. I had Mum, of course, who was doing enough panicking for both of us. Poor Mum, she'd been burdened with making the golf club rooms look 'nice but not weddingy'. We'd spent the day before trying to scrub sticky bits off the carpet and secreting away dusty fake gladioli. I tried to convince her (and myself) that it was very retro chic. A dappled beige carpet, beery-scented, stained-bar-towel brand of chic. Mum's white tulips and pale-pink cabbage roses didn't stand a chance. Her tasteful pale blue suit was hanging in the bedroom next to my 'elegantly understated' (boring) dress, longing for a snowy white marquee and a garden. She made us tea and tried to stay perky when Alison turned up to check I wasn't wearing red or something equally ruinous.

I started to fantasise about the bridal party that might have been, had I not been me. Had I been Hannah, for instance, I would have had a bevy of swished-up beauties bickering over who got to sit closest to me and take my posy while I was busy beneath the attentions of everyone in the room. (Gosh, I must hurry up and invite Hannah to lunch.)

Other than Ria, I was never very good with friends. Mum used to exclaim in shrill tones how much I enjoyed my own company, which was her way of saying my social skills were shithouse (also possibly a means of assuaging her own guilt over never producing a sibling for me). The truth is, I didn't like my own company at all and had an unhealthily terrible view of myself. I blame all the brown corduroy Mum had me in early on. I had the odd friend in infant school. With the emphasis on odd. Mum used to invite children over if she felt sorry for them. Like a painfully shy girl with a built-up shoe, and a boy who had to burp to talk. Then, in Year Four, I was accepted into St Catherine's on a music scholarship and in waltzed Gloria Mirrin with her blue mascara, her wildly exciting view of the world and her music.

On the wedding day it was just after eleven when she waltzed in again, this time bearing French champagne, a camera, a pink tulle dress, *The Best of David Bowie*, and Paul the hairdresser. 'Shut up,' she threw at me before I'd had a chance to say a word. 'This day needs some tarting up. I've just been to the golf club. Dear God, what were you thinking? It's like someone's Great Aunt Bev's organised the annual frugalism conference in there. Mrs M,' she shot at my clearly relieved mother, 'I've arranged for my aunts to meet you there in half an hour to help lift the place. They're known around the traps as the Glitter Sisters. They know what they're doing. We've got four hours and thirty-five minutes before race time. Let's go.' Mum looked suddenly happy and pink, which I realised with a pang is how mothers of only-child brides should look. She got her coat immediately, along with her box of silver cutlery and a candelabra.

I looked at Ria and said, 'What a dick I am.' She just nodded, poured champagne and turned up Bowie's 'Life on Mars'.

While Mum and Ria's Glitter Sisters were flinging frippery about at the golf club like footloose wedding fairies, Ria and I laughed and danced and sang and talked and primped and preened, and I realised that even though I'm an only child, I actually do have a sister.

We were fashioning a small veil out of an old lace curtain when Mum came back all jumpy and excited and Dad came in from golf. We hopped into our finery and Paul the hairdresser took a picture of the four of us together in the good room. It's still one of my favourite pictures ever, even though I'm wearing purple eyeshadow. (It was a thing then; Ria said it brought out green eyes – she doesn't get everything right.) I must try calling her again. (Find Skype password.)

Hugh and I were married in the church by a nervy new minister in transition lenses. He shook like a leaf while his black glasses slowly faded to grey. We tried not to laugh. A friend of Ria's played Pachelbel on the flute. The congregation sang 'All Beautiful the March of Days', led by Ria, in full voice, and the minister, whose lenses had cleared and whose confidence seemed bolstered by not wanting his singing thunder stolen by the small loud woman in pink tulle. This time Hugh squeezed my hand and let out a laugh. We giggled a bit during our vows, the words of which I don't remember, but I assume they were standard and brief. We kissed and laughed a bit more and it was done. Husband and wife.

Ria hugged me violently, punched Hugh hard in the arm and said, 'It'll be one to the nose if you don't stay good to her.'

I've just looked up the standard Church of England vows. Head, body, mind, love, trust, sexual union, joyful commitment, children, good times and bad, la la la, unity, loyalty, forsake all others, faithful . . . wait – sexual union? Our minister didn't say anything about sexual union; I'm positive he didn't. He would have been too embarrassed and Hugh and I would have totally lost our senses and laughed all over the altar. I would have blushed and everyone in the church would have known that I was thinking about Hugh's penis. Anyway, those traditional vows do assume quite a lot, don't they? What if a couple don't want children? What if they can't? I didn't give our words a second thought; neither of us did, we were so busy trying not to laugh.

Perhaps the minister should have added, 'And you must accept with good grace and minimal grouchy yearnings that you cannot reasonably flirt with intent with anyone again, nor can you experience that loin-achingly amazing lustful sex that you get when you first consummate a chemically charged relationship.'

Anyway, when we arrived at the golf club for the reception, I cried. And laughed. It was the most loving, valiant and hilarious effort to polish a turd I'd ever seen. Ria said later that they'd tried the tasteful tack, but the beige brick internal walls triumphed so they went 'the fully tacky tack' and filled the room with pink carnations and gypsophila. I mean *filled*. It was like an eighties fairy garden in there. And someone had 'borrowed' a haul of white concrete swans and three swan tyres, which were also filled with flowers. Nothing was spared – golf trophies were adorned, the cake was a cloud of flowers, even the deer heads on the walls had carnations behind their ears. And by the time the entrée was served, Mum had some in her hair, which indicated considerable champagne consumption. In our state of excited hilarity, Hugh and I thought it simply (tizzily) perfect.

Now I wonder whether it seems like a bit of a joke. Me there, with my lace curtain veil and all those carried-away carnations.

Alison was horrified. 'Dear God, this is appalling. Are you getting married or putting on a comedy show?' she scoffed, looking disdainfully at the decor as though it might rear up and grubby her navy frockcoat with glitter. As it happened, she later cracked her tooth on a pink candied almond.

Hugh's speech gave the day some sincerity, thank goodness. He managed to control his mirth for long enough to stand before our guests and say really nice things that made my mother cry and even seemed to satisfy Alison (pre–almond incident). Things like:

- 'Susannah floated around university with absolutely no idea of how mesmerising she is. I was fascinated. I'd never met anyone like her.'

Goodness, did he really say that or am I just playing Chinese whispers with remembered rememberings?

- 'Later I summoned the courage to talk to her and even ask her to play her viola. She was astounding. Up until then, music meant INXS, Stealers Wheel and the Carlton footy club song. Now I actually enjoy Classic FM, which says a lot about my extraordinary wife.'

My extraordinary wife. I remember the room sort of swayed when I heard those words. Surely they weren't words for bumbling old me. But they were, and for a minute I was terrified the wobbly world would blurry away like one of those cheesy cinematic transitions. I wonder if he didn't mean extra-ordinary.

- 'I never thought I'd be the sort of person to recite poetry, but I'm an engineer and words are not my strong point, so I'm turning to someone who knows better. My friend (also introduced to me indirectly by my wife) Charlie Baudelaire, who said: "Strangeness is a necessary ingredient in beauty." In other words, Susannah, you're a weirdo but that's why I love you.'

I wonder if he reflects on those words now. I think he's changed his mind about strangeness . . .

His closet interest in poetry continued. For my third-year composition I decided to adapt a poem to viola. I only knew TS Eliot and a bit of Wordsworth so I brought home *The Oxford Book of Verse*, and Hugh and I read bits to one another in plummy voices to see which might trigger some music. Days later, even after I'd settled on 'In the Park' by Tasmanian poet Gwen Harwood (she'd recently died and I was attracted to its simplicity), he was still reading poetry to himself.

In the end he handed the book back and said, 'Baudelaire's your man, I reckon.' I looked briefly at a translation of 'Les Fleurs du Mal' but from memory there were rape and poison and daggers involved.

Hugh ended his speech by producing my viola, which he had smuggled in. 'I knew Susannah wouldn't want to speak but I thought she might play for us. And then we can all get pissed.'

I had nothing prepared but, as I was making my way self-consciously to my viola, I caught sight of myself in a mirror and was struck by the fact that I looked kind of pretty. Even my hair was being polite as it peeked out delicately from under its curtain. So I played 'The Swan' from Saint-Saën's *Carnival of the Animals*. It's not a showy piece, no drama to it, and kind of sad if you read it that way, but the sweep of feeling I had right then was that eye-stinging, heart-singing kind of joy. Coral-coloured joy. Or carnation pink. *No rush any more*, the music said, *no more ugly duckling. You can glide through life with your head held high and your gorgeous husband at your side.*

Afterwards, I was startled by tears in Hugh's eyes, and by Ria saying, 'You've never been an ugly duckling, you nincompoop.'

Of course, later they couldn't get me off the viola. I played 'Sweet Thing' by our man Van, then some hops and jigs and *vivace* pieces until Hugh reminded me I should really have a dance too, with him. Back then the instrument was like another limb. I wasn't all that balanced without it. But even when I put it back in its case and danced with Hugh, I felt perfectly balanced . . .

I used to think I'd do it all differently, our wedding day, but now, having thoroughly examined it again, I don't think I would change a thing. Even the bit when Mum did a spontaneous speech about how pyjamas must never be allowed in a marriage. The whole fluffy fuss of it, now that I have a grasp on how effortful marriage can be, was perfectly warranted.

My Husband. Must press on with my Sparkle Project, channel extraordinary vibes and try to be fascinating.

WEDNESDAY 6th SEPTEMBER

Hugh is back in the state but hasn't actually come home yet. Is marriage just a series of texts about where the children are and whether we need milk until one of you dies?

SUNDAY 10th SEPTEMBER

Valda has fallen and broken her hip. I am sitting in the hospital beside her while she sleeps. She is heavily sedated and will probably have to have surgery to pin her hipbone. One of her legs is shorter than the other and she looks very small. I cried a bit because this has been her worst fear and because she's so lovely when she's asleep. She'll think this is the end of her; I wonder if it is? Poor Valda. Thank God Raffy is in and out of her house on weekends because she wasn't wearing her alarm and she might have been lying on the floor for hours and hours.

Hugh has to go back to Melbourne on Tuesday, for goodness sake. He promises it's his last trip for a long time. He has to front up to a Women in Engineering thing with April. She's going to talk about Antarctica. Hugh's been away so much he might as well have gone expeditioning. He said he'd come and see Valda and bring some lunch in for us. I'll have to try very hard not to radiate any of my cold feelings, but cold they are. And I'm just freshly warm from my wedding-day reminisce too. Such a shame.

Finally a letter from Ria! But not the joyful correspondence I was hoping for. I'll pop it in here to illustrate what I mean ...

Dearest Helen,

Should have phoned well before now but the days are full and when I find time to call it is too late and you'll be no doubt swinging from chandeliers or rummaging in the spice drawers.

Thank you, as usual, for having me. Always a pleasure to have a break from those peaceful and opulent hotel rooms with masseuse and mink throws when I can ditch with you, your smelly dog and smellier sprogs.

I hope you're over the impost of a new viola. I knew it was a risk but, Zannah, it had to be done. I have a very great deal of money. Hugh was talking about a maker in Adelaide but you had to have the best. It is the best. Have a feel of it when you can; it might teach you things.

Your children are also The Best. You have good bones, a nice house and silky hair. You have a life that doesn't press and everyone loves you. Scaffolding. Let it support you. Eloise loves you. She's just not a showy person; that's her nature, nothing to do with deep-seated traumas. And Hugh. Hugh especially loves you. I don't think you can see the wood for the trees any more but Blind Neddy can see how much he adores you. You're just too busy rootling around in those trees for issues. STEP AWAY FROM THE FUCKING TREES.

Maybe you just need some change. A new rhythm. Remember in first year we learnt that if there's no change,

there's no rhythm, no music, only the same old beat? I don't
mean your sex life either. That's had so much change you've
sent it into dissonance. Leave it alone, for fuck's sake. But
change something in YOUR life, in YOU. Yes, you have a lot
of children but not hundreds. They don't need you to be there
every single time they sniff. Do something for you.

  You probably hate me but you know I'm not one for
mincing words. And speaking of mince, your rissoles are
awful but I'll say again, your viola playing is sublime. SUB.
LIME. No one can do what you do with that daggy old
mourn-wielding instrument. I have been hugely and patiently
respectful of your extended creative pause but, for fuck's sake,
enough is enough.

  Anyway, loved our time, sorry I spoilt the ending.
Love you.
Always and always, Your Gloria. xxxx

PS Tell Mary-Lou that turquoise is nowhere on the spring
catwalks. Tell Jimmy I met the fast bloke from Fantastic Four
and got his autograph (enclosed). Tell Raff yes and Eloise no.
Tell Hugh I bought a punching bag, my hooks are mean and
I'll always know where his nose is.

Of course I don't hate her, but she can't understand. She's a musical prodigy with the confidence of an American bulldog. And
no dependents other than a few potted cyclamen. I am feeble
and weevily and needed to bits and my hands know not the bow.
They are ruined by dishpans and covered in thwarts. And my
rissoles are NOT awful. They were just a bit burnt. Better than
underdone.

Anyway, I'm very busy being here for Valda. It's so unlike Ria to be so instructional. I mean, she's naturally bossy but this is like a letter from your teacher. I've had to read it twice. I'll read it again. Am I missing something?

Valda hasn't moved. Better check she hasn't died while I was being cross with Ria.

She is awake. I leaned right over her to see if she was breathing and for a moment I thought she wasn't. Then she suddenly opened her eyes and said, 'Boo!' and laughed her head off. That woman. She is no more demented than me. That's probably not saying much.

LATER:

April brought me in a sandwich and a coffee. Hugh was caught up with something so she offered. I barely recognised her because her hair was straight and blonde! And she was wearing a pencil skirt. 'April!' I said. 'You look lovely.'

She blushed and said, 'Thank you. Just trying to be more corporate for this presentation. It won't last. My hair will be frizzy by this time tomorrow. And when I'm in Antarctica I'll probably grow a beard.'

She's really nice. I pretended not to see her blush; I know what it's like. We're all trying to be something we're not, aren't we?

Valda is trying to live.

I have sent Ria a flower emoji in a text. And a rainbow, which is the closest thing to an aurora I could find.

TUESDAY 12th SEPTEMBER

Hugh's gone. Needless to say, we didn't have frenzied, desperate goodbye sex.

Valda has had surgery and come through it well! She's not out of bed but she's sitting up and we watched quiz shows on the telly. Her marbles are intact, it seems – she knew everything from Rasputin to Bach and women's cricket. She must be feeling better because she said, 'That bossy nurse smells like boiled cabbage, a semitone away from fart.'

She had a visitor pop in – a tiny woman who looks older than Valda, if that's possible. She walked in tentatively and said, 'Valda Kent?' and Valda did a little happy sob, held out her hands and said, 'Daphne? Ahhhh, *O fortuna velut luna statu variabilis*.' They laugh-cried and embraced. So I made my leave. I'll go back with the children after school.

O fortuna velut luna statu variabilis means 'Oh fate, as change-able as the moon'. I know it from the Orff cantata 'Carmina Burana'. Valda and Daphne must have gone to school together. I love to think of them as young girls . . . I miss Ria. And Latin. Schools are not what they used to be. All that time we had to get to know one another without computers.

To be fair, I only knew Latin when it was pertinent to music, or in the form of Ria's insults.

Anyway, I'm sitting in a café in between buying socks and knickers and having to claim health insurance and not being late for school collection. You think you only just renewed everyone's knickers when you realise your ten-year-old is wearing size seven. The odd-socks bag is fuller than anyone's sock drawer. I should ask Ria to compose a piece of music called 'Where do the odd socks go?' It would have universal appeal. Well, perhaps not in equatorial climes.

LATER:
In other news, Eloise says her tummy hurts. Has she caught something from the hospital? Please not gastro. There's never a good time for gastro.

THURSDAY 14th SEPTEMBER
ELOISE HAS HER PERIOD! Mustn't write. Must go and be a loving mother. Dear Goddy God, my little girl is becoming a woman. At thirteen????!!! I was fifteen, I think. Have I been feeding her too much chicken??? Will she stop talking to me altogether and pierce her nose? Anyway, I'm going in with hot water bottles and analgesia. I've let her stay home, mostly so I can make sure she doesn't get chased behind sheds by any boys. And to read her a story and pretend she's still my baby. Sniffity sniff.

I'm calling Ria later. She should know. Hugh's still in Melbourne but I rang him immediately. He said, 'Right . . .' but I'm sure I detected emotion in his voice. I thought he might say he'd fly home early but he didn't. Of course, putting off important work affairs because of one's daughter's first period would be ridiculous. Nevertheless, there is mild panic in the air, mostly mine. All mine. Although Mary-Lou has wide eyes and Rafferty got in the car without hurry or harry, so that's saying something about the gravity of the situation.

☆

LATER:

Ria's not answering. Left message saying, 'Alert! Alert! Godchild experiencing menarche. Send positive affirmations immediately. And some for her too. Can you believe it? Please call.'

Hugh hasn't checked in to ask how we are. You'd think he'd be more concerned. His daughter has essentially just had her childbearing faculties developed. Not to mention tummy aches, etc. And my overwhelm. Eloise has beautiful hands. They're not anything like mine, which look like pig farmer's hands. They are long and elegant and piano-playing and I can't believe that they grew inside me. That whole beautiful, lengthening person grew inside me. How can she be so grown? How can this be?

. . . I remember how she sat in her cot and I put my hands out to her and she looked at them like she'd never seen them before . . .

Meanwhile the woman-child in question is predictably unfazed. I've been at her bedside with open palms and the invitation to ask anything. She said, 'Can I go to the late movies with Rebecca next week?' and then laughed and said, 'Stop stressing, Mum. It's fine. I'm fine.'

So I laughed too and said, 'Sorry, bit flummoxed.' And she leaned into me so I could say, 'Please don't rush, darling. Childhood is the best hood of all.' She nodded. And I thought about getting her to sign a contract but decided that would be pushing it, so I got her some beef consommé instead and talked about iron. She got a bit eye-rolly but the air remained warm. No one can be too annoyed when there's a hot water bottle involved.

Valda is well. I phoned in. She has asked for her music. I'm actually missing her morning arias in the next-door distance. Might take some consommé in to her later too. Except she'll know it's from a can and deal me more attitude than a dormitory full of hormonal teens.

REALLY LATER:

I'm having a glass of wine alone because Aunt Flo has come to visit and, like many spontaneously visiting grumpy aunts, she calls for wine.

Any excuse really. Last Tuesday I had a glass because I'd switched moisturiser to a coconut oil–based one as opposed to petroleum and I decided that the reduction of chemicals absorbed through my skin deserved some extra alcohol absorbed through my stomach. And what a novelty to drink on a Tuesday. People are always saying to break the rules. Second glass.

LATER:

Need to close my eyes and sleep, but there's a niggly feeling that there's something I should write down. Also I'm hungry but I'm not sure what for. While I wait for that important something to come back to me, I have to say . . . Oh, wait. I've forgotten that too . . . wait . . .

. . . I don't know if this was the important thing but I'll say it anyway: when I say two glasses, they are big ones. Probably more like three actual standard drinks.

I've just tipped out the rest of the wine in disgust. I know how I'll feel in the morning – crappy and annoyed. I will die early. Soon I'll be swigging whisky with breakfast and using concealer on my cauliflower nose.

I just coughed. An unexpected cough with a sort of burp at the end. Quite a burp, actually. More burp than cough. A burp. I burped. Just now. I never burp.

Go to bed, Burpy Parks . . . I've got as far as removing my clothes. Where are my pyjamas?

Actually, while I'm nude and before I put pyjamas on, I should go in and seduce Hugh. Might just have some Doritos first. Oh, wait. I don't have any Doritos because some wet blankety person in this house never buys junk food. That'd be me. It'll have to be lentil chips. Yuck, lentils, those sanctimonious little twerps. I bet they cause bloat.

BACK UP THE TRUCK. How can I seduce Hugh when HE'S NOT HERE? Hahahahahahaha. What a silly old dumbo. What's on the telly? Ah, *Antiques Roadshow* . . .

LATERER:

Holy God, Jimmy just walked in all sleepy and found me sitting here fully nude, eating chips and watching *Antiques Roadshow*. I don't think he was very awake, thank God. Extra thanks because I said, 'Oh, please just go to bed. Jeez, can I get no privacy in this place?' And then when he lingered in front of the telly I added, 'Go on, off you fuck.'

Dear God, have I swung completely off my rocker? Who says 'off you fuck' to their own child?

FRIDAY 15th SEPTEMBER

Headache this morning. Deservedly so. Jimmy appears to have no recollection of the *Antiques Roadshow* incident, so that's something.

I've been extra nice to him anyway. The hangover of shame has long outlasted the headache, let me tell you. Imagine if something had happened to one of the children and I couldn't drive them to hospital?! Third-degree burns, anaphylaxis, toxic shock???

Hugh hasn't called. Can't blame him. I wouldn't call me either. And Ria still hasn't answered even though we've had a PRETTY BLOODY HUGELY IMPORTANT DAY IN ELOISE'S LIFE, might I say. She shouldn't be the one to be sulking. She's the one getting all bossy about trees ET CETERA.

Anyway, THINGS TO DO (because I seem to have been bestowed a day with nothing in it other than headachy shame):
- Do proper grocery shop (evaporated milk, Jif).
- Develop photos from phone – storage levels critical!
- Uniform order forms due tomorrow (WTF? – it's September, you morons. Just ignore the Christmas decorations in Woolies.)
- Reply to invitations – think of excuse not to go to mothers' group spring picnic (everyone else so together, successful and fit).
- Chemist – ask why skin is coming off elbows. (Will there be new elbows underneath that don't have the texture of scrotums?)
- Find Raffy's good shoe.
- Call internet people and try not to shout.
- Hide all children's devices until they tidy their rooms, especially under beds.
- Make something new, exciting and nutritious for dinner (broccoli).

- Take some of said exciting nutritious food over to V's freezer – find out when she's home and what about care?
- New lingerie before Hugh gets back? THINK ABOUT NEXT SPARKLE PLAN.
- Pluck eyebrows and scan for chin hairs.

Oh, dear. I need a little lie-down after thinking of all that. I'll never get it all done. Hugh will return to chaos. (Mum would approve, at least.) Actually, looking back over the list, Hugh will be none the wiser because it's all stuff he can't see. Even if I stretch myself fully and get it all done, there'll still be dust on the skirting boards.

There's the one thing that I would really, really like in the bedroom – for Hugh to make the bed and vacuum under it. Without my asking him. If he ever washed the sheets, I swear to god I'd have an orgasm.

LATER:

I've just discovered some old vinyl records in Mary-Lou's doll's house. She's taken out all the furniture and laid the records down in the bedrooms and covered them with little blankets. What is the meaning of this?

LATER AGAIN:

I'm not much closer to solving the record mystery. I stood Mary-Lou in front of the doll's house and said, 'Is there anything you'd like to tell me, darling?'

She looked guilty and said, 'No, thank you, Mummy.' So I had to open up the doll's house and say, 'Are you sure?'

She thought for a minute and then said, 'Shhhh. It's a very big secret.'

'What do you mean?'

'Valda asked me to creep them away (little creep re-enactment) so that no one burglars them when she's dead from a broken hip.'

'But, darling, she's not going to die just yet. And now you're the burglar.'

'No, I'm the hero. I'm going to make sure they go to the world.'

'What do you mean?'

'I can't tell you any more, please, Mummy. I was meant to be the hero. You can't tell Valda you found them.' And her eyes welled up with tears, so I didn't press.

I didn't know what to do so I left the records in the doll's house until I can talk to Hugh. He always has a sensible perspective. The records are in paper covers, no labels. In the tiny bathroom I also found the sticky tape, a box of bandaids and the spare key to the car. Hmmm.

Hugh still hasn't called, so I sent him a text message that said, 'Are you dead?' He replied with a smiley emoji, which surprised me because I didn't think he was an emoji sort of person.

I've also texted Ria: *I got pissed on a Tuesday and today I skipped assembly. CHANGING RHYTHMS and all!* because maybe she's waiting for an acknowledgement of her letter. No response yet despite further messages from me – four tulip emojis and one cheeky ghost.

SATURDAY 16th SEPTEMBER

I've had a very strange phone call from Mum. She called from golf, which she never does. Then she didn't seem to have anything to say.

She wanted to talk to Hugh, said she'd tried his number but it goes straight to voicemail. I explained that he's not home until tomorrow and she sounded quite agitated. 'Anything wrong, Mum?' I asked.

'No, darling. Just got a birdy on the sixth, actually. Waiting for the other slowpokes so I thought I'd phone in and send love. Lovely day. Are you busy? Good to be busy.'

Then she went on about her gardenias, said goodbye and hung up. I smell a fishy fish. Her voice sounded like she had something caught in her throat. Perhaps she's feeling bad about the birthday viola and is scheming with Hugh to send me to one of those health retreats where no one's allowed to speak to you for two days and you eat spiralised zucchini and come out transformed, patient and moderate.

Still no reply from Ria. She's extending the silence for full instructional impact. Or perhaps she's coming to the health retreat too. Perhaps she's waiting for me there.

THURSDAY 21st SEPTEMBER

Without you, I'm just a sad song,
I'm just a sad song.
My notes are loud and startling,
As they carry across the water of my tears.

I wonder whether it's possible to cry every bit of water out of your body so that you shrivel up and fall to bits and blow away in the wind?

MONDAY 25th SEPTEMBER
Perhaps she's waiting for me there.

I can't find her here. There don't seem to be any trees to search in. Can't even see the trees. What happens when you can't see the wood *or* the trees, Ria? When you can't see for tears. What happens then? What happens to the music when you can't hear it? Can you answer me, Ria? I had so many more questions for you.

Should I have asked? Should I have known?

And, Ria, I thought . . .

Perhaps she's waiting for me there.

But you'd already gone.

Everybody was somewhere, flapping about, trying to work out how to tell me before some news headline screamed it at me. And no one wanted me to be by myself at the end of a phone line. Alone with the children and such a horrible big bombshell. Ria's brother Mac tried Hugh, then phoned Mum; Mum tried Hugh, then phoned Dad as she sobbed her way home from Richmond Golf Course. Dad made it in time. Poor Dad, not his brightest moment, not his scene. He hates a tear. And his Saturdays while Mum's at golf are his sacred and peaceful pottering days. How to spoil a peaceful pottering day.

I was still trying to work through my to-do list and had happily let the children go off to the park with Josh and Isobel. I was up to making something with broccoli, which was bolognaise with hidden broccoli. *Remember, we used to make it with cinnamon and chilli and we'd strain the tomatoes?*

'Zannah, love, I'm sorry. I have some terrible news,' Dad said, when he found me at the stove.

'Oh, no. It's Valda, isn't it? Poor Valda.' My voice wobbled because to my surprise I felt very, very sad. 'I was just about to take her some bolognaise with broccoli. That would have done her good.'

And Dad said, very gently, with a hand on my arm, 'No, Zannah. It's not Valda. It's Ria. They're saying she killed herself.'

And there must have been some sort of creature in my chest because it punched me in the throat and doubled me over and sent up an ugly, ancient wail. And started the tears that won't seem to stop.

But, Ria, there were still roses and ocean and birds and sparkling wine and days. Still days: some of them not yours to take.

Lament

I'm sitting in the car outside the supermarket. I've just done the groceries. People, I suppose, have been doing their groceries these last weeks as per normal. Which seems so very wrong. Life goes on even when it doesn't. The days have piled up in the wash basket, sent up the weeds and eaten all the food in the pantry. These wet and grainy days of tears and sigh. There wasn't even a wobbly bean in the bottom of the crisper drawer.

What does Ria think about it all? I have her note here, folded up inside my Sparkle Pages, which are now struck-through with pointlessness.

I've read the note only once, when it arrived in the post a few days after I'd been told of her death. Like a missive from beyond. And now, outside the supermarket, while people are keeping on and ordinary things are doing their ordinary thing, I'll read it again.

Dear Susannah,

I have Motor Neurone Disease. Look it up if you don't know it. It might as well be called Major Nightmare Disease. I couldn't tell you because you would have tried

*making everything all right. And I might have believed
that you could, just long enough to lose all control. No one
needs me lingering around and dribbling on things. Least
of all me. I can't watch my hands fumble the piano keys,
Zannah, and they've started already. It's only the second
secret I've ever kept from you, I promise. I know you
understand. I know you'll be sad and do that crying face but
just remember it's really fucking ugly. Talk about me and
don't forget me but then get on. And don't be sad for me.
I've done everything I ever wanted to do. I'm only afraid of
living now.*

*I'll haunt you somehow, my dearest friend. I'll watch and
I'll know and don't forget that everyone's still waiting for that
key change.*
*Always and always and ALWAYS, Your RIA. Xxx (INSERT
CHEEKY LITTLE GHOST EMOJI HERE)*

Outside, the people are still doing their people things. I'm doing my ugly crying face. There's a chance the wind changed a while back because this is how I seem to look now. My family has started to look away.

Is Ria here somewhere? It's quite a still day but in the top of a nearby tree I can see a breeze. Is that something? Who said something about the wind and goodbye? When does the haunting happen, Ria? Are you watching now? And who'd have thought I had so many tears? I can't see the memories either. They are clouded with the strange fact that you're gone. But you were just here. You were just here. And you always said always.

☆

Oh, but Eloise has camp coming up so I have to think about dehydrated food and where the sleeping mat is. The crying might stop if I just don't think. Eloise hasn't cried.

What's Ria's first secret?

THURSDAY 12th OCTOBER

On the goodbye wind came a cold, cold sigh. And it put out your fire.

This isn't something I remember knowing. I suppose, when things get broken, bits and pieces can make their way back in through the cracks.

DON'T THINK.

SATURDAY 14th OCTOBER

Mary-Lou and I are sorting out her wardrobe. School holidays. She has four stripy blue T-shirts and no shorts that fit. I will have to get her some shorts. The weather is warming up.

WEDNESDAY 18th OCTOBER

Pine bark has arrived. Valda has been moved to the rehab ward. April has gone to Antarctica. She sent Hugh a photo of bioluminescence.

THURSDAY 19th OCTOBER

Today while I was busying myself in Valda's room, she said, 'Unspent sorrow will sour, curdle and clog up the sink. Eventually things will burst.' She patted the chair next to her, then thumped it and said crossly, 'You will go pop.' I sat. 'Think about her,' she said. 'Thinking has never been a trouble for you in the past.'

And we sat in absolute silence but for the tick of the clock. At first I thought, *Well, this is ridiculous. I could be doing parent help.* Then I went a bit blank and listened to the sound of Valda breathing. She was staring straight ahead and, after a minute, closed her eyes. I closed mine too. And found myself drawn to the dark, icy pond inside my head. I dipped a toe in. It hurt. The tears threatened. (How can there be any left?) I recoiled, and Valda put her hand on mine. Firmly, as if to make sure I didn't sink.

There is music. Humming? There we are, Ria and me. We might be thirteen. I'm in a green cotton dress. We're standing on the lawn of a beautiful sandstone house with pretty laced verandahs. It must be one of the families that Ria's mum Netty worked for. She'd sometimes take one of us with her if there were big gatherings. There are huge rolls of hay dotted about the paddock beside and lots of people around. A garden party? Christmas? There's something sticky about the memory – icy poles or fizzy cordial. Probably something Netty had bribed us with to stay out of trouble. We are standing together, avoiding the gaze of people, leaning in on one another, like Siamese twins joined by shyness. Someone is trying to get us to play a game. There are roses and punch and laughter and a string quartet. The violist has a perfect blonde, flicky-out ponytail, a silver bangle and a humble, kind smile, which she sends to me. I smile back and imagine myself with a viola and a ponytail. The brothers call us sissies or something. We hide behind a nearby tree so we can listen to the music without being bothered. There, we whisper and laugh and listen to the happy chatter of birds. They might be saying that everything is all right. We pretend that the house with the laced verandah is ours, that we are sisters and the viola player is our governess. We decide that we will stay there forever and ever, always and always. The humming is louder now, a song, sung by a shimmering soprano that sounds like water.

And I opened my eyes then, because the sound of that singing was so close and so real. And it was real. Valda was singing. I don't know what it was she was singing but it was so, so beautiful. '*Why mourn,*' she sang, '*since death presents us peace, and in the grave our sorrows cease?*'

I didn't feel the tears but they were all over the place and it was searingly wonderful to have shed them for something other than sadness. Valda. Valda, the soprano: the keeper of that silken, searching voice – a voice I'd heard so often wafting and dancing from her windows in the mornings. She was still sitting beside me but her gaze was on something far, far away. When the song reached an end she blinked, sniffed a little sniff and took a sip of tea.

'Valda,' I breathed. 'You sing.'

'I do.'

'Opera.'

'Yes.'

'You didn't tell me.'

'You didn't ask. People never ask for the stories of the wizened and wise.'

'I've heard you, from the window in the mornings. I thought you were a recording.'

'Ah, I have been enjoying those showtunes. They're very common but easier for my old vocal folds.'

'What was that you just sang?'

'It's an elegy, set to music. It always brought me comfort.'

'Did you sing on the stage, Valda?'

She sighed. 'Yes. Sometimes. But not since Neville . . .' She looked at something very far away.

A nurse came in then, all bustle and boss, and said, 'Time for your walk, Mrs Bywaters.'

'It's Kent,' Valda snapped. 'Valda Kent. And I've been all the way around the lake, thank you all the same.'

I kissed Valda on the cheek and left them bickering. But to think that Valda can sing like that!! I suppose she sings now to bring Neville back. I don't remember her singing while he was alive. Did she perform onstage until he died? That's not so long ago. Must ask her next time.

I'm grateful for that old memory of Ria and the birds. Memories can polarise even as they go through the washes of time and fade. Then you can pop them out to brighten up grubby greys and ponds of sable sadness. They can stir up trouble, though. It's properly dark outside now and I'm wandering, wondering, as my mind does at this hour. Why, if under the tree with the birds Ria can whisper secrets, couldn't she tell me this one? No one was with her when she was diagnosed, nor afterwards in what must have been a quicksand of despair. She didn't tell her brothers, her work people or me. I can't bear the thought of her alone with that horrible heavy secret. Can't bear.

Ria's brothers weren't surprised that she hadn't confided in them, but they couldn't believe I didn't know. I should have known. Damn it, Ria, I should have known. They cried for you, those big noisy boys. All three of them. Imagine! Mac, with those shades on, his teasing mouth all upended. Trent and Bax, who'd brought their little tiny sister home for a Tasmanian funeral, as you'd wished. They had the enormity of you etched into the lines of their faces. Did you see? Were you there, laughing and calling them sooks? I'm sorry I didn't play at your funeral. Even Hugh tiptoed the idea up; he said everyone would expect it. Henry played the cello, though. He was amazing and he had tears all the way down to his fancy shoes, bringing everyone undone. He played the requiem from your *Charlotte's Web* adaptation. Oh and oh! I know you'll be cross it wasn't me. But I can't stop these tears. And my heart is broken, Ria, and you know where that takes the music. The viola would have been strung with my heartstrings and the bow laced with icicles. The instrument might have screamed, or been weakened to some sort of prickly *glissando* harmonics. No one wants their funeral music to be violent. Frederick Federici died from a heart attack just after singing a final note of morbid old Faust.

She said that this MND is the second secret she's kept from me. What is the first? Perhaps she's coming back to tell me. Tears. Stop thinking.

Raffy says he knew Valda could sing like that! Should I talk to my children more?

SATURDAY 21st OCTOBER

We got presents from Ria today. A posthumous present. (You are really creepy, Ria. I suppose you left instructions for Joseph. For goodness sake. How many personal assistants have to undertake posthumous duties?) She organised her ashes to be swished through five glass paperweights, for distribution between her brothers, Hugh and me. Mine has delicate sweeps of white and a blue the colour of her eyes. (Is that particular blue the colour of grief?) Hugh's has yellow. They're horribly kitsch. Ria must have laughed when she was planning those. I wish I could have been there for that. I should have been there.

Hugh studied his for ages, as if something might glimmer and wink at him from the greyish grains that are all that's left of the physical Ria. My dearest cheerful, unflappable Hugh. This has flapped him. Today he cleaned the loos, without being asked. That's how flapped he is. He said, 'Do we have any rags?' And I replied, 'No. Just use the toilet brush.' And he said, 'The what?'(!!!) Has he never noticed the brushes beside toilets the world over?

I think he's cleaning the loos because it might surprise me enough to stop my crying, which must by now be irritating him terribly. Why can't I be one of those people who can't cry no matter how much they immerse themselves in memories? I've had to put a virtual sphincter on my memory valve, but it's very leaky.

Hugh got on the next flight home the minute he heard about Ria. I almost envy the flurry of activity he would have had to enter once Mum had reached him and broken the news. By the time he got home I was in a sort of petrified state where everything on my to-do list seemed ridiculous. And where the things on my should-have-done list were horribly not done. Like stopping Ria from injecting herself with her neighbour's insulin. I'm not wording this well. I'll put it into Hugh's words:

'When I got home there was an easel set up in the kitchen but no paints, some vegetables chopped, your mother re-ironing my shirts, the children not watching telly and you in the bath. But the most disturbing thing was that there was no music. That made me cry.'

Our stereo is usually on constant shuffle, sometimes with the volume so low it's like a subconscious murmur. I don't remember turning off the music.

He came, with his tears, into the bathroom and found me sitting in the bath with my chin on my knees. I was trying to think about honey and how bees love capeweed and capeweed honey is apparently delicious and that's good because even pesty old capeweed is good for something. And all the while, my stubborn tears flowed into the water. I glanced up at Hugh but his face was so sad that he looked like someone else and I had to turn away and think about potato salad and whether it should have bacon.

'Susannah,' he said, in a shaken whisper that reminded me about Ria not being just mine. I stood up all dripping and put my arms around him. And he stepped into the bath in his unironed suit and sat down with me in my tears. Then we looked at each other and laughed a little bit. Then we didn't and Hugh said, 'Ria would be laughing,' so we laughed again. And once we'd gone quiet and thinky and the water had cooled off, he said, 'Some people are probably too good for this world, Zannah.' Which is the most spiritual thing he's ever said and hints that perhaps he has listened to my years of intangible tangents.

When we came out of the bathroom and Hugh went to the laundry to shed his dripping suit, Mum said, 'The meatballs are on and Jimmy's done a picture of a tree stump.' And we all had a brandy.

Later that night, in bed, Hugh held me in his arms until I went to sleep in them. It's the first time in a very long time that we haven't had a lying-down cuddle and then had to move apart because someone couldn't breathe or someone had bad breath or a numb foot. Or an erection. He just wrapped my body in his bandage limbs, pulled together displaced things and breathed newly spun love into the echoey space within.

We haven't made love like that in such a long time.

MONDAY 23rd OCTOBER

It was the first day back at school today, only it wasn't. We arrived at the school gates to find them closed. School goes back tomorrow because today is a student-free day. Both schools. I phoned Eloise, who I'd put on the bus, and she said, 'School's not on today, is it?' And I said, 'No.' And she wasn't cross, which made me cry again.

Eloise didn't cry at Ria's funeral, of course. Everyone else did. We sat up the front of the cathedral and Mary-Lou gazed up at the brass angel-shaped lectern and whispered, 'Is Ria here, Mum?'

'She's in there,' whispered Jimmy, nodding at the coffin, his eyes huge.

Mac, Trent and Bax had insisted on the coffin being there. 'People might not believe us otherwise,' Trent said. I didn't like it. Ria wouldn't like it. I couldn't sit in that crowded cathedral and not picture her in that box, with all those disruptions in her neurotransmitters now sleeping, their job done. And the flowers on top were all wrong. Too much. But her brothers had brought her all the way home so I understand, I suppose . . . I hope she thought to pop her cyclamen in a sink of water before she went.

Neither did Eloise cry when I told her Ria had died. Dad had to fetch the children back from the park and he brought them all in, breathless and waiting to hear why they'd been summoned home. Mary-Lou said, 'I can beat Pa at running and he said we can have blackcurrant cordial.' So Mum got them blackcurrant cordial, extra sweet, while Dad hid in the living room. Raffy stared hard at my puffed, smudged face so I said, 'Ria died, darlings. She died yesterday, I'm so very sorry to say.'

Rafferty wailed an infant cry that fractured the pieces of my heart and sent splinters into my throat. Beside him, Mary-Lou shrieked in fright and Dad came back in to take her. Mum took Raffy in her arms and Jimmy pushed his face into the small of my back.

'How did she die, Mummy?' Jimmy asked, tears spilling from his eyes.

'She was very, very sick,' I said. 'Only we didn't know.'

And Eloise? Eloise stood absolutely and completely still. Then she vomited blackcurrant into the sink, washed the sink and loaded up the dishwasher . . .

So we're all back home again. A bonus holiday day. We might sort out the pantry. Hugh is at work. Spring has turned cold and windy and blown a lot of blossom away.

WEDNESDAY 1st NOVEMBER

This morning Raffy gave Eloise a (sharper than friendly) pinch and a punch for the first day of the month and set off a full-blown war. So I screamed at them. Screeched and screamed and screeched again. In front of Hugh.

I even got the wooden spoon out and told them to pull down their pants so I could spank them. Raffy cowered but Jim screwed up his eyes and bravely bared his bottom. I threw down the spoon and cried and stomped away and did a lot of picking up random mess and thumping about like a grumpy hair-shirted martyr who has mercifully spared bottoms and is not about to spare stray Lego bits or worn-down pencils.

Hugh pulled a 'settle-down' face and sent it my way like a slingshot. It stung. I screeched at him too. 'Maybe you could turn off the telly and support me by being the bad person for once. You're always the goddamn goodie.' His settle-down face turned surprised and then thunderous. He turned up the telly. I turned it off and faced him.

He looked at me. 'Do you want an argument?'

'No. I want someone to pick up their own SHIT for once, and maybe do the dishes or offer to take me away somewhere or drive me to a lake with a clinker rowboat on it.'

He rolled his eyes.

'And don't ROLL YOUR UNROMANTIC EYES AT ME!'

'You do want an argument, so come on, let's do this. Tell me what your problem is.' His exasperated hands were palms-up in front of him. I felt the world tilt.

'I don't have a problem, you have a problem,' I said, and started to stomp away because I could feel myself sliding, along with any hope for rational and measured responses.

'Okay. Well, what's my problem, Zannah?'

'Exactly. What is your problem?'

'Don't walk away. You started this.'

'I did not. You started it with your eye-rolly, settle-down face.'

'What?'

'Want me to get a mirror? You should see yourself. You look like Jimmy when he spent all his money on that remote-control car and then realised it wasn't the one he wanted. Terrible shame when you get a Mazda but you could have had a Maserati.'

'That's it. I can't talk to you,' Hugh said. 'You can walk away now. No. Actually, I'm walking away.' He got up.

'No! I'm walking away. You stay and gaze at your precious telly that you're in love with.'

I'm not good with words when I'm angry.

The only thing I could do, amid the prickling shame, was hitch up the tatters of my pride and stomp off on my warpath, picking up mess along the way. If nothing else, temper tantrums can be very productive. Although I think I threw away Jimmy's maths improvement certificate.

When my stomping took me into the laundry, the washing machine said *shoosh shoosh shoosh* and made me lie down on the floor to rest my racing, roaring heart. There I realised how terribly tired I was, and that perhaps those cool slate tiles with a pillow of odd socks would be a good place to stay, possibly forever. I wondered from the middle distance whether that moment might mark the proper start of the unravelling.

I seem to have been unravelling for years. It's a wonder there's any ravel left. Must almost be down to the hard, blank spool.

Then the washing machine reached the end of its cycle and there was quiet, with no music. And I thought about how I'm another year older and that 'I, Susannah Parks, have lost the spark in my marriage. And I need to find it.' And I lay there for a little bit longer before getting up and going to find my Martha Wainwright CD so I could play 'Bloody Mother Fucking Asshole' and dance to a different beat.

And then Hugh announced that he was taking the children to Bouncy World so that I could have some breathing space and I stopped feeling sorry and thought, *Great. Mr Goodie is also Mr Fun.* And they left. Now I've done ironing and sighing a lot, as well as the usual tears, because God forbid I use my breathing space to just breathe.

If it were me who had died, Ria would never do all this crying. 'Don't blubber,' she'd say when I got a bit shiny in the eyes over something.

'I'm not,' I'd say with a sniff.

'Bullshit. I can read you like a sook.'

When her mum died she cried once, then taught herself to bake. She made a spectacular vanilla and custard cake called a tractor cake. It was big enough to feed everyone, including my family and all her ravenous brothers. For three years she baked everything from cake and caramel slice to lemon delicious and cream puffs. Then one day when I rattled her cake tins and found them empty, she said, 'No more baking.' After that, she composed her first award-winning piece of music, a sorrowful sonata for flute and viola that won us first place and fifty dollars at the Hobart Eisteddfods. I wanted to spend it on lunch at Sizzler but she used it to buy a microphone. We rigged it up to the Christmas tree base and drove our families mad with silly, teasing jigs and impromptus. 'She drove us so mad we started calling her Mozzie,' Bax said during his eulogy, 'but I'd do anything to hear her playing piano in the next room again. Anything.' They did call her Mozzie, or Mozz, but just as often they'd call her Glory. She variously called them cockshiners, douche-nozzles, negatons and smells. Glorious little Gloria Mirrin, biting everyone's heads off, touching them up and putting them back on more squarely.

Perhaps I'll go and ~~write a sonata~~ make a tractor cake.

☆

PS Ria loved Martha Wainwright. She gave me that CD. I love how Martha's music seems to be full of secrets. Listening to it is like wandering through attics. All our attics are full of secrets, I suppose.

SATURDAY 4th NOVEMBER

Today we had Jimmy's birthday party. It was not my most triumphant mothering moment. Jimmy wanted to invite his whole class to come along to the cinema complex, kill one another with laser guns and eat hot dogs, sweets and cake. I said yes. Then I paid an extortionate amount of money to watch Jimmy shoot everyone (including his siblings, his father and me), claim the prize, brag about his new 240-dollar sneakers (I said yes to those too) and not thank Mary-Lou for her present (a finger-knitted wristband in his footy colours with a card that said *I am very glad your not ded*).

He did thank his friends for their gifts, so that's something, but as I watched him swagger about, I found myself worrying that at this rate he could turn into ~~a complete cockhead~~ a slightly arrogant teen. Hugh must have been thinking the same thing because he said, 'That boy's going to need a face full of acne before he trips over his ego.'

Yes, a little puncture to the self-esteem wouldn't go astray. Nothing too scarring – perhaps not acne – just an unfortunate trouser split or something. A little tumble down a peg or two. Giving him exactly what he wants is not going to help. I even paid extra to have the birthday cake supplied, so he wasn't even subjected to the usual humbling experience of my cake decorating. (Once Eloise got a Dolly Varden with a chocolate–zucchini cake skirt. I was trying to sneak in some nutrients. The zucchini possibly wasn't grated finely enough.)

☆

Anyway, between laser traumas, parental shames and a few too many Smarties, I find myself back in the wardrobe. Should I put some work into the Sparkle Project? It's November already. Jimmy is eight. 'Tick tock, motherfuckers,' Ria would say, if she wasn't so gone. Perhaps I should delve back into Hugh's and my archives again. It seems pertinent to record the parenting bit of our history, anyway. The bit where the happy couple have done the sunset thing and awake to find the sun has of course risen again, and there is a terrible lot to do.

Hobart, 2003–2004

Our busy careers whipped up again soon after our wedding (we had a three-day honeymoon in a beautiful Swansea guesthouse where the pipes resonated a rich baritone throughout the night and the seaweed brought a nasty smell in on the morning breeze). S Mackay became S Parks (eventually; there were a lot of forms to fill in) but everything else stayed much the same. We still worked hard and played hard and let our sundries pile up in the spare room. I still talked to Ria most days about Life off the Island, still dreamed intermittently about flying away.

Then I got pregnant. It was planned. Ish. I just went off the pill and put it out of my mind. 'It'll happen if it's meant to, then we'll cross that bridge,' I said, like a twit. No one tells you that the baby bridge is like something constructed by Dr Seuss. Even Hugh, my structural engineer, didn't anticipate such willy-nilly-ness; his coping strategy included patting my head and taking on extra work. From the moment of conception my body did an abrupt about-turn; I was nauseous most of the time. The thought of coffee made me ill, I couldn't look at salad, everything about me became feeble – my voice, my gait, my work. My fingers swelled up, my head felt heavy on the chin rest and in the orchestra I moved from first to second viola.

In my spare time I ruthlessly threw everything away from the spare room (including Caroline Smedley-Warren, the poor love; she looked disapproving but resigned) and worried about whether fresh paint could hurt tiny lungs. I rearranged the kitchen so that for years Hugh would open the plate cupboard and find the cups. Barky wouldn't leave my side because he thought I was packing up to go away, when in reality I'd stopped daydreaming about packing up and going away; instead I was thinking about nesting and putting down roots and how to stay. Also about breast pumps, prams and whether Vegemite was a legitimate form of vitamin B.

And still I was telling everyone that there was no way I would be changed by motherhood. Mum looked worried and Alison sniggered. Because of course I was utterly and irreversibly changed forever.

I went into labour two weeks before my due date, while shopping at Baby World. Mum had offered to buy us a pram and instructed me to meet her there. She was late. Late enough for me to feel a bit woozy among the nursery linens. All the shelves filled with shoulds loomed over me. You *should* have a car seat with luxury velveteen, you *should* hang black-and-white mobiles above the cot, you *should* dress your baby in stripes, *should, should, should*. My palms felt damp. I tried to distract myself by using a meditation technique recommended by the scary prenatal nurse (scary not because she was fierce or bossy but because she sometimes wore fairy wings and barely spoke over a whisper). The idea was to visualise flowers opening. I closed my eyes and had managed to open three daisies and a violet when Mum's voice, very close and unnaturally quiet (much like the nurse), said, 'Boo.' I did a small scream, a large jump and a little bit of wee.

'Oh, darling, I'm sorry,' said Mum. 'I was trying not to scare you.'

'But you said boo!'

'Just a tiny little boo, to alert you to my presence.'

'I've done wees on the carpet,' I hissed.

'Don't panic. I'll say it was me. Or we could just . . .' She glanced furtively about, took a bib from a nearby rack, popped it over the wee and stood on it. After a moment she picked up the bib. The wet spots were gone. 'Golly, they're very absorbent bibs. You should get some. Not this one, though.' She put the damp bib back on the rack.

'Mum!' I clutched at her arm.

'Oh, don't be such a square, Susannah. They've had worse than that in Baby World, I'd imagine.'

'Mum,' I said again, looking at another small dribble at my feet. 'I don't think it's wee.'

And that's how Mum frightened Eloise into the world, then told everyone forevermore about her granddaughter, the baby very nearly born at Baby World. (It wasn't 'very nearly' at all. Eloise was born via normal delivery eleven hours later. She didn't appear the slightest bit startled. I was, though. Very.)

That was Boxing Day 2004, the same day that 230 000 people were killed by a tsunami in the Indian Ocean. And that was the day, once I got over my outrage at what women and their vaginas are subjected to in childbirth, I was walloped by a love so intense that it swept me up and took my breath and sent things clattering down around me. Is motherhood a natural disaster?

MONDAY 6th NOVEMBER

I got a message from Hannah. On my phone yesterday afternoon. She said how sad she was to hear about Ria and wondered whether she could pay us a visit. Oh, God.

What I don't want is someone crying on my shoulders. Lord knows I do enough of that. Also house chaos and terrible yellow bathroom. I bet Hannah doesn't have piles of crap on the end of her kitchen bench.

Hugh thinks it's a great idea. 'Didn't we say we'd invite them over for lunch anyway?' We did. This means finding all the parts of me and putting them back together. At least temporarily. And food preparation. I'll work up to calling her back.

Hugh bought me a bag of Clinkers. Remember those? Sort of like chocolate-covered chalk? For a minute I looked confused but then he said, 'Just until I can get you to a lake,' and I remembered about the dinghy thing. I suppose it's his way of smoothing things over again. I should make a smoothing gesture too, but that would probably lead to sex and, frankly, I'm not in the mood. And I'm all distracted about Hannah and lunch. So I just looked pleased with the Clinkers, leaned into Hugh and said, 'Thank you.' That'll do.

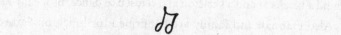

Modulation ♡

WEDNESDAY 8th NOVEMBER

Halloween-themed disco at school. I didn't know about it until last night (Jimmy said he gave me the letter but I don't remember) so they had to go as ghosts. Then two of the sheets I'd grabbed turned out to be fitted ones. So there was a fight over the flat sheet, which ended in Raffy and Jim having to be puffy ghosts, as if they were wearing those bubble skirts from the eighties. Or jellyfish. Also there was a slight stain on Raffy's back. For God's sake, Susannah. It's one thing to embarrass yourself but it's quite another to humiliate your children. Jimmy hid behind a black cat and a skeleton and refused to dance. Broke my heart.

Also Hannah and family are confirmed for lunch on Saturday. I will be calm, make a simple but classy meal and wear a classic shirt dress. None of Hannah's children would ever be sent to a school disco dressed as a puffy, wee-stained ghost.

God, I hope it wasn't a sex stain.

FRIDAY 10th NOVEMBER

Can't write because no time. It's almost midnight and I've just finished straining the ~~sourcrout~~ ~~seurcraut~~ ~~sourkruat~~ dammit, pickled cabbage. Honestly. I should get a job so I can buy in food. But then I'd worry about additives.

SUNDAY 12th NOVEMBER

Where to begin about yesterday? From the beginning, I suppose.

The de Montagus arrived exactly on time. Hannah's husband, Charlie, is not the mannered gentleman I imagined. He's a proper pommy larrikin, extremely tall, with a round face that's flushed with good nature. And he shouts everything. 'CAN I USE YOUR LAV, PLEASE?' he said shortly after arriving. The children slunk about, looking at our guests with bewildered expressions until he made them all tell him their names and swiftly gave them new ones. 'RIGHT, WHO HAVE WE HERE? ELOISIANA, JIMMY SWAGGART, RAFFERTY RULES AND MARY-WHERE'S-THE-LOO. VERY PLEASED TO MEET YOU. THESE ARE MY CHILDREN, WALLY-WIZZER AND THNEE.'

Gazelle Emily and her smaller sister Gazelle Nell rolled their eyes but laughed. We all laughed. Mary-Lou dutifully showed him to the LAV. Everyone else tried saying 'Thnee'.

His shirt was crisp and clean and cut beautifully, the only hint of gentility about him. I wanted to hug him for so expertly putting paid to any ill-ease. 'I'm really, really sorry about your nose,' said Eloise to Emily, and Emily said, 'It's fine.'

'She met a boy because of it,' Charlie said. 'He asked her whether she'd walked into a door and if the door might need sorting out.'

'*Daaaaad!*' Emily blushed deeply until I wanted to hug her too. I have an affinity with blushers. One day I'll give Emily some green face primer. And April, she's a blusher too.

Hannah and Hugh shared a warm greeting, with hug, which I tried not to watch but then did because the act of looking away was obvious. So I looked away and then looked back, which was even more obvious. But I got to see some clear shyness on both sides, which is something I didn't think either of them were capable of.

Hannah didn't blubber on about Ria, nor did she get all awkward with my tears. She just gave me a bowl of homemade guacamole and a card saying:

> *Dear Susannah, this comes with my deepest sympathy for your loss. Ria was a rare force of nature and I know that you will be missing her terribly. I have vivid memories of your friendship, like when the two of you came to a party dressed as a horse, and when you played the footy club song at the end-of-season dinner.*
>
> *And when Ria's mum died and you made her guacamole and made sure everyone left her alone with the piano.*
>
> *Not many of us experience friendships like that. I'm so very sorry. Hannah.*

(I'd forgotten about Ria's guacamole phase. I didn't make it. I bought it from the deli, but it's kind of Hannah to say so. And I'd forgotten about us going as a horse. I was the rump.)

I didn't wear a classic shirt dress, but a spotty frock, which felt lovely until Hannah arrived in her beautifully cut, spotlessly clean jeans, T-shirt and loafers. Then I was a party-cake decoration. A gaudy bauble. How can jeans and a T-shirt be so goddamn chic? She looked like a model in an airport. Expensive but effortless.

When Hannah came into our house, she said, 'Oh, I love all your things. So much character! Sometimes I think I shouldn't be so minimalist. And I love West Hobart – those views!' Which could be construed as, 'Bloody hell, your house is cluttered, and don't feel too bad about not living in Battery Point.' But I choose to take the compliment, especially as it came across as entirely genuine. I do love a mantelpiece. (Ria's paperweights are on the mantelpiece in the sitting room. It seems wrong to put them in the study to hold down papers.)

Hannah said, 'I always wished I could be as cool as you and Ria, but I always worried too much about my appearance.'

I couldn't believe it. I said, 'No! But you had perfect hair one hundred per cent of the time. And a proper grown-up job.'

There was a very uneasy moment when I went out to the barbecue to look for the kitchen paper and Hugh and Hannah were deep in a conversation that stopped when I arrived. I flummoxed about, said, 'I love kitchen paper,' went red and scuttled away. Sauce with your awk, anyone? I can only conclude that they were either 1) talking about me, 2) talking about their sweetheart days or 3) scoffing about my vol-au-vents. (French doesn't always equal classy, apparently.) They have a history. I can't begrudge them that.

After the children had all eaten and headed outside, we were finishing off our lunch when Jimmy came running in and said, 'Mum, Raff's taken everyone to Valda's and he's being a show-off.'

'What? Is that where you all are? At Valda's?'

'Yeah.' Jimmy shifted uncomfortably. 'He's showing the stuffed owl and the photographs.'

So I bowled over next door and found that the children had indeed found the key and invited everyone into Valda's house. They were all in the living room: Jimmy and Nell poring over photographs on the floor, Eloise and Em sniffing a decanter of sherry, Raffy leaning over Valda's old record player, the owl looking disdainfully down from the mantelpiece.

'What's going on?' I yelled and everyone jumped.

Eloise dropped the crystal decanter stopper onto the carpet and said, 'Shit.' Mary-Lou gasped. Jimmy laughed, then didn't. He knows when my face means business.

'You can't just let yourselves in. Eloise, you're the oldest. You should know better.'

'Raffy said we were allowed.'

'HEY, NICE MAPS,' came a booming voice from behind me. Charlie. He saw the business in my face too. 'COME ON, NELL AND EM. OUT.'

From the record player came a crackly recording of a soprano. It faded in and swooped around the room like a divine calling, its static only enhancing its otherworldliness. We all stopped and listened. The owl might have turned its head.

'It's Valda singing,' said Raffy proudly. And he picked up a photograph off the floor and said, 'This is her as Silvia from *Ascanio in Alba* at Her Majesty's Theatre in 1943.'

I'm not sure which flabbergasted me more – his admirable Italian pronunciation or the photograph of a very young, very beautiful Valda, in full nymph regalia. There were other photographs too. Valda Kent, it seems, was quite a star. I took a long moment to marvel at the fact, then turned to the trespassing issue at hand.

'Put everything back where you found it, please.'

'YES, COME ON, YOU LOT,' said Charlie. 'WE'LL GO AND PLAY TOTEM TENNIS.'

'Boring, Dad,' sneered Em and Charlie lowered his tone to say, 'Now.' They obliged. Apparently quiet Charlie means business too.

Raffy took the record from the turntable, put it back in its sleeve and tucked it under his arm. 'Put it back, Raff,' I barked.

'But these are ours,' he protested. 'They were in the doll's house.' (Oh, thickening plots!)

Mary-Lou piped up. 'I rescued them from the burglars.'

I raised my voice (but didn't yell because Charlie). 'Put them back on top of the record player, right now. It's where they belong.'

Raffy put them back, but then gave Jimmy a shove. 'Dibber dobber. You always ruin everything.' Jimmy's fists clenched.

'Jimmy,' I said, my voice a warning. It went unheeded and, quick as a flash, Jimmy gave Raffy a neat uppercut to the belly.

'Ooof,' said Raffy, and went down to his knees, gasping for breath.

'Jimmy!' I said, genuinely shocked. Jimmy looked at me for an instant, his face as stricken as mine. Then he ran. 'Stay in your room!' I called after him.

'I'm so sorry,' I said to Charlie. 'Sorry, Nell and Em. That's not like him —'

'Ah, that sort of thing happens at our house all the time,' said Charlie. 'Doesn't it, girls? Always bashing one another senseless.'

The girls rolled their eyes at him. We collected up the sobbing Raffy and trailed home.

Hugh poured us some drinks, we nibbled on grapes and listened to Charlie tell funny stories. I told a story about Hugh taking me to see a rare Tasmanian koala in New Norfolk one April Fool's Day. We all laughed and laughed and I thought, *look at us, having a lovely lunch with friends, being hilarious and together and sparkly. No one would guess Hugh might rather be in Antarctica. And perhaps, just perhaps, he'd rather be here.* I got some marinated olives out of the fridge.

I eventually went in to check on Jimmy. He wasn't in his bedroom, nor did he come when I called him. I instructed the other children to search for him and went back to lunch. 'Tell him there's sherbet for the ice creams,' I said, having another sip of wine. I hoped it would take the children a bit of time to find Jim so they wouldn't all troop back in to bother us.

They didn't. They stayed out in the garden and played while we nibbled at cheese platters and talked. Eventually Mary-Lou came back in for drinks and I said, 'Is Jimmy all right?'

'I don't know,' she said. 'He's not with us.'

'But did you find him?'

'Nope.'

'What? Where is he, then?' I asked, getting up.

'I'll go,' said Hugh.

'I'll go too,' said Charlie, and they went outside, still deep in conversation about football.

So Hannah and I sat at the table alone and I said, 'God, sorry,' and felt brave enough to thank her properly for the Ria card. A tear escaped. I apologised. 'They get away from me, the tears.'

She rummaged in her handbag for a moment and produced a gold mascara wand. 'It's a really good waterproof one. Keep it. I have more.'

'Thank you,' I sniffed. 'That's a really nice gesture. Most people get carried away with casseroles and things but can't really look at me.'

She did look at me then, in that properly seeing way. 'You haven't changed a bit, you know, Susannah.'

'Really? Nor have you. Actually, you have. You're even more glam.'

She laughed. 'It's probably just the name.'

And then, once we established that Charlie isn't actually landed gentry or a European heir, she asked me to guess what Charlie's job actually is. I'd got through teacher, auctioneer, tour guide, stockbroker and children's entertainer when I heard Hugh reprimanding Eloise outside. 'Put down the badminton. Jimmy is missing.'

Jimmy is missing. I tried to shut down my thoughts and close the catastrophising doors before irrational things ran out, but my body wouldn't listen. It panicked.

I coordinated a shrill but strategic and thorough search of each room of the house. Not a sign of him. Hugh appeared concerned. It was becoming clear that there was no point looking in the garden any more.

'We'll check the street,' said Charlie, his sunshiny face just a little clouded.

'He'd rarely go out the gate on his own,' I said, with a ripple in my voice. Hugh shot me a glance and his concerned expression deepened.

'Let's keep calm,' he said sternly. *But he's only eight*, I thought, with my heart beating right up to my cheeks.

Rising panic: 'Jimmy! Jimmy?' I called on the street, trying not to let my voice overflow. I could hear Hugh's voice echoing mine, and from over near the Hadleys', Josh's and Isobel's voices chiming in. Charlie's booming yelled from Valda's house. 'Jimmy! JIMMY?!'

Full-blown panic: I went to the park, starting to feel convinced that someone had taken him. It happens. The whole world is captured by the horror of it when it does. They hold their children a little bit closer. I was drinking wine and wishing he wouldn't be found. Must hold them closer. *How long ago was that? A car driving fast could be long gone by now. Long gone.* Heart pummelling, eyebrows prickling with the cold sweat of fear. *This is my fault, my fault. Oh, please not this again . . .*

I stumbled on along streets and streets. I passed a group of teenagers, a woman pushing twin babies in a pram, an elderly couple. None of them had seen a little boy in a green T-shirt. The couple offered to help but by then I'd started to run. The flight bit of fight or flight, I suppose. *Duty of care, duty of care*, my feet pounded out on the pavement, and I wondered whether I was meant also to pound on doors and ask if anyone had seen my little boy.

My little boy. I had an image of a baby, sitting up in her cot, twirling the ear of her toy rabbit and staring into space. I could smell the urine warmth of the room. I ran harder.

I almost ran into a man on a corner. It was Father Graham. 'Susannah?' he said in alarm. 'Are you all right, dear?'

I tried to rein in my voice, but it got away from me and by the time I'd reached the end of, 'We can't find Jimmy,' it had billowed into a siren. My knees threatened to go; Father Graham held on to me.

'Let me help,' he said. 'Where are you searching?'

'I don't know, oh, I don't – I don't know.' I couldn't get my breath.

'Sit here a minute. You need to sit.' He led me to a low wall, under someone's maple tree, and perched me on it.

'Take a minute. There, there,' he said, sitting next to me. So I breathed. He smelled of teacake. 'Just get your head clear so we can think.' His voice was like teacake too. Soft and warm. I held his arm and tried to catch my breath, catch my thoughts.

'This,' I gasped at him, 'is very, very bad.'

He patted my hand and said, 'Have a quiet think, then we'll look. I'll say a prayer.' We sat. Above us, birds chattered. I remembered Jimmy snuggling into Ria while we listened to those birds at Collins Bonnet and I thought, *Not now, Ria, please*. Not now. But Ria's voice was in my ear anyway, clear as the river. *I think they're saying that everything's going to be all right*.

And while my thoughts were still rounding the bend, my legs took me to my feet and back into a run. 'The birds!' I called to Father Graham. 'Henry's birds!'

Poor Henry, I must have given him such a fright. I burst into the shop, all sweat and clatter and gasp. He was with a customer but stopped mid-sentence. 'Susannah?'

I wavered at the sight of him, had to fight the urge to lie down on the cool, creaky floorboards and delay any dashed hopes. 'Have you seen Jimmy?'

'Jimmy? No.' He came towards me. 'No, I haven't.'

I walked on, through the book room and out the other side to Henry's courtyard and the aviary where, in his favourite green shirt, his eyes all huge and extra beautiful, Jimmy sat. Blessedly, wonderfully sat. There, there.

I took him in my arms, held him and whispered, 'Thank you,' to the birds and then, 'Thank you,' again and aloud to Ria, along with a kiss blown to the sky. And then I hugged Henry and sobbed with relief and guilt and all the other things. Sobbed and sobbed and sobbed.

Jimmy was gone, we calculated later, for over three hours.

Henry called Hugh to collect us; he wouldn't let us walk home. I was a wreck, I suppose, curled up in Henry's overstuffed chair with Jimmy clutched to me. Henry worried the teapot beside me and Father Graham, who'd arrived a bit after me, tried to get Jim and me to eat apple slice. 'You gave your mother a terrible fright,' Father Graham said to Jimmy with a smile. 'Aren't you lucky to have someone who loves you so much? Isn't he lucky, Henry?'

'Yes,' said Henry.

'Sorry, Mum,' whispered Jimmy. He touched the spots on my dress and added, 'And I'm sorry I punched Raff. I'm completely horrible. Everyone thinks so.' I pulled his head to my shoulder and rubbed his hair. 'You're not *completely* horrible. You just lost your temper. It happens. Everyone has something at least a tiny bit horrible about them.'

'I can hear your heart,' he said. I could too, beating its scold on my breast.

'Your poor heart,' said Henry gravely.

When Hugh arrived, he surveyed the scene and said, 'Jim, you worried us, mate. Look at Mum.' They looked at me. My hands trembled. Hugh sighed and said, 'This sort of thing happens all the time.'

'It does,' said Father Graham. 'I ran away once: packed a case and went to the river. Mum knew I'd be home when I was hungry. Actually, I got bored first.'

'I should have checked where he was,' I said. 'It was hours before we noticed. What if —'

'Well, it didn't,' said Hugh firmly. 'Whatever you're going to say, it didn't happen.' He was cross now and looked suddenly very tired. 'It was all of us. We were all in charge. He's fine. Come on. Let's get you home.'

Jimmy climbed into the car and before I could get in, Hugh said, 'I told Hannah and Charlie about Eloise.'

I went cold. '*What* about Eloise?'

'About when she was a baby.'

'Oh, Hugh, no.' The tears threatened again. 'Oh, no.'

'I'm sorry. We were a bit hysterical. It must have seemed —' He paused.

'Insane?' It came out in a shriek. 'Ridiculous?'

'Unusual,' Hugh said, touching my hand. 'Disproportionate. I felt I had to explain.'

'That's our private thing,' I hissed. 'We hardly know them. God, Hugh. We haven't even told our children. Not even Eloise.' I crumpled inside. That tiny baby girl peered suspiciously at my hands.

Hugh said, 'Well, maybe we should.' He got into the car. I swallowed everything down and got in too, being careful to close the door softly. Any more jarrings might have shattered me. In the car, I reached behind me to Jimmy and squeezed his hand.

'Sorry, Mum and Dad,' he said.

'WELL, HELLO, STRANGER!' Charlie said to Jimmy when we walked back into the house. They were cleaning up. The other children were watching a film. They turned to look at Jimmy and me, fascinated.

'How were the birds, Jimbo?' asked Raffy kindly. He looked as though he'd been crying too.

'We're having a search party,' said Mary-Lou. 'You can join in, Jimmy.'

Eloise looked warily at me.

'Why don't we have a drink?' said Hugh.

Hannah got some facial wipes out of her handbag and handed them to me. 'You go and freshen up; I'll do some nibbles.' She gave me a kind smile and touched my shoulder and I stared at her. There were tears coming from her eyes too. She sniffed and said, 'I think I'm traumatised by your trauma.'

In the bathroom, I looked at my puffed face and at Hannah's waterproof mascara and felt bewildered. *Perhaps*, I thought, *one day I could try giving some of my darkles to other people. Hugh can't take on any more and they're spilling out of me everywhere.*

Is there a chance that he's actually, clinically, had enough? Have I?

God, what a miserybags I am. I must look at the day's bright sides:
- We found our missing boy.
- Henry hugged me back.
- Valda Kent!
- Hugh and Charlie definitely bonded. Over bottles and bottles of red wine. (Oh, dear.)
- The mascara is Chanel.

MONDAY 13th NOVEMBER

Still feeling a bit bruised. I'm not sobby but I'm wearing the waterproof mascara. Tears are my constants these days.

Hannah is still feeling hungover. She sent me a text that said: *Thank you for a very memorable day except that I don't remember the last bit. Feel like shit today so I see why. See you soon?* (The word 'shit' was actually an emoji poo. I love that she's not too glamorous for emoji poos. She did a question mark at the end there, which indicates she might like to see us again soon. This is a miracle.)

She and Hugh and Charlie got very drunk after the trials of the day. They are fun. I drank a bit of wine but was terrified

I might recount the whole Eloise thing in horrible hammy detail. My floodgates are already very leaky; people are sure to drown if I open them. Anyway, we should recount family secrets to family – i.e. children – before anyone else. I nearly didn't send the children to school this morning because they're so precious.

Henry phoned. He left a message saying, 'Susannah dearest, two things: one, I have a thumb drive for you of soothing country songs. Trust me, better than therapy. And two, I have a dear little edition of *Jane Eyre* you might like. Not valuable but gorgeous. It's all yours. Swing by. Kiss, kiss.' Bless him.

I wish I could talk to Ria. RIA, I WANT TO TALK ABOUT ELOISE. But I must shut up, stop thinking and do my jobs before school ends. I'm taking the children to visit Valda, and Hugh's bringing dinner into the hospital. Valda Kent!

Don't forget – prune juice, drycleaning, book Barky's grooming, thank you letter to Father Graham for prayers. Take up praying?

PS Charlie is a part-time librarian! He is also the 'lead parent', meaning stay-at-home dad, because Hannah earns a squill being a brand consultant. I wonder how she might rebrand me.

TUESDAY 14th NOVEMBER

Take it out of my hands, oh, please, just take it out of my hands. There's no good time for this, it will never fit with my plans. But it's so cold it burns my skin, just take it out of my hands ...

Who sings that song again? It doesn't matter. It's today's theme song regardless.

☆

Yesterday the children and I talked to Valda Bywaters about Valda Kent. We heard about the olden, golden days of her mother teaching her music, of her performing at the Theatre Royal and, once, Carnegie Hall! Daphne was with us too; they used to sing together. Great friends. Daphne lives in Devonport but she's here staying with her granddaughter. I listened and listened and got blissfully lost in their days. I wish Henry had been there. And Ria.

But here's what else happened: once Hugh had arrived with fish and chips for everyone, I said, 'I'll give you back your records, Valda.'

'What records?'

'The ones you gave to Mary-Lou.'

She looked surprised. 'Ah, of course that's where I put them. I do forget things. Yes, they're me. Doesn't matter what happens with them really, but at odd times I get it in my head that they might be of value.'

'Of course they have value, Valda,' Daphne tutted.

I agreed. 'Priceless. I'll get them copied and archived and they'll last forever. Do you have any recordings, Daphne?'

Daphne smiled. 'One or two. Not solo, though. Valda had the voice.'

Valda added, 'Ah, but Daphne had the beauty.'

'Yes,' said Daphne. 'Your nose was always a shame. But I'd have given anything for your whistle notes.'

'Do you still sing, Daphne?' Hugh asked.

'Ah, no. I was a smoker. Too many bouts of bronchitis. We didn't know it was bad, did we, Valda?'

'Daphne lost her range, and her gift. It was terrible.' Valda looked pointedly at me and said, 'Susannah is a gifted violist, Daphne. But she gave it up.'

I tried not to wince. Valda went on. 'She's terrible at mending, her garden's a mishmash and she makes awful egg sandwiches, but her music! Her music is something else.'

'But you haven't heard it,' I said.

'Yes, I have,' she snapped. 'Rafferty played it to me. Something you played with the TSO? Something for the Queen?' She waved her hands around in the air dismissively.

'I haven't played for the Queen,' I said.

'"Bohemian Rhapsody" by Queen?' offered Hugh. 'That was a great one.' I was shocked he'd remember. I loved that performance too. It came just as the orchestra had offered me full-time permanency, about a month before I discovered I was pregnant with Eloise. I bought a Carla Zampatti gown for that performance. My life had started to feel like one of those flying dreams.

'Whatever,' Valda said (which proves she's been spending too much time with Raff). 'It was very, very good, Daphne. But oh, well. Anyone who can walk away from that talent doesn't deserve it anyway.'

'Valda!' said Daphne. 'My word, you can scathe. I don't —'

But she was interrupted by a clear, firm voice saying, 'Oh, Valda, please will you just shut up? Just leave it alone, fucken oath.' And then I realised with surprise that the voice was mine: my voice, with extra strength. And swearing. People gasped.

Valda looked completely taken aback just for perhaps a millisecond before she said, 'My dear girl. It's not fuck-en, it's fuck-ing.'

Hugh laughed nervously. Then Daphne put a neat hand over her mouth and giggled. But that newly strung, resonant voice of mine went on: 'I had a terrible thing happen too. I didn't get sick. I'm sorry for that, Daphne, but I can't play any more because of it.'

There was silence for a moment. Daphne's hand was still covering her mouth. My hands were trembling. Jimmy, who was sitting next to me, touched my arm. Raffy's big eyes looked up at me. Mary-Lou leaned into my arm. And then Eloise said, 'Mum? What terrible thing?'

I put some shaky fingers into Mary-Lou's hair, let them play with the silky curls. I let my tears come and then I looked through them into a little nursery room in a Newtown house, a room that was just the right temperature for a baby. On the wall was a black and white frieze with the alphabet and a series of framed manuscript papers containing the original composition for the 'Starlit Sonata' – a gift from Ria. There was a cot with a bottle, some fluffy toys, blankets. And a baby. All, all alone.

I wiped my eyes and looked at Hugh. He nodded. And so I took a deep breath, the sort of breath you'd take if you haven't taken any for a long while: right up from your feet. And I spoke:

'Darling, something happened when you were a baby. After you were born, I took some time off from the orchestra, but when you were six months old I went back to work. I was travelling a bit, Dad was just getting the business started; we were busy. We hired a full-time nanny to take care of you. We were there in the mornings and home in time to give you dinner and put you to bed. I tried to be there most weekends, but I wasn't always.' I stumbled on the lump in my throat. I looked at Hugh. He gave me a tiny smile. I closed my eyes for a moment and looked at the black-blue inside of my lids in case there might be something written there that could help. There wasn't, so I opened them again.

'When you were nineteen months old, just over a year after I'd gone back to work —' I paused and swallowed. 'I came home at midday with a nasty cough that was disrupting rehearsals. I found

the dinner cooked and the washing folded. I found you in your cot.
You were awake but quiet, sitting up. You had your bunny and
your blankets. You were sodden. And the nanny wasn't there.'

There was a gasp from Raffy. I shuddered out another deep
breath. 'I went to you, I put my hands out and you . . . you just
looked at them as though they were something completely foreign.
You didn't smile. You just stared and stared at my hands, and then
you reached out and touched them with one tiny finger, as if checking
to see that they were real.' My tears starting coming then. I looked at
Hugh; he had some tears too.

'I got you out of bed. I changed you. You'd had terrible nappy
rash for a long time and it was very sore. But you didn't cry. I called
the nanny and she answered straight away. She sounded just the
same. All bright and capable. She said you were sleeping and that she
was just folding the washing. She told me to have a great afternoon. I hung up. I called your dad and he came home. We sat on the
couch with you and we waited. And four and a half hours later, she
came back.'

'Where did she go?' asked Jimmy.

'She'd been going to a second job. She'd been putting Eloise in
her cot every weekday at ten o'clock and leaving her there until half-
past five. Five days a week.'

Both Daphne's hands were over her mouth now. Folded over
one another like an X. X for wrong. I looked at Eloise. 'Everyone
said how amazingly good you were. I was so proud of our perfect
baby – she sleeps through the night, she's so quiet, she never cries.
But you never cried because no one ever came. No one ever came.'

Through my tears, I could see Eloise moving towards me: a
rippling, slender mirage, impossibly tall. She put her arms around
me and Mary-Lou and said, 'Mum, it's okay, it's okay.' And then

Raffy joined in, wriggling his arms around my legs, then Jimmy, then Hugh. Hugh cupped a hand around my head and pressed his lips to my cheek. He sniffed. I felt his tears.

WEDNESDAY 15th NOVEMBER

Sparkle notes: nothing startling but Hugh and I lay in the spoons position last night. We were awake and we didn't talk, not at all. I could hear his blinks. We lay there for a long time and his breath on the back of my neck was filled with the words we didn't have to say. There were no crackling sparks keeping us awake and we fell asleep like that.

This morning when we woke up we had moved apart in the night and as Hugh was getting up he said, 'How often do you think about it? Eloise?'

I touched his back and said, 'It kills me at least once a day.'

And he said, 'Me too.'

He got up then. And suddenly I didn't feel warm and spoony any more. I thought, *I don't believe you. And, did you sail away to Antarctica from pregnant me and three babies and think about it every day? Didn't you want to stay close as close? Or did you need to apply ice to the wound? Did you think about it this year when you had plans to leave us again?*

2012

I hated the time when Hugh went to Antarctica. Hated it. By then we'd moved into West Hobart, had three children and deeply immersed ourselves in domestic affairs. Hugh was making the transition into his own forensic practice, but before he did, he decided that some wild oats needed sowing, in the South Pole.

'Zannah, what do you think about a season in Antarctica?' he asked one Easter when we'd taken the children camping on Maria Island. It was a March Easter, one of those postcard-lit autumn days when the sun is low and gets into everything and you want to skip up hills. I was feeling altogether intrepid, having brought two children and a toddler on a camping holiday (drive to Triabunna, get on ferry, put a tent peg in) so I said, 'Well, I'm up for anything these days,' and held up my toilet trowel.

He laughed, then didn't. 'I've often thought about going, and once I'm entrenched in my own business there probably won't be the chance. And they're advertising for a supervising engineer . . .'

'Are you serious? And leave all this?' I made a grandiose gesture around Maria's particularly fetching landscapes. Jimmy sneezed onto my shirt.

'It'd be a five-month season in Davis Station, leaving in October.'

I looked at him properly. Frowned. 'You have to be joking.' If hackles were visible, he might have seen mine go up like warning flags.

But instead he started talking rapidly about what an opportunity it would be, great for his career blah blah blah . . . I don't really know the detail because my brain filled with umbrage that must have foamed up and blocked my earholes. I dragged him a distance away from the children and hissed, 'You mean to tell me that I've been waiting all these years – that I ditched my going-away dreams to stay here with you, bear your children, wash your shirts, prepare your food and be generally broken in, tamed and domesticated, all the while wondering when we might at least temporarily migrate north, only to find that you've concocted plans to move south? SOUTH! Without me!'

'Jesus, I didn't realise it's all been such a trial for you,' Hugh said angrily. 'I thought you were happy.'

'And I thought you might one day take me away.'

'Well, clearly now's not the time —'

'No, clearly not —'

'Not the time for us all to go.' He was shouting now.

I raised my own voice. 'Right, so when you get back from Antarctica, how about I gallivant off to Vienna with Ria for a season, just me?'

'If you go for music, then great, terrific, I'm all for it.'

'Oh, and what, you'd get a nanny, would you?' He was silent then. My voice was softened by sob. 'You'd let them have those enormous biscuits from the school canteen,' I said, because I couldn't think of anything else. 'Barky would die of thirst and no one would floss.'

He rolled his eyes and said, 'Wouldn't hurt them to be less looked after.' His face was tight, and somehow different from the face I knew so well.

I think we both left that conversation with a bit of Antarctic ice in our hearts. And if I'd looked, his beautiful autumn eyes might have taken on a grey tone. Perhaps he's truly never seen me the same way since then. Thick rankles are not very attractive, I suppose.

Later on that Maria trip, I took Eloise up the Bishop and Clerk track and she fell on the scree. I had to carry her all the way back to Darlington. It took us hours to reach Hugh and the boys and, by then, Hugh was worried. But I felt sort of reinforced. 'Mum rescued me,' Eloise said, and Raffy gave me a pat and said, 'Well done, brave Mummy.'

On the ferry back to Triabunna I said, 'You should go to Davis Station, Hugh. I can see it means a lot to you. But, for goodness sake, don't get trapped down there, don't dedicate your life to penguins, don't forget about us and don't fall in a crevice.'

He squeezed me tight and said, 'It's just an application at this stage. I probably won't even get in.'

But of course he did. And a week before he left, I discovered I was pregnant again. And perhaps we did fall into a crevice, or at least a rut. Regardless, I unfolded my brave face, sent him merrily off on his stream and determined to be all cheery and capable. But Hugh had set up some rigid scaffolding for us in the form of Alison, Laurence, Hire-A-Hubby, Jim's Gardening, Mum and Dad, so I didn't get a chance to be capable. I'd be gathering myself together in the sickly mornings after a sleepless night with restless Jimmy, and Alison would show up, rested and coiffed, with a basket of bakings and remedies and trilly advice. She'd cast an eye at the state of things, wipe Raffy's nose, braid Eloise's hair and throw away the cold raisin toast. She taught me the meaning of officious. Also, how hopeless I can be.

Sometimes Laurence would come over and say that a tree branch looked dangerous or put a broken wheel back on the wheelie bin. Then they'd leave again, all buoyed by their do-goodery. Then Jimmy would cry and Raffy would get bored and break things. Eloise was just disturbingly stoic. I'd overuse the clothes dryer, have nightmares about tree branches falling on the children and wish *Play School* went for longer. At the park I envied old people their freedom.

Mum and Dad were only moderately better; they were good at whisking the children away so I could tidy up in my own time, or sleep. But everyone would return from thrilling adventures, the children would be filthy, exhausted and wide-eyed from seeing fairies or catching a fish, and I'd be elevated to a new level of boring. Boring and bored, I suppose. I longed for my music but it was a yearning that felt altogether wrong, fraught with danger. What if the music took me away too?

By the time Hugh finally arrived home from his intrepid, life-changing adventure, our house was sparkling and the wheelie bin wheels were fine, but mine had fallen off. The sight of him with a beard, my relief and my sense of injustice combined and made me feel faint. He said, 'It's so good to see you. You look different somehow.' We laughed because by then my belly was swollen with Mary-Lou. But it was more likely to do with having all my self-belief chipped off.

MONDAY 27th NOVEMBER

We've reached that time of the year when the teachers stop setting homework, you stop worrying about iodine supplements and times tables, and you start collecting loo rolls for Christmas craft. When the days stay warm until eight so you have to have a gin and tonic on a Monday. When you feel as though it's time for the year to have a little lie-down.

But it can't because Christmas. And because the Sparkle Project should be drawing to a close. And sparkles remain elusive (unless you count the tinsel Mary-Lou has been flinging around everywhere in readiness for the Christmas tree).

Hugh is an exception. He doesn't seem to be winding down at all. I'm not sure how he could have absented himself from work for another Antarctic trip . . . I fear I've renewed my bitterness on that front; perhaps I should stop the recollecting now. I think it's clear where our history gets a bit dark and cumbersome, and 'Remembering is only a new form of suffering,' said someone once.

To be fair to Hugh, though, he's been very loving lately. Not passionate, just supportive-style loving. Kind. He's been kissing me a lot. Actually, more like pecks, as if just reminding me he's here, even when he's work-distracted. So that's nice. Different, but nice.

Funny things they are, pecks, when you think about them. If kissing is scientifically proven to be an early manifestation of basic human desire, what is a peck? An IOU? Dr Folds says we're all meant to kiss our beloveds for at least seven seconds if we want to keep our flames burning.

TUESDAY 28th NOVEMBER

Eloise flatly refused to go to school today. And I didn't argue. They've entered the 'consolidation' stage at school, which means they all pretend to finish off projects but are actually cleaning out classrooms and going on excursions to Richmond Gaol, etc.

So we went Christmas shopping. Her suggestion, clearly. I have never thought about Christmas shopping in November before. It turned out to be an unexpected delight. Eloise put her head on my shoulder for a second when we were walking through the mall: a tiny, leaning bit of it's-okay-thank-you-I-love-you, which almost brought me undone. Tenderness from a teenage daughter is a bag of pink diamonds and a punch in the heart.

I took her to an extravagant restaurant and we laughed about how suspicious Mary-Lou is about Father Christmas while Jimmy is sailing along in blissful, fairy-lit belief. Then out of the blue she asked, 'What happened to the nanny?'

I swallowed a painful lump of half-chewed chicken salad. I looked around for water.

'Did she get arrested?'

'No.'

'Why not?' Eloise frowned. 'Isn't neglect a crime? She had a duty of care. I looked it up.'

I flinched at the words 'duty of care' and put down my fork. 'She was very young. Twenty-two. She was the oldest of eight children. That's why I hired her. A lifetime of experience, I thought. Her father was chronically ill and her mother was an alcoholic. I don't think neglect registered as a thing.' I sighed. 'She was doing three jobs to support her family. It's no excuse, but I didn't like to see her charged. Dad agreed. We made sure she'll never work with vulnerable people again.' My voice cracked on 'vulnerable'.

Eloise was staring at me, her head tilted: fascinated, distanced, grown-up.

I looked back at her and said, 'It was *my* duty of care.'

'But, Mum,' she said, 'weren't you busy? Music was your job, wasn't it?'

'You were my job. You were my life. Music took too much.'

She frowned. 'Ria told me that you'd go mad without your music. Are you going mad, do you think? You can be weird sometimes.'

I coughed on nothing. She waited. Her eyes were kind but serious. A simple question. God, she's so black and white, it hurts my eyes. 'I don't think so, darling.'

'Okay,' she said, satisfied. 'Well, I wasn't meant to say but Ria also told Raffy and me that you change people with your music, and that you could probably change the world. That's pretty cool.' She smiled a proper, big, Eloise smile. I love that smile. 'And just so you know, I don't have any hard feelings about your work – I don't even remember – so whenever you're ready.' She did a little viola-playing mimicry, then took a mouthful of soup, swallowed and said, 'Tracy Chapman changed the world with her voice. This soup needs salt.'

But I sold my voice for a manicure and some nights in a haunted house. And it's too late for me to change the world.

THURSDAY 30th NOVEMBER

Nothing to note. And I just don't feel all that inclined to sit in the wardrobe. Really, chairs in wardrobes are for not-clean, not-dirty clothes and wet towels.

Although I can be a bit of a wet blanket at times.

FRIDAY 1st DECEMBER

It's December – *eeeeeek*! This is the moment when we panic about all the things not done and we make a things-not-done list and run around half-doing everything. Badly. The December List. I'll make mine here, as proof:

- Mulch garden
- Christmas pudding ingredients
- Get photos printed and put them in an album
- Wash curtains
- Air bedding
- Nativity costume (not fitted sheets)
- Optometrist!
- Find lost printer cartridge receipts
- Buy Mary-Lou a new schoolbag before next year
- Bicarb soda for smell in car?

- Hugh's birthday present
- Retrieve Sparkle Project from Too-Hard Basket.

I might as well cross off the washing of curtains and the photo albums; they are just perennial To-Do list items. One must have pies in one's skies.

Hi-ho, hi-ho . . .

WEDNESDAY 6th DECEMBER

Right, so I'm well into the December List. I even got the photos printed! Four hundred and sixty-eight of them. I've put them into albums to give to Hugh this afternoon for his birthday. Hugh's birthday is the perfect time to fire up my resolution again. It's seen some bumps and twists but I refuse to leave this year with less sparkle than the last.

Hugh's been just as busy as I have, getting the year wrapped up and tied in a bow, so there's been little time to move beyond pecks. But so little time, so much old flame to reignite (which reminds me, there's a bit of burnt toast stuck in the toaster). I think I'm going to have to bring out the big guns, so to speak. The flame throwers. Time is short and I'll be damned if I'll let this resolution waft away and disappear into next year. Will deploy secret weapon and report back . . .

LATER:

So I didn't attack Hugh with a flame thrower but I did give him a (dum-di-dum) blow job! This is not such a secret weapon after all; everyone knows that a blow job is the quickest way to a man's heart.

The blow job gets quite a bit of bad press among women, actually. I mean, I'm never in raptures at the prospect of giving one, but they serve some important purposes:

- It seems to be, in a man's eyes, the ultimate expression of love. They will be genuinely thankful in ways never seen by the likes of chopping onions and folding smalls.
- They are useful preludes to significant requests such as pet insurance.
- They are relatively quick (particularly if the job hasn't been done since his last birthday).
- There will be no surprise postliminary drips from bits.
- They can actually be, if you block out the fact that there is a penis in your mouth, quite horny, actually.

Before said blow job, we had a nice family birthday dinner at The Don Camillo (Hugh's favourite) at which we presented Hugh with his five photo albums, one from each of us. (I know, how organised.) And then it was early home because school tomorrow and once the children were in bed I led him into the pantry and surprised him by pulling down his trousers. He did get a shock!

I kissed his stomach and thighs and it wasn't long before his penis was responding with little nudges on my chin, as though it was nodding its agreement. And when I did actually start with the in-mouth part, I was surprised to feel a sudden desire jolt through my body. It was only a few minutes before his breaths became gasps and he sent me a warning on a whisper. I stopped, held him but moved my face clear. (I just can't swallow. *Erk.*)

Afterwards he said, 'Susannah, that was really, really nice, but don't feel you have to, you know . . .'

'I don't feel I have to,' I said. 'I enjoyed it.' And I meant it, actually.

'But about the spark thing, your resolution,' he stroked my cheek. 'We've had a tough year, there's plenty of time for all that. Let yourself get through it all.'

But we kissed and there was definitely some newly generated sparkle there, so I took a moment to feel a bit smug.

But perhaps he's right. Perhaps a marriage is a thing that generally muddles along with the occasional sparkle but no actual hot sparks, until you make them. And as long as you know how to make them when the need or desire arises, you'll be okay. I can just whiz him into the pantry for a quick blowie and presto! Instant passion. Occasionally you might stumble into some passion, and then you can just delight in the spontaneity. For the rest of the time we should all be recording our family history (the good bits), making up photo albums filled with happy memories and carrying our children on our backs when they hurt their knees. Aren't those the things that keep it all together?

We don't have to be constantly overwhelmed with desire; no one would ever get anything done. It needn't underwhelm us either . . . I suppose we just need to be whelmed. Orderly, motherly, productive and content. Content in the whelm.

And another thing: I should stop trying to express in detail the ins and outs (!) of our sex life. The best way to describe it is not to describe it at all. The beauty of lovemaking is the intimacy of it, the thing between you and your love. It's the act, not the description. That must be why there are ugly words like scrotum and vagina and root, so we SHUT UP about our private lives.

Therefore, after all these months of attempting to detail our sex life in frequent despatches from the front (bottom), I am going to stop. Now (for fuck's sake).

☆

Gosh, it's been a while since I've felt so insightful. There's a refreshing clarity of thought here in the whelm. Mostly I'm like the hard, blue half of an eraser that's meant to rub out ink but just makes smudges.

WEDNESDAY 13th DECEMBER

And, joy-joy-jingle-jingle, Eloise begins her Christmas holidays this afternoon. Ho ho. I'm clutching a rocking-chair moment while I can.

School has said that I can take her home early from final assembly – if I so wish. So I will (even though there's a good two hours between final assembly and the end of school in which I might well get some exercise, find a job, make a ~~croquenbusch croquenbush~~ soufflé or wash the curtains).

I am very much looking forward to spending more time with her. The others don't finish until next Thursday so there's scope for all sorts of bondy moments. We could go on some outings, think about what Christmas baking we might do this year, etc. It'd be good to veer the children away from the errant commercialism that is Christmas. Perhaps we could make everyone's presents. Valda suggested those oranges with cloves stuck in that people can hang in their wardrobes. I'll keep one for me. It might have a smudging effect on this wardrobe, detoxify it of any inappropriate thoughts I might have had here.

Valda isn't doing well in rehab. She wouldn't get out of bed today. Her nurse says she is 'impossible'. I know what she means.

'Can I get you anything, Valda?' I said.

She sighed and said, 'Bonox, I suppose,' and then told me again the story of Neville and the Bonox. 'Once Neville drank too much of a Russian white spirit called vodka and the next morning he thought he'd die. I gave him Bonox and it saved his life. He said after that it was his duty to protect me forever. I never went anywhere without him after that.'

'How romantic,' I sighed and she gave me a hard look.

One of her bad days.

Hearty old Bonox. I wish I had some Bonox for my heart. Or botox, for that matter; a frozen heart is preferable to this leaping, dipping, cracked one.

Anyway, off to be personable, logical, caring and productive. Perhaps I should study nursing?

FRIDAY 15th DECEMBER

I had a Very Sad Day yesterday. I even bought some Bonox but it evidently does nothing for that horrible feeling you get when you can't ever see your best most beloved friend ever, ever again. I can hear her, though, I suppose. I put some of her music on late last night, very quietly in the wardrobe. Hugh must have been awake because he got out of bed and came in and hugged me. There were already tears, of course, but the hug brought on proper crying, partly because it felt so nice to be snuffling into his chest without anything chilly between us. Also because it's so rare for him to know that trying to fix things is for structures and appliances, and that shut-up-and-hug works best for sad people.

I cried and cried and cried. He sat on the floor next to the rocking chair and leaned on my legs and we listened to more of Ria's music. I embellished it with varying degrees of sob. Hugh cried too. I stroked his cheek and said, 'Do you think we'll ever not be sad about Ria?'

'No,' he said. 'We'll always be sadder than we were before. Maybe a bit wiser too.'

That sounds right, I think now, from my small distance of two months. Perhaps the pain, while it stops shooting, just softens and turns into a slightly wonkier form of normal. And we all go on, somewhat misaligned, and with more shadows in our years. Absence is such a presence.

He kissed me then, on the rocking chair and through my tears. (I don't think he notices them any more, like cracked tiles in the kitchen.) The kiss had some unexpected passion in it, and went on for much, much longer than seven seconds. And then the passionate kissing turned into proper horniness, sudden and sharp. I won't be elaborating because I'm all about the action not the description now. Suffice to say, WOW. It was amazing. Also, this is the first time in ages that Hugh has initiated sex. Apparently extreme emotions can turn into sudden desire, known as 'the grief horn', but even so, there's more proof that we can access passion when we need to. There are quite a lot of sparkles in the Susannah vase. By New Year's Eve it'll be positively iridescent.

WEDNESDAY 20th DECEMBER

Eloise hasn't been quite as engaged with our mother–daughter time as I'd hoped. She's spent a lot of it talking on the phone to her friends, meeting up with them, then coming home and talking to them on the phone again. She's not being unpleasant or distant or rude, just, I don't know, thirteen, I suppose. Very nearly fourteen, for goodness sake. I'm trying not to appear desperate but I must have been gazing wistfully at her too much because yesterday she picked up one of my hands and held it to her cheek for a long moment, then kissed it. Then she stole my toast and skipped off to meet Rebecca at the pictures.

I looked for a long time at my hands and then rubbed some lavender lotion on them. Lavender and tears.

Today, having directed myself to stop adding the weight of my need to all the other pressures placed on teenage girls these days, I buggered off to help Mum and Dad with their Christmas preparations. They're to host this year but have asked if I can step in as a sort of event manager. I think they want to keep me busy. I'm happy to. Mum's quite distracted – she says it's because her hollyhocks have rust and the cat's had to start anxiety medication, but I suspect it's because there's a parcel under the Christmas tree with a French postmark. She has too much bounce and glow for her distraction to be coming from worry. I wonder if she's upped the botox, or whether extra admiration has an uplifting effect on the skin. I wouldn't know. Dad saw me eyeing the parcel and said, 'It's a Fabergé Christmas bauble or some ruddy thing. Doing the trick already.'

Anyway, helping with Christmas is a timely boost to my inner glow and renewed family focus, and it means that I can add a few guests to the invitation list. I'd quite like to ask Hannah and Charlie as this is their first Christmas since they moved back here. Mum's already asked Henry and Valda. Charmian? Father Graham will be busy with Jesus's birthday, etc. but I might ask him as well. Oh, April will be fresh back from Antarctica so we should ask her too. They won't all be able to come, of course. Such short notice.

Who else can I ask? Isobel and Josh? Mum said, 'The more the merrier.' And the busier the better, I suppose. And perhaps it will counter any horrible pains we'll have over not having Ria in the world for Christmas. She always used to skype the children in her Father Christmas get-up and read them their sins. 'Jimmy

Benjamin Parks, you are guilty of eating all the neenish tarts and blaming your farts on the dog,' etc. And her Christmas mixed tape – she always sent me a mixed tape, on cassette, of the best music of the year. I can't bear that there won't be one this year . . . must stay busy.

THURSDAY 21st DECEMBER

Nearly everyone can come! I hope Mum's sorted out the cat.

Isobel and Josh are the only ones who can't. Isobel turned up this afternoon with a little bag of shortbread and this (!!):

'I'm sorry. We're taking the children away for Christmas. We have some things to talk through with them.' She paused, and I noticed that her eyes were shadowed with dark, that her hair was unusually stringy. 'And, Susannah, I have to tell you that we're putting the house on the market. Josh and I are separating.'

I think I just gaped at her for a full ten seconds. I really couldn't believe it. 'Not you and Josh, surely not.' I was properly floored. And dismayed. What chance do any of us have if the best couple in the neighbourhood can't love one another enough?

She gave a little sad smile. 'I worked really hard at it, but in the end, I just can't keep up with Josh.' She started to cry. 'He has such drive – I mean, his sex drive, his ambition, his commitment to quality family time; honestly, I just want a good rest, in a tracksuit, eating bad food.' She sniffed. 'Sorry, I'm not devastated. I'm sad – for the children, and for him. But mostly I'm so, so relieved. Is that terrible?' Her mascara ran. I wondered if I should pay forward Hannah's waterproof Chanel.

'No. I've heard it said that if you put too much strain on your heart, it will fail,' I said.

'Yes!' She laughed. 'I have to look out for my heart. Cardiac tissue never heals. Any longer and my ankles would have swollen up.'

'Or your vagina walls would have worn away.' Then I clapped my hand over my mouth and added, 'God, sorry. That was inappropriate.'

But Isobel was laughing: proper belly laugh, cry laughing. 'You are hilarious, Susannah. You really are. You always make me smile.' *Do I?* 'And you're right. My vagina needs a break too. I once suggested he have an affair, but he's so loyal to perfection.' She sighed. 'I'm so ready for some perfunctory living.'

Poor Isobel. You're only perfect until your facade crumbles, aren't you? She needs some good plain cake and some ants in her sugar.

Meanwhile, if they're the only refusals, Mum and Dad have eighteen people for Christmas Day!!! What was I thinking (for Christ's sake)? I haven't told Hugh exactly how many people are coming because he'd be all 'what the bejesus?' about it and ring all the warning bells instead of the Christmas ones and I'll fall to inadequate bits. I'll just pretend I can do it until it's done.

I have ordered two Christmas puddings from Hill Street Grocer, Mum is doing salad, Alison is bringing condiments and brandy butter. I just have to manage the turkey and the pink-eyes and the nibbles and the drinks. And the Florentines to have with coffee. And the crackers. The children can decorate the table.

Jingle-jingle go our bells.

SATURDAY 23rd DECEMBER

Everyone has officially started holidays, including Hugh. This morning we all pottered about together being productive. It was a nice feeling. The sun shone and the children played – actually played. They tramped dirt into the house, ate all the chocolate stars from the Christmas tree and demanded pizza for lunch but Hugh yelled, 'STOP BEING SO SELFISH. Mum washed the floors this morning.' And he shook his head and smiled at me. We felt like a team again, with a remnant throb of that amazing wardrobe sex. (I don't think I'll hang a cloved orange in there after all.)

We had a family outing to the botanical gardens. With Valda. It was one of those glorious, golden afternoons, the sort that heats up the jasmine and sends the happy sounds of family summers out across the scented suburban air. Out-and-about air. It had us packing up a picnic lunch and sitting under a giant oak. The children went off to play, leaving Hugh, Valda and me in warm, bird-chirpy silence. Hugh had the paper; he read us a bit now and then. We drank apple cider. Valda complained about it being too fizzy. I looked up into the trees to see if I could find the birds, and the tears welled and spilled, like only tears with the siphon of real heartache can.

Valda patted my hand and said, 'Birds dream, you know. They dream about their songs and have little dream rehearsals so that the next day, their singing has improved.' Hugh glanced up from the paper, gave me a little smile. Valda helped herself to a shortbread and the birds kept rehearsing. I thought about some Ria things, and some Eloise things, nibbled cheese and discovered a coarse hair on my chin that I cared about. The tears dried and someone walked past wearing a tulip-shaped hat.

Grief is an ordinary thing. I should do a little bit of it every day. I wonder, could I put it on my Things to Do list? Should I rehearse my chirp until it's real?

☆

But then, on the way home, Raffy said, 'Mum doesn't like her new viola.' And Valda said, 'Well, she hasn't tried to like it.' And I was suddenly tense again. We passed a young woman strolling in a floaty shirt dress and thought, *I wish I could be her, strolling in a floaty shirt dress with no apparent baggage, but here I am, with all my baggage, in a hot car that smells like the inside of schoolbags.* I was feeling anything but floaty. Feeling shirty, actually.

'Don't forget my mail next time,' Valda said once we'd settled her back in her room and made her tea.

'Old mole,' I said to Hugh on the way out. He kissed my head and we went home to where the children were brushing their teeth without being asked.

It's one step forward, two steps back at the moment.

Before bed I made a half-hearted attempt at turning my shirty into flirty, but was relieved when Hugh didn't seem to notice. He ran me a bath and closed me in the bathroom, which is probably the ultimate act of love anyway.

SUNDAY 24th DECEMBER

CHRISTMAS EVE! No time for much other than preparations. Hugh's been making breadcrumbs for stuffing while I'm decorating the gingerbread house (possibly too ambitious but oh, well) and we are SO TEAM.

Dissonante ♪♪

MONDAY 25th DECEMBER

We're about to leave for Mum and Dad's but I just want to have a little lament about Christmas presents. Remember when they were The Most Exciting Thing of the Year? That excitement the night before Christmas was so palpable it could be bottled and doled out on a Monday morning with the school lunches. I remember it well, but I no longer feel it. I'm sad about that. More untimely *nostos algos*. This morning, the children's presents for Hugh and me included: a pine cone with googly eyes, a clay snowman that looks like a poo, a laminated haiku about beards and some blue coconut ice. I know I should be more grateful.

I gave Hugh the photo albums, which he loves, but of course there's not a single one of anything to do with Antarctica and this is quite a stark omission when you view the albums all together. Oh, dear.

On a positive note, the children got electric toothbrushes from Father Christmas so their teeth might sparkle. And an enormous new spring-free trampoline from Hugh and me. Jimmy and Mary-Lou will be able to do their acrobatics, Eloise can sit on it with her friends and Raff can lie on it. And, mostly, I won't have to think up as many activities. Or worry about spring-related injuries.

Everyone's happy . . . The trampoline is clearly not a selfless offering but I'm a bit over the quest for inner glow and am fast-tracking outer sparkle. I have six days left. I'd better get on . . .

LATER:

Oh . . . This morning (aeons ago) I was at Mum and Dad's looking proudly over the beautiful tinselly dining table and thinking how so much Christmas sparkle surely contributes to overall sparkle (despite trampoline selfishness). And now? Now I'm hiding in the wardrobe again and everything is ruined and ruined and ruined. The girders have corroded, the noggins are lousy with rot and everything, everything is falling down.

And though a full report is a terrible blight in these Sparkle Pages and its mostly hopeful notes, a full report is what I will give. Because I must face up to the music. All the hideous, horrible music.

While I was gazing upon the resplendent table setting, Hugh came into the dining room, saw that we had both extensions on the dining room table and had set up another smaller table and said, 'Jesus, how many people are coming?'

'Eighteen, including us but not including Jesus,' I said proudly, because it all looked so nice.

'Who?' he asked, so I reeled off everyone. When I got to April, he looked aghast.

'No, no, no. We're not having April,' he said. 'Are you sure she said yes?'

'Yes, I'm sure,' I said. 'She doesn't have family here, Hugh. Of course she's coming. She sounded really pleased to be asked.'

Then he went a bit pale and said, 'Can you come outside, Zannah? I have to talk to you.' And for a wavery moment I thought,

*Oh, God. He's terminally ill. No one ever says, 'I have to talk to you'
unless they're dying. Or leaving. Oh, God.*

'What's wrong?' I asked. 'Are you sick? Is the business in trouble?'

'No, Susannah.' He glanced at the children attaching silver balls
to holly. 'Can you just come outside, please?'

'Are you going away? You're going away.' I had a sudden vision
of him sitting cosily alone with a book in Mawson's Hut.

'No. Please just —' He beckoned.

Mum trotted in and said, 'Now, children, where shall I put this
beautiful Fabergé egg? It's too good for the Christmas tree.'

I wished terribly that I could stay and talk about Terrence Squirrel
and eggs and things other than Antarctica, but Hugh took me by
the arm. I followed him outside and when we got to the clothesline
I said, 'If you're going away, then perhaps you could take us all with
you? We could all do with a change of rhythm.'

'Susannah, I'm not going away. I'm sorry, I know this is the wrong
time and place but April can't come for lunch with us, and I can't not
tell you any more – something happened, Zannah, in Melbourne just
before she went to Mawson. Just before Ria . . . Anyway, April . . .'
He rubbed his eyes and took a breath. 'April kissed me. I kissed her
back. It happened twice. Then I stopped it. I didn't start it but I knew
she had, you know, feelings, and I let it happen. I would have told
you sooner, but Ria . . . and I should have put a stop to it before it got
to that. I'm sorry and I need you to know that I love you, it's not a
thing, and it will never, ever, ever happen again.'

And I think he was saying some other things but I didn't hear
them because I felt suddenly nauseous and had to concentrate very
hard on not being sick. I clutched a trouser leg that was flapping
from the clothesline and raised my hand in a stop sign. He stopped.
From the kitchen I could hear Ryan Adams singing 'Come Pick Me

Up' and I wished Dad didn't share my taste for sorrowful music. I wished we were home and Valda was singing from her windows and drowning things out. I wished that April hadn't appeared and Ria hadn't disappeared and I'd never started to meddle with our lives. I screwed up my eyes and wished all those Christmas wishes. *Take me back a year,* I thought. *Take me back.* I felt butterflies in my stomach. The ones that tell you to run. There were sparks too. Angry, fatal, voltage sparks. I heard them crackling. *Those are no-good sparks,* I thought. *He's given all the good ones away.*

'Susannah?' Hugh whispered.

'The turkey needs me,' I said and went back inside, trying to walk steadily but probably not because my mind was in a snarl-up of guests arriving and turkey basting and having to plaster up my cracks with make-up for the sake of the children, and wondering if my bell earrings and festive dress might mean I could climb into the Christmas tree and hide until it was all over. And then came the terrible, crashing thought that, actually, it probably was all over.

I put myself in Mum's powder room for another few minutes of head-whorls (with tears), then I wiped my eyes, fluffed up my hair, brushed my eyebrows and emerged with hugs for the children. I said things like, 'Isn't this exciting! Everyone will be here soon.'

By twelve-thirty everyone had arrived. Alison and Laurence with their respective snips and silence, the de Montagus with their gratitude, Henry with his familiar warmth, Charmian and her curiosity, Father Graham and his dear beans. And April, looking gracious with pretty pink cheeks, exciting Antarctica tales and a Christmas hamper. They all threatened to scatter the brittle pieces of me.

We had the handing-out of the presents. Hugh gave me some perfume, Valda gave me a pair of hand-stitched, lavender-filled bags to put in my shoes, Mum gave me some lacy knickers and a whisk. And then Jimmy handed me a large heavy parcel, which I opened to reveal Hugh's painting of the Susannah albatross. 'Dad and I made the frame,' he said proudly. I cried some tears that weren't happy tears, even though most people thought they were.

Then Charlie boomed, 'Well, I think Susannah and Frannie should be given a trophy for inviting us all today, but this might do instead,' and he handed me a bottle of Veuve Clicquot. I would have quite liked a trophy as well. After all, I'd given April some Christmas shortbread and not a knuckle sandwich.

At lunchtime, even though Valda avoided mentioning the dry turkey (self-basting, my arse), complimented Mum on her honeyed carrots and gave us an exquisite rendition of 'The First Noel', I couldn't find my cheer. In fact, I felt jealous! Of Valda! I checked myself and said, 'Valda, thank you. That was truly lovely.' The words felt like stones.

Alison was thrilled to see Hannah, of course. She was all, 'Oh, Hannah, you can't be a day over thirty,' and, 'Nice to meet you, Charlie, but I can't pretend I'm not a bit cross with you for nabbing Our Hannah.' *Getting along like a house on fire,* I thought, then imagined the house bursting into flames.

All the time I felt the pulsing, contained want of April from across the table. And all the time Hugh watched me. So did Mum, apparently, because she caught my arm at the kitchen sink and whispered, 'Darling, you've been taking deep breaths all day and you keep rubbing your hands. What on earth's wrong?'

'Oh, you know, I've never been a very relaxed entertainer.' She looked suspicious but I couldn't say anything because cracks. I just swigged some champagne and smiled. She frowned.

I was still in the kitchen (with the champagne) when Hugh came in, cupped my face for a second and said, 'How are you doing?' It might have been better if I'd thrown a wobbly then and said, 'Not good. Really terrible, actually. No one gave me a trophy and I'm wondering whether I should just surrender to being the hired help and step aside for the April and Hugh show. I mean, you two have so much in common so that's bound to be a happy ending.'

But Raffy bounded in and so I turned away towards the dishwasher and did a sing-songy, 'Very well, thank you! Lovely old Christmas.'

And I drank some more champagne, let everything bubble away inside me and wondered whether I should just get really pissed and bury myself in the discarded wrapping paper. With any luck I might get put out with the rubbish. But instead I started saying things like, 'Tell us a bit more about yourself, April. What do you do other than work work work? Henry likes country music – all those lonesome hearts and long dusty roads. Do you have time for hobbies?' and 'Tell us all about Antarctica, April. Everyone, April's fresh back from the South Pole. I'll bet Hugh's been anxious for details. I hear you saw some phosphorescence.'

'Yes,' said April feebly. 'And the Aurora.'

'Oh, fabulous,' I gushed. 'Sea sparkles, sky sparkles, sparkles everywhere and all around.'

Then there was a bit of an awkward silence into which Mum said loudly, 'I nearly got you a budgerigar, Jimmy, but then I thought, no, a sandwich press is much more useful.' She looked at Charmian. 'He loves his toasties.'

'Hugh would have liked to have gone back to Antarctica,' I said. 'Except he has a terrible case of albatross. Did you see any down there, April? Albatross?'

And Mum said, 'Alison, tell me, do you mind showing me how to make a shandy? I quite fancy a shandy.'

And Alison looked down her nose and said, 'I wouldn't have any idea, Frances.'

'Oh, Alison,' I said. 'Would you stop being so snooty about us, please? We've never been good enough, have we? And anyway, Mum hates being called Frances.'

Please behave, said a distant voice to my heart, but it didn't listen.

'Oh, that's all right. I quite like it these days,' said Mum. 'Frannie's a bit too close to Fanny, isn't it?' And people forced out a laugh.

Then Father Graham said, 'How's your new viola going, Susannah? Henry showed me the bow. What a beauty.'

And cheery, beery Charlie called out, 'DID YOU BRING IT ALONG?'

'I brought it!' said Raffy, with his eyes suddenly shining and his cheeks very pink.

'PLAY US A TUNE,' boomed Charlie. Raffy darted from the house, banging the front door behind him.

Things get a bit blurry after that. I have vague, melting memories of me turning my gaze to Hugh for a long moment and my eyebrows stinging with overwhelming fury.

'Oh, well done, Raffy,' said Alison, with a smile in her voice. Mocking. 'A tune, please, Susannah.'

'Yes!' said Charmian, clapping her hands as Raffy wafted back in and towards me like a mirage, the viola case between us.

Rumpenda asinis eorum, said Ria from elsewhere, far away. *Shove it up their arses.*

'No, Susannah,' said Valda in a kind voice, and I realised I'd repeated the Latin words aloud. Kindness in Valda commands attention so I paused. She shook her head. 'Don't . . .' But it wasn't quite enough.

I took the case from Raffy's tentative hands, threw open the clasps and wrenched the viola from its velvety bed. 'A tune?' I said. 'Rightio then.' Without even attaching a shoulder rest, I raised the viola, and after a moment's pause for effect, I launched into a crazed frenzy of horrible scratches and squeaks and tonal clashes, enough to make dogs run and humans recoil.

I hurt with shame, recounting this. I've committed a travesty against my beloved music: shown complete disrespect to an innocent instrument and violated its trust with a shocking assault. Ria would be utterly furious if she could see what indignities I forced upon the viola she'd helped lovingly create. *Oh my God, Ria. I'm so, so, terribly sorry.*

But on and on I went, until I felt an old familiar fizz in my hands that might have softened the performance and turned it into something else, something lost and almost found. But in the moment, that feeling felt like a threat. And so, before it took hold, I stopped abruptly, and said, 'There you are, a new composition. A little impromptu called "Ode to April and Hugh".'

'Susannah —' Hugh stepped towards me.

'No, don't,' I said, pointing the bow at him like a weapon. 'I am not a building, my damp cannot be removed, and you can investigate my weak spots all you like but they cannot be fixed. Experts say that damaged hearts will never heal.' Then I shoved the instrument back into its case and stormed out of the room. (But something was so undone and unresolved that it was like leaving a parenthesis off one end of an aside.

See, such tension. So I stormed back in and said, 'And incidentally, if you'd like a composer's interpretation, you could just take it as a very raw playing of the heartstrings, if you like, and a final *poof!* of the spark.' And then I stalked once again from the room and out of the house and all the way to the park, where I sat on the bench and tried to hear birds but couldn't because of the enormous pounding in my head.

And the people I left behind? I can see them all now and the shock in their faces is so acute it looks like trauma.

So there we are, then. I don't know where to go from here. Merry Christmas?

TUESDAY 26th DECEMBER

I've apologised to our guests. Via text. This is a cravenly act but that's apparently my forte these days so I'll just run with it, I think. I didn't message Alison, though. She's been awaiting my downfall for years and is no doubt in raptures. I didn't message April either. I don't even have a teeny-weeny sorry for her.

I've had replies:

> Hannah: Take care and see you
> soon Xx

I think that's probably the last I'll hear from the de Montagus. Denting Hugh's car is far more graceful than putting on a show of demonic possession and scarring everyone forevermore.

> Henry: Oh, I wanted to call but hadn't quite
> worked out what to say. I feel very sorry. I hope
> you feel better soon, please say if you need
> anything. Charm and Father G send love too.
> Henry

I wonder whether Father G dabbles in exorcism.

I've apologised to the children too. I didn't let Hugh talk to them about any April foolery because I just want them to think I mixed things up, that I was all wrong about anything to do with April and Hugh. Mary-Lou squinted up her eyes and said, 'Are you and Dad going to be drivorced? Sally Pedder's mum and dad are drivorced and now she gets two houses and gummy bears in her lunch box.'

So I made myself laugh and said, 'Of course not, darling. I'm sorry. I have to never, ever drink champagne. I got all silly over nothing and I'm very sorry. Will you forgive me for my terrible behaviour?'

Eloise said, 'Will you let me off next time I'm very, very badly behaved?'

'I'll still love you,' I said.

'I still love you,' said Jimmy.

'I'd still love you even if you ran through the school playground in the nuddy,' said Mary-Lou, who thinks nudity is hilarious.

'I'd still love you,' said Jimmy, ever competitive, 'if you ran through the school playground in the nuddy and shat under the swings.'

'Oi,' I said. 'Don't say *shat*.'

'Well, don't screechy about with the viola and yell at Daddy,' he retorted.

'Deal,' I said.

'And please don't ever do poos in the school playground,' said Raffy.

'Okay.'

Hugh laughed in a feeble way. And I wondered whether, if I squinted my eyes, he might have looked a bit like the Hugh who loved me once. But I can barely look at him at all.

Eloise hasn't said much but I know she knows. She's been sufficiently occupied, though. I gave her my credit card and sent her shopping with Mimi and Rebecca because today is her fourteenth birthday. She couldn't believe her luck. I can't believe my shame. It's filled me right up. It's filled twenty viola cases. It's filled the vase with horribly grey-brown water. It's her birthday and I've been so weird that her father has been compelled to kiss a lesbian. (She's not a lesbian. Apparently we all just assumed that. She's just brave. Antarctica brave. And she's also, I realise, an electrical engineer with a PhD, which means she's a doctor of sparks.)

Oh, I wish and wish and wish like never before that I could just be normal. With useful, kept-warm hands.

WEDNESDAY 27th DECEMBER

I let him talk. A little bit. He came to bed after me last night, and at first I pretended to be asleep but I could feel him lying there looking at me.

'Say what you need to say before you burst,' I said to the dark. 'Be gentle.'

He took a deep breath. 'Wait!' I said and sat up, turned on the light. I needed to check his face for untruths. Then I lay down again and whispered, 'Go.'

'Will you stay calm?'

'I don't know.'

'That was some performance, Susannah.'

'I was hoping to outperform you,' I said. 'How do you think I went?'

'I think you went close.'

'Silly Mummy,' I said in a cold, ugly voice.

He took another breath. 'Will you let me explain a bit more?'

I stayed silent, so he continued. 'We were in Melbourne. The judge had just decided to award damages. We were excited —'

'Stop!' I screwed my face up on a vision of elated April flinging herself at Hugh, his hands on her . . . I tried to talk to my heart. *Be calm, be calm, here's some oxygen . . .*

He paused, but went on. 'It was just a kiss. The second time was the following day and I stopped it before it even really started. It hasn't happened again. It won't happen again. I promise. Zannah, you're my only . . . the only one.'

I sat up and said, 'Have you been messaging one another a lot?' I remembered his emojis.

'Yes. For work. Mostly.'

'Do you ever send her the kiss-blow emoji?'

'What? No. I don't know. I might have.' He cleared his throat. 'Susannah, there's no excuse, but she was so enthusiastic about everything. She wanted to know all the things I know. She admired me. It's my stupid ego . . .'

'Funny, isn't it,' I said, 'how she wears a ring on her little finger to remind her to put integrity before her ego?' I picked up his left hand and touched the gold band on his ring finger.

'Zannah . . .'

'How long did you kiss her for?'

'What? I don't know.'

'Approximately.'

'I don't know. Maybe ten seconds, if that.'

I put my hand over my mouth.

'Zannah, are you going to be sick?'

'No.' But I vomited through my hand and all over the bed.

'Oh, Zannah. Oh, no. I'm so sorry. It was nothing —'

'Don't you dare tell me it was nothing. Nothing doesn't look like this.' We looked at each other – his stricken face, my green one – the mess on the bed. I gathered myself and the bedclothes up and made for the bathroom.

'Zannah, I promise it was just kissing, I don't know what I was thinking.'

I said, 'Shut up. I want to go home.'

It's a terrible thing to feel homesick in your own home. It's after ten and I'm still in my nightie. In the wardrobe. I must try to move my parts. Perhaps to the garden.

LATER:

Mum came over this afternoon with a cake for Eloise and a hamper of food. She found me in the garden violently shearing dead heads off the daisies.

'Hello,' she called. 'I have cake and goodies for the birthday girl. I didn't think there'd be much of the sort happening here.'

'Thanks, Mum,' I said.

'And speaking of cake,' she said, 'didn't you take the cake on Christmas Day? What a spectacle. It was hideous. You certainly didn't inherit your histrionical streak from me.'

'But, Mum,' I said. 'Hugh kissed another woman – he's been having an emotional affair with April.'

'What? Just a kiss? By the looks of you, I thought he'd got someone pregnant.' She took the shears from me. 'Goodness, leave the poor daisies alone. None of this is their fault.'

'I'm so angry with him,' I said as the old tears fell.

'And I don't blame you, darling, not for a minute. He absolutely did wrong by you. And April.'

'I don't care about April.'

'Anger is a good thing. It's there to shield your sensitive parts, but the problem is that your sensitive parts are extensive, aren't they?' She tucked a piece of my hair behind my ear. 'So your anger has to be enormous.'

'He deserves every bit of it.'

'You're right. That Hugh Parks is evil to the core. I've always known it. Men like him are the scourge of society: lecherous, conniving and grubby. I say we find him and give him what he deserves. Revenge is ours!' She held the shears aloft and gave the air a few snips.

'Mum, this is not a joke. I feel really betrayed.'

'Actually, revenge is quite a good idea. Go and find yourself someone to kiss. Settle the score, spare the daisies, move on.'

'Mum.'

'It seems to me you've had quite the emotional affair with yourself of late anyway, darling, sorry to say.'

'What?'

'I'm your mother. I've been watching. I saw you in that leopard-print dress.'

'Mum, Hugh has been dalliancing with another woman!'

'Well, go and get a divorce, then,' she said. 'Quick smart, neat and clean. Best for the children.' She watched me turn white and then held my face by the chin. 'He's a good man, Susannah. He loves you. You love him. That's your umbrella; get under it with him, snuggle up and weather the storm.'

Mary-Lou, Raffy and Jim ran into the garden then, and Mum said, 'Oh, look. Here's a pair of wellies and a macintosh. All the better. Hello, darlings. Where's the birthday girl?'

They left me in the garden. The sun peeped out from behind the trees.

THURSDAY 28th DECEMBER

I'm in the wardrobe with the new viola at my feet. I just opened the case and whispered a little apology speech. It was, 'I'm sorry I called you ugly. You're really not. You remind me of horse chestnuts when they've just popped out of their husks and they always make me smile. I'm sorry I dismissed you. But mostly I'm sorry I used you to say such horrible things. In such an inarticulate way. I broke all my musician rules and I have no excuses.' Then I closed the case up again and made myself think.

Perhaps I have outperformed Hugh's bad behaviour. Yes, he kissed April twice, indulged in some textual intercourse, did the wrong thing, but I've just had a read back through this diary and dear God, I'm so irritated by me. I was the one baring my soul to a wardrobe man and fantasising about divorce. I was the one being altogether careless and neurotic with our sparks. And now there are none. If I were my one and only, I'd go and kiss a bright, supple, environmentally aware graduate too. Hugh has probably done us all a favour. I will stop thinkering about with our family. Stop blurring myself with sentiments and none-such and let everything just be. Even if that means it will fall.

So there we are, then. Herein lies the end of the Resolution. Almost a year of trying far too hard. And now, all the low notes have drowned out the high notes, and my work here is surely done.

SPARKLE PROJECT ABORTED.

Scordatura

♩♩

Two things have happened to make me pull myself out of the too-hard basket. (It's cavernous and scary in there, with a pile of holey school tights, a filthy oven and cobwebs in the cornices.)

This is the first:

I was at least brave enough to slink over towards Valda's house yesterday, but I lost my nerve at her hedge and stopped, backtracked, stopped again. Then I heard, 'I can see the top of your doleful head. Bring it back and open its trap.'

I wanted to run, but she was right. Doleful I was. So I walked to her steps, stood before her and delivered an impromptu, clumsy but heartfelt speech. Something like: 'Oh, Valda. I know I was awful. And you singing so beautifully and so merry for a change. I mean, you're often merry, just not *so* merry. And your song was a gift, a lovely holly-wrapped but not prickly Christmas gift. I can't explain my actions. I think I went pop!'

She waited until the pause was long enough for my discomfort to bloom and then said, 'Come closer, please. I want to tell you a story.'

So I meekly sat in the chair beside her and waited while she set aside her knitting and repositioned herself.

'Neville hated me singing, you know. Hated it.'

'No!' I was aghast. 'But how could he?'

'Oh, he liked it well enough at first. The first time he saw me it was from an audience at the Odeon when I was sixteen. He said he thought he'd seen an angel.'

'He was very charming,' I said, remembering the sepia photograph on the wall in Valda's hallway of the two of them walking along the street, dressed formally in hats and coats, with the candid smiles of a couple dashing off to begin their glamorous life together.

'Yes, he was,' said Valda. 'He charmed me. I was swept. We were married when I was nineteen, right when the Conservatorium received an opera tutor from Vienna after the war. Just as I was told I might go somewhere.'

'What happened?'

'I think Neville found himself to be very, very jealous.' She sighed. 'I don't think he could help it. He was cross about anything to do with my career. He found an idiot doctor who told me I wouldn't conceive if I continued to place such exertions on my internal organs.'

'What?'

'I believed him. I did so want a baby. We tried. But it wasn't to be. That was hard. Neville blamed the voice training. Of course it's codswallop but he really believed it. He couldn't bear to hear me sing. And in the end, four years after we were married, I stopped.'

To my dismay, Valda pressed her fists to her eyes and gave a little sob. My heart hurt.

'Oh, Valda,' I said, taking one of her hands. It was cold. 'I thought you stopped when he died, not when you were married.'

'I started again when he died.' She laughed. 'After his funeral. It was a pitiful sound at first, I tell you, but I haven't forgotten how to open my false vocal folds.'

'So no mutual respect, gentle handling, kindness and conversation?'

'Not much.' She sighed. 'Those were the things I wished for, but . . .'

'The old bastard.' I was still amazed.

'To be fair,' she sniffed, 'it was different then. Women were there to tend to their husbands. And he was a good man in many ways. I was only frightened of him a few times.'

'Well, that's a few times too many. You should never, ever be afraid of your husband,' I said.

She sighed and said, 'Oh, well. When he got weak and ill I wasn't afraid any more. And I didn't look after him as well as I might have. Sometimes I put him in respite care just so I could listen to music and go to the pictures. And once I put earthworms in his chocolate cake.'

'You could have left him, Valda. You could have had a glittering career.'

'But I did love him,' she said, a tear spilling over. 'And I'd made my vows. I didn't have the choices you have today.'

Spoilt by choices . . .

We sat for a few minutes in silence and then she picked up her knitting again and said, 'Well, don't just sit there with your teeth in your head. You have some mending to do.'

I can't believe it. All along, that nasty old Neville had taken Valda's voice, that wonderful voice . . .

And the other thing is this:

Ria's oldest brother, Trent, turned up this morning with an enormous, Christmas-wrapped parcel. Enormous.

'I don't know what it is,' he said apologetically. 'I hold no responsibility, but it had strict instructions to get it to you before Christmas. Sorry it's late but we weren't sure, after the paper-weights . . .' He looked uncomfortable. 'She had some dumb ideas, that one. And we kind of skipped Christmas this year, you know . . .'

The children and I (Hugh was over at the Hadleys' helping Josh pack up his garage) helped Trent carry the parcel inside. There was much excitement. Mary-Lou skipped alongside and said, 'It's probably going to be a horse.'

'I hope it is,' said Trent, with a wink at her. It reminded me that he was the gentlest brother, the one who winked at Ria like that and always called her Glory. 'Just let me know if you want me to come back and take it away again. Good to see you, little Susie.' He gave my shoulder a pat and I tried to smile, but it came out all wonky.

It wasn't a horse. It was Deborah Smedley-Warren; I knew as soon as I saw her petite beige feet, identical to her sister's. We slid her out of the box and stood her up against the wall. She was wearing Ria's Father Christmas costume and holding a sign that said, *Merry Christmas to my dearest favourite hooligans, may your days be daisy and your bum-trumpets trumpety. Love Deborah and Ria. PS Please check my sack.*

We found a hessian sack at the bottom of the box and inside it was a squashy turquoise unicorn for Mary-Lou, a *Star Wars* Lego set for Jimmy, a boxed set of Australian music for Raffy, a pearl brace-let for Eloise and a Leatherman pocket knife for Hugh. And for me, a cassette tape.

I left the children with Deborah and their presents and retrieved my old cassette stereo from Raffy's room. I took it into the wardrobe and, with shaking hands, put the cassette in. The tears had been trickling since we found Deborah but now they positively streamed in anticipation of the music. It wasn't music, though. It was Ria's voice. Or rather, the voice of Caroline/Deborah Smedley-Warren. 'Hello, Susannah,' said the voice. 'I've decided to move down here with you if you don't mind. Bit miserable up there in cold, lonely London. And I have a feeling you might need me.' Ria laughed then, and I gasped with the nearness of it. Then she said, in her normal, dear voice, 'Hi there, Helen Burns. I hope this has reached you before you sobbed all your guts out and died a terrible eviscerated death. I know you've been crying too much. You've never been one to bottle up your emotions. But I want to say that you should stop now. You'll dry yourself up and that won't do the passion any good. How's that going? Have you serenaded him yet? Have you picked up that glorious viola? You know it doesn't have any guilt-baggage steeped into it, so it'll be easy to play. Spruced-up spruce is not nearly as absorbent as un-buffed sycamore.'

There was a pause, and the sound of a deep breath.

'Ah, the viola,' came her voice again, weighted now, perhaps labouring under the weight of tears. 'Have you noticed that lots of those dead composers wrote for viola at the end of their lives? Maybe it's the perfect instrument for telling all their secrets and finally letting go.'

Ria laughed again, then, 'Fucking hell. I sound like a complete tosser, and I'm not telling you anything you don't know, just that it seems to me now, towards the end of your year, you should just let all the secrets out. Don't you think? In the best way you know how. And if you don't remember what that sounds like, I have all your recordings right here in one place, so you can remind your-self 'til the cows come home. The first piece isn't you, obviously.

It's me. It's called "L'Albatros" and it's an adaption of the poem by Baudelaire. He wrote about an albatross being a beautiful, huge-winged bird who was extraordinary in flight but a bit of a bumbler on land because its wings got in the way of walking. Reminded me of you, with your great long viola arms. And if I need to spell it out even more: for fuck's sake, have another look at that painting Hugh did of the albatross, okay? I'm signing off now. Love you, Helen Susannah Burns. Don't disappoint me now. Always and always, your Ria.'

'L'Albatros'. It was a simple piano piece, not long – about three or four minutes, perhaps. A fantasia. High and slow, sustained, grace-ful. Then lower and elegant, exciting. But a crash and the music turned comical and clumsy, ambiguous *andantino*. I thought of Ria's failing hands on those beloved keys of hers. But then a sort of escape and a catch in your heart and a slowing, a relief. And then an onwards sort of feeling, with a very light *arpeggio* that made me think of a shiny day and a sequined sea.

'Exilé sur le sol au milieu huées,
Ses ailes de géant l'empêchent de marcher.'

I looked it up, the poem. And, dammit, now I'm crying for a fictional albatross. And a bit for me, with my bumbling arms and my nowhere hands.

I listened to the whole cassette. All my compositions, all the recordings of the TSO we did in the ballroom at Government House in Hobart, my cadenzas, the hurried etudes we had to record at the Con, the silly little fantasias Ria and I made up together. She'd kept them all. I just closed my flooding eyes and listened.

The last two pieces were her beautifully polished version of the 'Starlit Sonata', followed by my original. She always loved an extended coda.

'My most favourite sound,' came Hugh's voice when the last note had gone. I opened my eyes to find him standing in the doorway. 'I like your version best. Ria's is more lightweight, or something. Would that be right?' He looked suddenly shy.

'Yes,' I said.

'When we were looking at violas for you, and talking to the luthier, I learnt that it's the world's most imperfect instrument. In its upper register it splutters; down low it grumbles. It needs strings half a foot longer for complete resonance but then it would be unplayable.'

'Yes,' I said again.

'He said that he's tried to perfect it, but some things are better left alone. He said that in its limitations and tempers and troubles, there are the most wonderful possibilities.'

For a long moment we didn't speak. His eyes were shaded with a desperate need to make things better. I've seen that exact shading before. Years ago, that terrible afternoon when we sat on the couch with our baby girl and waited for the nanny to come home. Right now, he stepped towards me with his arms heavy at his sides and said, 'So I won't try to jump in to improve our structures, but I want you to know that even when I'm not beside you, I'm not going anywhere without you. It's been high adventure so far, and I want quite a lot more.'

'And perhaps,' I said, 'I never should have tried to manufacture passion.'

'Yes, because listen . . .' He pressed rewind on the cassette player, hit play on the 'Starlit Sonata' and we listened again to the tender, sparkly recapitulation. 'There it is,' he said, taking my hands and putting them to his lips. 'The real thing; it's been here all along.'

We leaned on each other for a long time before I sighed and said, 'But I do have work to do. Do you think you could help me?'

SUNDAY 31st DECEMBER

Dear God, Ria, Granny, Grandpa, Nanny, Pa, Neville, Jesus, Mary, Joseph, the patron saints of everything and anyone else in the upperlands who might have some influence on the universe, help me make everything all right. Help me not to trip over myself and bugger things up any more.

Finale

MONDAY 1st JANUARY

Right. It's the New Year and I know I am meant to have made my final notes in this diary by now, but I have this last bit to tell . . .

Henry hosted a big New Year's Eve do at Lettercello. There were crowds of people. Hugh and I packed up a picnic, the children and Valda and took our smarting selves along.

We arrived to find a large party in full swing. The French doors had been opened out to the lawns and people were moving freely between the shop, the courtyard and the green. Henry, unusually flushed with excitement, rushed to welcome us. He smiled so widely at us that I had to give him a hard stare. He coughed, ran his fingers nervously through his hair and whispered, 'Your mum and dad are out on the lawn by the linden tree.' I tried not to faint.

We found them. Mum said, 'Hello, darling. Let's sod this year right off, shall we?' and gave me a glass of champagne and a forehead kiss. Dad winked at me and said, 'You right, old soldier?' and 'Better not overdo the bubbles tonight, Zannah-doo.' We settled onto picnic rugs, we ate, we chatted. I traced 'oh dear' and 'Ria?' on my leg with my finger. Hugh reached down and gave me his hand, and when I looked at him he smiled. With crinkles.

And then there were the fireworks, and while everyone oohed and aaahed I could close my eyes and do a little bit of praying because after the last whizzy spinny thing, it would be time . . .

I received the nod from Henry and had to let go of Hugh's hand. Before I slipped away he caught my arm and whispered, 'You'll fly.'

I stopped under a tree in the shadows and waited. A few very long minutes later, Henry found me and we weaved through crowds of people into the shop. There were only a few familiar faces, I noted with relief. Hannah's and Charlie's were two of them, Isobel another. They hadn't seen me. Everyone was blessedly busy being festive and tipped-up and happy. Behind the counter at the centre of the shop, Henry gestured to the floor, smiled and did a few tiny excited handclaps. I sat down next to my brand-new viola and took it gently from its case. 'Made especially for Susannah Parks,' I whispered to myself. Henry fiddled about with a microphone while I closed my eyes and tried to ignore the clamour of my heart.

'Excuse me, everyone,' he said a moment later. 'Pardon the interruption, but could you all please gather where you can see me? I'd just like to say a few words.' The party simmered lower and moved forward. 'I wonder whether,' Henry continued, 'on this eve of a brand-new year, you might all indulge me a little. You all know how shy I am with my cello.' (Cheering from the crowd.) 'Well, I thought I might impose upon myself to play you a little festive tune, as a way to say thank you for your support of Lettercello this year.' (More cheering) 'And then I thought, actually, no. You and these walls have heard enough from me.' (Boos from the crowd.) This deserves something much more rare and special. So, I'm thrilled to present you all, my wonderful customers, friends and family, with something *very* rare and *very* special . . .'

There was a lengthy pause at this point because during Henry's speech I'd had a mild-to-moderate panic on the floor and, having put the viola back into its case, was peeking around the corner of the counter, sizing up the prospect of crawling through everyone's legs, out the French doors and into the night never to be seen again. (*Mother of four vanishes on New Year's Eve, friends and family report erratic and selfish behaviour, and display a sense of relief*...) The panic turned into terror when I peered through the forest of legs and saw my family standing just inside the open doors. All of them. And Raffy staring directly at me. He looked alarmed and tugged urgently on Hugh's hand. Hugh leaned an ear down to Raff and then jerked a glance my way. He smiled, nodded, gave me a wink.

An urgent whisper came from Henry. 'Susannah?' I ducked back in behind the counter and tried to breathe. Henry joined me. 'You know what you're doing. You just have to trust yourself.' He knocked the microphone stand and it swayed. Things were moving rapidly into awkward amateur territory. Henry looked at my terrified face and added, 'But if you really can't, I'll take over. It's your choice, Susannah.'

Choice, choice, choice... I gasped some breaths in through my nose. And for a second I thought I could smell the theatre. Henry popped up again and faced the party. 'Bear with us, everyone. Chat amongst yourselves for a minute but don't go away...' He kept talking. I squeezed my eyes shut, but the cursed tears came. 'Oh, fuck off,' I said to them.

'I really hope,' came Hugh's voice in the dark, 'that you're not talking to me.' I opened my eyes. He was crouching beside me. 'Because I'm not fucking off anywhere.' He brushed the tears from my cheeks, which made more come. 'You can do this.'

I sniffed. 'Everyone expects a lot. I expect a lot. There's so much expectation. And I won't be enough. My fingers won't know what to do.'

Hugh took my fingers in his very warm hands and said, 'You, Susannah Parks with all the sparks, are more than enough.'

'Oh, no, Hugh. I'm so sorry. You're the enough one. You always have been and I'm sorry. I'm sorry I was searching for insufficiencies in you. I was looking for holes to match all mine. A tatty dress doesn't go with a well-cut suit.' I rubbed at the stupid tears and added, 'It's unbelievable how enough you are.'

He smiled at me, with his whole dear face, and said, 'Shut up and be brave.'

But before I could, Rafferty appeared beside us. He gave me a smile and reached down to pick up the viola and the bow. Then he stood before the crowd, gave a funny little curtsey and began to play!!!!!!

Can you believe it? He played, actually played! And played well! The tune was familiar but I couldn't place it at first, and I didn't try to think because I was so mesmerised by the sight of him. Raffy. Playing viola. I was dumbfounded. I looked at Hugh. He was equally amazed. We were still sitting on the floor but we shuffled out from behind the counter to get a better view. I searched all over the boy with the viola for my languid Raff but he wasn't there. Beautiful posture, smart tones, smooth transitions. But the best thing was the little smile on his lips and the flush in his cheeks.

I found myself humming along with the tune as he played and then, with a lurch in my chest that made me gasp then sway, I realised what it was.

'Hugh,' I whispered, clutching his arm. 'Hugh?' He looked at me. I squeezed. 'It's my "Lullaby for Eloise".' I put my hand to my face to brush away the tears, but there weren't any there.

At the end, we stood to applaud him – his first standing ovation. I heard Charlie's loud whoo-hoo above the crowd. Mary-Lou danced around and Jimmy cheered without a trace of let-me-try-that. Eloise was watching me, her eyes all bright. I smiled at her and she gave me a little nod, then a bigger one, and I realised that Raffy was handing the viola to me. There was more cheering. Charlie was quiet, though. I could see his nervous face, Hannah beside him. *They think I might ruin things again*, I thought. In front of them was Valda, seated but head high, her eyes bright. *What a beautifully long neck*. Proud. She had her arm linked in Daphne's, who was sitting beside her. They both looked younger.

So, with Henry's help, the viola under my arm and my trembling hands clutching the bow, I found the microphone and hoped it wasn't picking up the pounding of my heart. The room went completely silent and I put the unfamiliar viola under my chin.

If there's no change, there's no rhythm, only the same old beat.

I stared at the floor and then glanced out to the audience and Valda told me later I looked just like a possum in the headlights. I caught sight of Hugh's face. He was the other possum, the one about to see his best friend get hit by a car. For a moment my mind went to Peter the Possum and, with sabotage in its sights, threatened to wayward completely away.

'He who loveth best, playeth best.'

☆

I saw Hugh's face again. I saw Ria at the piano and I heard her say, *I'll lead you in, Helen Burns. Stay brave.* So I announced to the crowd, 'This is a piece called the "Starlit Sonata",' in a loud and stilted voice that didn't sound like mine. I swallowed, took a breath, let myself think, and looked at my family. 'I wrote it for Hugh. And, as it turns out, for all of my family.' Then I whispered to the viola, 'No dissonance, all consonance, let's follow.' And then I began to play . . .

Dear Mum,

I want to tell you that you are better than fireworks, much, much, much better, with more whiz-bangs. There was a giant whiz-bang in my chest when you played your viola. You gave me tears.

I am sorry I secretly played your viola. It was in the wardrobe and Ria said she thought it should be played so it wouldn't get stale. She said to wash my hands because the oil in my skin isn't good for the bow. I always did, I promise. Ria helped me on Skype. We found your lullaby music and she helped me read it. She cried when she saw it. I'm learning 'Sweet Thing' by Van Morrison too. Your new viola is easier to play than your old one but I'm going to save up for my own. Maybe a bit smaller.

We kept it a secret because we were waiting until I had some good technique and a whole song to show you. And I was scared you'd be cross. I'm sorry to have secrets.

Now that we don't have Ria, can you teach me your viola, please? I want to one day be able to play what you played, that music that made everyone go still. I want to know how you play that. Thank you, Mum.
Love from Raffy. Xoxoxoxoxoxo

Dear Zannah,

I know you've been writing in a diary and I wanted to add something from me, so you could refer back to it as a side note to your reflections on the year, from a reliable source. Also because I don't think my spoken words can do justice to how I feel and what I want to say.

I've already told you that seeing you play again was amazing. It was out-of-this-world amazing. I know you said your fingers felt huge and you mucked up parts but, trust me, the 'Starlit Sonata' never sounded so good. I heard the stars; I heard how they falter, then shine. I heard your tears too. And, with your hands sometimes unsure of Ria's new key, I heard all that incredible hope.

But what was even more amazing than the music was you. The look of you, with that music in your face, was better-than-anything amazing.

I'm really sorry I haven't helped more to bring you to your music. I'm not good with things that don't go back together the way the manuals say they should. I realise that helping probably meant just being there more. I should have been there. I really hope I'm the only one you'll ever choose to be disappointed by.

Would it be too fix-it of me if I took you and the children away, on a world trip, to all the places you've wanted to go? I thought, since you and the Susannah-Viola seem to be making friends, that we could go to the places where she was born – Switzerland, Canada, Wales? But wherever you like. We could improvise. What do you think? Are they repairs you'd be happy for me to make? I should have taken you away sooner, but I don't think it's too late.

Let's put you in the sky, Susannah-Albatross, my chancey little
sparkling star.
Love (and a lot of passion) always, H xxxxxxx

PS I'll always be grateful for the bee in September.

♩♩

Coda

I can't well say how it felt to play again. Perhaps my music said that best. My hands are back, though: fumbly, but here. Ria's hands are too; her piano was just underneath, catching the little falls. And when I relaxed a bit and closed my eyes midway through, I saw again that magnificent Aurora.

And Eloise, my little-big, black-white girl, was all blush and silver with feeling and feeling and trailings of tears. I held her face in my trembling hands and brushed the tears away, the way I've wanted to all this time.

And Hugh. His amber eyes were bright with it all: with the year trickling away around us and the children writing their names in the air with sparklers. He kissed me for about seven and a half seconds with his eyes wide open and all the butterflies came out.

The good butterflies.

There has been sex. Quite a lot of it, actually. I know that this is not the new status quo; I know that passion will wax and wane. There'll be more patches of no sex, then we might have hurry-up-then sex and birthday sex and we-should-have-sex sex. Occasionally we might have mind-blowing sex. None of it will benefit from too much overthinking.

Lately there's been a lot of what-would-I-do-without-you sex; that's a really good kind. But I'm prepared for the not so good, the little cold bits. Marriage and motherhood is like any other art form, with its demands on patience, endurance and time. Its ups and downs, the welter and the whelm. We have six personalities in this house. There will be loggerheads and odds. But contrary motion is a simple device that dramatically improves a piece of music.

Actually, I have been doing a bit of composing. Just one piece so far: a simple little *bagatelle*. It was meant to be for Raffy to try, but all these thoughts of passion, etc. inspired me to write some lyrics. (I was never a lyricist so this is a new and wavery thing.) And these ones turned out to be not all that suitable for a child's playful tune. So I'll just put them here instead, as a little *mezzo* note in between the highs and lows: an end point for the Sparkle Pages, and this resolutionary year . . .

My heart, it sang soprano once,
Against the brilliant stars,
But now it sings contralto
And it's stronger for the scars.
There is loss, there's ice and frost,
There's fog and blinding storms,
But also there's a place for me
That's sparkly, safe and warm.

Silly. Hearts can't sing. My hands can, though, and do, every single day.

♩♩

Fermata

The End.
   (Also the middle.)

♫

Acknowledgements

THANK YOU:

- To my brilliant mum and dad. This book wouldn't be here
  if I wasn't here, with a functioning brain and a wayward
  imagination. So thanks to you both for sorting that out.

- To a big sister who helped grow that imagination in our
  enormous garden, among the mulberry trees. Em, I'm sure
  I've popped some of your piercing observations into these
  pages and claimed them as my own, much like when I stole
  your Fimo creations and gave them to my friends. Sorry
  about that.

- To my husband, Richard Dick Dickie Ben Curly Fezzle
  Bignell, I am so grateful to you for never, ever expressing
  dismay that I choose to write a lot and occasionally prance
  about on stages with microphones instead of milking the
  cows. Also, thank you for not ever complaining when I burn
  the guinea fowl.

- To my children, E, B, and L, for being naughty enough to
  provide me with material and nice enough to leave me the
  heck alone sometimes. I love you even when I yell.

- To Maggie Mackellar (words-can't-express sort of thanks)
  for being precisely the mentor and friend I needed and
  need, for saying it's okay to shut the door and keep my

bottom on the chair, for introductions and for being so sensible when I'm floating about in other worlds singing musical theatre and listening to Amy Shark.

- To Fiona Inglis, who was the first to endure the whole first draft, take a huge leap of faith with me and make it all seem achievable, thank you to you and all at Curtis Brown Australia and UK.

- To Faye Bender for your efforts across the world.

- To Nikki Christer. You were the very first to read some of the Susannah words, offer encouragement and keep me going.

- To my wonderful, enthusiastic publishers, Kimberley Atkins and Ali Watts, for reining me in and cleaning me up.

- To editor, violinist and wordsmith Amanda Martin for your musical insights and sensitive management of Susannah's quirks. Also Elena Gomez, Celine Kelly and Emma Schwarcz for your clever editing and sharp eyes. To Madison Garratt, Louise Ryan, Louisa Maggio, Emily Hindle, Alysha Farry, Debbie McGowan and everyone at PRH who has contributed and made me and Susannah feel so welcome.

- To Jude Elliot, who brought my voice out of my head and insisted I could, even when I couldn't; to Adrian Smith, who reminded me not to do anything stupid like grow up; and to Father Terry Rush, who quite literally gave me space.

- To the people who helped, inspired, tolerated and spurred me on in small-enormous ways – Des Vernon, Tom Flood, Posie Graham-Evans, Monica McInerney, Dominique Hurley, Richard Sprent, Matthew Annells, Gaye Wright, Caroline Bignell, Molly Archer, Kelly Pummeroy, Hannah Bale, Anita Schleebs, Maggie Sakko and all the gorgeous, long-suffering readers of megoracle.com.

- To Samuel Taylor Coleridge, Charles Baudelaire, William Blake, TS Eliot, Martha Wainwright and Dodie Smith for their works, and to concert violist Jennifer Stumm for her insights.
- To Kate Miller-Heidke and Tim Minchin, who feel like friends and who sang to me as I wrote this book, thank you for inspiring other friends like Ria.

And thank you so very much to booksellers for selling and to readers for reading. Put this book to your chest and imagine it's me giving you a little thank-you hug. Probably don't kiss it or anything though; that would be weird.

'A boisterous tale
of music, friendship
and women's rights.'
Books + Publishing

'Never a dull
moment.'
Country Style

Once in
a while,
everyone
needs to
be heard

THE
ANGRY
WOMEN'S
CHOIR

'A mighty fun read.'
Jessie Tu

'An unputdownable
celebration of
all women.'
Brisbanista

MEG
BIGNELL

Freycinet Barnes has built herself the perfect existence. With beautiful children, a successful husband and a well-ordered schedule, it's a life so full she simply doesn't fit.

When she steps outside her calendar and is accidentally thrown into the generous bosom of the West Moonah Women's Choir, she finds music, laughter, friendship and a humming wellspring of rage. With the ready acceptance of the colourful choristers, Frey learns that voices can move mountains, fury can be kind and life can do with a bit of ruining.

Together, Frey and the choir sing their anger, they breathe it in and stitch it up, belt it out and spin it into a fierce, driving beat that will kick the system square in the balls, and possibly demolish them all.

'If you have forgotten why you're angry, if you've forgotten that you are angry, this laugh-out-loud, sob-out-loud, sing-out-loud book will remind you.'
Minnie Darke

'Funny, sad, relatable, full of people who continue to breathe well after the last page.
A beautifully nuanced read from start to finish.' MARTA DUSSELDORP

WELCOME
TO
NOWHERE
RIVER

If we never get lost,
we can never be found...

MEG
BIGNELL

By the bestselling author of *The Angry Women's Choir*

Long past its heyday and deep in drought, the riverside hamlet of Nowhere River is slowly fading into a ghost town. It's a place populated by those who are beholden to it, those who were born to it and those who took a wrong turn while trying to go somewhere else.

City-born Carra married into Nowhere River, Lucie was brought to it by tragedy, Josie is root-bound and Florence knows nowhere else. All of them, though familiar with every inch of their tiny hometown, are as lost as the place itself.

The town's social cornerstone – St Margery's Ladies' Club – launches a rescue plan that turns everything around and upside down, then shakes it until all sorts of things come floating to the surface. And none of its inhabitants will ever be the same again.

This is the highly original and heartfelt story of a place where everybody knows everything, but no one really knows anyone at all. Brimming with heart and humour, this is a delightful novel that celebrates the country people and towns of Australia.

Discover a
new favourite